SWEET DESIRE

Declan pulled Daria close again, and she didn't resist. "So your favorite color is red. Sparkle would say red symbolizes everything that's hot and sensual."

"Hades says it symbolizes blood and the fires of Tartarus."

"I like Sparkle's take on it better."

Time to feed his senses. This was what made his existence bearable. But he'd learned centuries ago to mask the intensity of his need. A little playfulness made the women he had sex with relax and laugh.

"How about a red surprise to celebrate our connection?" Declan visualized what he wanted and then willed it to take physical form.

Her startled gasp was all the reaction he'd hoped for. "How'd you do that? Is it real?"

"Sure is." He hoped his little demonstration would give her pause when she thought about dragging him off to Tartarus. But then again, he'd enjoy a battle with another immortal. With *her*. Certain battles could be sexy as hell.

"Well, at least we don't have to worry about anyone seeing us. I hope no one comes along, though. It would be hard to explain away a wall of Red Hots."

Nina Bangs

One Bite Stand

LEISURE BOOKS NEW YORK CITY

A LEISURE BOOK®

January 2008

Published by

Dorchester Publishing Co., Inc.
200 Madison Avenue
New York, NY 10016

Copyright © 2008 by Nina Bangs

ISBN 10: 0-8439-5954-1
ISBN 13: 978-0-8439-5954-3

The name "Leisure Books" and the stylized "L" with design are trademarks of Dorchester Publishing Co., Inc.

Printed in the United States of America.

10 9 8 7 6 5 4 3 2 1

Visit us on the web at www.dorchesterpub.com.

One Bite Stand

CHAPTER ONE

Memo: to all harpies
Subject: dress code
The Depraved Fashionistas Department must approve
all harpy clothes. Choose a wardrobe that complements
your grotesque harpy image and wear it with pride. Refer to the Harpy Handbook, section four, page sixteen,
if you are unsure whether your clothing meets company
standards. Punishment for noncompliance will include
one year of wearing a zombie's castoffs. You will then
realize that, yes, it can get worse.
    Remember, you are the public face of Tartarus.

HADES THE BENEVOLENT

"Forget Hades's memo and tell me why I feel this way,
Kal." Daria stood at the window folding and unfolding
her hands.

Her brother looked up from his laptop. "Explain."

"I'm sweating. I *never* sweat. My heart's pounding. I'm
breathing hard. And I have this pressure in my stomach." She swung to face her twin. "What's happening
to me?"

"Either an unexpected birth or you're going to throw
up." His lips tilted into a smile. "Relax, sis, this isn't worth
a panic attack. It's just a job."

"It's a job I have to keep. Too much depends on it." Kal
didn't understand. Harpies didn't get callbacks. It just
never happened. Job interviews always ended badly. Usu-

ally with the interviewer doing lots of screaming before taking a header out of a tenth-story window.

"What if he takes one look at me and decides I'm too much of a bad thing?" Was that fair treatment? Uh, no. Sure, harpies had a rep for stalking the unsuspecting, who quickly became the unwilling when said harpies dragged their uncooperative butts off to Tartarus. But still, the corporate world needed to develop a little flexibility in its hiring practices.

"He'll love you." Kal wore his humoring-my-sister expression.

Still, knowing how rare this chance was, Daria wasn't about to mess up. "I can't believe this Ganymede guy hired me. It's too perfect. I get to be mean and ugly and someone pays me for it." She frowned at her twin. "What's the catch? Why me?"

Her brother shrugged. "The gargoyles were on strike?"

She pulled on her boots as she thought over the situation. "No, really, what were the chances of this job coming along just when I needed it?"

Kal paced restlessly. "No big deal. Aunt Ocypete stayed here last year. She met this Ganymede. One look and I bet he knew she could whip an army of Viking berserkers into shape. Why do you think Rome fell? Aunt Ocypete was leading the barbarian hordes."

"And?" She walked to the mirror and studied her image. Did her boots and dress work together?

"So when he needed someone tough to manage the Woo Woo Inn, he called her for a recommendation." Kal paused in his pacing. "Who the hell names a guesthouse the Woo Woo Inn? Come to think of it, she never did tell us what happened here last year."

Daria didn't really care what had happened. She had the job. Now she had to make it work. She leaned forward to get a closer view of her face. "Omigod, look at my face. I can't go down to my first night on the job looking like this." She could see her title of Harpy Hopeful turning to Harpy Hopeless real fast.

"You look fine."

"Uh, fine is *not* fine. My employer specified mean and gruesome."

"He didn't use the word *gruesome*."

She ignored him. "To pass the harpy test, I have to be a vicious, cruel, violent, and *butt-ugly* being that is half woman and half giant vulture. I'm required to snatch victims and carry them off to Tartarus. I can take human form while in pursuit of clueless prey. I memorized that from the Harpy Handbook. If I'm not gruesome enough, I'll get marked down. I need a more grotesque, more wickedly depraved, more heartless bitch image. Pull some of *those* out of your mysterious box of amazing makeovers."

"Calm down, sis."

She sighed and let some of the air out of her frenzy. "I'm sorry. It's just that Mom is looking forward to me joining her. It's the start of a family tradition. I can't blow it."

Her brother threw her a sharp glance. "Why all the insecurity?"

How could she explain it to him, all the years of not being good enough in the eyes of the other harpies? No one had bothered him because he wasn't expected to join Mom. Not his fault, but the truth.

"I was never on the fast track to success. You know, the other kids teased me a lot, especially Eris. Never ugly enough, never nasty enough."

"Why the hell didn't you ever tell me about that? I would've made sure she left you alone."

His anger on her behalf was real and it warmed her. "Harpies have to learn to defend themselves. Besides, I eventually took care of the problem." She smiled at the memory.

Kal wasn't happy with her answer, but he couldn't argue with it, so he headed for the door. "I did what I could with your face, but you don't want to scare the crap out of the guests. You can't afford to get fired." He still looked ticked. "Besides, your bone structure doesn't lend itself to grotesque. Look, I knocked myself out on your total image, so appreciate it and stop whining."

"Maybe braces would—"

"No."

"Um, how about if my ears stuck—"

"No."

"You could have hairs growing out of my nose and—"

Kal exhaled deeply, a sure sign of fast-fading patience. "This Ganymede person who hired you doesn't want a troll welcoming guests. We're here to find someone you can snatch and take back to the underworld. Keep your eye on the goal, and forget about everything else."

Daria ratcheted down her glower a few notches. "I guess so." She chanced another glance in the mirror. Pale face, colorless lips, and black eyeliner that made her look like a frightened raccoon. Coarse red, blue, and purple hair that fell almost to her butt. A few interesting piercings, and some dynamite tattoos. It would have to do for now. And Kal was right. She needed to keep her job as night manager at the Woo Woo Inn until she passed her test.

She trailed him out the door and walked down the stairs with him. "You know, if you'd tell me how you make your magic, it'd save us tons of time. While I was turning myself into Lady Loathsome, you could be scoping out our victim." They'd had this argument before. She always lost.

"Not going to happen, sis. I'm the only one who can do what I do. A little gift Mom gave me to make me feel okay about never getting a shot at being a card-carrying harpy. Guys don't qualify. Sexism. Gotta love it." His smile was a bitter twist of his lips.

Daria immediately felt guilty. Not a positive harpy character trait. She'd have to nurture her inner bitch. But not with Kal.

She caught a glimpse of them both as they passed a hallway mirror. Fine, so mirrors were an obsession. Daria never met a mirror she didn't embrace. A weakness. She felt compelled to check out every one. Maybe this time she'd be ugly enough, horrific enough to live up to her mother's standard. But it never happened. Probably never would. One peek at Mom and humans had nightmares for weeks. Now, *that* was greatness.

She pushed the mirror from her mind and concentrated on cheering Kal up. "Your talent is totally unique, Kal. Have I told you lately what a genius you are?"

He was six-feet-plus of toned muscle. Kal didn't try to hide that. He'd saved his magic for his face. It was scarred, blotchy, puffy, and made her want to look away. And it was all fake. Kal's real face was gorgeous enough to make women do astonishingly stupid things.

He smiled, but it didn't reach his eyes. Amazing eyes, really, if people could get past his repulsive face. Violet like Dad's eyes. Kal hated them.

"No crooked teeth tonight?" She felt bad for Kal. At least she was the right sex. Too bad neither of them had the genes to conform to the official harpy look. Without Kal's magic, she couldn't begin to compete with the harpy candidates who were naturally hideous.

"I won't be smiling so I don't much care what my teeth look like." He guided her toward the registration desk. "As of right now, you're the official night manager of the Woo Woo Inn."

She couldn't help the queasy feeling. This job would decide her place, if any, in the harpy hierarchy. Smoothing her dress, Daria stopped at the desk. Taking a deep breath, she smiled at the woman staring at her with wide-eyed horror. Good. First impressions were important.

"Hi, I'm Daria Abarr, and this is my brother, Kal. I spoke with a Mr. Ganymede on the phone. He hired me as his new night manager. I'm supposed to start tonight."

The woman continued to stare.

Uneasy, Daria slid her gaze to the chubby gray cat crouched on top of the desk and the brown dog sitting on the floor beside it. The dog offered her a happy tongue-lolling grin. Well, at least someone was glad to see her.

The woman finally blinked, and then she glared at the cat. "Explain."

Daria glanced at Kal. He shrugged. There was something off about the woman and two animals. She could ID most nonhumans, but this little group confused her.

The cat stood, stretched, and yawned. "I couldn't take a whole summer of you bitching and moaning about having no one to practice on. You needed a challenge, babe, so here she is." He speared the woman with a hard gaze. "And no, I won't do the talking-in-people's-minds shit. It's demeaning."

Daria frowned. A shifter, maybe? But she wasn't getting shifter vibes from the cat. What about the dog? Was he . . . Whoa. She was a *challenge*? What did that mean?

Before Daria could ask, the dog stood and whined at the woman. "Can I go outside? Can I, can I? I bet all the bunnies are out. Can I chase them? Can I, can I?" His tail wagged his whole furry behind.

"Now look what you did, Mede. Trouble thinks he can talk out loud too. Fine role model you are." The woman narrowed her eyes to amber slits of fury. She spared a glance for Daria. "Would you excuse us for a minute?"

Daria and Kal nodded. They moved far enough away to be out of normal earshot. But harpies had excellent hearing. Was that Daria's fault? Of course not. She listened.

"You hired a *harpy*? I don't believe you, Mede. I was supposed to do the hiring. What will Cindy and Thrain say when they get back? My God, she looks like an *American Idol* reject."

Kal winked at Daria. "See, someone complimented you already."

Mede offered the woman a cat shrug. "You'll find out in a few weeks. Hope they have great sex in Paris. It'll put them in a good mood. Besides, we have more important things to worry about than our new night manager. Declan checked in tonight."

The woman didn't lose her mad, but at least she seemed diverted for the moment. "Can anything else go wrong?" Her expression said no.

The dog was now bouncing up and down, ears and tongue flapping in the breeze. "I smell bunnies out there. Bunnies, bunnies, big fat *bunnies*!"

The cat padded toward the screen door. "I'll take the kid outside for a run."

The woman looked so angry, Daria expected her red hair to go up in flames. "Don't you *dare* try to escape. You hired her. I wanted a nice normal human for the job."

The dog nosed the screen open and charged into the night. His barks faded into the distance.

The cat paused at the door. "You scared the last 'nice normal human' away. That's why I hired the harpy. Deal with her." And then he was gone.

The *cat* had hired her? Mede must be short for Ganymede. Wait. Scared a human away? What was that about? Uh-oh, complications on her personal horizon. When Aunt Ocypete had picked this place for her test, all she'd said was it might present a few difficulties. She'd never elaborated.

Daria hadn't expected to meet three nonhumans. And they knew what she was. She'd have to lull them with her friendliness and bubbly personality before trying to fly off with one of the guests. This was tough stuff. She needed a primer. Reminder to self, order *Bubbly for Dummies* from Amazon.

The woman walked, no, *swayed* over to Kal and her. If Daria had wanted to project sexy—which she didn't— she would've asked this lady to lay a few lessons on her. It wasn't just the woman's walk, it was her total package. Oozing sexual invitation from every pore, she was a predator dressed for the hunt. A really short black skirt, clingy barely there top, and killer stilettos made for a more potent package than a pheromone cloud.

Of course, Daria didn't care, because she'd never met a male who could tempt her away from her primary goal of making it to the top.

The woman stopped in front of them and smiled. Sure, the smile was insincere, but even an insincere smile from her would bring most men to their knees. Daria glanced at Kal. Her brother was scowling at the woman. Yay, Kal.

The woman invaded Kal's personal space and gazed up at him from those strange amber eyes. "Hi, I'm Sparkle Stardust. You've got a body women would love to touch."

She demonstrated by smoothing her fingers over his bare arm. "Too bad about your face." She tilted her head to stare at him from a different angle. "Is it real, or are you playing with smoke and mirrors?" Sliding her fingers along his jaw, she offered him a smile that didn't even pretend to be innocent. "So, what is Kal short for?"

The only hint that Sparkle might be getting to her brother was a tic in his left eye. Amazing she'd had even that much effect. Kal was the king of calm, icy self-control.

"Kallias. And my face is what you see. Accept it, because it won't be changing any time soon." He kept his gaze trained on Sparkle's eyes, refusing to let it drop to her scooped top.

Good thing. Sparkle's scoop was definitely a double dip. That path would lead to madness for any man dumb enough to look down. Daria jumped in to distract Sparkle from her brother. "So, what do I do first?" She tried on a perky grin. Was she doing it right? Harpies weren't known for their perky anything.

"What you do first is explain why a harpy wants to be the night manager of an inn that caters to guests interested in the paranormal." Sparkle rolled her eyes in mock thought. "Wait. Could it be you hope to carry off one of our guests in your sharp little talons? I understand you get brownie points if you snag someone powerful. Think your chances are good here?"

Sparkle paused to change conversational directions. "By the way, the whole concept of half woman, half vulture is really gross." She leaned closer. "You have good bone structure, though. I can work with that."

Uh-oh. Daria didn't want anyone but Kal messing with her face. She felt the first stirrings of panic. Sparkle's eyes gleamed with the fervor of the total zealot. Daria needed to guide her back to the main topic. "Nope, wouldn't even think about carrying off any guests. Kal and I just wanted a break from the same old, same old." She gulped back a nervous laugh. "I was kind of surprised you recognized us. What are you guys?"

Sparkle studied her long, bloodred, perfect nails. "Mede, Trouble, and I are cosmic troublemakers. We're ancient beings with unspeakable powers. We wreak havoc on the universe whenever we have a spare moment. And if you try to grab one of our guests, I'll rip your wings off." She never lifted her gaze from her nails.

Forget friendly and bubbly. Harpies had the wicked-temper thing nailed down. Daria didn't take threats from anyone. She speared Sparkle with a stare that had a lot of Mom in it. "If you catch me in harpy form, we'll see who tears what off."

The corners of Kal's lips turned up in silent approval.

Sparkle finally looked up from her nails. For a moment, Daria wondered if she'd blown her job before she'd even started. Then Sparkle smiled, and Daria heard Kal suck in his breath. Sparkle would never be a harpy contender.

"I like you, Daria. You've got attitude. In fact, I'm going to make you into someone the Woo Woo Inn can be proud of."

Daria growled low in her throat. "You will *not* mess with my face."

"That'll come later." Sparkle's gaze grew thoughtful. "The Goth gear has to go. No representative of the inn can run around in a black, pixie-hem dress with rabbit fur trim and six-inch split-heel platform boots accented with rubber spikes and silver studs." She closed her eyes. "Give me a minute for the nausea to pass."

"Rabbit fur?" The male voice was deep and definitely menacing.

Sparkle's eyes popped open at the same time Daria and Kal turned to the man who'd walked up behind them.

Good grief, he was a walking, talking mountain. He had to be at least six feet five inches of bulging muscle and in-your-face aggression. Light reflected off his shiny bald head and the diamond stud in his ear.

Daria glanced down at the hem of her dress. Rabbit fur? Who knew? "Um, I guess so."

From his angry huff, that wasn't the right answer. Luckily, Sparkle stepped in to head off violence. "Hey, Mel. Good to see you back again this year. Don't sweat the rabbit fur. We'll get rid of that right now."

Before Daria or Kal could react, Sparkle bent over, grabbed the rabbit fur, and ripped it from the dress. Luckily, it hadn't been sewn on too well and came away in one piece.

Daria opened her mouth to register lots of loud outrage, but then she caught Sparkle's pointed stare. The stare said, "Let me handle this."

Remember your job. She settled for a vicious death glare. Kal looked more puzzled than angry. That was Kal. He always thought things out before reacting. She was usually the impulsive one.

Sparkle hit Mel with her sexiest smile. "See, all gone. Give me your car keys, and I'll have someone take your bags up to your room. Why don't you go relax in the parlor? Daria will bring your room key to you once your luggage is taken care of." Without giving grumpy Mel a chance to respond, she pointed him toward the parlor.

Scowling at Daria one last time, he handed over his keys and ambled away. Everyone gave a collective sigh of relief.

"He's a were of some kind." Kal shifted his gaze to

Daria. "I think I'll wander over to the parlor too. See what's happening there. Will you be okay?"

"Sure." Maybe. Daria was beginning to see why Ganymede wanted someone mean and ugly. If the inn's nonhuman guests were like Mel—who probably shifted into a bull elephant—then he'd need someone with an intimidation factor of ten. The ugly part? Ugly added to her perceived menace. Perceptions were important.

Sparkle beckoned for Daria to follow her. "You're about the same size as me. Let's see if we can find something else for you to wear." She held up her hand before Daria could object. "And no, you don't have a choice. Each summer Mede and I run the Woo Woo Inn while the owners go on vacation. Mede may've hired you, but he doesn't always think in terms of guest satisfaction."

Daria was feeling a little surly. "He specified ugly. Well, ugly is a package deal. It's not just about my face. Get rid of my dress and boots, and part of what makes me *me* is gone."

She caught Sparkle's muttered "Thank God."

Reluctantly, Daria followed Sparkle to her room. She couldn't afford to defy the cosmic troublemaker just yet. Daria made sure she shielded her thoughts before allowing herself a few indulgent fantasies. All the fantasies involved Daria carrying a kicking and screaming Sparkle Stardust off to Tartarus. She glanced down at Sparkle's stilettos. Hades didn't stock designer shoes in the underworld. The thought made her smile.

Once inside Sparkle's room, Daria forgot about everything. She turned in a slow circle. "This is . . ." Words failed her.

"Sex is my thing, sister. I'm the best at what I do in the cosmic troublemaker world."

"And that would be?" Daria exhaled deeply, trying to

relax before the sexual overload made her head explode. Paintings that were way beyond explicit hung from the walls. Candlelight reflected off red silk and velvet everything. The scents of sex and desire filled the air. And if she were anything other than a mean and ugly harpy, the soft music would've made her want to perform exotic and kinky acts on the first male she met.

"I bring sexual chaos to the world." Sparkle flung open her closet and scanned the contents. "First I find two people who're completely wrong for each other." She glanced over her shoulder and offered Daria a sly smile. "Then I manipulate them. By the time I'm finished, they're so into lust I have to stamp 'Superheated Combustible' on their bare butts."

Daria made a rude noise. "You can only do that if you're dealing with weak humans."

Sparkle's smile widened, revealing straight white teeth. Daria wondered if she'd been a shark in a previous incarnation.

"I'm sure you'd be a lot stronger than any human. Why don't we place a small wager on exactly how strong you are, hmm?" Sparkle pulled a few things off their hangers before bending down to choose a pair of shoes.

Daria had opened her mouth to say no and then closed it. Kal was always reminding her to think before she acted. It wouldn't hurt to listen. "What kind of wager?" Was she suspicious? You bet.

"At the end of each night, we'll get together. If you survive the night without a lustful act, you can make me do one thing." Sparkle thought about that. "Let's amend that. You can make me do something that doesn't involve seduction. I'm the string-puller, not the puppet. Besides, Mede's my guy." She dumped the clothes over a chair and put the shoes on the floor. "If *you* give in to temptation, I get to improve you in some small way." Her voice sounded only mildly interested as she once again studied her nails.

Daria knew she should say no, but she'd never made a bet with anyone in her entire existence. And this was way too easy to pass up. Besides, it would give her a chance to practice random acts of cruelty. Mom always said she'd never make a true harpy until her heart was as small and hard as a prune pit.

"You have a deal." Daria walked over to get a better look at the clothes Sparkle had chosen. "So what are my duties?"

Sparkle stepped between her and the clothes. "Oh, this and that. Basically just make sure the inn is running smoothly and the guests are happy." She pushed Daria toward the bathroom. "Go in and take off your clothes. Hand them out to me and I'll give you your new outfit."

Daria wasn't dumb. She pretty much figured Sparkle didn't want her to see the clothes because she knew Daria would hate them. It didn't matter. She'd play the game. And when she came out of the bathroom, she'd grab her own clothes, run up to her room, and change again. Then she'd try to avoid Sparkle for the rest of the night.

Once inside the bathroom, she stripped, handed her clothes out to Sparkle, and then slipped into the black silk pants and purple top before putting on the gold sandals. Ugh. Mom's screams would be heard all the way from Tartarus if she could see her only daughter in this outfit.

And she just might, because Daria knew there was a judge planted among the inn's guests, someone who'd be grading her during these two weeks, or as long as it took her to capture her prey. It wouldn't be another harpy. Too obvious. She just hoped that he, she, or it didn't have a camera phone.

Daria tried to tug the purple top higher. No luck. Most harpies were flat-chested. She wasn't. Some nights you just couldn't catch a break. "Why purple?" Not that it mattered.

"It matches part of your hair." Sparkle sounded distracted. "Look, I have to go. The cook's having trouble with tonight's menu, and I have to find someone to take care of Mel's bags. When Ganymede comes back inside, he'll tell you what to do. Oh, and don't forget to take Mel's keys to him in the parlor. They'll be on the registration desk."

Well, well, her luck had turned. Daria grinned. Maybe she'd just change back into her own clothes right here. Opening the bathroom door, she peeked out. No Sparkle. She peered around the room. No clothes. What the . . . She stalked to the closet and yanked the door open. She shoved Sparkle's clothes aside. Sexy, sexy, and downright sleazy.

Daria slammed the closet door shut and stormed from the room. She headed for the stairs. "Bitch, bitch, bitch," was her mantra all the way to her door. Her explosive harpy temper whipped around her until the air crackled with its energy. She wanted to change into harpy form and hunt down the sneaky, clothes-stealing viper.

She barely controlled the urge to kick down the door to her own room. Her hand shook as she unlocked it and went inside. *Calm down.* No way would she pass the test if she blew everything her first night on the job. And as much as she wanted to snare Sparkle Stardust for Hades, she admitted the cosmic troublemaker would be hard to take down with Ganymede and Trouble in her corner. She'd have to find someone powerful—because powerful got her more points—but also someone who was alone.

She took a deep steadying breath. Okay, she was over

it. She'd change out of the purple abomination and go down to start work.

Daria was trying to decide which of her equally yummy doomsday fashion statements she'd change into as she pulled open her closet door.

The closet was empty. She growled low in her throat.

"Someone's feeling the need to bleed."

CHAPTER TWO

Declan Mackenzie sat alone. That's the way he liked it. He studied the inn's guests gathered around the blazing fireplace. From the comfort of a recliner tucked into a shadowy corner of the Woo Woo Inn's parlor, he watched them watch each other.

The nonhumans checked each other out, deciding who wasn't a player and who could kick ass. The humans glanced around the room, wondering if any of their fellow guests were vampires or werewolves. Declan could tell them there were lots of worse things that stalked the night.

Sure, it was warmer closer to the fire, but he was okay with the chill of the room's darkened corner. It matched the cold inside him. Call it boredom or just the uncaring that came after too many years of the same routines, but Declan just didn't give a damn about much anymore.

He closed his eyes as he slid his fingers over the recliner's smooth leather. Hope wasn't completely gone, though. His senses could still bring him pleasure, could still warm the frozen places in what passed for his soul.

Opening his eyes, he yawned. A human reflex. He wasn't human. Hadn't been for about nine hundred years. But it demonstrated so well how he felt that he couldn't resist. He'd visited the Woo Woo Inn for about twenty minutes last year. This visit wasn't half as entertaining. Not yet, at least. It promised to improve once he found his prey.

Movement at the door to the parlor caught his attention. A big bear of a guy had walked in. He paused to glance around the room, and then he headed for Declan's corner.

Damn. Declan automatically raised his mental shields. No one, human or nonhuman, could get past them to read his thoughts or ID what he was. He didn't smile as the man dropped onto the chair across from him. A weresomething. Declan didn't care what kind.

The man grunted at him, the universal guy greeting.

Declan nodded, but didn't offer to start a conversation.

"Just got here. They're taking my stuff up to my room. You been here before?" He didn't sound too interested in Declan's answer.

Good. Declan wasn't here to make friends. His job was pretty straightforward. Hunt. Kill. Go home. He shrugged. "Last year. I didn't stay too long."

"Great setup they have. Turned this big old Victorian mansion into a place where people who like to talk about paranormal stuff can get together. Does a huge business."

"Yeah. Great concept." Declan didn't elaborate.

"I'm Mel." Grinning, he leaned forward and stuck out a massive paw of a hand.

Declan exhaled wearily. Not that he needed to exhale, but if he wanted to be accepted as human, he'd better remember all those little human habits. Like breathing. Evidently Mel didn't get the message, because he continued to grin at him.

Declan hesitated. His name wouldn't mean a thing to anyone but the one he hunted. And if that person was in the room, he or she probably already knew his identity. The only thing his target might not know was the extent of his power.

"Declan." He grasped the other man's hand. At the

same time, he did a quick walk-through of Mel's mind. Nothing there to hint that he was the one Declan hunted. But Declan did find something that made him smile for the first time.

Mel settled deeper into his chair and the conversation. "Some of the people who come here really think they're vampires or werewolves." He shook his head sadly. "You're not one of them, are you?" He sounded relaxed, but his gaze had sharpened.

Checking me out to make sure I'm only a harmless human, Mel? Declan's smile widened. "Nope. No fur or fangs." He was batting five hundred on the truth-o-meter. Not bad. "I'm into UFOs. Heard there were some great group discussions going on about sightings around here. New Jersey's a long way from L.A., but I go wherever the action is." He didn't give a flip about UFOs. On the other hand, he'd be real interested in finding a UFK—unidentified freaking killer.

Mel nodded, but he looked like he'd lost interest. Declan didn't pose a threat, so Mel could move on. "Be careful out in the woods. Could be some crazies running around. Wouldn't want you going home with holes in your neck from a vampire wannabe." His laugh was as big as the rest of him.

Declan acknowledged the joke with a grim smile. If he didn't feed soon, a few of the inn's guests might be going home with their own unique souvenirs of their stay at the Woo Woo Inn. "I'll be careful. You won't find me out in the woods at night." He'd be there, but Mel had zero chance of seeing him. "I'm just dipping my toe in the paranormal pool."

"Uh-huh. You make sure you don't get that toe chewed off, you hear?" With that cheery warning, Mel started to rise. But something caught his attention, and he paused.

Following Mel's gaze, Declan watched the woman who'd entered the parlor scan the crowd. When she spotted Mel, she frowned. Then she headed toward them.

Interesting. After nine centuries, it took a lot to make that word pop into his mind when he saw a woman. "Sex" was his pop-up ad of choice. But anything that interested him staved off the coldness for a while.

From the neck down she was all warm curves. Those gold sandals made her legs go on forever. Her head? Definitely belonged to another woman. All the color in her face must've faded into her hair, because the hair was a multicolored mess. And the black circles she'd drawn around her eyes made her look Night-of-the-Living-Deadish. Now, why would a woman who dressed like that . . . ?

The push of magic as she neared him surprised Declan. He narrowed his attention to a tunnel of focused concentration, stripping away the magic to find the essence of what lay beneath. Most of the beings in this room, human or otherwise, would see nothing more than a pale woman with really bad hair. But thanks to nine hundred years of experience and the power he'd inherited from good old Dad, Declan *knew*.

He leaned back and smiled. The smile wouldn't reach his eyes. Whatta you know, a harpy. Harpies dealt in death. But there was something off about this one. An exploratory probe of her thoughts bounced off strong protective shields. Smart woman. You never knew who wanted to play in your mind.

Okay, so she wasn't as horrific looking as a harpy should be. Made sense, though, to tone it down if she expected to mingle with humans. Sending guests screaming into the night would earn her a quick boot out the door.

But she shouldn't be able to clean herself up that well. And the magic he felt wasn't her own. Strange.

Could she be the one? Harpies were dedicated collectors for Hades. He'd keep her on his radar.

She stopped in front of Mel and shoved some keys at him. "Your car and room keys. Enjoy your visit, sir." Her expression said, "Want a free ride to a vacation spot in Tartarus?"

"Hmmph." Mel took the keys and started to walk away. Then he paused to look back at her. "Good thing you got yourself a different dress. Don't go sewing any rabbit fur onto this one. Oh, and do they still have that brown dog here?"

She nodded and Declan would just bet she had her teeth clenched.

Mel's face split into a happy grin. "Terrific." And then he left.

The woman watched him go. She took a deep calming breath before turning to study Declan. "Can I get you anything?"

He shook his head. "What's with the rabbit fur?" Declan smiled at her, the special smile he saved for women he wanted for a night. It got lots of use. He accepted the power of that particular smile. It was just another tool.

The tool didn't work this time. She didn't smile back as she studied him a little too intently. *Don't get your hopes up, sweetheart. You won't be carting me off to Tartarus.*

Would he make a good candidate for a trip to Tartarus? Daria wasn't sure. He felt human. A human would be okay. But there were nonhumans in that group by the fire. One of those would be a lot more impressive. Besides, she didn't want to snatch just anyone. She was looking for someone evil, someone worthy of Hades's attention. It didn't matter how physically powerful her victim was; once she was in harpy mode it was all over. But if she wanted a challenge, she'd choose someone with powers beyond the mere physical.

"Mel didn't like the fur trim on my dress. It was rabbit fur." She shrugged. "I thought it was fake. What do I know?"

He nodded, and then flashed that smile again. Wow, powerful stuff. He was heat lightning and hot summer nights. Why that comparison? Why not compare him to the heat of Tartarus? No, her description was right. This man was of earth—primal, raw, exciting.

She felt the pull of sexual attraction, that heavy feeling low in her belly and the urge to clench her thighs around his hard male body. Surprising. *Disturbing.* She couldn't afford any distractions while she was here.

"I'm Declan Mackenzie. And you are?" He raised one dark brow.

She almost forgot to answer, lost in the dark fall of his hair, the brilliant blue of his eyes, the hard planes of his face, and a body his black T-shirt and jeans did nothing to disguise. Her gaze slid over the leather duster he'd dropped on the floor beside his chair. Unusual coat for this setting. "Uh, Daria Abaar."

"Intriguing. Daria is Greek. What would Abaar be?" His expression promised that everything about her interested him.

Abaar would be the first name she'd come to in the phone book. "This and that. I have a mixed ancestry." Kal and she were the products of Mom's one-night stand with Apollo, so yes, mixed would be about right. If Mom had lusted after an uglier god, or Apollo had been less drunk that night, then her brother and she wouldn't need magic to fit in. "Have you met any of the other guests?"

"Other than Mel? No. But I will." There was something in the narrowing of his eyes and the thinning of his sensual mouth that hinted at savagery. Human or not, she was looking at a predator.

"Well, if you need anything let me know." Time to put some distance between Declan's sensual pull and her unsettling awareness. She'd make sure none of the other guests needed anything while she scoped them out for a one-way, all-expenses-paid flight to the underworld. Kal was with the group by the fireplace. He'd give her his assessment when they got back to her room.

Daria almost didn't hear the frenzied barking in the distance. There was something desperate in the sound. The only dog she'd seen here was Trouble. He must've found his bunnies. Strange. He didn't sound happy about it. She was prepared to ignore the dog, when the barking turned to terrified yelping. *Hmm.* She looked around. Declan and she were the only ones close enough to the window to hear the noise. But he was human, so no enhanced hearing.

She drifted toward the hallway, undecided about what to do. Ganymede was with the dog, wasn't he? On cue, the cat padded past her headed for the kitchen.

Daria intercepted him. "I think I hear Trouble barking out in the woods. He sounds a little upset."

Ganymede glanced around to make sure no one was near enough to hear them. "He found some rabbits. He'll be okay. It's too early in the night for anything dangerous to be out there." His gaze turned sly. "They're all still in the parlor." He glanced at the kitchen. "Gotta go. A bowl of ice cream is calling my name."

"But what if—"

"You're the night manager. If you think he needs rescuing, take care of it. Oh, and stay away from the old church. There's something bad there. Might be dangerous even to you. Wouldn't want to have to scare up a new manager." With a dismissive wave of his tail, he answered the ice cream's siren call.

"That went well." Daria watched Ganymede disappear into the kitchen before sticking her head out the front door. Not that she cared what happened to the dog. He wasn't even a real dog. Besides, she had work to do, a victim to choose.

She allowed herself a moment to wonder about the old church. Dangerous to her? She didn't think so. Curiosity was an unfortunate harpy weakness. Before she winged her way back to Tartarus, she'd visit the church. Otherwise her need to know would eat at her long after she left the inn. She considered chasing after Ganymede and asking a few pointed questions, but just then the dog's frantic yelps escalated to terrified cries.

With a resigned sigh, she stepped onto the porch and let the screen door swing shut behind her. Mist was creeping across the inn's front lawn and winding in snake-tail tendrils around the trees in the forest beyond. The dog's cries echoed in the foggy darkness. Totally spooky. Totally her kind of night.

Once she found the right direction, she ran as fast as she could in the stupid gold sandals. She could move a lot faster in harpy form, but no use taking the chance that a guest might spot her. Besides, it sounded like Trouble was headed her way.

She wove around trees and leaped over fallen branches. Daria bet the sandals had *handmade in hell* stamped on their evil soles. To make sure she didn't trip and go splat, she kept her attention on where she was putting her feet.

The small clearing with a pond in the middle of it caught her by surprise. She paused as the sound of bodies crashing through the underbrush reached her. *Big* bodies. Maybe Trouble had run into a bear. Did they have bears in the New Jersey Pine Barrens?

Just then, Trouble streaked out of the woods. His eyes were wide and panicked as he raced up to her. "Big bunny, big bunny, big *big* bunny." And then he hid behind her.

She blinked. What the . . . ? Daria held that thought as a second animal burst from the forest. "Omigod." It looked like a pit bull with rabbit ears and a fluffy white tail. The monster bunny snarled at her as it drew closer. *Wow, impressive canines. Vampire Bunny?*

No way could she let that thing get Trouble. Ganymede and Sparkle would fire her behind if anything happened to him. And no, she wasn't doing this because it was the right thing to do. Harpies were heartless. She peeled her lips away from her teeth in her own snarl. Hunting was in her blood, and one oversized cottontail wasn't enough to intimidate her.

She gathered herself as Horrible Hare tried to leap around her to reach the terrified dog. Jeez, the ground seemed to shake every time those huge hind legs thumped down. He was in midleap when Daria grabbed him by the scruff of his neck and hoisted him into the air.

Shocked, he hung there for a moment. Daria allowed herself a moment of triumph. She might be in human form, but she could still take care of bully bunnies. Not that this was a normal bunny. Normal rabbits didn't have fangs, and they sure enough didn't grow to be the size of pit bulls.

"I'm putting you down now. A smart move would be to leave the dog alone." She released him, ready to react if he attacked Trouble or her. "I bet you're an insecure little wuss in human form. Find some other way to affirm your manhood."

With a really unbunnylike growl, the rabbit changed.

"What the hell do you think you're doing, lady?" Mel loomed over her in all his naked glory.

She did a quick scan. Okay, not so glorious. Daria gulped hard, forcing her stomach out of her throat and back down to where it belonged. "I'm saving the kid here from a jerk who should pick on someone his own size." The "kid" sat staring at her with hero worship gleaming in his big doggy eyes.

"Maybe you need to keep your nose out of other people's business. And the mutt's as big as I am. Difference is, he's a coward. So I got a kick from chasing him. What's the big deal? Don't see any blood." His gaze turned assessing. "You got a soft spot for the young and clueless?"

Something about his expression made her uneasy. "Nope. No soft spots. Except for my job. I'm the night manager. No chasing or intimidating goes on while I'm on duty."

His grin told her he'd chase whatever he felt like chasing. "I like turning the tables on things that think because I'm a rabbit, I'm easy prey. It makes me feel all warm and fuzzy inside. Know what I mean?"

Yeah, she did. Maybe she'd just scoop him up right now and cart him off to Tartarus. She deserved a few warm, fuzzy moments herself. Mom would be impressed that she'd gotten her man on the first night of the test. Best of all, he was mean and powerful enough to satisfy Hades. How many more chances would she get to catch someone like him alone in the woods? No witnesses except Trouble, and she didn't think he'd tell anyone what happened.

She looked around to make sure. And met the amused gaze of Declan Mackenzie. *Rats.*

"I saw you rush out the door. Thought you might need help with something. Guess you have everything under control, though." He moved from the shadows, Mr. Tall-Dark-and-Sinister. His black leather duster was a punctuation mark at the end of the sentence that said, "I'm a sexy, dangerous male animal."

Daria just stared at him. How much had he seen and heard? What if he'd caught Mel changing? She took a deep breath. *Think*. He must've missed that part of the show. He wouldn't be this calm if he'd seen the whole thing.

Mel's gaze darted between Declan and her. "Look, I like running naked through the woods. I'm into all that one-with-nature crap. I should've been more careful, though. Didn't think I'd bump into anyone. Sorry." He didn't sound sorry as he nodded at Declan and then strode into the forest.

Daria bit her lip as she worried the problem. She'd made two big mistakes. First, she should've done some hysterical screaming when Mel went all naked, hairy, middle-aged guy on her. Second, she shouldn't have picked him up. Maybe she could've just stumbled into his path. She hadn't acted like a human female. Mel had probably already put the pieces together. She wouldn't get another shot at him. Worse yet, he might blab to someone else. If he did? There went her element of surprise. Great. A blown cover on her first night. *Way to go, stupid.*

"Huh. I could've sworn Mel didn't like you."

While she'd been calculating her dumbness quotient, Declan had moved into her personal space. Being this close to him was like floating in a lake of steaming water. As long as she was bobbing along on the surface, it was all good. If she started to sink, though, she'd go really deep before hitting bottom. Drowning in all that male yumminess might be fun, but it couldn't be good for her harpy career. And her career was all that mattered.

"Guess I was wrong." Declan went on. "He got naked pretty fast, so he must like you. A lot." He slid his gaze the length of her body, and his smile was a sensual twist of his lips. "So do I."

"What?" She narrowed her eyes as she got his meaning. "Whoa, there. It was just like he said. I was busy looking for the dog when this guy burst from the bushes with all his danglies hoppin' and boppin' to their own tune. I mean, my jaw dropped all the way to here." She waved her hand somewhere in the vicinity of her waist to demonstrate exactly how far said jaw had dropped. "And while I was picking up my jaw, the dog found me. So I can go back to the inn now with my jaw tucked underneath my arm."

"Hmm." His smile said, "Yeah, sure."

She opened her mouth to blow him away with an angry retort. But she closed it again as Ganymede padded out of the forest.

"Yo. I felt all this guilt about sending you out into the scary woods alone." He'd chosen to explain things in her head.

Made sense if he didn't want the human sex god to hear him. It also said something about his power. He went up a notch in her estimation.

"So I left my ice cream melting while I checked things out." He paused to bat at a bug. *"Okay, so I didn't feel guilty. Sparkle made me come."*

Declan seemed oblivious of Ganymede's conversation. He wandered over to the edge of the clearing. "I think I'll walk a little before I go back to the inn. Seems to me the property map by the door showed an old church in this direction."

"Um, I think the church is off-limits to guests." But not off-limits to nosy employees.

"I know." His smile was a slash of white in the darkness.

"So I don't think you should go there."

He stared into the darkness. "Why don't you go back to the inn with the dog and make believe you don't know where I'm going, hmm?"

Daria fought to hold back a gleeful giggle. *Yes.* "I guess if you're determined to go there . . ." She shrugged. "I wouldn't be doing my job if I didn't go with you. The inn has a duty to keep its guests safe." *Gag.*

Declan speared her with a stare that warned of approaching storm clouds. "Maybe it isn't too smart wandering around alone in the woods with a strange man."

She offered him her perkiest smile. "Strange women could be just as dangerous." More than he'd ever know. Lucky for him he was human and not particularly evil, or else he might be on his way to say hi to Hades.

He gave in with an irritated grunt. As she walked beside him along the wooded path with Trouble and Ganymede at their heels, she let her imagination run amok. But that would have to be the only thing running amok, because her test was serious business, not to be sidetracked by broad shoulders, a great face, and muscular everythings.

First, she'd strip slowly with lots of wiggles and wanton intent. Then she'd watch him slip out of that leather coat. He'd pull the T-shirt over his head while she admired how the play of moonlight and shadows defined his bared body. Maybe she'd help him get rid of his jeans and . . .

Declan glanced at Daria. She seemed lost in her own thoughts. Good. He reached for Ganymede's mind, and when he found it, he got right to the point. *"Let's hear the story one more time."* He would rather have had this talk while they were alone, but he'd make do with what he got.

Ganymede didn't pretend to misunderstand. *"Your first*

guy showed up two weeks ago. Said the council was thinking of relocating here from Scotland because the American Mackenzies were out of control. The council figured they could police the clan better from this side of the Atlantic. He was scoping out the inn as a possible headquarters."

"They're a bunch of control freaks." Declan had defied the council by settling in the States a century ago. And he was the only one on the council who thought clan members should be allowed to live their lives the way they wanted. He drove the other members crazy. But they were afraid to throw him off the council. He allowed himself a grim smile. They had good reason to fear him.

"Yeah, well, anyway, a few nights after he got here he went into the woods and never came out."

Declan nodded. Teilo. Not too smart, but tough in a fight. He wouldn't have gone down easy.

"We searched. All we found was a finger with the council ring on it." Ganymede's eyes gleamed in the darkness. This wasn't his cute-kitty look. "Whatever took him left the scent of wolf behind. New Jersey doesn't have any wolves. Sparkle questioned the three weres who were staying with us. None of them did it."

"Okay, then the council sent Sceolan here to find out what happened." Sceolan was tough and smart. After losing Teilo, he would've gone into the woods armed to the teeth. And he could've taken out a werewolf without breaking a sweat.

Declan had told the council to send him, but Sceolan had wanted to go. Teilo had been his close friend for a lot of years. And even though centuries separated him from his Viking roots, Sceolan still believed he should rush in weighted down with weapons and berserker rage to avenge his friend. Great in theory, but it hadn't worked.

"He lasted three days, then the same thing. He went into the woods at night, and all we found was his finger with the damn ring." Fury simmered just beneath the surface of Ganymede's voice. "We didn't have any werewolves staying at the inn that night."

"Why didn't you shut the place down?"

Ganymede offered him a cat shrug. "No good excuse. We couldn't bring in the cops. Whatta we say? There's a were-wolf in the woods? He ate someone, but he left the guy's finger and ring behind. Guess the metal got stuck in his teeth. And you can't floss after every meal." He glanced away. "Besides, it looks like the victims are all council members."

"Still . . ."

"Look, bloodsucker, after the first killing, I went into the woods every night. No one messes with me. I kept the guests close to the inn where Sparkle could watch them. The second guy decided to go hunting without telling me. By the time I got to the church, it was too late." The long pause was fraught with all kinds of menace. "I'm spending every freakin' night at that church until I catch whatever's doing this. And when I'm finished, there won't even be a finger to mark its end."

"Cindy and Thrain don't know about this, do they?"

Ganymede's silence was his only answer.

Declan stared into the forest. There was almost a full moon tonight. Whatever lurked in the darkness had a taste for the Mackenzie council. "You shouldn't have let Daria go into the woods alone."

"She's a harpy. She can take care of herself. Besides, nothing's happened to anyone but you guys."

Declan settled into silence while he tried to work up some fear. Nope, didn't have any. Too bad. Those that had the sense to be afraid lived to have the crap scared out of them another night.

He'd stopped trying to hang on to his emotions a lot of years ago. What was the use?

He looked at Daria. "You've been quiet for a while. What're you thinking?"

"Hmm? Oh, nothing much. Just daydreaming about stuff that'll never happen." Her smile was all about secrets.

Declan returned her smile. She wouldn't be too happy to know that when she smiled it canceled out the multi-colored mane and raccoon eyes.

Ganymede stopped at the edge of the forest. Smothered by brush and vines, an old ruin of a church stood in a clearing. Yellow crime tape stretched from tree to tree around the edge of the woods. Signs warning that the clearing and church were off-limits were nailed to at least a dozen trees.

"The fingers were inside the church."

Declan nodded.

"Wish the bastard would try to take us on now." Ganymede's voice was thick with his need for battle. *"He's never seen what a pissed-off cosmic troublemaker can do."*

Daria rubbed her arms. "Something doesn't feel right here. So what happened?" She leaned across the tape to get a closer look.

"A crime, I guess." He felt the wrongness too. It was like a darkness rising from the ground—cold, deadly, with a thick slickness that slid across his skin. He controlled the urge to rub his hands against his jeans. What the hell was it?

"You know, maybe it's time for me to go back to the inn. I can't do my job out here." She tugged at Declan's sleeve. "Come on, let's go." Trouble leaned against her leg, a low rumbling growl vibrating in his throat.

Must be a potent threat if it made a harpy jumpy. Declan couldn't do anything while she was here. He'd come back once he'd made his plans, and then he'd see what the big bad could do against someone who had a little more in his tank than Teilo and Sceolan.

The voice caught them just as they were turning away. It seemed torn from the earth itself, a deep growl of savage satisfaction. "You came, as I knew you would."

Declan swung to face the church. Beside him, Ganymede tensed. Daria sucked in her breath on a startled hiss. Trouble barked, but he didn't try to crawl under the yellow tape. Maybe his brain would grow into his body after all.

"Who are you, and which of us are you talking to?" Seemed like reasonable opening questions. Declan's voice echoed back at him in the thickening fog. His follow-up question would be about funeral arrangements. Did the asshole want to be cremated or should Declan just shove the body parts into a hole?

The chuckle oozing from the ground was pure evil. "I've waited overlong for you, Declan Mackenzie. Come to me now."

Ah, Declan finally felt an emotion. This guy was creeping him out. "Why? So you can do to me what you did to Teilo and Sceolan?"

"No. They were only a means to draw you here. Come to me *now*."

That would be a no. Declan would come back alone and find out what the hell was going on before he destroyed the thing lurking under the church. "It's been great talking to you, but I have plans to make." He was counting on whatever was here being bound to this spot. They'd be in a world of shit if it decided to chase them back to the inn.

"Let's go." He turned away from the clearing.

A roar of fury shook the ground beneath them. Declan's reaction to the threat was instinctual. He felt the slide of his canines as he spun to face the danger. Peeling his lips back from his fangs, he hissed.

Daria's startled gasp reminded him a second too late that he was supposed to be human. Well, hell. He clasped her hand and dragged her away from the church. Trouble gave a frightened yip as he raced toward home.

When they had almost reached the inn, Declan chanced a glance at Daria. She stared at him from wide eyes.

"You're a vampire."

He grinned at her. "Yeah. And you're a harpy."

CHAPTER THREE

"Hey, now that everyone knows everyone else, I can talk out loud. What the hell was that back there?" Ganymede padded ahead of them, tail waving in the air. "Not that it scared me, but it's my job to know all the monsters in the woods. After I talk things over with Sparkle, I'll go back to make sure no idiots . . . er, guests go sightseeing around the church."

Declan was a *vampire*. How had she missed that? And what did that thing at the church want with him? Harpies didn't shudder, but tonight was special, so she indulged herself.

Ganymede rolled on, oblivious of all undercurrents. "You gotta draw it into the open, bloodsucker, so I can eyeball it. Can't destroy it until I ID what kinda entity it is. Sorta fixated on you, isn't it? Wonder why? And what's it doing underneath the church? If it wanted you, it coulda made its move last year when you first showed up. Oh, and why's it bound to the church anyway? Lots of unanswered questions. We need answers fast."

Declan rubbed a spot between his eyes. "Maybe it didn't have the power last year. Maybe it wasn't even here last year."

"Vampires don't get headaches." Daria tore out her mental page dedicated to Declan Mackenzie and started a new one. At the very top, she noted: add to list of candidates for possible relocation. A vampire was fair game. And vampires were evil by their very nature, weren't they? Hades had even mentioned vampires in his last memo. She thought about adding "too hot to ignore," but decided against it. She didn't want that particular reminder every time she accessed his page.

"When I was human I got these big, head-banging migraines. You *never* forget that kind of pain. If I were still human, I'd have one right now." His expression said it might just be named Daria. He smiled at her. Lots of fang showing. "Hey, Ganymede, maybe you'd better rethink closing down the inn. Cindy and Thrain will kick your furry butt out the door if they come home to find that something ate their guests."

Daria tried to concentrate on what was under the church. She couldn't. Declan was a *vampire*.

Ganymede glanced over his shoulder, his cat eyes gleaming in the dark. "Understand this, vampire, *nothing* messes with me. I take care of what's mine."

"And that worked so well for Teilo and Sceolan. Look, I appreciate your help, but this is council business. The entity back there killed two of us. Its meal ticket stops with me." Declan's voice was filled with quiet menace.

Whoa. The church monster had killed two *vampires*? "Hey, I didn't know that—"

"Don't want to start a pissing match in front of the little lady here, but when you take this thing down, I'll be there." Ganymede's tail whipped back and forth as he continued along the path.

Okay, Daria was going to end all nine of his miserable lives. Just for giggles. *Little lady?* He was kidding, right? Her mouth opened and words came out before she could think about their impact on her new job. "Um, I don't think a cute little kitty like you will be much help against the big bad monster back there."

Ganymede looked up at her, and something absolutely

terrifying glowed in his amber eyes. She sucked in her breath and stepped back. Uh-oh, *scary* kitty.

"Cute. Little. Kitty?" The cat held her gaze as everything in the forest stilled—the wind, the movement of animals and insects, *life*. And then without a whisper of sound, all the trees within a hundred yards of them fell down. Just fell down. Instant crop circle.

Declan and she stared at the cat. Ganymede turned away as though nothing had happened and continued across the new clearing. "See, I've got no self-control when I get ticked. Sparkle says I need to go to one of those anger management classes. Me? I say it's bad to repress all that mad. Don't know how I'm going to explain those trees to Cindy and Thrain when they come home, though."

"Forget the trees. We have more important problems." Declan sounded like a frustrated adult trying to reason with a couple of kids.

Probably because that's how Ganymede and she were acting. Daria subsided without saying anything else. But she wasn't thinking about the "big" problem. Sure, she was curious about whatever was under the church, but the fact that Declan was a vampire took center stage. Why? Maybe she didn't want to know the why.

Hmm, come to think of it, now that she knew he was nonhuman, she could add him to her list of possible judges as well. It wouldn't help her chances of passing the test if she tried to carry off the judge. So her first order of business shouldn't be choosing a victim, but finding out who the judge was. Complications. She didn't need them.

While she'd been thinking, Declan had turned his attention back to her. "So what's a harpy doing at the Woo Woo Inn? And don't tell me you're not here to snatch someone. The question is, why not choose someplace easier, someplace where no one would know what you are?"

"No one *was* supposed to know what I am. How did Sparkle and you figure it out?" She'd kept her shields up. No one should've been able to get past them.

Ganymede glanced back and gave her what passed for a cat grin. "Sparkle knows shoes and people. She loves hooking up the unhookable. And as challenges go, harpies are big game. I'd bet she's come across a few of you guys before."

Daria nodded. That made sense. Sort of. She glanced at Declan. "Okay, how about you?"

He didn't look at her, focusing his gaze instead on the path ahead. "Dad wasn't a vampire." A long pause hinted that Dad was much more. "He passed down some of his power to his only son. I can strip away surface illusions to see what lies beneath."

Surface illusions? What did that mean? When the silence stretched out, Daria figured he wasn't going to volunteer any more info about his family, so she turned her attention elsewhere. "I'm still not clear on my duties, Ganymede. Sparkle and you have been pretty vague."

Declan put his hand on her arm, and no matter how impersonal it should feel, it didn't. The slide of sensation wrapped around her awareness with a warning that touching him back would be a huge mistake. But she wanted to. She definitely wanted to.

"How about answering my question? Why *here?*"

Declan sounded casual enough, but she sensed a deeper interest. She wondered what was behind it even as she prepared her lie. "Aunt Ocypete said this was a great place to relax. I figured I could work here for a while and wind down a little. Even harpies need some R & R." Not really. When she reached Mom's level, she'd have to maintain eternal vigilance, always on the lookout for vic-

tims. "I don't know what Aunt Ocypete's definition of re-
laxing is, but this isn't mine."

They reached the inn before he could comment. Daria
thought about doing some night manager stuff, whatever
that was, but decided to stick with Declan and Ganymede
instead. Blame her insatiable curiosity.

Sparkle was in the middle of arguing about nail color
with one of the guests when they walked into the front
hall. She allowed the woman to wander away as she fixed
Ganymede with a tense stare. Daria figured the cat was
filling her in mentally on the night's excitement.

A tiny smile played around Sparkle's mouth as she cast
a glance Daria's way. "Any lust-induced touches happen
out in the woods?"

Daria remembered their bet. She returned Sparkle's
smile. "No." It was a good thing the bet didn't include
thoughts. But there'd be a few *rage*-induced touches if
Sparkle didn't return her clothes. "I want all my stuff
back. Now." She left the "or else" possibility hanging in
the air.

Sparkle ignored the demand and the implied threat.
She sighed. "I mourn your lost opportunities."

Opportunities? Daria wasn't going there any time
soon. "Oh, and I still don't know what my job is."

Sparkle didn't look interested in any conversation
without sex in the topic heading. "Boring, boring."

"I think you need to shut this place down." Declan's attention returned to Ganymede. "Whatever is under that
church might be bound now, but who knows when it'll
get powerful enough to escape. And you can't stay on
guard 24/7. If it gets loose, it might decide to vary its
menu. After all, one council member every few weeks
isn't too filling."

Sparkle put two fingers up to her forehead and closed her eyes. "I sense a seismic event coming. Cause—two hard heads bumping." She opened her eyes and grabbed Daria's hand. "If you're going to work here, you need to see the place. Let's take a quick tour. I guarantee when we get back they'll still be going at it. You won't miss anything."

Daria took in the light of battle in Ganymede's eyes and decided to go on the tour. Who knew, a perfect victim might pop up along the way. She trailed after Sparkle.

"Parlor. You've seen it. Big room, fireplace, yawn. Ignore the chimney sweep ghost." Sparkle started to drag Daria away. "All the woo woo stuff is good for business. People don't go away disappointed when they come here."

"Chimney sweep ghost?" Daria stopped walking.

"No biggie. He got stuck in the chimney a bunch of years ago." She shrugged. "The house was empty. He died. Don't worry, he doesn't make much of a fuss. A little cursing, a few complaints about his crappy minimum-wage job, and pieces of coal dropping into the grate. Nothing major. Two lovers trapped in the chimney would've made for more fun." She turned away from the parlor. "Let's go on to the kitchen."

That poor spirit. Daria caught herself before more sympathetic thoughts polluted the waters of her harpy soul. But she was still thinking about the spirit when they reached the kitchen.

"This is Katie the cook. She practices Wicca. Katie might be a sweetie"—Sparkle's expression said *not*—"but her broom is armed and dangerous. Don't cross it." Sparkle gave the short woman a finger wave. "This is Daria, Katie. She's our new night manager. Be kind."

The cook was a dinosaur on a starship. She fit in with the old-fashioned look of the rest of the house, but she commanded an army of new stainless steel appliances. Katie scowled at Daria. "We'll do just fine together as long as you stay out of my kitchen." She peered at Daria. "Need to do something about your face, gal. I can give you the name of a good plastic surgeon."

Daria brightened. Katie *was* a sweetie. That was the nicest thing anyone had said to her since she'd arrived.

Sparkle didn't give her a chance to thank Katie as she hurried her on to the library. "I like this room. All dark and manly." She sniffed. "It even smells like a man. Old leather. And someone used to smoke a pipe in here. Cindy has hundreds of books on paranormal stuff."

"What's this?" Daria reached down to open a book resting on the desk. "*The Advice Book.* What kind of advice?"

"Everything. We don't have time—" She started edging toward the door.

The book thought they did. "Oooo, you're the first ones to visit tonight. And two good ones you are." The cackle sounded a little fiendish. "Harpy, lots of destiny issues coming your way soon. What you think you want, you don't want; and what you really want might kill you. But go for it."

"What?" Daria blinked.

"Sparkle, big change ahead. You could lose your way. And a new nail color won't fix it." Another cackle.

Sparkle reached over and slammed the book shut. "That thing gives me the creeps."

"A talking book? Where'd that come from?"

"Who knows? It just showed up one day and Cindy let it stay. She's softhearted that way. I'd bond with it more if it gave sensual advice." Sparkle glanced at her watch. "Look, we only have time for one more room. My sensitivity session starts in five minutes."

Daria almost walked past the guest bathroom until

Sparkle grabbed her hand and pulled her inside the small room. She glanced around. Nothing special. "Why here?"

Just then the toilet started flushing. And flushing, and flushing, and flushing. At the same time there was a rap on the mirror. Startled, Daria glanced up in time to see a message in red appear on the glass surface. *Let me out!*

"Uh, I think someone's trapped in the mirror." Daria figured this was as bizarre as it got. A human would have to be in desperate need to brave this room.

Sparkle shrugged. "We've invited it to leave, but it just keeps writing messages and flushing the toilet. The flushing will stop once we're gone. I wanted you to see this so you'd know why guests run screaming from here trailing toilet paper behind them."

"Why not break the mirror to free the entity?"

Sparkle shook her head. "Seven years of bad luck. Can't take the chance. Besides, it might not work and then you've ruined an antique that cost megabucks."

She was right. Daria straightened her spine. She was a harpy. Harpies didn't give a flip about the suffering of others. No more saving anyone, even Trouble.

Sparkle hurried away, leaving Daria to walk slowly back to where Declan and Ganymede were still arguing. She stopped to peer into the dining room. Guess she'd have to find out on her own what lived in here. Later.

Daria sensed their anger even before she reached Declan and Ganymede. It was too late to turn and walk away, so she joined them.

"The Woo Woo Inn doesn't close down for anything as long as I'm in charge, bloodsucker. I'll blast that thing outta the ground if I have to." Ganymede's ears were flat against his head and his tail whipped from side to side.

"Yeah, and how long do you think you'll stay in charge

once guests start disappearing? And I don't think the return of one finger will satisfy the grieving relatives. *Their* fingers will be busy punching in the numbers of their lawyers. What will Cindy and Thrain think of that?"

Ganymede hissed.

Declan showed fang.

"You know, I bet you guys could work out a compromise if you'd stop going all aggressive with each other." Daria, the voice of reason.

Ganymede turned angry cat eyes on her. "Go manage something. That's what I'm paying you for."

Okay, now *she* was ticked. "Fine." Turning her back, she walked away.

"Someday you're going to find out you're not as almighty powerful as you think you are. Last year it was Sparkle that saved our butts, not you." Declan turned and followed Daria.

Ganymede was royally pissed. He wanted to kill something. Through his rage he heard a noise. Cocking his head, he listened. It sounded like . . . No, it couldn't be. Panic drove his anger away in an instant. It sounded like an ice cream truck.

Someone shouted from the parlor, "Hey, take a look out the window, it's a freaking ice cream truck."

"Woohoo! An ice cream man. Let's eat him." The werewolves.

Ganymede was in charge. He should go in there and tell the wolves to keep their mouths shut in front of the humans. But he couldn't. All he could hear was the ice cream truck. Playing "Don't Be Cruel."

"What's an ice cream truck doing here this late?"

"Way to go, Elvis is in the house."

"Let's get some ice cream."

The voices rolled over him while he stood frozen. He watched the guests stampede out the door to get ice cream. Ganymede just watched.

And when everyone had gotten a cone and wandered back inside, Ganymede waited. *He knew.* The ice cream guy had come for him.

Ganymede wouldn't give him any satisfaction. He'd go to meet him. Cosmic troublemakers didn't run and hide. He stared at the front door, and when it opened, he walked onto the front porch with legs stiff from tension.

The ice cream guy was sitting on the porch swing. He looked at Ganymede from serene eyes. Ganymede had never been able to tell what damn color those eyes were. But he did know they were deep and penetrating and they saw to the core of his black soul. Okay, not so black anymore. He'd toned it down a lot since they'd first met.

"Well, well, Ganymede. It's been a while." He still had all that dark hair that flew in every direction and a fuzzy beard.

He had a deep soothing voice. Ganymede hadn't forgotten that voice, any more than he'd forgotten the first time he'd met the ice cream guy. "Nine years." Ganymede fought to keep his attitude. "So how's the goodness-and-light business doing? I never got a name from you last time, so how about I call you Chill? It goes with the ice cream crap."

"Business is passable. And give me any name you want." There was a hint of laughter in his eyes.

"You don't have to worry about me. I still have some of the goodness-and-light you gave me last time. I'll let you know when I need a refill." Ganymede said the words even as he felt despair setting in. Chill wouldn't be here if he thought everything was okay.

The man shook his head. "You should know better, Ganymede. Lying doesn't work. Last time we met, you were working for the forces of darkness. The Big Boss gave you a second chance, allowed you to keep your cosmic troublemaker job because it meant so much to you. Everything was great for a while, but recently you've been falling back into old ways."

"Yeah, yeah, I'll try to do better." He couldn't help it. The guy brought out the sullen in him.

"You've promised before, Ganymede." Chill stared into the darkness. "Now you'll have to make a decision about your future."

This couldn't be good.

"You have to give up cursing, threatening to kill things, and Sparkle Stardust."

"Fine, I can do . . ." Ganymede choked. "Sparkle?" His voice was a strangled gasp.

"Afraid so. She's not a good influence on you. Sparkle is selfish, vain, and fixated on sex." There was no condemnation in Chill's voice, only a sad statement of facts.

"Yeah, but she's—"

"Your choice, Ganymede."

"What's on the other side of 'or'?"

"Or you'll no longer be a cosmic troublemaker. You'll be an ordinary Joe going to an ordinary job each day."

"*Human?*" No. The Big Boss couldn't do this to him. "Wait. I can't choose. I—"

The ice cream guy rose. "Now. Make your choice, Ganymede."

Panic took all reasoning power from him. He couldn't give up Sparkle. But being a cosmic troublemaker was everything to him. Why get up in the morning if you couldn't mess with someone's life?

Chill waited patiently.

Ganymede hated him with a white-hot intensity. "I'll give up Sparkle." Every word was torn from his heart.

Old fuzzy-beard nodded.

"I'll check in now and then. Oh, and every time you curse, I'll take away one of your treats. Juvenile but effective." Mr. Goodness-and-Light walked back to his truck and in a few minutes the strains of "Don't Be Cruel" faded into the distance.

Ganymede stood there a long time. How would he go on without her there to joke with him, insult him, and make awesome love to him? How would he tell her? The thing under the church didn't seem like such a big deal anymore.

Declan thought about getting up and leaving the parlor. He'd come in here to calm down and try to think through what had happened at the church. But now Sparkle was having some kind of sensitivity session. He didn't need it. Declan didn't get close enough to anyone for them to care whether he was sensitive or not. But he tuned in for a minute.

"Quality time with the ones you care about is precious. Use it wisely." Sparkle was in harem-girl mode tonight. She wore loose black silk pants and a fringed top that wouldn't be within shouting distance of her navel any time soon.

"Yeah. Play Monopoly with them even if you always lose Park Place," put in Harvey the werechicken. "My uncle asked me to come over for a game last year. I was too busy. The next night a wolf ate him." He glared across the room at the three werewolves.

The werewolves waved at him.

"Uh, yes." Sparkle frowned.

Declan grinned. He'd bet that wasn't the direction she wanted her discussion to head.

"You, back there, what do you and your special friends"—read lovers—"do when you're all cuddled up together?"

The woman Sparkle pointed to was a great-looking redhead. A demon. She smiled at Sparkle. "We play with souls."

Not the right answer. Sparkle frowned.

Declan lost interest in the session as Daria walked into the room. She spotted him sitting in his favorite dark corner and came over to sit with him. She pulled her chair close so she could talk without bothering Sparkle. There was a lithe sensuality to her walk that would horrify her harpy heart if she knew.

"What's Sparkle talking about?" She spoke in a quiet, husky voice that was so sexy he wanted to drag her to the floor and make love to her in front of Sparkle and her whole sensitivity crew. Sort of a hands-on demonstration.

Whoa. Not his usual in-control response to a woman. "Relationships." Close enough.

She nodded. "Emotional relationships don't work for me."

"Me either." He was torn. It was okay for him to be cold, but he wasn't sure how he felt about her being the same way. "I avoid them. Too transient. Too many what-ifs and might-have-beens." Humans freaked out when they discovered what he was. Besides, they died too soon. And the women of the Mackenzie clan? They knew what he was and ran like hell when he got anywhere near them.

"Does it bother you?" Her interest was real.

It made him uncomfortable. Women enjoyed the sexual pleasure he gave. They didn't care about his feelings. And that was fine with him. He shrugged. "My emotions have dried up over the centuries. So I guess, no, it doesn't bother me." He met her gaze. "I'm surprised about you, though. You're a sensual woman. Are you sure there's no one special back home?" He allowed himself a smile he knew had more than its share of sexual intent.

"No." Daria looked horrified that she could exert a sensual pull on any man.

He smiled. She probably checked herself out in a mirror each night to make sure she was ugly enough to repel everyone.

Would she understand his attraction to her? Probably not. Getting lots of bright and shiny presents put on his bed was exciting. When he opened them up and found they were all empty? Not so exciting. Nowadays, he wanted something interesting and amusing inside the boxes. Glossy wrapping paper optional.

Declan allowed his gaze to glide the length of her body. He saw her tense. She'd noticed. His smile widened. Her body was worthy of the shiniest party paper. Her face? Not as bad as she'd like, he was sure. In fact, he'd bet Sparkle could create a few miracles from the neck up.

"What do you think is under the church?" She'd decided to steer the conversation out of dangerous waters.

"I don't know." Whatever it was, it wanted him. It had killed two council members to get to him. And at the edge of his consciousness was a memory he'd managed to suppress for nine hundred years.

"I hope Ganymede doesn't regret not listening to you."

Thoughts of the church and what was under it grew fuzzy around the edges as Daria shifted, her thigh pressing against his for a nanosecond. That's all his body needed. His emotions might have faded over the years, but his senses had grown far more acute. Any touch from a woman he wanted woke the sexual beast in him. He growled low in his throat.

He wanted to slip that purple top off her. Then he wanted to unhook her bra, freeing her full breasts. Then he'd cup those breasts before lowering his head to run his tongue across each nipple.

"I think Ganymede's the kind of guy who'd need to be sitting on a mountain of fingers before he'd admit he made a mistake." He spread his legs, relieving the growing pressure and drawing Daria's attention. He felt the slip-and-dip of her gaze skim his thigh and pause *there*. There acknowledged the attention by hardening its resolve.

"I suppose." Her gaze skittered away.

Her scent. It was of warm woman and suppressed arousal. He could feel her tension, her I-want-but-don't-want turmoil. Good. The longer she made him wait, the more erotic excitement she'd bring to the moment when he buried himself deep inside her.

She looked back at him. "I'm curious. Why were you here last year?"

He shrugged. "I'm a member of the Mackenzie council. The council is sort of the ruling body of the Mackenzie clan. Our headquarters is in Scotland, but we live in different parts of the world. There was a clan rebellion at the Woo Woo Inn, so all five of us had to show up to put it down."

She raised one pierced brow. "Rebellion?"

"It's not important. I didn't give a damn about the rebellion, but the rest of the council is pretty rigid when it comes to clan laws." He grinned. "Sparkle Stardust carried the day for the rebels, and I went home with the rest of the council."

"Sparkle?" Puzzled, she pursed a surprisingly sexy mouth.

"One cosmic troublemaker against five vampires? What'd she do?"

"She removed their sexual organs until they agreed to leave everyone at the Woo Woo Inn alone." He grinned at her. "Sparkle left me intact because she thought I was cute." He winced. That sounded almost playful.

"Wow." Daria shook her head. She looked like she didn't quite believe him.

"We need to talk, Daria." A hard male voice interrupted them.

"Later, Kal."

"Now."

Declan controlled the slide of his fangs as he stared up at the tall guy who looked like he was wearing a fright mask. A male harpy. Unusual. He'd only seen a few during his lifetime. Daria seemed at ease with him. A lover?

Declan's unexpected surge of emotion felt a lot like jealousy, or what he thought jealousy must feel like. He hadn't experienced it in centuries. Not since he realized he liked sex but not the stuff that followed.

Declan smiled at the harpy. A mere baring of his teeth. "I think the lady said no, pal." This Kal guy was close enough for Declan to realize the magic he'd sensed on Daria belonged to him. What did that mean?

"Okay, okay, I'm coming." Daria stood.

Kal walked away without another word.

Declan's thoughts were a jumble of possibilities.

Daria took a last glance at Sparkle, who waved at her. Then she glanced down at him. "See you later." And she hurried away.

Running away won't do you any good, harpy lady. He sometimes thought he had a little werewolf blood in him, because when the prey ran he couldn't control his need to pursue.

Werewolf.

And suddenly a thought so horrible hit him that he forgot where he was and the woman walking away from him. The memory he'd been dodging for nine centuries hit him smack between the eyes.

Fenrir? No, it couldn't be. But if it was, God help them all.

CHAPTER FOUR

Memo: to all harpies
Subject: quality control
Quality Control reports that harpies have flooded Tartarus with lying politicians. This type of prey offers no challenge and lowers the tone of our great company. Harpies are encouraged to be the best they can be. Go out and get a vampire, a werewolf, or at least a spammer. Punishment for dumping any more dishonest politicians on Hades's doorstep will include listening to Rush Limbaugh day and night for six months.

Remember, you are what you snatch.

HADES THE PATIENT

Kal was waiting for her at the registration desk. "Your clothes. I don't know where they came from, but get out of them before the judge sees you."

"Can't. Sparkle hijacked my wardrobe and left me with this. I'd yank out her fingernails one at a time, but then Ganymede would fire me."

"There has to be something you can do." Her brother didn't sound sympathetic.

"Fine. I'll do something." Harpy temper alert. "See if there's a felt-tip pen in one of the drawers." She waited while he fished one out. And then she methodically drew smiley faces all over Sparkle's sexy top. She handed back the pen. "Happy?"

The hint of a smile softened his face. "Creative. Had a tough night, sis?"

"You have no idea. Now, what's so important it couldn't wait?"

"Eris is here." He waited for her reaction.

"That *witch*." Aello's daughter, Daria's competition, the most conscienceless climber of the harpy corporate ladder, the grossest of them all—*she* wouldn't need any artificial ugly upgrade—was *here*.

"Where is she?" Obviously not nearby, because wherever Eris went, people fled. No, Daria didn't hear any screams of horror or see anyone running for their lives. "I thought she'd targeted a maximum-security prison for her challenge. Two contenders shouldn't be hunting in the same place."

"Eris never gave a damn about rules. She's here and looking to take top prize. You've got to ratchet up your act."

For the next half hour Daria worked at the desk and tried not to think about Eris. But it was tough not to remember all the teasing, all the taunts the other harpy had thrown her way over the years.

"I'm so sorry your stay was cut short." Daria smiled at a sweet-faced old woman who was waiting to check out. She was surrounded by five rolling suitcases and three scary minions.

The sweet-faced old woman didn't smile back. "Ghosts in the chimney, spirits in mirrors, bossy books, things that grab the food right off your plate. It's too busy around here." She drew her lips back from her fangs to express how much she really hated all that busy stuff.

Daria sighed. She really wasn't cut out to be a manager—lots of smiling and acting nice, both offensive to her harpy sensibilities.

Okay, a little honesty. She wouldn't mind smiling or being nice to Declan. No excuses, she simply liked the guy. And that might be the exact reason he should be her test subject, to prove she had what it took to snatch anyone Hades wanted. *Please, please let someone more evil, more powerful, more perfect pop up.*

Daria pushed a strand of hair from her face and looked around. Guess that was it for the night. As soon as she took care of a few more things, she'd hunt up Eris and have a calm, quiet talk with her.

"You're being too nice." Her brother, Kal the grump.

He'd been hovering around her, sort of like the ultimate fight manager, suggesting cutting verbal jabs as various guests stepped up to the desk to ask questions, check in or out—tell that woman a little butt goes a long way, tell that man he has to stop buying his clothes at thrift shops—and scowling when she ignored him.

Now the bell had rung, and he was moving in to get her ready for round two. Kick her if she ever took her brother anywhere with her again. *Uh, hello? He's the only one who can make you look like a harpy.*

"It's my job to be nice to them."

Kal thought about that for a few beats too long. "Yeah, you do have to keep this job. What comes next?" His expression said it'd better involve her being vicious or violent, preferably both. "There're a lot of people here. One of them is the judge. You've got to prove you can embrace your inner cruelty, sneer at goodness, and—"

"Okay, okay, I get it. The meanest of the mean, the rudest of the rude, that's me. Sheesh." She watched a pudgy balding man head her way. Human. Now, what did he want?

Would this night never end? She still had to make sure all the guests had what they needed, check on the cook, get her clothes back, and confront Eris. *Then you can think about Declan.* She pushed that thought aside. Too soft, too . . . human.

With Kal breathing down her neck, she didn't even try to dredge up a smile for the guy. "Leaving?"

The man offered her a toothy grin. "Hell, no. This place is great. I just wanted to find out how I could get a peek inside the walls."

She blinked at him. "Inside the walls?"

"Yeah. Oh, I'm Walt Hendricks, professional debunker, and this place is a freaking treasure chest."

"Debunker?" She glanced at Kal. He shrugged.

"That's me. I go around proving that vampires, were-wolves, and stuff like that don't exist. It's all phony."

She fought back a grin. "The world needs more people like you."

"Thanks. This lady said she heard noises coming from the cellar. Thinks they're ghosts. So I went down to the cellar to check for rats. No rats." Walt frowned. "There were three guys who went down with me. Got really ticked when we didn't find any rats. Said they were pretty disappointed with the situation here. Asked me if I knew any place that *did* have rats in the cellar. Don't know what their thing was. Probably don't want to know."

Daria made a mental note: *three werewolves will probably check out.* "This is my first night on the job. You'll have to talk to Sparkle Stardust about the walls."

He nodded. "I've got a nose for anything fake. Bet those rats are in the walls." His eyes gleamed with the fervor of a zealot. "This place is getting a rep for being the real deal when it comes to paranormal crap. That's why the big business. The Woo Woo Inn won't be a draw once I get through with it." Looking like the self-righteous jerk he was, Walt strutted away in search of Sparkle.

"Well, between Walt Hendricks and the monster under the church, Cindy and Thrain will be lucky to have a business by the time they get back." Where was her so-what attitude? Jeez, she was actually outraged on the Woo Woo Inn's behalf. Go figure.

"Who cares?" Kal ignored anything that didn't impact their goal. "We need to talk about this Declan guy. Stay away from him."

She raised one brow, which should've warned her brother. He ignored the warning.

"He's trying to hit on you, sis. No distractions, remember?" Kal's gaze followed the sway of Sparkle Stardust's behind as she walked to the door with one of the guests. "Besides, he's a human. You can do better."

"He's a vampire, and no, I can't do better. You'd have to be a woman to understand." Daria didn't make a habit of wondering about her brother's sex life, but she did now.

Maybe it was because she was reassessing her own sex life. Hers was practically nonexistent. Sure, she could've hooked up with lesser male harpies, but she was too focused on her career to feel any enthusiasm.

"A vampire?" Kal looked surprised. "Must be powerful if I didn't pick up on him. I'll add him to the list."

"Right. Your list." All of Kal's efforts centered on her rise to power in the harpy world. Always had as far back as she could remember. Daria had never thought about it before; she'd just taken his support for granted.

She thought about it now. He wouldn't draw the notice of any female harpies, because even with his magic, he wasn't grotesque enough to suit them. Kal took his harpy heritage seriously, so he wouldn't show his real face to human women. He didn't have any friends, because he was too involved with her career, and he just didn't fit in with the other males.

Selfishness was a desirable harpy trait. Then why didn't it make her feel good to know how selfish she'd been? Mom said "It's all about me" should be her mantra. Well, not where Kal was concerned. And that decision *did* make her feel good.

"Working up a list of victims isn't as easy as I thought it'd be." Kal's usual calm-and-patient persona was slipping.

She nodded. He never lost his temper with her. She'd seen him in action with others, though. It took a long time to light his fuse, but Kal didn't play nice once he got mad.

"I'm only considering victims who're alone. No witnesses. Any witnesses and you don't pass." He grew thoughtful. "Maybe we can use the vampire's interest in you against him. Get him alone and then snatch him." His smile wasn't a smile at all. It was all calculating harpy. "So I take back what I said about staying away from him. Go for it, sis."

Daria didn't understand the flutter of panic that thought brought. "Who else is on the list?"

"No werewolves. They're pack animals. Too many chances for a witness. A werecat. Leopard. Solitary. A big maybe. Five vampires, but they're traveling together. Again, a witness problem. A demon, but she'd be happy to visit Papa Hades. No challenge there. The cook is a witch. Could work if we can figure out how to get her away from her kitchen. The only cosmic troublemaker we have a shot at is the dog, Trouble. He's young and likes to run off by himself. Plus he's probably not as powerful as I suspect Ganymede and Sparkle are." Kal turned to the second page of his list. "I have a few more shifters to check out, along with a couple of unidentified beings. If we really get desperate, we'll grab a human."

She frowned. "The pickings sound pretty slim."

"That's why you need to concentrate on the vampire. I think he's alone. Alone is good. And he'll impress the hell out of everyone if you can get him."

"Yeah, I guess so." Personally, she thought snatching Mel the wererabbit or Walt the debunker would give her more personal satisfaction.

As if conjured by her own conflicted feelings, Declan came in from outside. Where had he gone? Had he visited the church again? Daria's need to know bothered her. But she was beyond denial, and besides, Kal had given his seal of approval to her interest. So it was all her brother's fault. There, blame assigned.

She wandered over to where Declan had paused to stare into a mirror. Daria stood beside him. He saw nothing, she saw too much. Even taking into account the image Kal had created for her, she couldn't compete with Eris. *Her* face was thin. Eris boasted at least three double chins. *She* had big eyes. Eris gloried in her small, beady ones. *She* had an ordinary nose. Eris never stopped bragging about her huge, hooked beak.

And she couldn't ask Kal to up his magic without taking the chance of uglifying herself out of a job.

"Do you miss being able to see yourself in a mirror?" Maybe that wasn't such a bad thing. If she couldn't see herself, then she wouldn't know how far short she fell of her goal.

Declan shrugged. "Sometimes. But I wasn't thinking about the mirror." He grinned at her. "Smiley faces?"

"Don't ask." She glanced away from him and caught her reflection in the mirror. Holy horror! She was *glowing*. Okay, not actually glowing, but his smile canceled all of Kal's hard work. No amount of magic could hide her joy in Declan's smile.

Daria coughed and cast a guilty peek in Kal's direction.

He offered her a thunderous expression as he mouthed, "Stop looking so damn happy." She shrugged. There were some things in life or death she couldn't control— Hades's bad temper, the daily afternoon temperature in Tartarus, and her glow when Declan smiled.

She sure hoped the judge wasn't lurking anywhere nearby, though. She looked around. A few shifters, one vampire, and Mel. The wererabbit ignored her as he studied the shifters. Probably choosing a new victim to bully.

To escape the storm clouds building around the registration desk, she linked her arm through Declan's and led him toward the parlor. "I have a few things to do. Keep me company?"

"Sure." Declan did the dueling glares thing with Kal before going with Daria. "Who's your friend?" Nope, he wasn't jealous. But he *did* want a night with Daria Abaar's sexy body wrapped around him. And if the male harpy got in his way? Bye-bye, harpy guy. A violent thought? You bet. That's because Dad was a violent-gene machine.

"My brother Kal."

Well, that sort of took the air out of his budding rivalry.

She talked about her night as they walked. He liked listening to her. She was the one person who could take his mind from the nightmare scenarios he'd been creating in his mind.

That thing under the church couldn't be Fenrir. For that to happen, coincidence would have to be piled on coincidence until they formed a complete impossibility.

"Did you enjoy your walk?" Her smile said, "Fishing, fishing."

"I had to feed."

"Oh."

"Don't worry, I didn't do any drinking on Woo Woo

Inn property. A few people in town will wake up tomorrow with a hell of a hangover."

"Sure." Her expression didn't give away how she felt about that. She stopped in front of a group of vampires. "Can I get you guys anything?"

Night Feeders. The lowlifes of the vampire world. Alone they weren't too powerful, so they traveled in gangs. The one closest to Daria grinned up at her. "You can get me a bag." His fangs were on full display.

She frowned. "A bag?"

"Yeah. You've got a killer body, babe, but I'll need to put a bag over your head so I can fuck—"

Before Declan could transfer thought to action, Daria took care of the problem.

She grabbed the guy's fangs, one in each hand, and yanked. Eyes wide, he came up out of his seat. "Here's the deal, dirtbag. I can pull real hard and tear your fangs right out of that useless head. Hmm, wonder if your brains would leak out of the holes? Oh, wait. No brains." She exerted a little more pressure and the vampire made panicky sounds. "You know, I bet no one has experimented to find out if fangs grow back when they're pulled out by the roots. Want to be part of that experiment?"

The captive vampire tried frantically to shake his head, but Daria had too tight a grip on his fangs.

The other Night Feeders started to rise. Declan lowered his shields and let them touch his mind. Shocked recognition drove them back into their seats. So his cover was blown. The Night Feeders were the least of his problems.

With a disgusted sound, Daria released the vampire and allowed him to sink weakly back into his seat. "Jerk." She turned to the rest of his group. "You want anything?"

They all shook their heads while they slid nervous glances between Daria and him.

Daria turned to the rest of the room. "Anyone want anything?" She was met with shocked silence.

"Well, I guess that takes care of that." She didn't look particularly upset.

"I have to talk to the cook. Let's buzz by the kitchen."

Bemused, he followed her, but whatever needed saying in the kitchen didn't get said. A small woman met them at the door and thrust a tray of food into Daria's hands. "It's time for dinner. Put these on the dining room table. Oh, and if something tries to grab one of my buttermilk biscuits, you snatch it right back. Those biscuits are only for paying guests."

He leaned against the wall and smiled as she made multiple trips from kitchen to table. She was one harried harpy. He'd bet this wasn't what she'd had in mind when she swooped down on the Woo Woo Inn.

The smile ended abruptly as he realized what he was doing. No way could he let her make him too happy. Yeah, he wanted sex, but that didn't translate into happy.

He curled his lip at the scent of rare beef and the sounds of hungry predators. Any shifters whose alternate forms were herbivores should probably control their need to change while they were here.

When everyone was finally served, Daria filled a plate and dropped into a chair at a corner table. He joined her. "Remind me not to go near the kitchen again. At least the vampires take care of their own meals." She glared at him. "You could've helped."

"Not and keep my street cred with the other predators."

"Sexist." She kept her accusation to one word as she gave in to her hunger.

Jeez, he even got a sensual rush from watching her eat broccoli. That was sick. Aside from her ability to arouse all his senses, what did he really know about her? "You said you weren't here to snatch anyone. Maybe you're not. Maybe you're moonlighting at a second job. Done any contract work lately?"

She paused with her fork halfway to her mouth. Carefully, she returned it to her plate. "Contract work?" He could see her processing that. "Are you asking if I'm working for that thing under the church?"

"It's a possibility. If it can't take a physical form, it might need help with the killings and finger removals. You and your brother deal in death, so you'd be logical choices for the job." He didn't want to react, but the momentary flash of hurt he saw in her eyes bothered him. "But it could be almost anyone here. Those Night Feeders, for example." He waited for her temper to kick in. It didn't.

"I get where you're coming from. In fact, I'm proud you think I'm capable of that. Harpies have violent natures. It's who we are. Just like your nature is to be a cold, bloodsucking fiend."

Ouch. He didn't get a chance to comment because suddenly her biscuit began to float off her plate. At the same time, he saw a dim outline hovering above their table. A kid? Maybe. He wouldn't even have seen the outline if it weren't so dark in this corner. Declan waited for her to grab the biscuit away from the spirit. She stared at it for a moment, and then looked away. The biscuit disappeared.

"The cook wouldn't be happy about that." He made his voice soft, no accusations in it.

She shrugged. "I didn't want it anyway." But she looked troubled.

Did she have a little conflict with her harpy nature going on? He let the subject drop. Probably because he had a few of his own conflicts.

She pushed her chair back and stood. "I'm finished. Let's go."

As they left the dining room, Declan noticed her brother sitting across the room. Kal didn't look happy. "So what's next?"

"Next is headed our way." She nodded toward the front door.

Sparkle cast them a speculative glance as she strolled over. Every male within sight watched that walk with lust in his heart, or elsewhere.

Declan looked at Daria, and for a moment thought he saw a touch of wistfulness in her eyes. His sympathy surprised him. Sympathy. An emotion. The Woo Woo Inn was cracking his hard shell, and that was dangerous. A hard shell kept bad things out and worse things in.

He realized that Daria's values had been turned upside down from the moment of birth. Ugly was beautiful. Violence was good. And all positive emotions were submerged for the greater bad.

Now, for the first time, she was seeing what the rest of creation considered desirable. Okay, so Sparkle was over-the-top and outside-the-norm, but she was damn good to look at.

Daria's moment of wistfulness—if it ever existed—disappeared. "The night's over, Sparkle." She glanced at her watch. "It'll be dawn in a couple of hours. I've had all I can take for my first night. I'm heading to my room."

Sparkle's slow, sexy smile heated everyone and everything around her, giving new meaning to global warming. When she turned that smile on him, Declan was able to appreciate it, but felt nothing more. Not like what he felt for Daria. Uneasy, he wondered exactly what he *did* feel for her. And why?

After centuries of one-bite nights that included sex, a few sensual sips, and the inevitable don't-look-back good-bye, he had his routine down. No emotion, just a feeding of his senses. Perfect. That's the way it would be with Daria. He'd *make* it that way.

"Have you progressed beyond meaningless chatter and sizzling glances?" Sparkle aimed the question at Daria.

"Nope. I practice a hands-off policy. Now give me my clothes back."

Sparkle nodded toward Declan. "How can you resist touching him? Mmm, all that warm male flesh just waiting for you. Think of his bare, muscular chest. First you could trace each nipple with the tip of your finger, then slide your palm over—"

"My clothes. Now." Daria's face had lost the pale look. She flushed, refusing to meet his gaze.

Declan frowned. What was this about? His senses were alive to Sparkle's suggestions, but what was left of his reason wanted to know why Sparkle was pushing so hard.

Sparkle ignored Daria's demand. Instead she turned her attention to him. "Forget her face. Look at that body. Think of stripping her down to hot, wanting woman."

He was thinking, he was thinking.

"Are you going to give my clothes back?" Daria's voice trembled, either from embarrassment or anger. He wasn't sure which.

"Um—" Sparkle rolled her eyes to the ceiling for inspiration. "No. And even though I applaud your attempt to accessorize with all those smiley faces, you really need some help from someone who has more fashion sense."

"Fine. So let's settle up tonight's bet. I won." Daria ignored the snarky comment about her fashion sense.

From the tone of Daria's voice, that didn't bode well for Sparkle.

Sparkle's sigh was filled with dramatic resignation. "Let me guess. You want me to give back the black cotton jammies with 'Hades Is My Hero' on the front."

"No." There was something in Daria's voice he hadn't heard before, a hardness that hinted at exactly how ruthless she could be. "We agreed if I won I'd get to make you do something."

"I suppose." Sparkle's expression grew wary.

"I want you to break a nail. *That* nail." She pointed to Sparkle's right index finger. "And you can't fix it for three nights."

"I don't think so." Sparkle's voice was cold. No calculation, no sensuality, no inflection. Just cold.

Daria shrugged. "Hey, it was *your* bet." The guests nearby stopped to stare. "If you want to back out, we can cancel the whole thing."

Sparkle never took her gaze from Daria. "Declan, would you get the nail clippers from the top drawer in the desk?"

What bet? He retrieved the clippers and handed them to Sparkle.

She took a deep breath and then clipped off the nail on her index finger.

Katie the cook gasped before hurrying back into her kitchen.

Then Sparkle lifted her gaze to Daria. Declan had thought she was frightening last year, but her scary index had just shot through the roof.

"You've made me very angry, sister."

Declan believed her.

"I was amusing myself up till now." Sparkle dropped her gaze to her ruined nail. "I just got serious." Turning, she walked away.

Daria looked at Declan. "I lost my temper."

"Yeah, I noticed."

"That was a mistake."

"No doubt."

"I guess you want to know about the bet."

"That would be a yes."

She walked to the screen door and stared into the night. "It was a stupid bet. I don't know why I made it."

"Sparkle is good at manipulating people into doing things they don't want to do."

"She bet me that I couldn't get through each night without one lustful act." She looked over her shoulder and grinned weakly. "She doesn't know me."

He could take that as a compliment—I had to fight hard not to touch you—or he could interpret it as a slam—I have so-so willpower, but it wasn't hard to resist you.

"Just a suggestion, but if you win tomorrow night, leave her nails alone. You don't want to send her over the edge."

She kept staring into the night. "I guess what happened to your council last year would qualify as sending her over the edge." Daria turned her head to smile at him. "Did she do it for real?"

"I don't know. But the other guys were doing a lot of running and screaming. Sounded like they thought it was real."

"And she thought you were too fine to mess with."

"Uh-huh. I think she said something about not depriving me because who knew when I might need all that wonderful male equipment?"

She threw back her head and laughed. Really laughed. The sound made him feel good, and that made no sense at all.

"I assume she gave everything back."

He nodded. "Once their favorite organs were back in place, they were gone."

She was still chuckling. "Sounds like a scary lady."

"Never underestimate her. Ganymede seems like a straight-ahead guy. Get him mad and he'll kill you. The end. Sparkle strikes me as someone who'll nibble you to death—a bite here, a bite there. Always when you don't expect it. You'll be just as dead as with Ganymede, only it'll take longer."

"Thanks for the warning." She yawned. "It's been a long night. Think I'll go up to my room."

Declan glanced at his watch. "Yeah, it'll be dawn in another hour or two. I have to see what I can figure out about our friend under the church."

She hesitated as though she wanted to say something and then changed her mind. "See you tomorrow night."

Declan watched her climb the stairs, and then went out onto the porch. He'd wait until he was sure she was settled in her room before he headed out to the church. Ganymede was probably still there, but that was good. He needed someone to get word to the council in case he didn't make it back to the inn.

CHAPTER FIVE

Daria watched from her window as Declan strode across the front lawn and into the woods. They'd both been lying.

She'd had no intention of going to bed before she talked to Eris. But that would have to wait until she found out what her favorite Mackenzie was up to.

A harpy's insatiable curiosity was a terrible thing. Daria thought about that as she followed him along the narrow wooded path. But a harpy's ability to rationalize made everything okay. So by following Declan, she might catch him alone and be able to snatch him. Or if that didn't work, she could save him from the thing under the church, because she didn't doubt for a minute that's where he was headed.

Daria frowned. She wasn't supposed to save anyone from anything. Mel the wererabbit had been an aberration, an unthinking moment when she'd let her hunting instincts take over. Besides, she would've lost her job if she'd let Mel have the dog.

Then she brightened. By saving Declan's butt, she was simply giving herself another shot at him tomorrow night. There. Harpy rules upheld.

When she drew close to the clearing where the church stood, she found a hiding place that gave her an unobstructed view of everything.

Ganymede and Declan stood behind the yellow tape arguing. Daria blocked out all extraneous sounds so she could hear.

"Look, bloodsucker, I don't give a darn what you want.

I'm staying right here close to the action. Cosmic troublemakers don't hide behind trees so they'll be safe."

Harpies did. Oh, not so they'd be safe. It was so they could be sneaky. Sneakiness was taught from the cradle in the harpy world. Wait. Something was wrong with Ganymede's comment. Darn? Ganymede was a *damn* kind of guy.

Ganymede plunked his bottom on the ground to emphasize his intention. "You need backup. I don't want to have to collect your finger in the morning." He stared at said finger. "Nice ring, though. Can I keep it if, you know, things don't work out?"

"I won't need backup. I have a feeling killing me isn't in the entity's game plan. But I won't do anything stupid. I'll stay out of the church. I just have to find out if it can materialize and what its agenda is."

Daria could see the amber glow of Ganymede's eyes.

"You're thinking if it can't materialize, it might have a few buddies hanging around to do its dirty work?"

That would be Kal and her according to Declan.

"Makes sense." Declan stared at the church. "Otherwise I don't know how it killed Teilo and Sceolan and just left their fingers. I've known beings that could kill from a distance, but leaving the fingers behind makes it more close-up and personal."

"You're sure they're dead?"

"Yeah, I'm sure. Council members are connected. I felt it when they died."

"Got it." Ganymede stood. "So give a shout-out to the bas . . . bustard."

Daria held her breath. Her stomach roiled with a mixture of excitement and worry. Harpies were addicted to the life-and-death stuff. But until she'd landed at the Woo Woo Inn, she hadn't known what real excitement was.

The worry part made her uneasy. She shouldn't care what happened to Declan, but she did.

Declan vaulted over the yellow tape into the clearing. Daria gulped. Without conscious thought, she gathered herself.

Whoa, she'd forgotten something. Quickly, she stripped off her clothes. Not so she could spare Sparkle's outfit, but because she'd need something to change back into when she returned to human form.

"Hey, you there, under the church. I'm here. Let's talk." Declan moved a little closer to the ruined building.

Ganymede abandoned casual in favor of readiness. He crouched close to the ground, his back end doing the little back-and-forth swing cats did when they were getting ready to pounce.

It's here. Daria felt the presence as a sudden rush of icy air that covered her bare body in goose bumps. Declan must've felt it too, because he hissed, curling his lips away from his teeth in a snarl that exposed lots of fang.

At the same time, he became true vampire. His eyes elongated and grew larger, their brilliant blue now a black that reflected no light, a death color. His body seemed subtly bigger, more muscular. But greater than these physical changes was the sense of power and danger that flowed from him, a warning that you didn't mess with an angry vampire.

"You were wise to return, Declan. It would not have gone well with those at the inn if I'd had to come searching for you." The voice was stronger, more menacing if possible; a deep rumble that almost seemed part of the earth itself.

Declan took a few more steps forward.

No! Daria's silent scream didn't stop him.

"Big talk doesn't mean a thing if it isn't backed up by a

big body with lots of teeth. And what the hell do you want with me anyway?" Declan grew still, that complete lack of movement a human or harpy could never attain.

"You wish for a big body with lots of teeth? I can certainly accommodate you."

The entity's laughter was hollow, humorless, and totally terrifying. Daria hoped it was all bluff.

That hope came up a supersized zero as the air shimmered and a shape emerged. Daria clapped her hands over her mouth to keep from shrieking. Nothing was supposed to scare a harpy, but she'd just found the exception to the rule. A big furry exception.

In front of the church's entrance stood the biggest wolf she'd ever seen. No, not a wolf, a werewolf. He was the size of a pony, his glowing red eyes contrasting with his gray fur. And when he opened his mouth to growl, his teeth were very white, very big, and very sharp. And she was very impressed.

"Okay, you've convinced me. You have a form. Now what do you want?" There was something strange about Declan's voice. Not exactly fear, but a deep horror that went beyond fear.

"You know what I want. The prophecy will be fulfilled. You cannot stand against me." With those cryptic words, the wolf padded toward Declan.

"Fenrir." Declan breathed the name, disbelief mingled with dread.

Out of the corner of her eyes, Daria saw Ganymede leap past the yellow tape. But she was faster.

Her change was instantaneous. First the searing pain, then a rippling feeling as she became a giant vulture from the waist down. Six-inch talons were perfect for hooking and carrying off the unlucky. At the same time, with a tearing sensation, powerful wings sprouted from her shoulder blades. Her transformation was complete. In this form, she doubted anyone could match her strength.

She launched herself into the air and then swooped down over Declan. He barely had time to glance up before she hooked the back of his leather coat and lifted him into the air. As she soared upward, the wolf howled his fury and leaped high, his huge jaws snapping shut mere inches from Declan's legs.

Declan didn't fight her, but she could feel the angry tension in his body. Daria carried him beyond the yellow tape just as an explosion ripped apart the silence and a blinding light lit the night. A quick glance assured her that Ganymede was doing his thing.

"Put me the hell down." Declan's voice was tight with anger.

"Gee, thank you very much, Daria, for saving my ungrateful butt." She dropped him from a little higher than she'd originally intended. Maybe the jar would knock some sense into his thick skull.

When she turned to see what was going on in the clearing, the wolf was gone and only Ganymede stood there. The cat turned those amber eyes toward her. For a nanosecond she felt the push of his power. She swallowed hard. Good thing he wasn't on her to-do list.

Not that he scared her . . . Okay, he scared her. It wasn't normal for anything to frighten a harpy, but she'd found two scaries within five minutes. Another weakness she had to work on. Thank the gods the judge didn't carry a fright-o-meter. This would be her little secret.

She returned to human form and immediately began to search for her clothes. The silence behind her crawled up her back, forcing her to turn around. Vampire and cat stood, eyes wide, staring at her. "What?"

"Hey, babe, lookin' good. Never saw a harpy with a

body like that." Ganymede's unblinking gaze didn't waver. "How about you, bloodsucker? Ever see anything like that?"

"No." Declan had the good sense to look away.

But before he did, Daria glimpsed sexual hunger in his eyes. And even with the threat of a bionic werewolf hanging over them, she felt a rush of happiness. Sure, she wanted him, but her joy wasn't just because of that.

As she pulled on her clothes, she examined her reaction. Only a few male harpies had ever desired her, and not with the red-hot-burning-love kind of desire. Daria felt proud that she didn't need male approval and interest, because, well, she wasn't waterfront property in the harpy world. Ugly was the yesterday, now, and tomorrow look for harpies. No use yearning for what you'd never have. But here was a man who looked at her with lust in his eyes, his heart, and parts farther south. This was so cool.

Daria frowned. What *wasn't* cool was having to put Sparkle's shoes back on. Then she returned to thoughts of Declan.

She hoped he wasn't the judge, because she intended to make love with him, and if he *was* the judge he'd have to mark her down for having too much fun on the job.

Was this a weakening of her commitment to be the best harpy she could be? No, she was just allowing herself a little more flexibility in how she reached her goal.

As Daria took a few tottering steps in Sparkle's ankle-breakers, she admitted she wasn't completely without guilt, though. She shouldn't be desirable to anyone in the mortal world, even a vampire. It made her unworthy of greatness in Harpyland. Come to think of it, why *did* Declan want her? Okay, he'd just seen her body, but he'd shown interest before that. Hmm, a mystery.

She glanced up to find Ganymede looking all broody as

he stared into the woods. Depressed? Ganymede and depressed didn't seem to go together. "Where'd the wolf go?"

"Back under the church, I guess. When he saw me coming, he just sorta sank into the ground. I tried to blast him, but he was too fast for me." Ganymede looked at Declan. "You know him? He sure knows you."

"Fenrir." Declan said nothing more as he started to walk back toward the inn.

"Hey, wait just one minute there." Daria ran after him. "Ganymede and I just put our lives on the line to save you. Maybe you owe us an explanation, huh?"

"I owe you nothing." He gave her a narrow-eyed stare. "And never pick me up like that again. Fenrir wasn't about to kill me."

Ganymede's disbelieving snort expressed Daria's thoughts exactly. "Could've fooled me, bloodsucker."

Declan didn't turn to look at them. "Fenrir doesn't have the power yet to break free of the binding, but he's close. It's me he wants, but keep the guests away from there anyway. You don't want any innocents nearby if that happens. Oh, and I won't need the help of either of you guys. I'll handle it from now on."

"Yeah, until I find your finger on one of my morning strolls." Ganymede mumbled his disgust. "Look, if you're not giving out any more info, I have to go back to guard the church until all the guests are tucked up in their beds. Remind Sparkle to bring me a snack—a piece of Katie's apple pie, a slice of that birthday cake from last night, and a couple of candy bars. Nothing heavy." He turned and padded back along the path.

Daria watched Ganymede disappear around a bend in the path before turning to Declan. "He won't try to take on this Fenrir by himself, will he?"

"Not much chance. I think Ganymede understands male pride. He knows I have to be the one to take care of this problem." He still didn't turn his head to meet her gaze.

"Male *ego*, you mean." She trotted a few steps to keep up with his longer strides. "And 'this problem' could take out half of New Jersey if he gets past you. Not that I don't have complete faith in your awesome vampire power or anything." All the sarcasm she could muster was packed into each word.

He made an impatient sound and then finally met her gaze. "Sit down."

"Here?" She glanced around.

"Here." He sank to the ground and reached up to pull her down beside him.

"Are there bugs? I can't see what's under those leaves. There might be bugs." She hovered uncertainly.

The corners of his lips turned up in the beginning of a smile, but Daria was too focused on searching the ground for signs of things that went scritch-scratch in the night to celebrate the break in his bad mood.

"I don't believe it. You're a dreaded harbinger of death and you're afraid of bugs?" His smile widened.

"Bugs are ugly, and they don't have any respect for harbingers of death." She thought about what she'd just said. "Not that ugly is bad."

"I'll get rid of the bugs for you." His gaze grew unfocused as he stared at nothing.

Suddenly Daria heard rustling sounds all around her. With a squeak of alarm, she watched small dark bodies emerge from everywhere—under the leaves, the roots of nearby trees, and even drop from overhead branches.

She took a deep breath, ready to scream and run like

hell, when she noticed all the bugs were moving away from them. Like a tide of many-legged lemmings, they flowed into the surrounding forest.

Daria stared in disbelief. "Let me guess. You're the Pied Piper of woodsy creepies. Have you considered a career in pest control?"

He watched her sit gingerly beside him before he answered. "It's one of my powers. I can drive things away. I've been doing it for nine hundred years."

His smile was bitter, and she had the feeling they weren't talking about bugs anymore. "You don't have many friends, do you?"

Oops, that was kind of rude. Not that rude was bad. For a harpy. She didn't want a harpy-to-vampire interaction right now, though. Daria wanted the man-woman thing going on. She'd better hope the judge couldn't read her mind, because that thought would mean instant disqualification. But in this place, with this man, she didn't give a flying flip.

She smiled. It felt forced, but at least her lips were curving up instead of down. "I understand. I mean, the no-friends experience. I've had to work on self-esteem affirmations my whole life."

"Self-esteem affirmations?" He looked puzzled.

At least that was a step up from insulted. "I have appearance issues."

"And they would be?"

Real interest gleamed in his eyes, warming her in a way a male's attention had never warmed her before. "My body's too curvy for a harpy."

"I noticed." The gleam softened to a sensual glow.

The sensual glow tied her tongue in knots. "I mean, curvy isn't a good thing when you have to fly. It's, um, an aerodynamics thing." Had that just come out of her mouth?

"Right. Aerodynamics. So I guess you need a spoiler to guide your airflow." He was openly laughing at her now.

Time to move away from body issues. "Then there's my face."

"It's not a harpy face." He seemed definite about that.

"Why not?" Sure, she didn't look like Eris, but Kal had worked hard on her.

He slid his gaze over her face. And where it lingered on jaw, cheek, and lips, she felt it as a feathering of his fingertips. "At first glance, someone would get an impression of unattractiveness."

"It's okay to say ugly."

"Not ugly." He frowned. "Never ugly. Interesting is the word I'm searching for. When I first saw you, I felt there were layers and layers to be stripped away and examined."

"Layers? Like a head of lettuce?" Fine, so she was leading him.

"You're not ugly. Discussion ended."

Okay, that should really depress her, but no matter how much she tried to sink into a sea of despair, little bubbles of happiness kept her afloat. This was not a good thing.

"Kal and I take after Dad."

Uh-oh. Declan's expression was way too thoughtful. She'd babbled six words too many.

"Let me pull this together. You both have the same father, and you both take after him. Because of Dad's side of the family, you have a face that lacks a certain gruesome harpy quality. I'd bet your father isn't a harpy." He didn't ask for her input as he made his deductions. "But you say that Kal takes after your father too. So why does your brother look like a real harpy?"

Because he's spent a lifetime working on his face. "Haven't a clue. Gee, it'll be dawn soon. Shouldn't you get back to the inn before that wicked old sun rises?"

Declan was beyond distraction. "I sensed magic when I first met you, but it wasn't yours, it was your brother's."

This was excruciating. She might as well hurry along the process. "Look, Kal and I are twins. Our father is Apollo, and Mom doesn't let a week go by without apologizing for not choosing an uglier god for us to call Daddy. Kal can never rise in the harpy ranks because he's male, so he's dedicated himself to making me a success. He received strong magical powers from Mom, and he's used them to make both of us more acceptable in the harpy world. He's done a better job on his own face, though."

"Wow." And that was a sincere wow. He might've eventually figured out she was artificially augmenting her ugly factor, but not that Apollo was her dad. Declan wondered if the old guy ever saw a female he didn't lust after.

"So, now that I've told you something intimate about my life, I think you should do a little revealing." She waited.

The words *intimate* and *revealing* sidetracked Declan for a moment. They conjured images of naked bodies entwined on a bed complete with tangled sheets and a night breeze cooling heated skin but not passion.

Okay, back to the real world, which was pretty crappy right now. All he'd meant to do when he told her to sit down was to distract her from questions about Fenrir, not end up blurting out his life story.

He wouldn't tell her about Fenrir, but it couldn't hurt to give her an abbreviated history of the Mackenzies. "The Mackenzie vampires have been around a long time, first as Vikings and later as Highlanders. We've been a powerful force in the vampire world for over a thousand years."

"Were you born or made?"

"Neither. We're born human and then become vampire in our late twenties. It's a natural progression, so we never have to go through the death process. I was twenty-nine when I changed."

"Can you only have kids while you're human?"

Declan nodded. "Clan members marry young. I married when I was fifteen. We had four children." Such a long, long time ago. He couldn't remember faces or voices. Sometimes when he was alone he wished he could. "So you won't have to ask, my wife died centuries ago, the victim of her own bad judgment in choosing the wrong midnight snack. My kids?" He shrugged. "Who knows where they are or even if they're still alive? Until recent times, it was tough keeping track of people."

"You should search for them. Family is important." She sounded militant about that. "I don't know what I'd do without Kal and Mom."

"How old are you really?" He knew harpies were immortals, but something about Daria conveyed a freshness, a vigor, that didn't feel centuries old.

She hesitated, and then tipped her chin up in defiance. "Twenty-eight. But even if I live to eight hundred twenty-eight, I'll still feel the same about family."

"No, you won't." She couldn't possibly understand how the centuries sapped life's energy and enthusiasm until the only things left were the senses. The enjoyment of all that was carnal still made existence somewhat worthwhile. When even that didn't matter anymore, it was time to die.

Her expression said she didn't believe him. "Let me get this straight. The Mackenzies are vampires, but they're not undead."

"Right. We change genetically, but we don't die."

"How old are you?"

"About nine hundred years old, give or take a century."

She blinked. "Incredible. When's your birthday?"

"I don't remember. Sometime in the spring."

Daria widened her eyes. "That's terrible. We have to give you a birth date and a party."

"Do harpies go around planning birthday parties?"

"Never." Then she brightened. "Sometimes we throw a party when one of us catches a biggie for Hades."

She amused him, but beyond that, she touched him. No one had ever cared about when he was born, and they sure didn't give a damn when he died.

"You're right, though. I can't go around making people happy." She bit her lip in concentration.

He tried not to think about its damp sheen when she released it.

"I'll have Kal set it up. He can do whatever he wants. He's not the one . . ." She let the rest of the sentence fade away.

Well, well. He'd known she had secrets, and she'd almost blurted one. "Kal setting up a birthday party for a vampire? Don't think it's going to happen, sweetheart."

"He'll do it. If I ask him. Besides, if you're going to deal with Fenrir—an unknown badass you won't talk about—you should at least have a few final moments of happiness."

He smiled. "You mean before all of me leaves this earth except for my finger?"

"That's not funny."

"I think I'd enjoy the party more if we were celebrating a victory over the forces of evil." Of course, there were degrees of evil. He didn't know if he qualified as a heavyweight on the badass scale, but he definitely had his moments.

"You're right. A birthday party now would be frivolous. We'll have it after the good guys win." She frowned. "You didn't hear what I just said. Good is *never* part of a harpy's title."

Enough about parties, he wanted the answer to a question. "Who're you trying to snatch, harpy lady?"

"No one." She looked away.

"Is it me?"

"Not at the moment." She wouldn't meet his gaze.

"Trying to take me would be a huge mistake." He gently clasped her chin, forcing her to look at him. "My father wasn't a vampire any more than yours was a harpy."

Her smile was bright and false. "Then we should celebrate our connection."

Their connection? He studied her wide eyes and didn't see their muddy color. He slid his gaze over her full lips and ignored her piercings. He dropped his attention to the swell of her breasts and forgot about her tattoos along with how dangerous she really was.

"Sounds good. Let's celebrate." He leaned closer. She didn't move away. "Got any ideas?"

"Um . . ."

"I agree." Wrapping his arms around her, he covered her mouth with his.

Kal had slipped up in his creation of the perfect harpy. Someone needed to tell him the real deal shouldn't smell of pine forests and spring breezes. Daria's brother also should've told her it wasn't wise to play with vampires if you didn't know their moms and pops.

Declan traced her lips with his tongue, anticipating their softness, their warmth. Then he transferred his mouth to her ear, whispering, "Tell me your favorite color." To encourage truthfulness, he gently nipped her earlobe.

She drew away slightly to stare at him. "Color? Red, I guess. Why?"

"Just curious." Before he could pull her close again, the roar of a lion split the night.

"Uh, don't the humans sort of wonder about noises like that?" She glanced around.

He shrugged. "Ganymede told me lots of humans who come here like to role-play. They bring their own sound effects. Some humans might like to think that's a real werelion, some just pass it off as a recording. Doesn't matter. The Woo Woo Inn is all about the strange and unexpected. That's why people come here."

"Which is it?"

"A real werelion."

She brightened. "I hope he likes rabbit."

"Uh-huh." Declan tried to pull her close again, but she resisted.

"Anything could be lurking around."

"I sent all the bugs away."

"Something larger, with eyes, ears, and a big mouth."

"I'll kill it." Declan was growing impatient to taste her. No, tasting was out this first time. Mentally, he slapped himself up the side of his head. What was he thinking? For him, there were *only* first times. He didn't come back for seconds.

Seconds and thirds led to women thinking there might be a "relationship." He didn't do relationships. Ever. His emotions had tanked long ago, so he couldn't offer any warm or caring moments to anyone.

Life was a whole lot easier if he kept his sexual encounters to a series of one-bite stands. It'd worked for centuries. No recriminations, no crying, no pain-in-the-ass emotional breakdowns. What could he say, he was a fun-and-run kind of guy.

"Look, I have a vampire's enhanced senses. I can hear Sparkle cursing you back at the inn. There're no living things anywhere near us."

"*Nowhere* near us?" Her voice was soft, but something dark and predatory flashed in her eyes, then was gone.

That's when he was sure. She was thinking of carrying his ass off to Tartarus. His vampire nature—the one that lived to hunt, terrify, and generally dominate all living things—thought their clash would be a blast. Daria was fascinating in so many ways. And the threat of danger she brought to the table made her even more desirable.

But a part of him that liked her and wanted to get to know her better—not sexually, because that would be a one-timer—hoped she'd decide not to try out any of her snatch-and-dispatch harpy tricks on him. He hadn't fought her back at the church because he'd realized she was trying to carry him to safety. If she ever mounted a serious attack, though, she'd regret it real fast.

He pulled her close again, and she didn't resist. "So your favorite color is red. Sparkle would say red symbolizes everything that's hot and sensual."

"Hades says it symbolizes blood and the fires of Tartarus."

"I like Sparkle's take on it better." He slid his fingers through the tangle of her hair. It wasn't nearly as coarse as it looked.

Time to feed his senses. This was what made his existence bearable. But he'd learned centuries ago to mask the intensity of his need. A little playfulness made the women he had sex with relax and laugh. Kind of like a killer whale balancing a beach ball on its nose.

"How about a red surprise to celebrate our connection?" He didn't give her time to puzzle through his comment. Declan visualized what he wanted and then willed it to take physical form.

Her startled gasp was all the reaction he'd hoped for. "How'd you do that? Is it real?"

"Sure is." He hoped his little demonstration would give her pause when she thought about taking him. But then again, he'd enjoy a battle with another immortal. With *her*. Certain battles could be as sexy as hell.

"Well, at least we don't have to worry about anyone seeing us. I hope no one comes along, though. It would be hard to explain away a wall made from Red Hots."

CHAPTER SIX

Daria couldn't appreciate the bizarreness of the wall because her brain, hereafter to be known as Command Central, was trying to put down a rebellion of the masses. The masses of sexual hormones that didn't give a flip about abstract concepts like duty, goals, and career.

"*He's alone. Snatch him. Gain great glory. Achieve goal.*" Her brain spoke in focused sound bites.

"*Woohoo! He's alone. Get naked and party until dawn. How many shots have you ever had at a hot bod who wants you this much? Uh, let me think. Oh, never.*" The masses spoke with one voice.

"Do you like the wall?" Declan breathed the question into her mouth, and when she parted her lips to answer him, he took full advantage.

She forgot about the wall as he explored her mouth, his tongue smoothing away any doubts, any ethical consideration about fraternization between harpy and possible prey.

He settled her body more tightly against his, the hard press of his cock and the magic he created with his mouth making mush of Command Central.

A harpy gave as good as she got, though, so Daria did some exploring of her own. She slid her tongue over the impressive length of each of his fully extended fangs, a stark reminder that he could fit into another category besides possible prey. Try dangerous predator. Yummy. She loved a man who was deadly in every way.

Just when her tongue was memorizing the texture and taste of him, he abandoned her mouth. No fair.

"The wall? You didn't answer my question."

To give her time to recall which wall he was talking about, he kissed the sensitive skin behind her ear and then traced a path down the side of her neck with the tip of his totally talented tongue.

For a rubber band moment that threatened to stretch her control until it snapped, he placed his mouth over the spot at the base of her throat where her life force pumped a frantic rhythm. His fangs were a firm pressure against her skin. She hadn't given him permission to . . .

Then he moved on. What she felt was relief, right? Absolutely. No way could she have any other reaction.

"Um, it's high." She shivered as he pushed up her top along with her bra, exposing her breasts to the cool night breeze.

Sure, they'd been exposed when she became harpy back at the church, but this was different. This time she was completely aware of his gaze on them, and, as she'd already discovered, his gaze was as intimate as any touch.

"All the better to remain private. What else?" He lowered his head to her breast and swirled his tongue around her nipple.

Her nipple hardened while the rest of her body liquefied. Was that physically possible? She didn't think so. "It's made from little red candies. They're symbolic, right?"

"Mmm. They're sweet, hot, and fun to nibble on." He demonstrated his nibbling technique by closing his lips over her nipple and nipping gently. "And their burn stays with you."

"Why—" she was down to speaking in short gasps "—that wall?"

"Because you're too tense, too focused on being a super harpy. I thought making love inside a wall of Red Hots would make you laugh, relax you." He transferred his attention to her other breast.

Huh? What he was doing to her body would *relax* her? He had to be kidding. Burying her fingers in his thick hair, she pulled him closer, if closer was possible. She didn't laugh, but she wasn't doing much thinking about her job right now either.

Reaching behind him, she slipped her hands under his shirt so she could splay her fingers across his broad back. Harpies didn't do a lot of touching, so the sensation of smooth male skin was a major rush.

She thought about stopping there, but that would be a waste of opportunity. And playing the opportunistic bitch kind of appealed to her tonight. Wiggling her fingers beneath the waist of his jeans—no underwear. Yes!—Daria worked her way south until she was finally able to clasp his awesome butt. She dug in, massaging a pattern of delight that shut even Command Central up. Daria was totally into the feel of his firm flesh beneath her fingers. Wonderful, amazing, but not enough.

Super harpy? She could dream. Right now, with him, she could only think about being super sexy. He made her feel sensual and . . . And what? If she lived in his world, that last word would be *desirable*.

He didn't give her a chance to feel conflicted about the word as he kissed a searing path over her stomach, pausing at the spot where Sparkle's borrowed pants began.

Don't stop, don't stop.

"You have a beautiful body." His breath was warm temptation against her stomach.

"No. Can't have anything beautiful." She was starting to pant as he slid her zipper down. Obligingly, she lifted her hips so he could work her pants over her hips. Her panties quickly followed.

When he moved lower on her body, she lost her grip on his bottom, so she anchored herself by taking a firm grip on his wide shoulders.

She should push him away, affirm her duty to be forever ugly, deny that he could find anything remotely beautiful about her, but Daria's will was seeping from her in a thousand small rivulets of doubt and desire. Instead, she leaned back to give him better access to her body.

"Why the need to *not* be beautiful? You could probably sneak up on your victims better if they were dazzled by all your positive points." Just in case she didn't get what points he was talking about, Declan reached up to roll one of her nipples between his fingers.

With a groan of pleasure, Daria expressed her appreciation for all the mind-blowing things his fantastic fingers could do.

She tracked his progress by the warmth of his breath when he spoke. Right now he was really close to where her massed army of hormones was attempting to hold off Command Central's assault. CC was armed with that dread weapon, *reason*.

He placed his mouth high on her inner thigh, and she clenched around the possibilities for his ultimate destination. So far reason wasn't making a dent in the hormones because there were just too darn many of them.

Daria figured she'd better answer his question fast before she lost the power of meaningful speech. "You don't understand. Ugliness is a part of our culture. You have beauty contests, we have ugly contests. It's who we are. Besides, a harpy's face throws so much fear into her victim that he or she can't mount any organized resistance." There, she'd burned her last working brain cell on that one.

She tried to spread her legs for him, but she'd forgotten that her pants were still bunched at midthigh. Well, she'd take care of that fast. Wiggling, she tugged at her pants, ignoring the twigs poking her in the behind. A harpy should be willing to suffer for . . .

She lost her train of thought—okay, the engine was still chug-chugging, but all her boxcars had rolled back down the track—as he slipped his fingers between her legs and *touched* her.

"Then change your culture. Look the best you can look and prove to everyone that a gorgeous harpy can be more effective than the old model. The easiest catch is the one that doesn't *want* to fight back."

Declan bent his head and she felt the slide of his hair across her stomach. She sucked in a deep breath and then exhaled shakily. He'd said something she needed to answer, but she couldn't think. She. Couldn't. Think! This had never happened before.

And the touching continued. He smoothed the tip of his finger over the most sensitive spot on her whole body. Back and forth, back and forth, back and . . .

Her breaths came in quick gasps. Her heart pounded out a message of need so intense it bordered on pain. *Think.* But thoughts came together and drifted apart, never staying put long enough for her to make a connection.

Shouldn't she be touching *him*, bringing him pleasure? But she didn't. What if she moved and he stopped doing what he was doing? She'd fold into herself and cease being.

He ripped the decision from her as he continued to tease the now really overexcited nub of flesh. Heaviness built low in her belly along with delicious heat and the anticipation of unspeakable pleasure. She arched her hips in an instinctive pleading for more, more, and yes, more.

The tipping point came so quickly it practically flattened her. He slid his index finger deep inside her, did awesome things with it until she cried out, and then withdrew it. Over and over again he tormented her while the pressure built, and then he added a second finger.

It was all over. She arched one more time as the first spasm stopped her breath, the pleasure so intense tears trickled down her cheeks. And when the first wave of her orgasm passed, she had only enough rational thought left to slap her hand over her mouth so her screams wouldn't cause someone to call 911. Then wave after diminishing wave of bliss rocked her until she lay limp but incredibly happy beside him.

Too bad Command Central had wrested control back from her hormones. She'd never experienced anything close to that. The few male harpies she'd sampled were untalented eunuchs beside Declan.

Fine, so a little honesty wouldn't hurt. The male harpies hadn't *been* Declan; therefore no matter how hard they tried, they couldn't compete.

That thought was so scary she immediately blanked it out. She'd already wandered away from the harpy mission statement rejecting kindness and random acts of helpfulness. Uncontrolled lust for possible prey would only compound the problem.

"That wasn't enough." He looked as if his comment had surprised even him. "I want you with all the bells and whistles, harpy lady, but not here and not like this." His soft murmur was filled with regret and a promise of so much more than what she'd just felt. "I thought here and now would be okay, but I was wrong. I want you to get the whole package when it comes to pleasure between us."

An unfortunate choice of words. *The whole package.* Her heart was still recovering from what his mouth and fingers had created. At the thought of his sexual package laid bare for her to play with, her heart skipped a beat and then picked up a new rhythm of arousal.

"Oh, I don't know. Don't put down what just happened. I can't imagine . . ." Wait. It had been *his* mouth and *his* fingers creating the magic. "Omigod, I'm so sorry. You did everything, and I just soaked it all up." A quick glance between his legs assured her that he was definitely experiencing sexual frustration.

He opened his mouth to answer, but closed it again as they both heard pounding footsteps drawing near.

"Damn." He helped her drag her clothes into place before pulling her to her feet.

First there was heavy breathing and then the sound of someone's panicked scrabbling at the wall. Finally, a wild-eyed face appeared above the top of the wall just before it collapsed amid an avalanche of Red Hots.

Tiny pellets of candy rained down on her. Daria put up her hands to protect her face. When the danger seemed over, she lowered her hands to find Walt the debunker on his knees staring up at Declan and her.

"What the hell are those things?" Walt's hands shook as he pushed himself to his feet and stared down the path. "Something's chasing me."

Daria ruled out Fenrir. Walt would be just another finger discarded along death's path if the werewolf had decided to sample a tasty debunker.

She frowned at Declan. "The third little pig would've built a sturdier wall."

"Do I look like I have bricklayer genes? I just needed the wall to stand up for about ten minutes. Was that asking too much? Who goes around climbing walls made from Red Hots anyway?" He looked grumpy.

"Ten minutes? And here I thought vampires were masters of long, sensual foreplay sessions. Talk about shattered illusions." She tried for a sulky expression, but she knew a smile was ruining her effort.

"I'll glue your illusions back together later." He didn't look grumpy anymore. The thought of all that gluing seemed to have restored his good humor.

They didn't have time to discuss the finer points of wall building because something else was coming down the path. Daria heard it before she saw it. An animal. Not small. From the sound of it, an animal that was leaping toward them with joyful abandon. Yes, she definitely sensed lots of joyousness going on. Did she know anyone who got his kicks from scaring people? Hmm. Uh, yeah.

So she wasn't surprised when Mel the wererabbit bounced into view. "Jeez, he's the Energizer Bunny plus ten."

Walt must've decided that Declan and Daria could protect him, because he gathered enough courage to whip out a camera and take a shot. "I don't really believe that's a rabbit the size of a dog. And I sure don't believe it has fangs like a damn vampire. A clever hoax, that's all."

Mel's final leap landed him in front of Declan and Daria. Walt had wisely put Declan between the "hoax" and himself.

Then the nonverbal communication began. Daria knew her expression said, "This is getting old fast." Declan seemed to feel an amused grin said it all. And Mel? He gave a belligerent glare that turned into an angry stare that turned into a look of sly, thoughtful calculation. It was the last expression that scared her the most.

When no one seemed inclined to say anything out loud, Mel cast Walt a last stare that promised they'd do this again when there was no one around to save his ass and then bounded into the forest.

Walt found his voice along with his courage. "See,

that's why I'm here. America needs to know about the fakes passing themselves off as the real thing. But I got a pic of the sucker. I'm going back to my room to take a long look at this 'rabbit.' I bet it's a dog with fake ears and tail. Don't know how they did the fangs yet, but I'll figure it out."

He met Declan's gaze and froze. Declan took the digital camera from his hand and calmly deleted the shot he'd just taken of Mel. Then he put the camera back into Walt's hand. "You won't remember this incident, Walt. You'll remember walking in the woods hoping to come across something interesting. You didn't find a thing. You wasted your night. Go back to the inn now."

Without another word, Walt obeyed.

Daria watched him until he was out of sight before turning to Declan. "You couldn't do that with another immortal, could you?" Of course he couldn't.

His smile was beautiful but didn't give her the assurance she wanted. She harrumphed before staring around her at the piles of Red Hots. "You can't leave these here."

He shrugged. "Sure I can." His attention wasn't even on the remains of the wall when the Red Hots just went away.

Very impressive. She knew he wanted her to ask how he'd done it, so she didn't. "You know, now that I'm thinking straight again I seem to remember you trying to convince me that beautiful was the new ugly. Was this thing that just happened between us—"she didn't want to give it a name while it was still so new, so exciting "—a way to get under my guard?" Even the thought gave her a sinking feeling. Why? She should be able to enjoy his body and walk away without anything touching the essential *her*.

"Hell, no." Anger. Not always a good gauge of truthfulness.

Did she believe him? Another thought intruded. If he were the judge, that's exactly the kind of thing he might try in order to trick her into denying her harpy nature.

But his fury seemed pretty sincere. "I don't know why you're so bent out of shape. I mean, that's what vampires do, don't they? You guys are master manipulators." And evil? Was he evil? Was he still on her list of potential victims? She was too confused to make a decision. Command Central agreed.

"You don't have a clue, lady." That's the last thing he said to her on their short walk back.

As soon as the inn came in sight, he was gone. She didn't even see him move. She'd forgotten that vampires had preternatural speed. Daria sighed. He had preternatural everything, including the ability to twist her common sense into knots.

"Mmm. That would make a fine offering to Hades. He's not human with that kind of speed. What is he, Daria?"

The voice spun Daria around. It was Eris, as nasty and butt-ugly as always. How could she have forgotten for even a moment that her chief competition was here? "He's vampire." *And if you touch a hair on his head I'll rip your arm off.*

The strength of her reaction to the other harpy's suggestion left her shaking. Where had that come from? Everyone was fair game among the harpies. The prize went to the strongest. And the cleverest. "He's not worth your effort, though. There're a lot of beings more powerful than him inside. Have you met Sparkle Stardust? Now, there's someone who'd *really* impress Hades." And her removal would get rid of a *really* big thorn in her side.

"Sparkle Stardust?" Eris looked thoughtful. "Maybe I'll have a look-see." But when she focused on Daria once again, there was sly wickedness in her eyes.

Eris sensed her interest in Declan, so he'd be her ultimate target. That was how Eris worked. Demoralize the competition and snatch the prize.

Daria's rage cleansed her of all doubts about who she was. She was harpy. And Eris wouldn't be doing any poaching in Daria's territory. "Why are you here, Eris? Maximum security too tough for you?" Her smile was no smile at all.

The other harpy snarled at her. "I could've chosen anyone I wanted from that pile of miserable, human offal." She glanced at the inn, her expression speculative. "But I got the word there were a bunch of nonhumans here." Her gaze slid to Daria. "More than enough for two harpies. A nonhuman will rack up more points with Hades." She shrugged. "Easy decision."

Who'd gotten the word to Eris? Daria shook off the question. It didn't matter now. Not only would she have to ID her judge and corner suitable prey, she'd also have to keep an eye on the meanest of all the harpy hopefuls. She envied Eris that distinction.

Time to set the record straight. "I was here first. This is my territory. If you stake out anyone I've chosen, then—"

"Then what?" Rage made Eris careless.

Daria saw the intent to change in Eris's eyes. Idiot. They were in full view of the inn. "Go ahead. Change. I want you to. That way anyone watching from the window can report your behind. Guess who'll be kicked out before she has a chance to pounce on even one victim?" Actually, Daria wasn't sure that would happen, but she counted on Eris believing it.

Eris looked uncertain as she glanced toward the inn, then decided a verbal attack would work just as well. Daria was ready. Eris would drag out the tired old insults she'd used to make Daria's life miserable ever since she was a kid. Her old nemesis had never matured past juvenile taunts. But Daria wasn't a kid anymore, and she had a few of her own insults lined up.

"Pretty face. You don't have even one real zit." Eris, pulling out the tried and true.

"Get lost a lot, don't you? You couldn't find your way back to Tartarus even if you tied a GPS unit to your butt." Daria, remembering Hades's complaint that Eris ended up at the Vatican instead of the Evil Entities Convention because she wouldn't ask for directions.

"You smell *nice*." Eris, surprised that Daria was fighting back.

"Gotten out of park yet? A pig could fly faster than you do." Daria, gaining confidence.

"You've got big boobs." Eris, getting desperate.

"A one-legged chicken could escape from you." Daria, sensing victory.

"A one-legged chicken could *not* escape from me." Eris, totally ticked off. She screeched her fury. Temper had always gotten the better of Eris's common sense.

Daria decided she might've gotten too caught up in the thrill of the moment. Eris looked mad enough to change right here where anyone could see her.

"Oh, goody. I'm always up for a catfight." Sparkle's sensual purr spun both Daria and Eris around. "No? How disappointing."

Eris snarled at Daria and then stomped toward the inn. Sparkle gave her a finger wave. "Bye." Then she turned back to Daria. "An old friend, I presume?"

"Something like that." Glancing down, Daria noticed Sparkle had wrapped the finger with the broken nail in a bandage. *Oh, give me a break.* The bandage was decorated with glitter. "A bit extreme, isn't it?"

Sparkle shrugged. "You said I had to break the nail.

You didn't say I couldn't hide it. I find the bandage less humiliating than everyone seeing nine perfect nails and one . . ." She took a deep steadying breath. Evidently the emotional trauma of a broken nail wouldn't allow her to continue.

Stop being a wuss. Say what you think. "You're a shallow woman. No one cares about your broken nail."

Sparkle raised one brow. "You have a problem with shallow? At least I'm not fooling myself into thinking I'm something I'm not."

Daria sighed. Touché. Since Sparkle's rebuttal had all kinds of layers she wasn't ready to explore yet, Daria backed off. "Forget it." She headed for the inn. She'd only taken a few steps, though, before she remembered. "Oh, Ganymede wants you to bring him some snacks. I can't remember what exactly, but I guess you know what he likes."

She nodded. "Aren't you going to ask why I came out here?" Sparkle's feline smile warned Daria not to ask.

"Okay, consider yourself asked."

"I didn't want to give you the news inside. Too many valuable antiques for you to throw."

Oh boy.

"I made a few little changes to your room."

"*Little* changes?" Daria narrowed her eyes.

"Very little." Sparkle didn't do sincere well. "And I've left some new clothes in your closet."

"You finished?" Daria's temper boiled just below the surface. Only the thought of losing her job kept her from snapping off the rest of Sparkle's nails. Then they'd all match.

Sparkle paused to think. "I suppose so."

"Fine." She walked away.

Sparkle smiled as she watched Daria enter the inn, her

back rigid with anger. Payback was a bitch. She wished she could be there when Daria got her first look at her room and new clothes. But she had to take Mede's snacks to him.

A short while later, Sparkle hummed as she walked the path to where Mede waited at the church. When she reached him, he was sitting staring into the night. He turned to look at her. "Hey, babe."

Sparkle stiffened. Something wasn't right. She'd spent time with Mede off and on for thousands of years. She knew him in all his many moods. What she saw in his eyes now wasn't good. "What's the matter, sugar-bunny?"

She put the paper plate she'd brought on the ground before unwrapping his fave candy bar, a piece of cake, and a slice of pie. Putting them all on the plate, she waited.

"Something's happened." He didn't look at her. "I got a visit from the goodness-and-light guy."

"Who?"

"Remember I told you about the time the Big Boss grounded me? I was working for the forces of darkness at the time. Having a hell of a time."

The pie disappeared from the plate.

Sparkle stared at the plate. "Where'd the pie go?"

Mede went on as if nothing had happened. "Anyway, I got in a tight spot and this ice cream guy showed up. Bailed me out. Then he told me the Big Boss was giving me another chance. But he attached some conditions. No cursing and no killing anything."

She nodded. "You called me in to help you a few years ago because you needed someone who could fly under the Big Boss's radar. I thought you said he wasn't paying attention to you anymore."

"Yeah, well, I miscalculated. The ice cream guy showed up tonight."

"I thought I heard an ice cream truck, but I was in my room making plans for Daria. I didn't want to interrupt my train of thought. What did he want?" She felt a stab of fear. Any visit from someone connected to the Big Boss was bad news.

"I named him Chill."

She just stared at him.

"He won't tell me his name, and I got tired of calling him the ice cream guy. So he's Chill. Ice cream is cold, get it?"

"Tell me, Mede. What did he want?" She braced herself.

"He said I'd gone back to my old ways: cursing, threatening to kill people." Mede looked frustrated. "That's not bad. Bad is blowing up planets, starting plagues, fun stuff like that. I haven't had any real fun for years."

That hurt. Sparkle thought they'd had lots of fun together.

"The bastard gave me a choice. Give up a few things or stop being a cosmic troublemaker."

The cake disappeared.

"Not be a cosmic troublemaker anymore?" She was outraged for him. "That's cruel. What did he say you had to give up?"

Mede couldn't meet her gaze. Not good. "Cursing, threatening to kill people, and . . . you."

"*Me?*" She felt like someone had stomped all over her new Manolo Blahnik stilettos.

"Yeah. He said you were a bad influence on me. Said you're selfish, vain, and fixated on sex."

"What's wrong with that?" An awful thought hit her. "You told him to get lost, didn't you?"

He finally met her gaze, his eyes pleading. "I'd be human, babe. No more cosmic troublemaker. It's who I am. I couldn't give that up."

Something heavy settled in the pit of her stomach. "So you chose your job."

"Yeah."

Sparkle tried to be reasonable. She really did. If she'd been in his place, she would've done the same thing. *No, you wouldn't.* "Spell it out for me, Mede."

He must've seen something in her eyes, because he looked panicked. "We can finish this job together. But then we go our separate ways."

"Just like that. No more days on your tropical beach while you make love to me in your golden god form. No more good times kicking butt and having fun together. The end." She'd skipped a few steps in the grieving process and gone directly to totally pissed. And if she bled a little inside, she refused to acknowledge it. "Fine. We'll finish this job for Cindy and Thrain. Then it's good-bye."

Sparkle turned away from him, stubbing her toe on a rock as she blindly headed back to the inn. She didn't look down to see if she'd scuffed the toe of her shoe.

"Sparkle. Wait. Oh, shit."

She knew if she looked back, the candy bar would be gone.

CHAPTER SEVEN

Memo: to all harpies
Subject: quarterly report
Productivity is down this past quarter. Every harpy must put more effort into meeting her quota. Inventory is low on cheating spouses. Refer to the Harpy Training Manual to find the most effective technique for trapping the elusive cheater in the act. Peeking in windows is encouraged. There will be a workshop on July 21 for those who need a refresher course on ways to recognize and stalk the guilty. Punishment for continued failure to meet your quota will be the big D. And no, we don't mean Dallas.

Remember the Tartarus motto: Whatever it takes, especially if it involves violence and mayhem.

HADES THE FAITHFUL

Sparkle had turned Daria's room into a torture chamber.

Posters of Declan lined the walls. Declan naked at the beach—on his stomach, his perfect butt coated with a light dusting of sand like a sexy sugar doughnut, and on his back with his fantasy-inducing cock resting against his muscular thigh.

She took deep calming breaths, but wherever she looked, there he was. The black-and-white shot of him sprawled naked across a massive four-poster bed with sheets tangled beneath his yummy body almost brought her to her knees.

Where'd Sparkle get all these pictures? Did Declan know Sparkle had them? Would Daria have the nerve to invite him over to see her etchings?

And his scent. It was everywhere. How'd Sparkle do that? Did she have a workshop out back where she made sexy, scented candles with names like Chris, Manny, and Bob?

And speaking of candles, there were at least a dozen of them. All lit. When she got past Declan's scent, she realized the candles offered fainter scents, like backup singers to the star attraction. She didn't recognize individual smells, but they all seemed aimed at raising her sexual hunger.

They were working. Or maybe it was just the cumulative effect of the posters and scents. Because she'd swear that as she gazed into the candle flame she could see Declan and her wrapped in passion on that big bed in the poster.

And then there were the sounds: quiet whispers in Declan's voice of what he'd like to do to her, what he'd like her to do to him.

Her respect for Sparkle's power shot off the chart.

Daria swallowed hard. She'd lose it if she stayed in this room one more minute. Maybe a shower would wash away the coating of arousal covering every inch of her, inside and out. She hurried into the bathroom and slammed the door shut behind her.

Silence. No scents. No posters. Weak with relief, she stripped off her clothes, stepped into the shower, and closed her eyes as warm water cascaded over her.

She wasn't prepared for the sensation of a male body pressed against her back. Not just any body. *Declan's* body. She'd never felt his bared length against her, but she recognized him, would always recognize him.

And that was the scariest thought she'd had all night. Daria didn't wait to see what he'd do or say. Opening her eyes, she plunged from the shower. A quick glance around showed she was alone.

Okay, this round went to Sparkle. Daria dried herself with shaking hands before pulling on her clothes. Then she fled the room. And as she'd done since she was small, she went searching for her twin.

Kal answered her frantic pounding on his door with a calm "Come in before you bring down the whole inn."

She stumbled into his room, only dimly aware that he wasn't wearing his harpy face. Why not? She'd ask him later. "I can't go back to my room. Sparkle sexed it up when I wasn't looking, and I don't know what to do. She put pictures of naked men on the walls—" no need to get specific "—and she's pumping in scents that'll trigger arousal." No need to tell him whose scent was in her room. And maybe she'd leave out the part about feeling Declan's body pressed against her in the shower.

Kal closed the door behind her. "You have to admire a woman who understands the nuances of revenge. She's going to make you pay for that broken nail."

"Maybe I should complain to Ganymede, threaten to quit unless Sparkle stops hassling me."

Kal shook his head. "Sparkle holds the key to his stomach."

"What?"

"Ganymede can't do his own cooking in cat form. Katie the cook told me Sparkle makes sure she keeps his stomach filled with his favorite foods. Ganymede and food have a loving relationship."

"So?"

"I hear the one time Sparkle decided to cook for the

inn's guests, food poisoning took on a whole new meaning. If she threatens to cook again, Ganymede will cave. You can't win that way."

"So you're saying I have to *stay* in that room?"

Kal exhaled impatiently. "The whole thing's a pain, but I don't see what the big deal is. Try to ignore it. Keep focused on grabbing someone. The faster you do it, the sooner we can get out of here. Until that happens, you need to keep your job."

"But I—"

"Look, if it really bothers you that much, we can trade rooms."

"No." If she was definite about anything, it was that Kal couldn't see her room. This had nothing to do with logic. It was purely an emotional reaction. "I'll deal with it." She could turn all the posters to the wall and blow out the candles. A little Vicks under her nose would get rid of Declan's scent. The shower? She hadn't a clue.

Kal flung himself across the bed. "Since I saw Declan come in ahead of you, I assume you didn't get a chance to take him."

She glanced away.

"Did you, sis?"

This was her brother, her twin, the only one she'd always believed would understand her. Still, she felt uneasy talking about Declan. "I had the chance."

He waited.

"I had the chance. I didn't take it." No excuses.

"The sex thing?" Now it was his turn to look away. But he was giving her an out.

"We were, um, involved. I lost sight of the ultimate goal."

"It happens." No ranting, no condemnation, just unconditional acceptance.

"As brothers go, you've got an A1 rating." She didn't say stuff like that much. Maybe she needed to say it more.

"Hey, you know I've always got your back, sis. But if this guy's your target, make your move soon. I guarantee Eris won't let any hellfire grow under her ass."

She nodded. Time to change subjects. "No harpy face tonight?" He usually kept his magic going even in private.

Daria cocked her head to study her brother. She couldn't remember the last time she'd seen his real face—violet eyes with thick dark lashes, a straight nose, and sensual lips. The faint shadow of his beard and an expression that said, "I'm dangerous so don't mess with me" made him look like a sexy pirate.

"Sometimes I get tired of the magic." He looked guilty. "Don't you ever wonder what it'd be like to just be accepted for yourself?"

She looked at him blankly. Shock made her speechless.

"Guess not. Forget it."

What could she say to that? Nothing came to mind, so she figured she'd better get out fast before he laid another bombshell on her.

She paused with her hand on the doorknob. "I haven't spotted the judge yet. Any ideas?"

"None." He seemed to make an effort to draw his mind back to Daria's test. "If you decide against the vampire, I have a few options for you."

"Sounds good. We'll talk later." Not waiting to find out if he had anything else to say, she left.

On her way back to her room, she thought over what Kal had said about being accepted for himself. That was the first time her brother had ever voiced any dissatisfaction with the official harpy party line—all harpies must be ugly enough to scare the hair off of Big Foot.

The only conclusion she could come to was that this was the first time either of them had spent even a few hours in one place talking to ordinary people. Okay, not-so-ordinary people. Always before, they'd only ventured out of Tartarus for short periods of time and never talked to anyone but each other. Didn't get to know the locals very well that way. Were the guests at the Woo Woo Inn corrupting Kal? Wow, a frightening thought.

She stopped thinking about Kal once she stepped back into her room. Humming to herself to drown out Declan's amazingly creative whispered suggestions, she methodically turned all the posters to the wall.

Then she blew out all the candles. No Vicks, so she dabbed a few drops of Eau de Yuck perfume under her nose. Kal had brought it along to make her smell bad—grossness should encompass all the senses—but she'd decided dousing herself with it would endanger her job security.

But no amount of climbing on furniture or crawling around on the floor revealed where the sexy talk was coming from, so she had to abandon the search.

Finally, she peeked into the bathroom. Fine, so she was a wuss. She'd use Kal's shower when she got up.

With that settled, she picked up the laptop Kal had insisted she bring, relaxed onto the couch, and hit the power button.

While it was doing its thing, she stared at the backs of the posters. Nope, she absolutely did *not* want to see yummy expanses of Declan's toned male body everywhere she looked. Yes, she had her priorities straight—career first and ogling last. *Nothing* could break her resolve. She was strong-willed, impervious to temptation, and able to resist taking even a tiny peek at his smoking-hot whatevers.

Sighing, she got up and turned all the posters face-out again. They were like a box of chocolate creams. Once the box was sitting in front of her, it was all over. End of story. She just hoped the judge hadn't set up surveillance equipment in here.

Before returning to the couch, she also rubbed off the smelly stuff under her nose. If she could see him, she might as well enjoy his scent as well. Never let it be said she was a hypocrite.

That done, she settled back down with the laptop. She Googled Fenrir and began reading.

A half hour later she sat staring at the nearest poster, but she wasn't seeing Declan. Memory played back the scene in which they'd confronted the werewolf. Fenrir. Everything she'd read filled her mind with gibbering voices that all sounded like hers.

And they were all very, very afraid.

Declan woke at sunset, but he didn't go downstairs right away. For once he was glad vampires didn't dream. He had enough nightmares to deal with while he was awake.

Fenrir. He couldn't wrap his thoughts around the how and why of it. Fenrir shouldn't be *here*. It didn't make any sense.

One thing did make sense. He'd probably overestimated his power when he'd said he could take care of the problem. Pride would have to be tossed, and he'd have to ask Ganymede for help. Ganymede was the most powerful entity at the inn. If the two of them couldn't take down the werewolf, then the world was in big trouble.

Since worrying about Fenrir wouldn't solve anything right now, he chose to think about Daria. What hadn't she told him? And did she really think she could drag him off to Tartarus? The mystery and challenge that was Daria excited him. But something else stirred in him. He liked being with her. Talking, fighting, and making love. Yeah, he was really looking forward to the making love part.

And as he pulled on his black pants and shirt before flinging his black leather duster over his shoulder—damn, he hated the council's dumb dress code—he chose to rationalize his decision to make love with Daria.

Sure, he never went back for seconds with a woman, but last night didn't qualify. Next time would really be the first.

Declan was halfway out the door when the pain began, a steady pressure at the back of his head. What the . . . Vampires didn't get headaches, didn't feel any pain unless they were wounded. He leaned against the door as he tried to cope with the forgotten sensation.

But the voice in his mind superceded the pain. *"Come to me, Declan. Tonight. I grow stronger, and you will not defy me."* Then the pressure was gone.

Yeah, like he'd do that. He locked his door and headed down the stairs. The pain and voice-in-head added a whole new dimension to the general weirdness of his life. He needed to talk to Ganymede right away.

Daria was coming out of the kitchen when he reached the bottom of the stairs. She looked a little harried.

"One of the things I'm supposed to do is check with the cook about the nights' meals. She's a witch, and she practices her craft in the kitchen. When I suggested the kitchen should be a no-magic zone, she got ugly." Daria cast a cautious glance behind her. "Ganymede couldn't pay me enough to mess with her again. She can change all the guests into broccoli stalks for all I care."

Declan would've made a few sympathetic noises, but his voice was momentarily unavailable. The outfit she was wearing had Sparkle Stardust written all over it. Short animal-print dress, a neckline that would've taken away his breath if he had any to take, dangly earrings, and heels that were so high he wondered how she could walk in them.

She seemed to forget about the cook as she narrowed her gaze on him. "We have to talk about Fenrir." Her tone said arguing would be useless.

Since she'd already seen Fenrir, Declan figured keeping her out of the loop would be next to impossible. "Is Ganymede in the kitchen?" Knowing Ganymede, nine out of ten times the answer would be yes.

"Yes. Along with the Dark Queen of Sex and Sin. I would've killed Sparkle right there between the pork roast and the apple pie, but that would've ticked off the witch. So I'll wait until later." She announced that matter-of-factly before spearing him with a warning glare. "Now explain your connection to Fenrir."

What the hell had Sparkle done now? Instead of answering, he motioned her into the kitchen. She followed, grumbling about vicious cosmic troublemakers, stubborn cooks, and secretive vampires.

Declan realized a moment too late he'd stepped into a war zone. Ganymede crouched on the counter, his face buried in a dish of ice cream, while Sparkle and the cook glared at each other over his body.

"Get that fat-assed cat off my counter. I don't have any recipes that include cat hair." The cook waved her spatula around to emphasize her point.

"That 'fat-assed cat' is in charge of this inn, and don't you forget it, Katie." Sparkle poked her bandaged index finger at the cook. She'd upgraded. Her finger was now wrapped in white silk. She'd accessorized by gluing two small rubies to the silk.

"Yeah, well, if the Health Department catches his royal tubbiness here, you won't need a cook anymore." Katie smiled at that thought.

Ganymede didn't bother to lift his head from the bowl.

Sparkle shot a sullen look at the cat. "He eats where he wants to eat." What was going on?

"Then I'll quit."

"Then I'll cook."

Ganymede's head popped up. "That's all right, babe. I wouldn't ask you to get all hot and sweaty over a stove." The cat's amber eyes widened. Probably remembering the horror of Sparkle's previous attempts in the kitchen. "Put the bowl on the registration desk. I'll finish there."

"Fine." Sparkle whipped the bowl from under his nose. "And don't call me *babe*."

Uh-oh. That didn't sound good. Declan trailed out of the kitchen with the others, leaving Katie smiling. She'd routed the enemy and was once more the supreme ruler of her personal kingdom.

Once settled on the desk with his bowl, Ganymede lost interest in the ice cream. Was that normal? The cat seemed pretty intense about his sweets. Declan checked to make sure no guests were standing close by.

Since everyone at the inn slept during the day, breakfast was served right after sunset. Most of the guests were in the parlor now waiting for Sparkle to lead the nightly meeting. After the meeting each guest would go his, her, or its separate way.

"Time to tell all, Declan. Fenrir?" Daria met his gaze and then let hers slide away.

Declan decided that more than Fenrir was bothering Daria. At least the sexual attraction thing was still going strong. He'd seen the flare of hunger in her eyes before she looked away. Good. He needed something positive to think about, because tonight was building up to be a major bust.

"So what does everyone know about Fenrir?" He wanted to explain as little as possible.

"I Googled him last night." Daria's expression said it all. Fenrir was trouble. "The oldest child of Loki, the Norse god of mischief and fire. Loki's a shifty character. Bad news for the other gods."

Ganymede looked awfully miserable for someone with vanilla ice cream coating his face and whiskers. "Yeah, but last I heard, Loki's chained somewhere. He's been out of commission for a long time." He began to clean his face with one gray paw, but his heart didn't seem to be in it.

"So what's that have to do with Fenrir?" Sparkle glanced down at her shoes. The toes were dusty. She didn't lean down to wipe off the dust.

Okay, full disclosure followed by semipanic, soon to be replaced by full panic once everyone understood the situation. "I was a Viking before I was anything else, and Norse myths say Loki will free himself just as Ragnarok begins."

"Ragnarok?" Sparkle stopped glaring at Ganymede long enough to look at Declan.

"The final fight between good and evil. Odin will lead the forces of good. So that means we'll have the ultimate battle of the gods." Daria looked troubled. "Guess which side Loki will be on?"

"Battle of the gods?" Sparkle showed a little interest. "That would make a kick-ass reality show."

Declan picked up the narrative. "When Ragnarok takes place, Loki, along with his three children by the frost giant Angrboda, will lead the forces of evil."

Sparkle looked thoughtful. "Evil *and* powerful? This Loki sounds like someone I wouldn't mind meeting."

Ganymede hissed. "Over my dead and decomposing body."

"That's a possibility." Sparkle threw Ganymede a cold stare. "So which way does the battle swing?" She didn't sound overly concerned.

"No one will survive."

"No more gods? So sad." Sparkle shook her head to show her regret over the loss of so many deities.

Declan exhaled deeply. "*No one*, Sparkle. No you, no me, no one. Supposedly, the universe will begin again, but we won't be a part of it."

"Oh." Sparkle frowned.

"Tell them about Loki's three children. The ones who'll join him to battle Odin's forces." Daria's grim expression must have mirrored his own.

"The prophecy can't be fulfilled unless Loki's three children join him in battle." Drumroll, please. "The kiddies are Midgard, a giant serpent, Hel, the Queen of Death, and our old friend Fenrir, a werewolf that frightened the gods so much they bound him to a rock a mile under the earth."

"Hmm." Ganymede looked like he had other things on his mind. "He's trapped under our church? How'd that happen? New Jersey isn't a hotbed of Norse gods. I guess a lot of the mob got whacked here, though, so maybe the gods said, 'Hey, if it's good enough for the mob, it's good enough for us.'"

"I don't know why he's under the church. I don't believe in coincidences, so I have to assume there was a reason why a Mackenzie ended up owning this place." He had a hunch Fenrir would be eager to explain everything to him.

"He showed up in my head right before I came down. He wants me back at the church. That can't be good." Declan decided against mentioning the pain. No one could help him with that.

"So when's this Ragnarok supposed to go down?" The chance for a good fight cheered up Ganymede a little.

Declan shrugged. "No one knows the year, but it'll start on the summer solstice."

"The night of June twentieth this year." Daria had done her homework.

"And this is . . ." Sparkle glanced at the calendar on the desk. "June fourteen."

Silence. Declan figured they could put the clues together without him. Armageddon in six nights. At least that was his conclusion since Fenrir had gained enough power to take physical form. But the werewolf still couldn't leave the church area, so maybe there was a chance for the universe.

"And your connection to Fenrir is?" Daria wasn't afraid to ask the tough questions.

"He's my father."

"Damn." Ganymede's eyes widened as soon as he said the word. "Check to see if my candy bar is still in the desk."

Sparkle pulled open the drawer. "Gone." She seemed to get lots of satisfaction from passing on that info.

Daria didn't seem to notice anything wrong between Ganymede and Sparkle. "What do you think he wants with you?"

Declan shrugged. "Who knows? We never had any contact until back there at the church. Hell, I didn't even know if the tale Mom told me about him was true. No one did. It was only her word. No proof. Guess I have proof now."

"What do we do?" Daria didn't know about anyone

else, but Declan's story made her harpy test seem sort of trivial. If the universe went away in six nights, there wouldn't be any harpy hierarchy to worry about.

"We go into the parlor so I can talk with the guests. They'll expect it. And until the world officially goes boom, life at the Woo Woo Inn carries on as usual." Sparkle seemed to reconsider her words. "Whatever usual is here."

Daria put her thoughts of imminent doom on hold long enough to take on Sparkle. "Wait up a minute." She grabbed Sparkle's arm.

Sparkle stopped as the others continued into the parlor. "Let me guess, you're still upset with your room's new décor." She didn't look even a little repentant.

"Forget the room. I want my clothes back."

"Clothes?" Sparkle did some deep thinking about that. "Oh, now I remember. I burned them. Can we go in now?"

"No." Daria beat down her need to throw something. Preferably Sparkle. "A warning. Don't mess with me again."

"Or else?" Sparkle looked really interested.

"Or else when I win our bet tonight, I might make you do something a little more extreme than breaking a nail." Daria allowed her smile to hint how evil her imagination could get.

Sparkle didn't smile back. "Then I'll just have to make sure I don't lose tonight." She started to walk away, but then stopped. "And don't push me, sister, I'm not in the mood." Not even a sexy smirk as she left.

What the . . . ? Something was wrong with Sparkle. She didn't have her usual wicked enthusiasm for making Daria's life miserable. Daria thought about that as she went into the parlor. Good thing Sparkle didn't know she'd done lots of lustful touching last night. *After* she'd claimed victory.

Declan had saved a spot for her on one of the couches. She sat next to him and tried to ignore the thigh-to-thigh pressure. Things got a lot tighter, though, as Walt squeezed down on the other side of her.

The debunker grinned at them. "See that bunch of guys over there? Someone said they're vampires. Can you believe that?" He chuckled. "I'm going to follow them tonight. Bet they'll just head into the woods with a case of beer and some crunchies. They'll spend the night talking about who'll make it to the World Series."

She glanced at the men in question. Her faves, the Night Feeders. If he wasn't careful, Walt the clueless could end up as the crunchy snack. And no, she wasn't worried about him. That would mean she cared. Caring wouldn't get her a seat next to Mom.

Besides, she had too many other things to think about. Like how were they going to keep Fenrir from gaining full power so he couldn't help Big Daddy destroy the universe? Now, *that* was a real worry.

Then there was Declan. In between him saving the universe and her passing her test, would they get a chance to . . . Daria shut off that thought valve before lust could come pouring out.

While she pretended to listen to Sparkle, Daria scoped out the others in the room. Who was her perfect victim, the being who was powerful and evil enough to get Hades's attention? She was just about ready to admit that Declan would never be her prey of choice. Kal could suggest someone else. What did that say about her commitment to the harpy test?

"Once again I might remind everyone the old church

is off-limits. Other than that, party like there's no tomorrow." Sparkle smiled at her audience, but her eyes were a little too bright, her smile a little too strained. "One never knows. It could happen. You wouldn't want to have any regrets."

Ganymede padded to her side. He sat down on her foot and then stared up at her. She jerked her foot from under him. Silent communication took place. Warning received.

"Well, did anyone experience anything paranormal last night?" Sparkle didn't look like her heart was in it.

A human raised a timid hand. When Sparkle pointed at her, she offered an apologetic smile. "This was probably nothing, but I heard a big explosion and saw a flash of light through the trees. I think it was coming from the area near the church." The woman glanced around, hoping for support. "Did anyone else hear something?"

One of the Night Feeders spoke up. "Me and the guys were doing a little hunting when we heard it."

Sparkle frowned at him. "Hunting? Guests are off-limits, you know." Distracted, she looked at Daria. "Make sure all the guests came back last night."

Then Sparkle tackled the big question. "You probably heard the Jersey Devil. He shows up once in a while, and the old church is his favorite stomping ground." She bit her lip as she tapped into her creative self. "That's one of the reasons to stay away from the church. The Devil doesn't do takeout too often, but when he does, he likes his food fresh. Sometimes he does Mexican."

She looked at a human guest named Carlos. He swallowed hard.

"Other times it's Italian." She stared at one of the

Night Feeders who called himself Geno until he smiled weakly.

"I think his favorite is Chinese." Sparkle glanced pointedly at an Asian family. "He's always hungry an hour later, though."

"What a bunch of crap." Walt's voice carried to every corner of the room. "The Jersey Devil is just a legend. There's no such animal. So what caused the explosion?"

Sparkle's gaze speared him, pinning him to his seat. "The sonic boom when the Devil slowed to under the speed of sound."

"Oh, jeez." Walt rolled his eyes.

Sparkle glanced at her watch. "Well, I guess it's time for everyone to get started on their evening. Remember that I'm leading a sensitivity session for nonhumans who want to coexist with other entities. Nonhuman wannabes are welcome. I try to be inclusive. Tonight's subject is betrayal and its consequences. We'll meet in the library."

Ganymede padded over to Daria and Declan. A few seconds later, Sparkle joined them. She pointedly refused to look down.

Daria didn't need anyone to beat her over the head. "What's going on between you guys?"

Sparkle took a deep breath. She looked around to make sure no humans were paying attention. "Last night an ice cream man showed up here."

Declan and Daria nodded.

"He's some kind of goodness-and-light freak. He told Mede he'd been a bad boy."

"Oh, jeez." Ganymede looked embarrassed.

"This guy said Mede had to give up cursing, threatening to kill things, and *me*." Sparkle seemed more sad than mad. "Every time he curses, he loses one of his sweet treats. What fun." A little vindictiveness shone through.

"Low blow, babe." Ganymede.

"We're both mature adults, so we'll continue to work together. But there is no more *us*." She slowly shredded a tissue she'd been holding. "Now I've got a session to run." Sparkle didn't give anyone a chance to stop her. She left the room so fast, Daria expected her to generate her own sonic boom.

Ganymede watched her leave. He looked a little lost. "I hope she doesn't do anything crazy. Sparkle isn't too big on self-control. I'm the steadying force in our relationship."

Ganymede was the steadying force? Daria thought that was scary.

"This guy must've threatened you with something big to make you break up with Sparkle." Declan looked sympathetic.

"It was give up my honey-bun or no more cosmic troublemaker."

Daria frowned. "Could he do that?"

"He can do whatever he damn well pleases. Oh, shit. I just lost two more candy bars." He got up and wandered away.

"Wow. Looks like this ice cream guy is the snake in Sparkle's personal paradise. Too bad." Declan glanced at Daria. "I guess you have manager stuff to do."

She nodded. "What do you have planned?" Daria needed to talk to Kal about a definite choice of prey, but she hoped Declan would stick around.

"I'm going out for a few minutes and try to clear my thoughts. I need to come up with a plan to stop Fenrir. Beyond that, I'm open to suggestions."

Okay, she shouldn't do this, but what the heck, she wouldn't be at this job long enough to build up a rep for dedication. None of the guests needed her right now, so it wouldn't hurt to slip out with him for a short time.

"Mind some company? We can knock around ideas." Did she sound too eager?

He smiled and instantly tapped into her inner slut. She wanted to fling herself on him and practice unspeakably erotic acts on his naked body.

"Sure. I need all the help I can get. Let's go."

CHAPTER EIGHT

Declan wasn't thinking about Fenrir. He was thinking about the woman standing next to him. The *dangerous* woman standing next to him.

On so many levels, she tugged at him. He felt the pull of her life force where it surged just below her soft, smooth skin. Arousal moved restlessly in him at the thought. Okay, that was a vampire being a vampire. Nothing to worry about.

But then there was his need to be near her. She was a scary mixture of strength and vulnerability. In a straight-up fight, no magic, she just might kick his ass. Beneath her attitude, though, he sensed someone trying to find her way. Maybe she was realizing there was more to existence than making Hades happy. He could hope.

See, that was not good. Hope was his enemy. Better to keep it simple. Harpies were bad news. Always. No exceptions. Enjoy her body and then run like hell. He needed to remember that. Because the times in his life when he'd deviated from his one-bite-stand rule had ended badly for him. He was good at wiping other people's memories clean. His own memories? Not so much.

He could control his need for blood and emotional closeness. He'd had practice doing that. To make up for depriving himself, though, he'd allow himself to have fun making love to her and foiling her attempts to cart him off to Tartarus. Funny, she'd had her chance to grab him last night when they were alone in the woods. He smiled. Maybe sexual attraction trumped even a harpy's work ethic.

But he was supposed to be thinking about Fenrir. If Dad managed to join up with Loki, Granddaddy would destroy the universe. Talk about family issues.

Declan figured he'd better move away from Daria if he expected to do any clear thinking. It was too warm for a coat, so he dropped his duster before stepping off the porch. He didn't need it anyway since he'd left his sword in his room. A bad habit to start. Lots of dead Mackenzies had gotten that way because of careless habits.

A few seconds later he wondered if he was about to join the list of careless and dead Mackenzies.

Distracted by warring thoughts of Daria and Fenrir, Declan missed the first signs he was under attack. He heard the woosh of air and the flapping of giant wings just before talons dug deep into his shoulders.

Pain ripped through him. He looked up. A harpy. *Not* Daria. Damn it to hell, why hadn't he put his coat on? If she'd hooked her freaking claws into the leather, he could've slipped out of the duster.

He fought past the pain as he pulled his power to him.

The harpy cackled madly. "See, Daria, I can take your precious prize right out from under your nose. He's mine now. I win, I win."

Declan didn't think so.

Daria jumped off the porch. "I knew you were stupid, but I can't believe you think you can get away with this. Let him go, Eris."

Major wow. Daria was into scary mode. His pride in her felt way too personal.

"I'm on my way to Tartarus. Wish me a safe trip. Wouldn't want me to drop him before I got there. Even a vampire doesn't bounce from ten thousand feet up."

He wasn't going anywhere with the queen of gross. How could Daria ever want to look like *that*? Time to free himself, though, before the harpy got too far off the ground. Fenrir's blood allowed him to fly, but he never liked to reveal his powers if he didn't have to. Surprise could be the deciding factor in a battle. Declan had a much more subtle way to foil this snatching. He focused.

"Damn, this guy is heavy." The harpy huffed and puffed, her wings beating madly, as she tried to rise.

"*Bitch.*"

Daria's voice was harsh with fury. And something else. Fear? No time to analyze now. A quick glance caught Daria's change from human to harpy form. Even the pain couldn't keep him from noting how hot she was from the waist up. Below her waist? He'd seen better. A vulture was just a vulture. Yeah, so her vulture form was bigger and her talons scarier, but he'd never been into bird watching.

"Ummph, oomph, arrgh!" The harpy had only managed to get him about a foot off the ground.

He looked up at her. "Guess someone needs to work out more." Declan forced the words through teeth clenched in agony. Then he renewed his focus, pushing his energy into the earth, where it took root, anchoring him in place.

She dropped him just as Daria slammed into her with what looked like a category-five force of angry harpy. Above him was a blur of talons, wings, and enraged shrieks.

One look at the porch, and he knew they were in trouble. Everyone inside had poured onto the porch to see what was happening. Walt was down on one knee taking pictures. Kal leaped off the porch and ran toward them.

Declan caught snatches of speech.

"Do something, Mede!" Sparkle had forgotten her mad for the moment.

"I am. Hey, you Night Feeders, I'm taking Daria. What odds will you give me?" Ganymede.

"I don't freaking believe this. But if it's for real, I'll make a fortune on these pics." Walt.

"This is way better than rats." The last words from one of the werewolves as all three changed and happily flung themselves into the air, trying to latch on to one of the harpies.

Then there were the assorted screams and curses from panicked humans. Declan's pain-fogged mind wasn't processing it too well. But he did have enough sense to grab Kal's arm as the harpy started to change.

"No. Don't add to what's going on." Declan pointed at the battle above his head, where a furious Daria was pummeling the other harpy. "I don't think she needs to be rescued. She'd want to do this herself."

Daria's brother looked up. She'd hooked her talons into the other harpy and was flinging her from side to side. Kal nodded and then glanced around. "Crap. How do we fix that?"

By *that*, Declan knew he meant the ring of interested spectators. "The nonhumans don't need fixing. They'll accept what they're seeing. But someone has to take care of the humans." It wouldn't be him. He was all focused out for a few hours until his shoulder wounds closed.

Meanwhile, Daria tossed her defeated enemy to the ground with a bone-crushing thud. The harpy immediately returned to human form. The last Declan saw of her was her flabby, naked butt as she raced for the safety of the woods.

The werewolves howled gleefully as they leaped in pursuit.

"Here." Suddenly, Sparkle was beside him. She pushed his coat into his hands. "Cover her up. Oh, and I'll give Daria something to put on your shoulders. Make sure she does it *personally*."

Declan sensed a wink, wink, nudge, nudge, but he was a little too out of it to be sure. He nodded, making sure he didn't move his shoulders in the process. "Right. Thanks."

Daria landed beside him. Kal and he stood together to shield her as she changed. Declan wrapped his coat around her as soon as she was back in human form.

She smiled shakily at him, but her smile died as she stared at his bloodied shoulders. "I should've screwed her into the ground headfirst. Are you okay?"

"Sure." Other than the excruciating pain? Yeah, he was fine. He was more than fine. For whatever reason, she'd leaped to his rescue. Even if she just wanted to save him so she could take him to Tartarus herself, he still felt great about how things had gone down.

"Hey, bloodsucker, how's it feel to have women fighting over you?" Ganymede had joined Sparkle. "I won fifty bucks from the Night Feeders betting on you, harpy. Way to go."

His expression said he wasn't as happy as he sounded. Declan suspected he was putting up a good front for Sparkle.

Daria frowned. "Betting on me?"

Declan didn't want to give her time to process that. "We need to get rid of a lot of memories."

"All taken care of." Ganymede glanced toward the porch. Everyone had gone back into the inn. "All the humans remember is hearing a lot of noise, but when they looked outside they didn't see anything." He shifted his attention back to Daria. "Sure hope you weren't planning on snatching one of the nonhumans. Now that they know harpies are in the house, they won't be taking any solo walks."

"Thanks for doing the memory-wipe thing." Declan figured it was time to get back to his room so he could take his shirt off before the blood dried and the material stuck to his wounds. "I have to clean up, but I'll need to talk to you later, Ganymede."

"No problem." Ganymede leaped onto the porch and waited for Sparkle to open the door for him. She went in and slammed the door in his face.

Kal peered at Daria. "You okay, sis?"

Daria nodded. "I can't believe Eris tried to carry Declan off right in front of me."

"Yeah, it was like a slap in the face." Kal shook his head. "She's always thought she was better than she is."

"Who's this Eris?" Declan climbed the porch steps and then opened the screen door. He winced when he moved his shoulders.

"She's Aello's daughter. Aello shares top-dog status with Mom and Aunt Ocypete." Kal followed them into the inn.

"Interesting." Declan looked at Daria. "Thanks for taking her out."

Daria stared at his shoulders and then glanced away. "I wasn't trying to save you because I'm kind."

He resisted the urge to smile. "I never thought so."

"I'm selfish and self-serving. She just can't come in here and take what's mine."

Mine. The word hung between them. Declan decided that, considering how he chose to interpret it, the word could mean mine to take back to Tartarus or mine to make love with along with lots of other good stuff. He chose to go with interpretation two.

"Selfish and self-serving. What else could a harpy be?" He waved off her follow-up comment and headed for the stairs.

Kal and Daria watched him until he'd climbed the steps, and then Kal rounded on Daria. "What the hell was that all about?"

She wasn't in the mood to listen to a lecture, even if it came from Kal. "That was about Eris trying to score higher than me on the test. You know she's a vindictive witch. She never got over that I could beat her at every level of harpy competition. She's a sore loser." She thought about that. "I admire that about her. Sore losers make good harpies."

Kal seemed to accept the explanation. "It's lucky you were on the spot or else Eris would be long gone."

"No, she wouldn't." Daria smiled. "I didn't save Declan. He saved himself. Eris couldn't lift him off the ground. I don't know what he did, but I was totally impressed."

"Then why'd you attack Eris? Why not just let the vampire take care of her? You know Aello will be out for revenge when she finds out you attacked her badass daughter."

"Haven't a clue." She wouldn't lie to her twin, even if a lie would get her off the hook.

"Be careful, sis." He looked troubled.

"Sure." Time to change the subject. "Who do you think the judge is? He must've gotten an eyeful tonight. And I'd really like to know who's helping Eris. Someone here is."

He shrugged. "Who knows? A man and woman checked in this afternoon. They're not human, but I can't make them. I have to believe the judge is already here, but I could be wrong. And anyone could be helping Eris. Probably nonhuman. She wouldn't lower herself to take help from a human. I'll see what I can find out."

As Daria watched him walk away, she realized something for the first time. He'd still made his face ugly, but tonight his nose was a little smaller and his ears didn't stick out. She wouldn't bug him about it, but she was curious.

"Oh, good, you're still here."

Sparkle's voice next to her made Daria jump.

"I was going to run this up to Declan, but there's something I have to take care of in the kitchen." The cosmic troublemaker's smile wasn't as vibrant as usual.

No, she definitely would *not* feel sorry for Sparkle Stardust. Daria glanced at her index finger. Still into designer bandages. "What is it?"

Sparkle pushed a tube into her hand. "I know he's a vampire, and I know he'll heal in a few hours, but right now he's in a lot of pain." She waited expectantly.

"And?"

"And he won't be able to put this on himself without moving his shoulders. I bet that bitch's talons went all the way through him. The cream will take away the pain until he heals." Her eyes gleamed with unmistakable challenge.

Daria took a deep breath. "I can do it. And every stroke of my fingers will be impersonal. Got it? Im . . . per . . . son . . . al."

"Of course." She widened her eyes. Innocence, thy name is Sparkle.

All the way up the stairs, Daria mumbled and grumbled while the bottom of Declan's coat dragged behind her. Sparkle was a sex-obsessed, calculating, manipulative opportunist. As a harpy, Daria admired that. As her victim, not so much. Daria almost stopped at her room to put on some clothes, but decided against it. Declan was in pain, and it was sort of her fault. A harpy had done this to him.

After pounding on his door until her knuckles hurt, she thought about going back to her room. No, that would be the coward's way out. Sparkle would take it as proof she didn't have the guts to stand eye to eye . . . Okay, eye to chest with him.

Hmm. She studied the door. She tried the doorknob. Locked. She gave it a little push. It popped open with a splintering of wood. Fine, so she'd given it a hard shove. Harpies didn't know their own strength.

He wasn't in the room, but she could hear the shower running behind the bathroom's closed door. So that's why he hadn't heard her knocking. She'd just wait for him to come out. Glancing around, she noticed the suitcase on his bed. It was open. Was it her fault harpies had curious natures? Of course not.

Walking over, she peeked inside. Lots of jeans and T-shirts. All black. Lots of lethal-looking weapons. Useless. Maybe she was wrong, but after reading about Fenrir, she doubted they'd do much good.

When she heard the water stop running, she hurried to the couch and tried to look coolly . . . impersonal. And if she didn't stop squeezing the darn tube so hard, it would burst and spew cream all over the room.

She was still working on the coolly impersonal expression when the bathroom door swung open. She smiled, a perky grin that said she was Nurse Daria here to tend the wounded warrior, and nothing else. *Stuff that in your impersonal pipe and smoke it, Sparkle Starshit.*

Her smile froze, though, as all of Declan filled the bathroom doorway. Naked. Very naked. She swallowed hard. *Maintaining impersonal attitude, here.* Daria quickly shifted her gaze to a painting of giant sunflowers.

Too late. She'd seen him.

Sighing, Daria abandoned the sunflowers for more fertile fields. She could stare at him forever. He looked that good. Was that an impersonal observation? Sure. It was an impartial assessment of the male body. Sparkle couldn't fault her.

"What're you doing here?" No attempt to cover himself, no shocked expression. Striding to his suitcase, he rooted through it.

"Um, Sparkle gave me some cream to put on your shoulders to help with the pain." She winced at the ragged tears in his flesh.

"So do it." He glanced at the door. "Wanted to get in here badly, didn't you?"

He didn't sound mad, he didn't sound glad, he sounded neutral.

"Yeah, okay." She took the top off the tube with shaking fingers. Good thing his back was to her, because *she* wasn't neutral at all. "Sorry about the door." She searched around for a plausible lie. "When you didn't answer, I thought maybe you'd passed out from loss of blood. I figured I'd better check on you. But when I heard the water running, I knew you just didn't hear me."

Before she moved up close behind him, she allowed herself one sweeping ogle. Looking at what Eris had done to him made her a little queasy.

Why? She was a harpy, for Hades's sake. She didn't faint when she saw mangled bodies. She'd earned an A in Blood and Gore 101. Maybe the sight bothered her because he wasn't just anonymous prey to her anymore. A disturbing thought.

But once she got past his shoulders, it was smooth sailing. The powerful line of his back narrowed to lean hips, with strong thighs and legs. And his butt was as close to perfect as she ever wanted to see. Anything more perfect would probably stop her heart. Really. Tight, firm, rounded in a totally male way, and made for a woman's hands to clasp. She knew what they felt like. She wanted to hold them again.

And talking about holding parts of his body, she could see the shadow of his heavy sacs between his slightly parted legs. From the look of his wounds, she'd have to put the cream on front and back. She sighed. Did a nurse's work never end?

Daria gave herself a mental head-shake. What was she thinking? She was using his injury to indulge herself. Sure, a harpy ought to take her pleasure where and when she wanted, but no judge was around, so she could admit that thinking about his body when he was hurting didn't feel right.

"Put on your jeans, and then I'll take care of your shoulders." Good. She'd gotten that out before she had time to think about it.

He looked over his shoulder and smiled. "I know what you're thinking."

Startled, she stared at him. "No, you don't. My shields are up." Then she realized he was teasing her. She relaxed and smiled back. "But if imagining makes you feel better, go for it."

His laughter was husky and sensual. "Oh, it definitely does, sweetheart." But he did pull a pair of jeans from his suitcase and step into them.

Once at least half of the temptation was covered, she stepped close to his back and smoothed the cream gingerly over his torn flesh. The wounds already looked like they were closing, but they must still hurt.

His muscles tensed beneath her fingers. She slid her tongue across suddenly dry lips. *Don't read anything into it. You just hurt him when you touched the wounds.*

So why then did she lean forward and slide the tip of

her tongue the length of his spine? And why didn't her action shock her even a little? Because it seemed the perfectly logical thing to do.

He shuddered. "You know how to take a man's mind off his pain."

"Turn around so I can put some cream on your front." What was in that stuff? It had a slightly sweet scent that made her want to lick it right off his yummy skin. She resisted the urge. Barely.

He obeyed, and for the first time she got a good look at his face. She'd been wrong. He wasn't neutral either. His eyes proved that blue could be a sizzling color. And when he smiled, he showed lots of fang. He was excited, she was excited, so what was wrong with them both being excited together?

No judge was hiding under the bed, marking her down for passing up another chance to get her vampire. Sparkle was nowhere around to see her touch him with a whole lot of lust.

The scent of aroused male and sweet cream combined to make her feel sort of drunk. Sure, she was operating a dangerous vehicle with impaired faculties, but just this once wouldn't hurt.

Dutifully, she spread the cream onto the front of his shoulders. She bit her lip, concentrating on the tactile sensation of the cream sliding over warm skin and hard muscle. The scent of the cream upped the level of her awareness until she wanted to climb inside him and lick her way out.

She settled for dragging the tip of her fingernail lightly around one male nipple before kissing a path over his awesome pecs and abs.

Daria swore their arousal was making the air heavy. That's why her breaths were coming in hard gasps. He'd buried his fingers in her hair and was holding her head to his stomach. She could tell him that if he was going to hold her head somewhere, she had a much better suggestion.

His jeans rode low on his hips, exposing his navel. She pounced on it, twirling her tongue round and round until he groaned.

Pulling away, she fumbled at the button on his jeans. With all that pressure building up behind it, unbuttoning him wasn't easy. But hey, a determined harpy could do anything.

For a moment, she glanced past him. Just in time to see one of the sunflowers in the painting wink at her.

She froze. Wink?

Declan sensed her sudden tension and turned to follow her gaze. "What's the matter?"

He'd dismantle anyone or anything that interrupted what she was doing to his body. Oh, what the hell? What she was doing to *him*.

Over the centuries, he'd gotten in the habit of categorizing sexual pleasure as something that affected only his body—like a great massage or a hot shower. If he believed all of these physical sensations never touched his inner self, were just surface things, he didn't give his emotions a chance to get involved.

His version of reality had worked for a lot of years. It allowed him to coldly ignore pain in order to kill what was hurting him. And it kept him from mistaking sex for love. He'd been around too long to get tied up in the love knot.

But he wouldn't lie to himself. Daria was tunneling through his surface layer and was dangerously close to a center he feared was a little too soft and mushy where she was concerned. He'd allow it. For now. But when it was time to leave, he'd walk away as he'd done so many times before. It might be a little harder this time, though.

She was still staring at the sunflower painting.

"You don't like sunflowers? I can make them go away, and then you can continue soothing my fevered . . . whatever."

"It winked at me."

His first instinct was to laugh. His second was to realize she must've seen something. Daria might be many things, but delusional wasn't one of them.

Delusions? He sniffed the air. "Sparkle gave you that cream. I don't recognize the smell. What's in it?" The troublemaker had been a little too insistent about Daria putting the cream on him personally. He knew she wanted the two of them to hook up—hooking up people was her thing—but would she be sneaky enough to give human nature a chemical boost? Sure she would.

"I thought of that. The smell of the cream along with . . . other scents was making me feel weird." She met his gaze. "In a really good way. But I'm not imagining what I saw. What's on the other side of that wall?"

He shrugged. "Another guest room, I guess."

"Let's go see." She headed for the door.

Leaving the room, he glanced at his door. Ganymede would have to fix it before Cindy and Thrain got home. He thought about Fenrir. Then again, if there was no inn to come home to, the door wouldn't much matter.

"I don't think this is a room. It looks like some kind of closet." She reached for the knob of the door adjacent to his. "Anyone who was in here is probably long gone."

He raised one brow. "And you suspect what?"

"I think someone was watching us through that sunflower."

"The sunflower. Right." He raked his fingers through his hair. "Why would anyone do that?"

Without warning, someone flung open the door, nearly knocking Daria down.

"Someone would do that so they could make sure Daria wasn't cheating on our little bet." Sparkle smiled sweetly as she strolled from the linen closet. "Once I realized you would head back to your room, Declan, I raced up here and drilled a hole through the closet wall into your room. It was too easy." She frowned. "I was disappointed. I thought they made these old houses better than that. Anyway, then I went into your room, drilled a hole in the sunflower, and made sure the hole in the painting lined up with the hole in the wall."

Declan swallowed his rage. Sparkle would enjoy it too much. Instead, he mentally strung together five of his favorite expletives. "Don't know for sure, but I think that's illegal."

Sparkle widened her eyes at him. "Well, I certainly wouldn't want to get in trouble with the law." She held up a small container he hadn't noticed before. "That's why I'm going to fill in the hole right now."

"I hope you have enough in that can to fill in the hole your head will make when I smash it into the wall." Fury made Daria's voice shake.

It took a lot to intimidate Sparkle Stardust. "Oh, get over it, Daria. I had to make sure you told me the truth about touching him with lust. Besides, I didn't see anything spectacular. Since all you have on is that stupid coat, you could've at least taken it off." She looked grumpy.

Declan let his temper slip a little. "Want to tell us why you think you have the right to spy on us? I'll need to explain it to my lawyer."

That got her attention. She shot him a considering look.

Daria moved toward Sparkle. "She'd better talk fast, because it's sort of hard to communicate after someone rips your tongue out."

"Hmm, I guess I'll have to write *You're Fired* on a piece of paper, then." Sparkle studied her index finger. The message, Have Sex Often, was spelled out in what looked like tiny rubies on her bandage. "Look, I don't know why you're so upset. I mean, you can't tell me you wouldn't jump at the chance to cheat on the bet if you could."

He expected Daria to explode all over Sparkle. Instead, she shifted her gaze away from the troublemaker. "Well, I wouldn't drill a hole through someone's wall so I could peek at them."

Sparkle radiated sly triumph. "You cheated last night, didn't you, Daria?"

"Nope. No lustful touches for me." Her glance at Declan said, "Keep your mouth closed."

"I'm a paying guest, and you drilled a hole in the freaking sunflower so you could spy on me. Ever hear of invasion of privacy?" Now he was *really* getting ticked.

It looked as though Sparkle had defused the situation with Daria, so she turned her attention to him. "This bet is important to me. She was so sure she could keep from touching you in a sensual way. I mean, that's a total insult to your sensually charismatic self."

Sparkle's gaze slipped to Daria for a moment. "Things were heating up in there. Way to go, sister."

Then she looked back at him. "The winner each night gets to change the other's appearance in some way. Hello? That's a biggie for me. My image defines who I am." She cast Daria a resentful glance. "Last night she won. Or so she claims. She made me break a nail. Tonight I won." Her eyes glittered with malice. "Am I a vengeful witch? You bet. I'm planning on major payback."

Declan decided not to react until he'd thought things through. But he did have one more thing to ask. "What was in that cream you gave Daria?"

Now it was Sparkle's turn to look away. "Oh, a little of this and a little of that."

"I bet lots of *that*." Daria's grumble promised she might be down but she wasn't out.

"Sparkle, if you were still speaking to Ganymede, would you have told him before you did this?" Declan remembered Ganymede's concern that she'd do something crazy. This qualified. "Would he have gone along with it?"

"No." Sparkle looked uncomfortable. "He'd worry about making Cindy and Thrain mad." She tried to look defiant. It came off a little sad. "But I'm in his rearview mirror now, so he doesn't get to give advice." Sparkle stared at the container in her hand. "I'll do this later." She went into the closet and set it on a shelf.

He raked his fingers through his hair. "We have to get those two back together again. Ganymede really is a steadying influence on her."

Daria offered a fervent "I hear you."

Silently, they watched Sparkle come out of the closet and close the door behind her.

Okay, time for him to beat feet out of here before his temper snapped. He'd leave the females to it while he put on a shirt and went looking for Ganymede. Afterward he'd figure out how to make love to Daria without someone watching them from the nearest painting.

"Ganymede and I have a few things to talk about." He looked at Daria, and he hoped his gaze told her they had a bunch of unfinished business.

Then he smiled at Sparkle, making sure he showed lots of fang. "Fix my wall and never let me find any holes in it again. Because if I do, I'll lose my temper. A pissed-off vampire can do lots of damage to a place. Thrain and Cindy might not invite you back."

Some of the satisfaction seeped from Sparkle's expression. "When you see Mede, tell him I threw away all the candy bars he had in *my* room. He can stay in the broom closet for all I care."

"Will do." Then he turned and walked away. Time to make a plan to stop Fenrir. He had six days before the universe went boom.

No pressure.

CHAPTER NINE

Anger warred with Daria's common sense. Sparkle had better hope Daria didn't win the bet any time soon. She thought a broken nail was a big deal? Ha. Sparkle wouldn't believe what Kal's magic could do to her I'm-so-sexy face. She might want to start shopping for designer paper bags right now.

"You're still mad." Sparkle stated the obvious. "You shouldn't be. We're a lot alike."

"We're nothing alike." Daria walked toward her room while Sparkle trailed behind. "I have to get dressed so I can return Declan's coat."

Daria unlocked her door, slipped inside, and tried to close it again fast. Not fast enough. Sparkle scooted inside just before Daria slammed it shut.

"Of course we are. We're both devious. I bet you put lusting fingers all over Declan after we settled up last night, didn't you?"

"No." Daria flung open the closet door and tried to pick something unflattering from Sparkle's wardrobe choices. Nothing looked like it would make a harpy fashion statement, so she just grabbed the first thing she touched.

"Oh, and we're both amazing liars." Sparkle bent down to retrieve a pair of shoes. "I think your other shoes are still on the porch. These will be wonderful with that outfit."

"The heels are too high."

"They're Alberta Ferretti satin and leather stilettos. Appreciate them for the works of art they are. They're sexy and they'll make your legs look gorgeous."

Daria wanted to beat Sparkle over the head with her "works of art," but she still needed the job. Mumbling a comment on Sparkle's parentage, she pulled open a dresser drawer, chose panties and a bra, then walked toward the bathroom with the clothes. "Any hope you'll leave while I'm dressing?"

"Why would I do that? We still have to settle up tonight's bet." She might be mourning Ganymede, but that didn't stop Sparkle from being the biggest pain she could be.

"Right." Daria took a quick shower. She would've tried to outwait Sparkle, but she still had a job to do downstairs. Once she'd put on her dress, she took a deep breath and left the bathroom.

Sparkle was still there, but she was not alone. Another woman had joined her. "Love the dress. Short, chiffon, halter top, and sensually understated."

The other woman nodded her agreement.

"Great." If she was brusque enough, maybe she could get back to work faster. Reluctantly, Daria slipped into the shoes.

"Too bad you have to take it right back off. I made a quick call while you were in the shower and almost cried with joy when Roxanne said she was available. Here, you can put these on after Roxanne colors, cuts, and blow-dries your hair." She handed Daria a pair of earrings. "And don't worry about not doing your job. I spoke to Ganymede. Someone's filling in."

The earrings dangled from Daria's nerveless fingers. "Color? Cut?"

"And blow-dry. Roxanne is a succubus. She instinctively knows what to do with a woman's hair to achieve maximum sexual impact. People make appointments years in advance so she can work her magic on their hair. Lucky for you, I was able to call in a favor." Sparkle glowed.

Daria could actually feel the cloud of impending doom forming over her head. "But a harpy never has good hair."

"This harpy will." Sparkle was all grim determination. "And don't think you can ugly it up after we leave. You have to keep it looking like Roxanne fixes it until you go back to Tartarus. Oh, and you can't cover it up either." She smiled. "That's where you made your mistake last night. You left me a loophole."

In panic mode, Daria visualized and then abandoned scores of escape scenarios—take harpy form and fling herself out the window, take harpy form and fling *Sparkle* out the window, take harpy form and beat Roxanne and Sparkle senseless with her wings.

But in the end, Daria caved because she couldn't think of an escape plan that didn't leave death and destruction in her wake. Ganymede would fire her, and she'd be kicked out of the Woo Woo Inn, leaving Eris to choose anyone she wanted as her victim. *Leaving Eris to choose* Declan *as her victim.*

And just before the horror began, Daria had a moment of perfect clarity. When she thought about getting kicked out, her first concern was for Declan and *not* her test score.

Two hours later, Daria had pretty much decided that Roxanne was her ticket to a passing score. Hades would grovel at Daria's feet to get the succubus as his chief torturer.

"There. Your hair is now a hunk magnet. Strange men will walk up to you in Wal-Mart and run their fingers through it. Want to take a look?" Roxanne was sweating from her efforts, but triumphant.

"No." Daria was definite about that. She, who couldn't pass a mirror without looking at herself, who would go out of her way to peer into any kind of reflective surface, did not want to see what disaster Roxanne had created.

Roxanne turned to Sparkle. Sparkle shrugged. "What can I say? Harpies are tough to work with. You did an incredible job, sister. Someday Daria will thank you."

"Not in this life." Daria got up, grabbed her clothes, and headed for the bathroom again.

"But I'm not done with her. I could help with her face. I think there's good bone structure under all the scary stuff." Roxanne took a step toward Daria.

Daria turned and bared her teeth at the succubus. "You. Will. Not. Touch. Me. Again." She went into the bathroom and slammed the door behind her.

When she came out, Roxanne was gone. Sparkle was sitting in a chair, one long leg crossed over the other. She swung it back and forth as she studied Daria. "When I win tomorrow night, we'll do something with your face."

"You won't win." No matter how much she wanted Declan, she couldn't give Sparkle power over her last remaining bastion of ugliness, her face.

Sparkle smiled, and for once it was just a smile. "You know, if you want something, you might have to give something up to get it."

"And your point is?"

"Declan wants you. A lot. Enough that he's lost that I-don't-give-a-shit-about-anything expression he had last year." Sparkle held her bandaged finger up to the light and the tiny rubies glittered. "He's a once-in-a-lifetime guy. Think about all your tomorrows. Without him. How many centuries before you get tired of being Hades's gofer and start thinking about what you threw away?"

"Wow, you're good." Daria was in awe of Sparkle's

power. The troublemaker could sense a weakness and exploit it while lying through her shiny, white teeth. "Let's get one thing straight. Declan wants to have sex with me. That's it. What would I do with someone like him?"

Sparkle lowered her lids and slid the tip of her tongue across her full bottom lip. "Oh, you do need my help, sister."

Daria had to get out of this room. Now. Even recognizing the game Sparkle was playing, Daria couldn't stop the graphic images forming in her mind.

The test. She had to focus on the test. Passing it was her ticket to the only life she wanted. Would *ever* want. And as she headed for the door, she tried to ignore the taunting inner voice whispering that real harpies didn't run away.

But as she was leaving, something occurred to Daria. She looked back at Sparkle. "What will *you* give up to get what you want?" Then she shut the door before Sparkle could comment.

Harpies were violent beings. Daria had never reached the level of viciousness Mom and Aunt Ocypete seemed to achieve naturally. But right now, Daria was feeling pretty mean.

She'd have to find Declan and clue him in to the new rules. He absolutely couldn't tempt her. Temptation included but wasn't limited to smiling at her, exposing large areas of bare skin in her presence, speaking in a sexy voice, looking at her . . . Hmm, this could be a problem.

But first, she'd expend some negative energy. When she'd thrown Eris to the ground, she'd caught a glimpse of Walt taking pictures of the fight. Ganymede had wiped memories of the incident from all human minds, but everyone seemed to have forgotten about Walt's camera. She hadn't.

Time to visit her favorite debunker. Stopping at his door, she knocked. She hoped he wasn't still downstairs.

Walt opened his door after the second knock. He stared at her from wide shocked eyes. Yep, he'd discovered what he had.

"We need to talk, Walt." She tried to sound calm and in control, but she was afraid some of her leftover anger was seeping into her voice.

"I came up to go through the photos I've taken since I got here. There're pictures on my camera. You, someone else, and a bunch of wolves. Only you aren't you. You're a . . ." He swallowed hard. "I don't remember taking those pictures."

Maybe she should get Declan to handle this. He could do what he'd done before. But then she looked past Walt.

The debunker had his laptop set up on the coffee table. His camera rested next to it along with the cable to download his pictures. Once they were on his laptop, it would take only a few clicks to e-mail them somewhere else. Once they were gone, no one at the Woo Woo Inn could get them back. If she left now, she'd just bet those photos would be in cyberspace by the time Declan knocked on Walt's door. If they weren't already.

Okay, it was up to her. Too bad she didn't have Delcan's talent for wiping memories. She'd have to find another way to delete the pictures and keep Walt from blabbing.

Not giving Walt a chance to close the door in her face, she stepped past him into the room and then shut the door behind her. "I want you to delete those pictures, Walt. They're fake. We staged them to put some excitement into everyone's night. But they're sort of embarrassing to me. I mean, what would my mom say if she saw them?" She tried for a nervous giggle.

It came out more like a growl. Oops. Guess she'd spooked Walt, because he rushed over to his camera and stood protectively in front of it.

"I don't think they're fake. I've got a feeling about them." For a moment he looked surprised those words had come out of his mouth. "Someone must've messed with my mind, though, because I don't remember any of this stuff. But my camera doesn't lie." He shook his head as if he could shake loose the missing memories.

Daria's rage was building. Not at Walt particularly, but at every crappy thing that had happened since she'd walked through the Woo Woo Inn's doors. He was going to give her a hard time.

"Oh, come on, Walt. Don't tell me you think I'm a—"

"Harpy. You're a freaking harpy in the pictures." His hands shook, but he didn't move away from his camera. "And there're no wolves around here."

She saw the exact moment he figured out that if there weren't wolves near the Woo Woo Inn, then the ones in the pictures must be—

"They're werewolves." He rubbed a shaking hand over his shiny head. "Those pictures are worth a fortune. I can send them to a lab and have them authenticated, prove they weren't done on Photoshop. Hey, maybe I'll get my own show on the Sci Fi Channel." For a moment he forgot to be afraid as the possibilities multiplied in his imagination.

Okay, no more Ms. Nice Harpy. Her anger exploded. This man was *not* going to spread pictures of her everywhere. She would *not* end up on YouTube where a bunch of idiots could make snarky comments about her. And he was *not* going to ruin her career. The judge would give her a big, fat zero if this got out.

"You like to debunk things? Well, debunk this." She'd had lots of practice stripping fast. Within seconds her clothes were off, and she became harpy.

Walt made strangled noises and reached for something to keep him upright. He collapsed onto the couch.

Her change completed, she dominated the room. She spread her huge wings for maximum terror effect and walked across to the camera.

When Walt looked like he might gather enough courage to make a dash for the door, she flapped her wings, knocking over lamps and assorted furniture.

She picked up the camera and carefully deleted the pictures. "There. All gone. Oh, and when you go home, feel free to tell everyone you saw a real harpy." Daria leaned toward him. "And if I see you taking any more pictures of things you shouldn't, I'll catch you alone somewhere and cart you off to the underworld. There's nowhere you can run where I won't find you."

Then she quickly returned to human form and pulled on her clothes. Walt watched her with slack-jawed disbelief.

Daria waved at him. "Later." Then she left.

She hummed to herself as she headed down the stairs in search of Declan. Scaring someone like Walt made her feel all gooey and happy inside. Too bad the judge wasn't around to see it.

Even finding Katie the cook taking her place at the registration desk couldn't kill her high. She grinned at Katie. Katie glared back at her.

It was only when she passed the first mirror that she remembered about her hair.

Declan sat at the kitchen table watching Ganymede working his way though a whole cherry pie. Amazing. He expected the cat to pop like an overinflated balloon.

The cook and Ganymede had worked out a compromise. Katie had set up a card table in the kitchen for when the cat wanted to eat there. The kitchen witch could take it down when she was doing her thing.

"Why aren't you out guarding the church?"

"Got bored and hungry. This Fenrir guy wouldn't talk to me. All the guests are back inside anyway. And Sparkle won't bring my snacks out to me anymore."

"Ah, the missing snack." Declan watched, fascinated, as the cat plowed through crust and filling, shoving the pie tin a little closer to the edge of the table with each bite. "Why don't you eat on the floor? It would be easier." He didn't give a damn where Ganymede ate, but he needed a little small talk before diving into the heavy stuff.

"I don't like eating off the floor. I'm in cat form. I'm not a cat. Do you eat off the floor when you're in bat form?"

Nice to be able to do mind messaging when your mouth was stuffed with pie. "I don't take bat form."

"Too bad. I always thought the vampire bat thing was kinda cool." Ganymede's whole face was buried in the pie. *"Bats eat bugs, don't they? Guess that's not so cool."*

Fine, small talk done. "Fenrir's gaining power every day. He's going to join forces with Loki at summer solstice. I don't think I can stop him alone."

That admission hurt. He'd always been solitary, and he'd always been powerful enough to take care of himself. For just a moment, he thought of Daria's comments about family. He should think of the whole Mackenzie vampire clan as his family, but he'd never been close to any of them. And once he became part of the council, most clan members steered clear of him. The council was *not* a beloved governing body.

"You asking for my help, bloodsucker?" Ganymede thought that possibility was worth pulling his face from the pie. His fur and whiskers were covered with cherry

filling. He sat up and began washing his face with one gray paw.

"Yeah, I guess I am."

Ganymede's amber eyes glowed with anticipation. *"Have a plan yet?"*

"None that would work. When I came here to find whoever had killed the council members, I wasn't expecting to come across anyone this powerful."

"Why does he want you?"

Declan shrugged. "I'm his son, so I guess he plans to use that blood tie somehow. Hope he takes disappointment well. I won't be cooperating any time soon."

"The two of you both showing up here still seems like a strange coincidence."

"Which means it's not coincidence. Loki the trickster is a powerful Norse god. The rest of the gods might've trapped him, but I wouldn't discount his ability to do some long-range planning."

"You never had any contact with either of them?"

"Not until now." Declan shoved aside childhood memories.

He'd had hope then. His mother's people were Vikings. *He* was Viking. And Viking fathers went away in their boats. But they came home again to their sons and daughters. His never had. Considering what Fenrir was, he'd been lucky. Declan drew the hard shell of his childhood disappointments around him.

Family had been important to him once, but nine hundred years stretched memories thin. He'd lost track of his own children. Sure, he'd tried to find them. And sure, it still hurt once in a while. Had they ever searched for him? Declan refused to go down that path.

"So how do we kill the monster? I figure if this Fenrir

doesn't join Loki, the prophecy won't be fulfilled and the earth will keep on turning." Ganymede reverted to regular speech now that his mouth wasn't full and his face was clean.

"Can anyone join this planning session?" Daria paused in the doorway before walking over to the table and pulling out a chair.

Her hair. The change had Sparkle written all over it. Daria's hair was barely shoulder-length now. It was warm brown with blond highlights, and tousled in a way that was totally sexy. He bet she hated it. Declan watched her sit, but words deserted him. They seemed to do that a lot when she was around.

"I just came from Walt's room. Everyone forgot about the pictures he took of my little dustup with Eris. He looked like he was about to download them onto his laptop. Once that happened, he was only a click away from sending them to the world. I had to take direct action."

"Is he still alive? A body could hurt business." Ganymede was a bottom-line kind of guy.

"He's alive. I don't think he'll be taking any more pictures around here. But he'll probably be hunting up Sparkle to give her a hard time." Her narrowed eyes said Sparkle deserved all the hard times Daria could send her way.

Silence. If Ganymede mentioned Daria's hair, he was one crazy cat.

"Hair's looking great, babe."

Declan winced.

Daria looked at Ganymede with death in her eyes. "Leave it alone, cat."

"Yeah, okay. I mean, I've seen lots better. Come to think of it, that style is pretty crappy on you." Ganymede turned panicky eyes to Declan.

"What he means is that your face is so noticeable that

it overwhelms your hair now. It's like the hair isn't even there. So basically, you're bald." Did that make sense? Probably not. But he refused to lie and say her face was grotesque, no matter what she wanted.

"Any thoughts on how to keep Loki from fulfilling the prophecy, Declan?" She'd just closed all discussion of her hair.

"None. The gods are pretty much indestructible. I guess gods can kill other gods, but none of us have god credentials."

"Speak for yourself. You've never seen me get serious, bloodsucker. What I did back at the church was just a warm-up." No one would ever accuse Ganymede of lacking confidence.

"Hey, I believe you. But we need contingency plans." Declan glanced at Ganymede. "Just in case he kicks your ass."

Ganymede looked surprised that anyone thought it could happen. "Yeah, yeah. So if it makes you happy, we'll figure out a plan B."

Daria seemed hesitant. "I hate to be the one to bring this up, Ganymede, but didn't you say you're not allowed to kill anything?"

"Shit. I forgot."

The rest of Ganymede's pie disappeared.

"So if we can't whack him, then we have to figure out how to keep him under the church." Ganymede didn't seem to think that was such a great idea. "Cindy and Thrain won't go for it. Too many fingers plus missing guests add up to trouble for the Woo Woo Inn."

"Will there still be a battle if Fenrir isn't there?" Lost in thought, Daria wound a strand of her hated new hair around one finger.

Declan shook his head to clear it of thoughts about her winding her hair around his cock. "I don't think so. In order for a prophecy to be fulfilled, all the elements have to be there. Loki alone isn't strong enough to destroy all the other gods. His two other children might help, but they need Fenrir's power and ferocity."

Ganymede looked forlornly at the empty pie tin. "I've gotta think about this, and I can't think on an empty stomach. Get the ice cream outta the freezer for me, bloodsucker."

Declan figured the cook was going to go ballistic when she checked her dessert supplies. He didn't intend to stick around to witness it. Digging a carton of Ben & Jerry's out of the freezer, he pried off the top and put the whole thing on Ganymede's table.

"Do lots of thinking while you're chowing down. I'm heading for the parlor." Declan glanced at Daria.

"I'll walk with you. I have to relieve Katie at the desk." She didn't make eye contact.

They'd almost reached the desk before she spoke. "Will it bother you if we end up destroying Fenrir?"

Trouble wandered over, tail wagging, and walked with them.

"No." *Maybe.*

"I guess you never knew him. He wasn't there for you and your mom." She reached down to pat the dog's head.

"My mother was a one-night, no, make that a fifteen-minute stand for him." *And now I'm following in his footsteps, or would that be paw prints?* Thank Odin, Declan hadn't inherited his dad's werewolf genes.

"It must've been hard for her."

"Not particularly. She parked me with whoever would watch me and followed her bliss." He knew his smile was bitter. "She was a liberated woman for her time. Of course, she became vampire right after she had me, and vampires didn't operate by all the rules humans did at that time."

"Do you have kids? And do you treat your kids like your mom and dad treated you?" Trouble cocked his head to one side as if trying to understand the conversation.

Surprised, Declan glanced down. He'd almost forgotten Trouble wasn't a real dog. He thought about his answer. Trouble might be a cosmic troublemaker, but he was only a child. "I have two sons and two daughters. But that was a long time ago." Were they still alive? He chose to believe they were. His few memories of them were old and faded around the edges, but he refused to let them go. "When they were little, they'd all come running into the house together and Grim would shout, 'We're home.' Grim was their spokesman and he always said the same words. Funny what you remember. I loved them." He tried to keep the softness from his voice. That was a different time. A time when emotions still ran strong in him.

Declan got the feeling he hadn't succeeded, because he felt Daria wrap her fingers around his clenched fist. She squeezed and her support was in the warmth of her hand.

"What're their names?" Trouble turned happy brown eyes up to him, oblivious of all undercurrents.

"My daughters are Bera and Finna. My sons are Alrek and Grim."

Trouble laughed. "Grim. Like the fairy tales. Where are they now?"

"I lost them."

"Then why don't you find them?" Trouble asked.

Declan was relieved he didn't wait around for an answer. Trouble spotted Mel the bully rabbit and slunk away.

Declan expected Daria to comment. She didn't. When

they reached the desk, she simply dropped his hand and smiled.

"I think I need a little fresh air," Declan announced. Would she understand that he wanted some space? "I'll be out on the porch."

Her smile said she understood that alone was a good place to be once in a while. "Don't forget to look up before you step off the porch."

"Will do." By the time he pushed the screen door open, she was talking to Katie.

He stood at the edge of the porch staring out into the darkness. Emotions? After so many years? Sure felt like it. First that touch of sadness for the good-old-dad who'd never existed. Then the sense of loss over his kids that he thought he'd packed away long ago.

His feelings for Daria? A little more complicated than he liked. Did he still want his one night? You bet. But he enjoyed being with her more than he should. Once she made her snatch and flew back to Tartarus, he might just miss her. He'd avoided missing anyone for lots of years.

He was so busy thinking about Daria that he didn't notice the pressure beginning at the back of his head until it slammed into him and dropped him to his knees.

His pain was the searing agony of a knife plunged into his brain. It blinded him, and if he'd had any breath, the pain would've taken that too.

"Declan, Declan, you try my patience. The time draws near when the prophecy will be fulfilled. I need you now. Come to me."

Fenrir's voice exploded inside his head, and if Declan could have ripped open his skull to let the voice out, he would have.

"Now, Declan."

The pain had taken his voice so he couldn't even call

for help. He seemed to have no will of his own as he climbed to his feet and staggered off the porch.

Trying to close the door on his pain, he pulled the ragged edges of his vampire power to him. He focused that power inward, fighting to force Fenrir from his mind.

He managed to slow down his drunken stagger toward the woods, but the pain didn't let up.

Help. He needed some freaking help. No voice to yell with, so he'd have to reach for someone's mind. Who? If only the pain would stop for a minute so he could *think*.

Ganymede. Powerful enough to hear him despite the pain.

The agony pounded, pounded, pounded as he tried to reach for Ganymede.

No go. He couldn't get past the pain.

As his legs continued to take him on a wobbling course toward the church, a wave of terror washed over him.

For the first time in nine centuries, he felt completely helpless.

CHAPTER TEN

Memo: to all harpies
Subject: expense accounts
Harpies can no longer charge unnecessary items. Accounting has stopped accepting receipts for BOTOX and lip plumper. They are not legitimate expenses. Harpies do not need disguises. That is cheating the company. Only Hades can cheat the company. Punishment for those who persist in handing in these receipts will be one year of daily bikini waxes.

Remember, the unadorned harpy face is a company asset.

HADES THE UNDERSTANDING

The guests were waiting for their last meal of the night. Lucky for them, their cook was able to multitask. Five minutes after quitting the registration desk and morphing back into a kitchen witch, Katie had conjured up a variety of mouthwatering food smells. Daria sniffed. No essence of singed cat hair. Ganymede must've escaped with his ice cream carton.

Everyone seemed happy and clueless. She expected that from the humans, but what about the nonhumans? Couldn't they sense the planet-shifting events happening around them? Guess not.

Mel edged up to her. "Seen that brown dog around?" Even after a night spent chasing small, helpless animals, he was still primed to make Trouble's life miserable.

She raised one brow. "And you think I'd tell you if I had?"

His smile was no smile at all. "You work here. It's your job to keep me happy."

"Not that happy." She turned from him, and came face-to-face with Kal. "Hey, brother. Having fun?"

He scowled at her. Nope, no fun going on in *his* life. She sighed and braced herself for a lecture. Not that she didn't deserve it; she did.

"I've decided on the wereleopard for you. She's alone, she's young, and she won't put up too much of a fight. I did a background search. She has an arrest record, so that should satisfy your need for someone evil." He should look more satisfied with his choice. "She'll get you more points than a human would."

"So why don't you look thrilled?" Daria frowned as a ripple of unease touched her. What *was* it? Psychic vibes usually passed her by, but she'd felt something. And that something wasn't good.

He shrugged and avoided her gaze. "Someone more powerful would've made an impact the judge couldn't ignore. Too bad you couldn't handle the vampire."

"Well, I can't," she said defensively. "Where's the leopard now?"

This time the ripple was a tsunami, a psychic punch in the gut. And the punch had a name. Declan. "Something's wrong."

"What?" Kal had been about to point out the leopard.

"Find Ganymede. Send him outside. Delcan's in trouble." She ignored the questions in her brother's eyes as she raced for the door.

Daria yanked it open and rushed outside. A quick scan told her Declan wasn't in sight. Trying to quiet her pounding heart, she stopped and listened. The faint sound of stumbling footsteps guided her into the woods.

Thank the gods for her enhanced harpy hearing.

Within seconds that felt more like hours, she reached him. He didn't even glance at her as he clutched his head between his hands.

"Declan, stop. What's wrong?" She grabbed his arm.

Shaking her off, he kept walking.

She pushed past him and turned to face him. "Speak to me. What's going on?"

His eyes had a glassy, unfocused look. The only thing she recognized in those eyes was agony.

"I'm not moving. Stop and I'll find someone who can take away the pain." Daria hoped she wasn't making false promises.

He didn't answer her, and he didn't swerve to go around her. When he walked right into her, she fell backward. Jeez, he was strong. If she hadn't rolled aside, he would've walked right over her.

It didn't take any deep thinking to realize where he was headed. The church. This was about Fenrir. Scrambling to her feet, she followed him.

She'd already stripped off her clothes and become harpy by the time Ganymede materialized beside her. Startled, she yelped.

"I can move through time and space, babe. Get used to it. So what's with the bloodsucker?" He glanced at Declan, who was still doggedly staggering down the path toward the church.

Later, when she wasn't frantic with fear for Declan, she'd be suitably impressed by Ganymede's power. "It's like he's in some kind of trance. He's headed for the church and nothing I've done has stopped him."

Ganymede didn't waste time arguing or asking useless questions. He just nodded and headed after Declan. Daria moved him up a rung on her cats-who-get-it ladder.

He padded around Declan and stood in front of him, much as she'd done. "Hold up, Mackenzie. You're going in the wrong direction."

Declan kept on walking.

Ganymede sighed. Suddenly a glowing wall appeared across the path. Declan slammed into it and stopped. Then he started trudging parallel to whatever was keeping him from Fenrir.

"Stubborn bastard. Crap, I just lost another candy bar." Ganymede's grumble echoed in the silent forest. "Pick him up and hold him still for me. The next step is tricky." The wall disappeared.

She hoped she could do that. Harpies had tremendous lower body strength. They needed it to carry heavy prey long distances. And their wings gave them the power to travel at preternatural speed. But she remembered how easily Declan had foiled Eris's attempt to carry him off.

It was tough getting into the air with all the trees. Her wings clipped branches as she rose over Declan. Then she dropped down, extended her talons, and grabbed the back of his shirt. Too bad he wasn't wearing his leather coat. Leather wouldn't rip like cloth.

Declan didn't even look up at her. With an inarticulate growl of rage, he ripped his shirt open. And as buttons exploded like tiny missiles, Declan walked out of his shirt.

Startled, Daria let the ruined shirt dangle from her talons for a moment; then she dropped it to the ground and dived for Declan again. Aha, this time she had him. She hooked her talons into the back of his pants, then flapped her wings madly to hold them both in place.

He didn't bother with the growl this time. Declan simply tore the front of his pants open, yanked them down, and stepped out of them. When his shoes got in his way, he clumsily discarded them too. No underwear to worry about.

Naked, he marched onward.

Folding her wings, she regrouped. In a calmer moment, she would have paused for silent contemplation of one of nature's most beautiful creations. But she wasn't calm. And there was nowhere else to grab him without sinking her talons into him. Nope, not going to do that.

She heard Ganymede's muttered complaint beside her. Then the cat padded in Declan's wake. Daria followed. Declan wasn't moving too fast, so it was easy to keep up.

Ganymede glanced up at her. "Looks like a compulsion. A strong one if it can work on our boy. He's fighting it, though. Now, here's what we're gonna do. As soon as we get beside him, you pick me up. Then you put your hand on his shoulder. Don't grab, because he'll just throw you off. Got it?"

"Got it." No argument from her. She was fresh out of ideas.

She reached Declan's side, and for the first time really absorbed his signs of distress. Sweat sheened his body, and he pushed his clenched fists against the sides of his head as though he could punch a hole in his skull to release the agony.

Daria put her hand over her mouth as tears filled her eyes. Crying? Absolutely not. Harpies never cried. Besides, what did she know about tears? She'd never experienced them before. For all she knew a blocked tear duct could be making her all watery. Or maybe an allergy to cat hair. She cast Ganymede an accusing stare.

And the heavy weight parked in her chest? Stress-induced. Mom had never told her how really tough all this test stuff could be. *You are so into denial.*

"Pick me up." Ganymede's voice was clipped and all business. This wasn't Ganymede the food-obsessed.

Not sure what to expect, Daria picked up the cat and at the same time put her hand on Declan's shoulder.

And everything ceased to be. When awareness returned she was in Sparkle's room.

Glancing around, she met Sparkle's astonished gaze. The queen of sex and sin was sitting on her red velvet couch. "Okay, you just impressed me to death, Ganymede." Daria scanned the room and found the cat sitting at the foot of Sparkle's bed. Declan sprawled across the mattress, every muscle taut as he strained against invisible bonds.

Since Sparkle seemed temporarily speechless, Daria addressed the cat. "Why'd you bring him to this room?" *And someone please stop the pain.*

"I could use a little help here." Ganymede glared at Sparkle and her. "I'm getting tired of holding him down. You guys tie him to the bed so I can concentrate on blocking the pain and stopping the compulsion. Why here? Sparkle takes her bed seriously, don't you, sweet-tart?"

"Always. I like to make love in a big, strong bed I can sink into." She rose from the couch in one lithe motion and went to her closet. Taking down a short robe, she wordlessly handed it to Daria. "With someone *not* named Ganymede."

From her tone of voice, Daria guessed she used the same words to describe her men. "Fine, so you like your bed. What about Declan?" Returning to human form, she wrapped the robe around her.

"The important thing about this bed is it's a four-poster, and it'll stand up to a beating. Sparkle's already given it lots of test runs." He looked at Sparkle. "Get something to tie him with, evil lady."

"We need to take away the pain *now*." Daria couldn't help it. That was the only thing she could think about. Getting rid of the compulsion would come next.

"We?" Ganymede watched Sparkle root around in a bureau.

"Fine. You." Who was quibbling about words?

Sparkle came back with what looked like custom-made handcuffs. With their comfy, crimson padding, they sure weren't police issue. "I'll take his ankles and you do his wrists." She handed Daria a set of cuffs.

Daria bit her lip as she dragged Declan's arms into a position where she could cuff each of his wrists to a bedpost. Wow, it took all of her strength just to wrestle one arm into position. And even knowing it was for his own good, she felt a stab of guilt.

This was bad, and she wasn't just thinking about Declan. Successful harpies never experienced pesky emotions connected with that totally useless human phenomenon called a conscience.

A harpy couldn't operate under any kind of stupid constraints that tied her emotionally to other beings. Her loving relationships with Kal and Mom were unusual in the harpy world, probably because Dad wasn't a harpy. Just one more strike against her among other harpies.

She was going to make a lousy harpy, because she was feeling all kinds of banned emotions: worry, grief, and worst of all, caring. And right now she didn't have the strength to push them away.

As Daria gazed at Declan's spread-eagled body, her only comfort was that he was so out of it, his mind probably wasn't processing many details.

Sparkle looked sympathetic, but Daria was too upset to judge how genuine her expression was.

"Mede and I will take care of him for now, Daria. Go to your room and get dressed. Then check on the guests. Katie served the meal a few minutes ago." She checked her nails to make sure all nine were still perfect. Handcuffing someone was hell on a manicure. "Get something to eat and by the time you've finished I'll have something to report." Sparkle's smile was all sweet understanding.

"But I—"

"You're the manager, and you should be there for our guests." Sparkle kept smiling, but some of her steel was showing.

Daria had no way to counter that argument. She couldn't very well say, "I'm a tough, heartless, harpy bitch, but his pain has turned me into a big, squishy marshmallow." No, harpies didn't beg. Turning, she left the room.

Ganymede stared up at Sparkle. "You could've let her stay. It'll only take me a few minutes to get rid of his pain. I could do it faster if it was an ordinary headache, but Fenrir complicates things. I'm betting the wolf drops the compulsion once he realizes the bloodsucker isn't gonna show. It's tough to maintain when the vic has Declan's kind of power."

Sparkle abandoned her I'm-okay and it's-business-as-usual mask as soon as Daria closed the door. Beneath her Sparkle persona she felt old, dry, and brittle. Mede had done this to her.

"We need to talk about the Big Boss, Mede." She walked over to the window and stared into the darkness. No way did she want to see his expression. Was she cowardly? You bet. Just add that to her selfish, vain, and fixated-on-sex list of faults. "I've always known immortals like us don't stay together forever. It's tough to maintain a relationship for thousands of years. But we've made it work by giving each other space."

No comment from behind her.

"Sure, I'm ticked at you for choosing immortality over me. But I get it." He didn't love her. The sex was great, and they'd shared lots of incredible adventures together. But it wasn't love.

What she was about to suggest scared her witless. "What if I told the Big Boss I didn't want to be a cosmic troublemaker anymore?" If they were both human, with a human's finite life span, would he want to spend those few years with her?

"Don't go there, babe."

That was it, then. It wasn't love.

Pasting a smile on her face, she turned to look at him. "Don't know what made me say that." She shrugged. "I wanted Daria out of the room because I have a few modifications in mind for Declan's compulsion." She studied her nails rather than meet his inscrutable-cat gaze. "What's his status right now?"

"His pain is gone and the compulsion is weakening. The pain was keeping him from fighting it." Mede's expression gave nothing away.

Sometimes she wished cats had more facial muscles so they could express emotion. She needed some emotion now. "I know what kind of power you have, so I want you to replace Fenrir's compulsion with one you create."

"A sexual one." He didn't have to make it a question. Mede knew her that well.

"What else? Make the compulsion specific to Daria. When Fenrir tries his trick again, I want it to act as a trigger for your compulsion. His won't have any effect once yours kicks in."

"Why should I do this?"

"Because you owe me." It was a small, greedy, cheap answer, but that's all he deserved from her. "Oh, and could you leave Declan in kind of a loopy frame of mind?"

Not waiting for his response, she headed for the door. "I'll go get Daria." By the time Daria reached the room, Mede would be gone.

"Why didn't you follow me tonight, Kal? I could've used your help. You haven't even asked what happened." It was tough carrying on a conversation when all Daria's thoughts were focused on Declan.

Kal finished drinking his coffee. He shrugged. "You were running off to help the vampire instead of ignoring him and focusing on your test. Maybe I didn't want to be a part of that."

"You're mad."

"I'm worried. This is what you've worked for your entire life, and I don't want you to blow it. The judge can see what I see. Eris is out there busting her butt trying to snatch someone."

"Yeah, and she has lots of butt to bust." When had that become a bad thing? In the harpy world, Eris's big butt was a source of pride. Daria was thinking like a human.

A smile tugged at Kal's lips. "Well, she's making it work for her. She tried to snatch a werelion earlier tonight. When she couldn't get a grip on his mane, she sat on him." His smile widened. "The lion bit her on the ass. Guess she'll be looking for other prey."

For the first time in what seemed like forever, Daria laughed. "I hope the judge got a front-row seat for the show." She scanned the dining room. Everyone was busy eating or talking except . . . She narrowed her gaze. Mel was staring at her. When she returned his stare, he looked away. "Kal, about the judge, what are the chances he might be a were?"

Kal followed her gaze. "Mel? What makes you suspect him?"

"I don't know. It just seems every time I turn around, he's there. I mean, he's the kind of judge the harpies would love—vicious, vindictive, and a bully."

Kal nodded. "I'll keep an eye on him."

"So, where's this wereleopard you've picked out for me?" She wondered how Declan was doing. Was he still hurting? Daria controlled her urge to push back her chair and rush to Sparkle's room. She pressed her lips together. Her job. If she didn't do it, she'd lose it. "I'll take a look at her and then I have some paperwork to do."

"I've changed my mind." He glanced away. "The wereleopard isn't good enough for you. If Eris is targeting a were, you have to go for something better. We'll try to isolate one of the Night Feeders. They don't have Declan's power. A vampire will be more impressive than whatever Eris drags to Tartarus."

She blinked. "But you—"

When he looked at her, she saw anger in his eyes. Why? Kal never got mad at her.

"Let me set it up, okay?" He pushed his cup away from him. "It's not like you're helping anyway. You'd think I was the one being tested." With that parting shot, he got up and left.

She knew she'd let distractions sort of mess with her focus, but this was only her second night here, for crying out loud. She'd get it together before the end of her two weeks. Of course, the universe would end before that if someone didn't stop Fenrir.

Well, the paperwork wouldn't do itself. Rising, she left the dining room. But instead of turning toward the registration desk, her feet took her to the small guest bathroom. Call it an impulse move. She didn't want to go up to her room, but she needed a few minutes alone to process what was happening.

Once inside, she locked the door and sat on the closed toilet lid. A perfect meditation throne. But before she could think one meaningful thought, the toilet started flushing and a familiar rap came from the mirror.

Sighing, Daria looked up to find the same message in big red capital letters on the mirror. *LET ME OUT!*

"Stop the flushing, for crying out loud." Who got mad at a mirror?

Surprisingly, the flushing stopped. Maybe no one had bothered to talk to whatever was behind the glass. "I feel your pain. Look at me, sitting in a bathroom so I can get my head straight. You're not the only one with problems."

Oh. Normal-sized letters.

"I'm having an identity crisis." She held her palms up as though balancing two destinies. "Am I Daria, successful harpy or Daria, desirable woman? I'm like an immortal yo-yo."

Bummer. Letters slanting downward to indicate depression.

"Yeah." She propped her elbows on her knees and held her head in her hands. "I keep telling myself I want to pass the test, but I don't do one thing to make it happen. I say I want to be ugly and gross, but I let Sparkle sex me up. If I were a dedicated harpy, I would've said to hell with the bet and not allowed Sparkle to touch me."

Sometimes we sacrifice our tomorrows for today. Smaller letters so they could all fit on the mirror.

Daria nodded. "You're right. And sometimes we sacrifice our future on the off chance a man we've only known for a few nights might be important to us. Is that dumb or what?" There, she'd finally admitted the truth. To a mirror. Hey, it was a start.

Our subconscious sometimes recognizes truths before we do. It was a big message to squeeze onto a small mirror.

Daria glanced at her watch. She had to get out of here in case Sparkle came looking for her with news of Declan. She stood. "Thanks for listening."

You're welcome.

But she didn't move. Who was she kidding? Not only wasn't she trying too hard to be ugly, but she wasn't doing much to build her rep as queen of the cold and callous. She'd never been cruel, so what made her think she could turn on the mean machine now?

She looked at the mirror. "Do you really want out of there?"

Yes. Really tiny letters signifying hopelessness.

Daria glanced around the bathroom. She opened the cabinet door beneath the sink and found a small plunger. Grasping it like a sword, she slammed the wooden handle into the mirror. Daria flung her hand across her eyes as broken glass sprayed the room.

When she finally let her hand drop, it was to find a glowing red orb hovering in front of her.

"Thank you. I won't forget."

The voice in Daria's mind was young, excited, and happy. Then the orb winked out.

She stepped over the glass and left the bathroom. Well, that had been an eventful little bathroom break. Sparkle was waiting at the registration desk.

Sparkle smiled her beautiful, deceitful smile. "You showed up just in time. Sit down." She pointed at the chair.

"How is he?" Daria didn't feel like sitting.

"Not so good." Sparkle sighed. "I think he's still in

pain. Mede did everything he could, but Fenrir is too powerful for him."

Daria's thoughts chased each other in ever-expanding circles. There must be something they could do for Declan.

"There might be one solution." Sparkle stared at Kal as he headed for the stairs. "Interesting. Your brother is looking better each time I see him."

"Forget Kal. What about Declan?" Daria wanted to pick Sparkle up and shake her like a castanet.

"Oh, sure. A vampire's most powerful impulses are connected to blood and sex. It's why I've always had an affinity for the glorious creatures." She slid a calculating glance at Daria. "I wonder how far you'd go to help him."

"Get to the point." Maybe she'd sic Eris on Sparkle. If she weren't so worried about Declan, the mental image of Eris sitting on Sparkle would cheer her up a lot.

"Okay, here's the deal. Declan is already hot for you. Mede said that someone has to trigger Declan's vampire lusts. Once he becomes vampire, his pain will disappear along with the compulsion."

Daria frowned. "Ganymede said that?"

"Absolutely."

"What do I have to do?"

"Do a sexy strip in front of Declan and then let the good times roll. Oh, and don't worry about the bet. We've already settled up for tonight." She smiled brightly at Daria.

"Let the good times roll?"

"Use your imagination, Daria. I know it's in there somewhere. Rusty, but still functional."

"And what happens when Fenrir does the same thing again tomorrow night?" Daria might be slow, but she could follow a bread trail.

Sparkle shrugged. "I guess it all depends on how much you want to help Declan. It's your call." Her gaze drifted to where Kal had disappeared. "I think I'll make sure all the guests are comfortable while you come to a decision. Don't worry about the paperwork. Declan is more important." And for just a moment she almost looked sincere. "I don't know about you, but I'm not ready for the universe to end."

Daria nodded. "By the way, I broke the mirror in the guest bathroom. My bad. Send me the bill." She walked away before Sparkle could say anything.

Strip for Declan? That was crazy. But Sparkle's reasoning made a weird kind of sense. He'd be stronger as vampire. But why hadn't he changed when he first felt the compulsion coming on? A question only he could answer.

Sparkle was wrong. There wasn't a decision to make. Declan needed help, and she'd help him. Daria felt a momentary twinge of guilt at leaving the paperwork for the day guy.

Guilt? Caring? Her engine was off the track before it even began to move. She'd spent a lifetime working toward bitch-goddess status; all it had taken was a few nights to destroy years of preparation.

Daria took a deep breath. She didn't have to make any final decisions right now. In the end, she'd be judged on the prey she brought back to Tartarus. A happy Hades was her ticket to a passing grade.

With that thought in mind, she started toward Sparkle's room.

"Excuse me. Could you help us?" The voice was young, perky, and cheerful.

No, no, no. Not now. Gritting her teeth, Daria turned.

A couple stood behind her. The woman immediately

snagged her attention. She had a strange kind of beauty that inexplicably gave Daria chills. Daria couldn't describe her eyes because she was so riveted by the woman's hair. Parted in the middle, her long hair was an instant attention grabber. One side was black, the other white. In her twenties, she wore jeans and a T-shirt that said Texas Tech. Her smile was wide and engaging.

"Hi. I'm Kiki and this is my brother Chris." She smiled up at the man next to her.

Under different circumstances, Daria would have given Chris a second look. Tall, slim, with longish blond hair and amazing black eyes, he was worth it. But she didn't have time now.

"So what can I do for you?" Daria managed to keep the impatience out of her voice.

"Oh, we're looking for someone. He's a friend of a friend. We know he's here, but we haven't seen him yet." Kiki looked at her expectantly. "Could you tell us what room he's in?"

Daria smothered a sigh. "I'm not allowed to give out room numbers, but I can let him know you're looking for him. What's his name?"

"Declan Mackenzie." Chris smiled at her. "He doesn't know us, but we're looking forward to meeting him."

"Um, I think Mr. Mackenzie went out for the night. He didn't say when he'd be back. But I'm sure you can catch up with him tomorrow night." Daria thought frantically as she lied through her teeth. Who were these people, and what was their connection with Declan?

Kiki made a moue of disappointment. "Bummer. Well, we'll make sure to hunt him down tomorrow. Thanks for your help." She glanced up at Chris, and they wandered away.

Daria focused on their retreating backs. Not human. But she didn't have a clue what they were. Certainly nothing she'd come across before. These must be the two Kal had mentioned.

Pushing thoughts of Kiki and Chris away for the moment, she hurried to Sparkle's room. Taking a deep breath for courage, she opened the door.

CHAPTER ELEVEN

What the hell had happened? Declan peered at the room through slitted eyes. Red velvet furniture. Red silk drapes. Erotic paintings. He glanced down. And he was freaking naked.

Where was he? Wherever it was, he felt pretty damn happy about it. There should be something he remembered, but right now all he could think about was how nice it would be to bury himself deep inside . . . someone whose name dangled just out of reach.

He knew his smile must look kinda goofy, because that's how he was feeling. Now, who was the cute little thing . . . ? Declan frowned. No, cute little thing was wrong. Sweet little thing wasn't right either. She wasn't cute and she wasn't sweet. She was—

The door swung open. A woman stepped into the room and shut the door behind her.

Yes! She was *this* woman. Old what's-her-name. He felt like hooting in triumph. Somewhere lost in the cotton candy stuffing his brain, he knew he wasn't a hooting kind of guy. So he didn't.

Whoever she was, she didn't look too sure of herself. She looked like she wanted to turn around and run back out the door. No. He didn't want her to leave. What *did* he want? Oh yeah, he wanted to bury himself inside her.

He felt the slide of his fangs.

And then he wanted to tap into all that hot life force pulsing just beneath the smooth skin of her throat.

Hunting instincts kicked in. He might not know much, but he knew he was a predator. So he'd just lie real still and wait for the right moment to pounce.

Lie real still? A little of the fuzz in his brain cleared. Enough for him to realize he wouldn't be doing a lot of pouncing any time soon. He couldn't move his hands or feet.

There wasn't much reasoning going on in his mind, so primal rage jumped into the vacuum. He fought whatever held him on the bed, but he fought it silently. Screams of rage would just alert other predators. He didn't know how he knew that, but he did. Arching his body, he yanked at whatever held him. Then he twisted his body before flinging it back onto the bed. The bed shook and groaned, but held firm.

Now he was pissed. He glared at the woman.

"Calm down, Declan. I know it hurts, but if you'll concentrate on me, I can make it go away." She walked to the side of the bed and offered him a tentative smile.

Hurts? He didn't know what she was talking about. But when he tried to tell her so, the words floated away from him.

"When you're back to being you, you'd better appreciate what I'm doing for you." She sounded almost mad. "I mean, sure I'm naked when I become harpy, but that's completely different from this."

Naked? He recognized that word. It sort of restored his good humor. If she'd slip out of her sexy clothes, he might get downright happy again.

She scanned the room. "Sparkle didn't expect me to do this without music, did she?" Wandering over to something in the corner that he couldn't see from his position on the bed, she made satisfied noises. "Okay, here we go."

Music drifted through the room. If only the stuff clogging his brain would go away, he'd probably know what it was. But he couldn't focus on the music. Not when the woman had returned to the side of the bed.

He caught her scent, a mixture of nervousness and female arousal. His cock reacted accordingly. He'd been hard since the moment she walked into the room, but now his sexual hunger got serious. Her gaze slid over his stomach and lower. She paused. He got harder. Then she glanced away. *Damn*.

"What do I do first? Harpies don't play sexual games like this."

Harpy. Did he know any harpies? Guess he did. His mind tried to process the info but didn't get too far.

As she began to move to the rhythm, she slipped the clingy little orange top over her head. "If a harpy wants a guy, she asks him to have sex with her." She did a little hip thrust that made him so hot he could feel sweat breaking out on his chest and stomach. "If he turns her down, she twists his head off. Harpies don't handle rejection well."

Reaching behind her, she unhooked her bra and let it drop to the floor. "I never asked anyone, so I don't have a long list of lovers. And the ones who asked me?" She shrugged, doing wonderful things to her full breasts. "Let's just say I don't twist off heads because of unmet expectations."

As his erection grew, his mind started to clear. Looked like the ones who said a man thought with his cock had it right. Daria. Her name was Daria.

While he'd been thinking about his cock, she'd kicked off her sandals, then started shimmying out of her short little skirt and panties.

She continued to move to the music, her breasts bouncing as she rotated her hips and shook her shoulders. "I'm starting to get the hang of this." Cupping her breasts, she rubbed her thumbs over her nipples until they were hard nubs.

He groaned.

Ever since she'd checked out the state of his arousal, she'd aimed her attention somewhere beyond his right ear. But when he groaned, she met his gaze with wide startled eyes.

"You're still in pain. Sparkle said this would help. I'll try harder."

If she tried any harder, his cock would explode.

Climbing onto the bed, she straddled his hips. Whoever this Sparkle was, he owed her.

"Sparkle said to let the good times roll." She offered him a smile that suggested those good times would definitely trump the pain he was supposed to be feeling.

He moaned to indicate that his discomfort was growing more and more unbearable. Could he help it if they weren't on the same page with their definitions of "discomfort"?

She leaned forward, her warm breath fanning across his skin. Too bad her hair wasn't a little longer. A big fantasy-fulfiller would be her hair trailing slowly over his erection, the feel of each strand sliding across the head of his cock and sending every nerve ending into starbursts of mini-orgasms.

Well, a vampire could only expect so much, and he had almost more than he could handle right now. Speaking of handling . . . He yanked at the bonds holding him to the blasted bed.

Touching her tongue to each of his nipples, she smoothed her fingers over his torso while making husky little murmurs of pleasure. "Getting rid of your compulsion shouldn't be so . . . stimulating."

Compulsion. The loud and very organ-specific demands of his body almost drowned out the word. But he did hear it. And suddenly all of the fuzziness and confusion were gone. He remembered. Everything. The pain so powerful he couldn't talk, couldn't gather his vampire powers to resist Fenrir's call, couldn't even *think*. And then the faint memory of Daria and Ganymede stopping him, of ending up here handcuffed to this bed.

What he couldn't remember was why Daria was crouched over him doing amazing things to his body. From what she'd said so far, he figured she thought "letting the good times roll" would end his pain and the compulsion.

An honest vampire would stop her right now and admit that he was fine. An ethical vampire wouldn't let her continue to put her mouth on his body in the mistaken belief she was helping him. A morally strong vampire would *not* let this go on.

Declan allowed himself a wicked grin while Daria was occupied kissing a path over his stomach. He was none of the above. And he wanted what she was doing more than he could remember ever wanting anything before.

Growling low in his throat, he gave his sexual hunger free rein. Bloodlust came along for the ride. If he weren't handcuffed, his sassy harpy would get the surprise of her short life. Nine hundred years of feeding his senses had taught him a lot about pleasing women.

Scooting lower on his body, she drew circles on his sacs with the tips of her fingers before cupping him in her warm palms. "Touching is such a sensual experience. Harpies aren't into a lot of touching. But holding you makes me want to . . ." She walked her fingers up his erection and did a tap dance on its head with her fingernails. Each tap of her finger was a shock wave of pure sexual pleasure.

Makes you want to what? He needed to know. He wondered what he should do. If he told her he was fine, she'd release him so he could touch her. But that didn't guarantee they'd end up making love. Once Daria decided she'd done her duty, she might just climb off him, get dressed, and walk out that door. Talk about sexual frustration. Nope, he'd suffer in silence.

Leaning over until her breasts pressed between his spread thighs, she swirled her tongue around his cock.

He sucked in his breath.

"I don't know about this. There's something missing. Not you." She patted his overexcited organ. "You're great."

Well, at least part of him hadn't taken an ego hit.

Suddenly, she straightened, the movement making her breasts jiggle. Great Thor's hammer. Mesmerized, he followed their motion.

Once again she positioned herself over his hips. Daria stared down at him. "I thought about tempting you with my sensual smile, maybe going for a few heated gazes. But I'm a harpy, so I don't think anything I try to do with my face would drive you wild with lust."

You have no idea. He clenched his whole body to control his need to thrust upward, driving himself into her.

Slowly, she lowered herself until he felt the head of his cock nudge open the door to his personal nirvana. Hot, wet, and tight, but still open just enough to make him believe a sensational welcome waited on the other side. He held the breath he no longer had.

She stopped. "You know, this isn't right."

What the . . . ? Of course it was right. It felt right to him. Didn't it feel right to her?

"Sure, it's supposed to help you get yourself together, but it's too much like taking advantage of you."

His psychic howl would probably break windows in China. *Take. Advantage. Of. Me. Please!*

Daria frowned. "No, I definitely can't do this to you." She looked like she was about to climb off of him.

He scowled up at her. "I'm cured. I'm okay. I'm better than okay. I'm freaking perfect."

"I know." She grinned down at Declan. It had been worth teasing him just to see the dumbfounded look on his usually in-control face.

"When did you guess?"

"When I felt you trying to decide whether to tell me you were okay. You went that weird kind of still for a moment. Vampires do that, but only when all their brain cells are firing." Fine, small talk finished. The major question was, would *they* finish now?

His smile made erotic promises at the same time his gaze delivered enough heat to send Sparkle's red velvet bedspread up in flames. He had serious lovemaking on his mind. "Try to walk away, harpy lady, and you'll see one crazed Viking who'll do his berserker ancestors proud."

Well, guess that answered her question. "We have things to talk about. Tonight could happen again." Did she want to talk now? Um, no. But Daria felt it was only fair to throw the thought out there.

"We make love first, then talk. Because I guarantee if you try to have a meaningful discussion now about anything not connected to sex, my body will tune you out. And my brain can't make it listen."

She glanced around the room. Sparkle had probably left the handcuff keys somewhere. Or not. "Looks like Sparkle took the keys to your cuffs with her." Daria reached over to give an experimental yank on the handcuffs using all her harpy strength. Nothing. *Rats.* "Help me."

Even their combined strength couldn't free Declan. He made a disgusted sound. "The cuffs and bed are probably Ganymede's creations. Other than Fenrir, he's the only one here with magic powerful enough to keep me in this bed."

"Guess you'll just have to lie back and enjoy it." And he *would* enjoy it. She'd make sure of that.

He didn't look thrilled. "Where's the fun for you if I can't do my part?"

"You foolish man." Once again, she positioned herself so she was poised above his cock. She savored the moment. "Running my hands over your bare body and putting my mouth anywhere I choose makes me happy with a sky-high capital H."

"I like steering the ship." He smiled at her, showing lots of fang. "Guess you already know that. But control doesn't seem too important when you're handing out pleasure like Halloween treats." His gaze was all about hunger and need. "Don't wait too long, sweetheart, or else I'll be nothing more than a pile of hot ash by the time you get ready to ride."

She'd wanted to make it long and luscious. She ended up making it short and sensational. Everything started out fine. No one could say she didn't have good intentions.

First, she teased his cock by lowering herself until just the head slipped inside her and then raising her body off of him. Up and down, up and down, until she was wet, hot, and clenching around the anticipation of taking all of him inside her.

Second . . . Okay, so she never got to second. With the hunting cry of the harpy, she swooped down on him and impaled herself on his long, hard shaft.

His harsh cry mingled with her little murmurs of pleasure as she lifted herself until only the head of his erection was still inside her and then slammed down on him over and over and over again. She gained speed as she felt the heaviness building low in her belly, the growing pressure that was almost there, almost there, almost . . .

There! She flung herself over the edge and hung motionless, locked in that breathless, paralyzed moment when sensation was too extreme to disturb with anything as mundane as breathing or moving. Then she plummeted downward on ever-weakening spasms until she lay emptied on top of his sweat-sheened body.

"And they talk about *men's* lack of stamina," she murmured against his neck. "Everything just sort of got away from me." Daria nipped his shoulder before lifting her gaze to his eyes. "Is this where I ask if it was good for you?"

She felt his chuckle vibrate through her.

"That's the most fun I've ever had tied up."

"How many times have you been tied up?" Probably none.

"A few times. Lovemaking has many windows, and I've looked through most of them."

"Poetic." Daria lifted her face and he took her lips in a long, drugging kiss.

"My senses have kept things fresh for me long after everything else became stale." His gaze grew troubled. "I think I have a problem."

Daria was instantly apologetic. "Omigod, I was so busy bouncing up and down on you that I never even thought about *your* needs. Biting is part of sexual pleasure for you, isn't it?" She was a selfish sex fiend.

"Relax. Biting enhances the experience, but what happened between us just now was a major wow without it." His smile was distracted. "No, my problem is much bigger. I've discovered once won't be nearly enough with you."

She felt ridiculously pleased. "And it usually is?" Fishing for compliments could get you dragged into deep water.

"Yes."

"And?"

"Find Sparkle and get me out of these cuffs." He didn't look like someone who'd just had fantastic sex.

Sighing, she climbed off him, took a throw from the couch to cover his hips, and pulled on her clothes. If he was going to be grouchy after something that great, then she was out of here. She didn't need Mr. Grumpy bringing her down.

"Oh, two people are looking for you, a Chris and Kiki. Nonhumans. Said they're friends of a friend. Something about them doesn't feel right."

He nodded. "I'll check."

As soon as she hit the hallway, reality crashed around her. They'd been in their own little bubble back there. Out here, Fenrir was still gaining power, she still had a test to pass, Eris was still being a pain-in-the-ass, Sparkle was still erasing Daria's harpy identity, and her brother was still acting weird. Oh, and she had to pay for an expensive mirror.

But she couldn't deal with her unending to-fix list right now. Dawn was near, so she'd better find Sparkle fast. Once free, Declan would go straight to his room. Daria wouldn't see him again until sunset.

Good. She needed time to pull herself together and decide what, if anything, had changed in their relationship back in Sparkle's room. Relationship? They didn't have one, couldn't have one if she intended to be somebody in the harpy world. Mom had spent one night with Apollo, but it had never qualified as a relationship. The thought of no relationship with Declan made her kind of sad.

She pushed relationship thoughts aside as she spied Sparkle walking toward her. Daria stopped and waited by the registration desk.

"Well, I'd say you look like a woman who's let the good times roll in a big way." Sparkle's smile was triumphant. "How's Declan?"

"Back to normal." Not one juicy detail would pass her lips. "Do you have the key to his cuffs?"

Sparkle didn't get a chance to answer, because Eris joined them.

"If it isn't the harpy traitor." Eris's beady little eyes blazed with contempt. "New clothes, new hair, and I bet you'll have a new face pretty soon. And you expect to sit beside your mom? I don't think so." Her multiple chins wobbled in outrage.

A few days ago, Daria would've put Eris through a window for that comment. But now she couldn't work up much of a mad because Eris was right. Daria glanced in the mirror behind Sparkle. Nope, she wasn't looking too harpylike right now. The scariest part was that her reflection didn't horrify her nearly enough. She'd just have to make a big splash by bringing in someone who'd make Hades's jaw drop.

"Go find another werelion to sit on." Daria decided if Eris made it physical, she'd heave her right into the middle of that crummy mirror.

Sparkle joined the battle. "You're a complete dumbass, Eris." Her eyes glittered with malice. "You think that ugly equals evil? Wrong. I don't care how disgusting you make yourself look; no one will ever mistake you for the real deal."

Eris's smile was small and spiteful. "The way I look is just part of the total perfect package. First, I scare the crap out of my prey, and then while they're frozen with fear I scoop them up."

Daria couldn't let that pass. "Like you did with Declan and the lion? Better hunt easier prey, Eris."

"At least *I'm* trying." Her sneer showcased crooked yellow teeth. "I don't want to be the bearer of bad news, Daria, but someone told your mom that things aren't going as planned here." She widened her eyes, which gave her an insane-serial-killer look. "Why, I bet your mom will be so worried, she'll show up to see what's going on." She held up her hands. "Don't blame me. I didn't do it. I got the news from my mom."

That thought horrified Daria so much, she forgot all about Eris. Who'd ratted her out? Maybe the judge, but judges usually tried to stay pretty neutral. If Mel were the judge, though, neutrality would be tossed. Kal? No, her brother wouldn't betray her. It could be almost any of the nonhumans staying at the inn. One of them might know Mom.

Since her comment didn't get the expected rise from Daria, Eris turned her poison tongue on Sparkle. "What do you know about evil, you sexed-up useless piece of crap?" Putting her hands on her hips, she laughed at Sparkle. "You spend your time tottering around on those silly heels and coming on to all the men. Who'd ever be afraid of you?"

She glanced at Sparkle's hands. "Oh, and that stupid bandage doesn't hide your broken nail. Everyone knows your nails aren't perfect." Inspiration struck. Eris practically beamed. "If they don't, I'll tell them. See, that's how afraid I am of little old evil you. Go ahead, do your worst, you stupid bitch."

Uh-oh. Daria backed up a few steps.

Ganymede bounded in from the parlor. *Bounded.* His chubby body wasn't made for vertical leaps. He must've sensed the seismic activity building in the hallway. One look at Sparkle's expression and he skidded to a stop beside Daria.

"Too late. This is gonna be bad."

His fear came across loud and clear in Daria's head. He pressed against her leg as they both watched with a mixture of horror and fascination.

Sparkle's eyes lit with an eerie amber glow even as she smiled at Eris. "You're about to learn a powerful lesson about evil, my fledgling harpy. It doesn't have to be violent. For example, I could put you on the floor right now and walk all over your pudgy body with my 'silly' heels. Afterward, you'd look like you'd been worked over by a giant hole punch. But that's not my style." She glanced at her hands. "Besides, I might break another nail." Looking up, she winked. "Powerful evil burrows into your psyche until it roots out the most frightening reality for you, and then makes it happen."

Eris wasn't even smart enough to be afraid. She just looked puzzled. "What the hell are you talking—"

A sudden shimmer that looked sort of like rippling water made Daria feel a little nauseated. When the shimmer stopped, Daria stood staring openmouthed. "Oh, wow."

Damn, that's my woman. Ganymede was batting zero. The *damn* would cost him another candy bar, and Sparkle wasn't his woman anymore.

For a moment, Eris looked confused. Then she noticed Daria's and Ganymede's stares. She glanced in the mirror. And screamed. Long and loud. The few people who still hadn't gone to their rooms rushed into the hallway to see what had happened. *They* stared.

"I'm, I'm *beautiful!*" Eris would have used the same tone to announce that she'd been stabbed in the heart. "This is a trick. It isn't real. It can't be." She babbled as she looked at her nails, perfect ovals of glistening pink color. Frantically, she broke them, but they reappeared immediately in all their perfect glory.

"My face!" She stared into the mirror while tears

streamed from her big blue eyes and trickled down her smooth flawless cheeks. With shaking fingers, she touched her full sensual mouth.

Sparkle rolled her eyes to the top of her head in fake thought. "Gee, guess you have a problem. This is almost like *Cinderella*. Do you think all your ugly stepsisters will welcome you back to the harpy fold?" She smiled and answered her own question. "I think not."

Panic lived in Eris's eyes. "This isn't forever, right? I'll be me in the morning, right?"

Sparkle looked bored. "Maybe. Maybe not. But then, what do I know? I'm just a stupid bitch." She turned to Daria. "You want the key to the cuffs." Reaching under the counter of the registration desk, she pulled it out and handed it to Daria.

Still in openmouthed awe at what Sparkle had done, Daria took the key without commenting. Sure, she'd wanted someone else to release Declan to avoid more of his bad temper, but she figured Sparkle would be busy with a hysterical harpy for a while.

"You let me go, you hear? My mom will kill you. I'll fix you, I'll carry off your dumb cat." Eris was descending into crazed threats.

"See me cower." Sparkle yawned. "You know, I'm disappointed you're not showing more gratitude. Look at you. Long blond hair, great body, gorgeous face." She shook her head sadly. "Hades would take your soul for what I just did for free."

The last glimpse Daria got as she walked away was of Eris throwing herself to the floor in a flaming harpy tantrum, but looking beautiful as she did it, of course.

Daria couldn't help it—she was smiling as she entered Sparkle's room. Declan was still on the bed looking as annoyed as a dark and dangerous vampire god could look.

GET UP TO
4 FREE BOOKS!

You can have the best romance delivered to your door for less than what you'd pay in a bookstore or online. Sign up for one of our book clubs today, and we'll send you **FREE* BOOKS** just for trying it out...**with no obligation to buy, ever!**

HISTORICAL ROMANCE BOOK CLUB

Travel from the Scottish Highlands to the American West, the decadent ballrooms of Regency England to Viking ships. Your shipments will include authors such as CONNIE MASON, CASSIE EDWARDS, LYNSAY SANDS, LEIGH GREENWOOD, and many, many more.

LOVE SPELL BOOK CLUB

Bring a little magic into your life with the romances of Love Spell—fun contemporaries, paranormals, time-travels, futuristics, and more. Your shipments will include authors such as KATIE MacALISTER, SUSAN GRANT, NINA BANGS, SANDRA HILL, and more.

As a book club member you also receive the following special benefits:

- **30% OFF** all orders through our website & telecenter! (Plus, you still get 1 book FREE for every 5 books you buy!)
- **Exclusive access** to special discounts!
- **Convenient** home delivery and **10 days to return any books you don't want to keep.**

There is no minimum number of books to buy, and you may cancel membership at any time. See back to sign up!

*Please include $2.00 for shipping and handling.

YES! ☐

Sign me up for the **Historical Romance Book Club** and send my TWO FREE BOOKS! If I choose to stay in the club, I will pay only $8.50* each month, a savings of $5.48!

YES! ☐

Sign me up for the **Love Spell Book Club** and send my TWO FREE BOOKS! If I choose to stay in the club, I will pay only $8.50* each month, a savings of $5.48!

NAME: _____

ADDRESS: _____

_____

TELEPHONE: _____

E-MAIL: _____

☐ **I WANT TO PAY BY CREDIT CARD.**

☐  VISA   ☐ MasterCard.   ☐ DISCOVER

ACCOUNT #: _____

EXPIRATION DATE: _____

SIGNATURE: _____

Send this card along with $2.00 shipping & handling for each club you wish to join, to:

Romance Book Clubs
1 Mechanic Street
Norwalk, CT 06850-3431

Or fax (must include credit card information!) to: 610.995.9274. You can also sign up online at www.dorchesterpub.com.

*Plus $2.00 for shipping. Offer open to residents of the U.S. and Canada only. Canadian residents please call 1.800.481.9191 for pricing information.

If under 18, a parent or guardian must sign. Terms, prices and conditions subject to change. Subscription subject to acceptance. Dorchester Publishing reserves the right to reject any order or cancel any subscription.

"Took you long enough." He watched as she unlocked the cuffs.

Where was the sexy man of a short while ago? "Sorry. Hey, you missed a real demonstration of power." She watched him swing his feet to the floor and stand. The throw slid to the floor.

He took her breath away. She'd never get tired of watching the play of hard muscle beneath smooth skin. Clenching her fists, she resisted the urge to make a fool of herself by clutching at his perfect behind. Sparkle would really have to sweat to improve on Declan Mackenzie.

"Yeah?" Whatever his thoughts were, they weren't on Sparkle and they weren't particularly happy.

"Eris insulted her, so she made Eris beautiful. Can you believe that?" Daria refused to let him sour her mood.

She'd made awesome love with a vampire she was beginning to care about a little more than she should, and she'd watched Sparkle make Eris eat dirt. She was happy. Tomorrow would be time enough to worry about the caring part along with all the other disturbing things on her personal horizon.

"I believe it. Remember, I saw Sparkle in action last year." He looked around the room. "Where're my clothes?"

Daria clapped her hand over her mouth. "Oops. I left them in the forest where you dropped them. They weren't in great condition, though, after you ripped them off. I'll go get you some."

"Don't bother. No one will see me."

She bit her lip. He wanted to walk through the inn naked? Let him. What did she care? "I don't know what your problem is, but if this is the way you always act after making love, I can see why women don't invite you back for seconds."

Daria headed for the door, ready to make an

outraged-harpy exit. As she put her hand on the door-knob, she turned to give him a parting blast and . . .

Declan was gone. She blinked. Just to make sure he was really gone, she checked in the bathroom, and even though she felt really silly, the closet. Yep, he'd left the room. Well, well, little by little she was learning her vampire had lots of hidden talents.

As Daria reached her own room, dawn was lightening the sky. But she had one more thing to do before falling into bed.

Sitting on the couch, she opened the laptop she'd brought from home. The Web was a fun place to keep in touch with this world. It was also a great tool for finding people.

Methodically, she Googled the names of Declan's children: Alrek, Bera, Finna, and Grim. She hadn't quite decided what she'd do if she found them.

CHAPTER TWELVE

Declan stood on the porch looking up at the full moon. The werewolves would be out in force tonight—howling, chasing small animals, and pissing on tree trunks to mark their territory. He smiled. People who romanticized werewolves forgot about the pissing.

The werewolves staying at the inn were a bunch of college kids. Anything larger than a rabbit was probably safe from them. They were long on enthusiasm but short on experience.

Unlike his werewolf father, who was probably gleefully gathering his energy to zap his son with another compulsion. Declan didn't think he could go through that again. That's why he had to confront Fenrir tonight. But he wouldn't do it alone. When ego bumped up against reality, reality won. Ganymede would be out in a few minutes, and they'd go together.

While he waited, he thought about Daria. Okay, so he'd been thinking about her ever since he'd risen at sunset. He hadn't liked appearing weak in her eyes. First, she'd carried him out of danger's way back at the church. Then she and Ganymede rescued him from the compulsion. Worst of all, he'd been helpless to take part in their lovemaking while he was cuffed to that damn bed.

Sure, some people got off on the bondage stuff. He didn't. For better or for worse, he was über alpha with all its attendant hang-ups. It was *his* job to keep the female safe, win every fight, and generally be a dominant jerk.

Then shouldn't it follow that a strong woman wouldn't attract him? Daria was a strong woman, and she attracted the hell out of him. Go figure.

"Yo, bloodsucker, are we hunting werewolf tonight?"

Startled, Declan glanced down. He was getting careless if he didn't hear Ganymede coming. "It's time to test-drive our talent and hit Fenrir with everything we have. If it doesn't work, we run like the devil and then come up with a different plan."

For a moment, amusement lurked in the cat's eyes, and then it faded. "I can't kill him. The goodness-and-light jerk will be watching. But I can grab his attention and then maybe you can get in a lucky shot."

Declan nodded.

"Understand, bloodsucker, that I'm not doing this because I'm a good guy or anything. I'm a selfish bastard. I like coming here in the summer, so I don't want anything messing with my vacation time. And I sorta get a kick outta matching wits with a god."

"Gotcha. Same here. This is all about revenge. The council can't let anyone kill its members and go unpunished. I only care about saving the universe because if it goes, I go too. It's all about me." And they were two world-class liars.

Ganymede started to say something, but turned to look at the door instead. Declan sensed Daria a moment before she opened it and joined them.

She was like a hot shower to his greedy senses. The heat she brought steamed up his common sense while all his blood surged to the surface. Well, at least to one particular surface. Even dressed down by Sparkle's standards,

Daria made him want to howl at the moon along with the werewolves.

"Let me guess, you were going to confront the big bad wolf without me. How do I know? You have guilt written all over your sexist faces." Accusation was in her narrowed eyes. She held up her hand to stop any comments. "No, you don't have to explain. I get the picture. Me, helpless female. You, mighty warriors."

Nine hundred years of experience had taught Declan *never* to agree with a woman when she used that tone of voice.

Thousands of years had taught Ganymede nothing. "Hey, babe, things could get rough out there. You don't want to get that great outfit all torn and dirty. We'll tell you what happened when we get back."

Declan could actually hear her grinding her teeth. "I have on jeans and a T-shirt. I'm wearing running shoes. Okay, so the jeans and T-shirt are sexy, but they belong to Sparkle. I don't care how torn or dirty they get." She dropped to her knees and got in Ganymede's face. "Look at me, you cosmic doofus. I'm. A. Harpy. I'm the deliverer of death, the harbinger of the hereafter, the meanest of the monsters. Don't you *dare* tell me things could get rough."

"Cosmic *doofus?*" From Ganymede's expression, Declan figured no one had ever dared call him a doofus before. Guess there was a first time for everything.

Declan thought of himself as a pragmatist, but it was tough keeping that attitude when Daria's life could be in danger. Just because she was immortal didn't mean she was invulnerable. Everyone had weaknesses. And he was beginning to realize her well-being was important to him.

"And if we say you can't come?" Declan thought he knew the answer.

"I'll follow you."

Declan looked at Ganymede.

Ganymede glared at Daria. "What does a doofus know? Let her see what real war is like." He did the equivalent of a cat sniff. "I'm paying a manager who doesn't manage. Don't know what that's about."

Declan had his doubts about the "real war" description. This was going to be more like an exploratory salvo, a mutual exchange of power to see who blinked first. It would be great if Fenrir went down tonight, but he didn't think it would be that easy. Gods tended to be resilient.

"Sparkle said she'd watch things for a while. She's in a good mood listening to Eris whine and beg for her old ugly self back." Daria stood. "Oh, and you'll need me if Fenrir hits Declan with another compulsion."

Ganymede looked thoughtful. "Yeah, you have a point."

Declan drew his coat around him as he led them into the forest. His sword rested against his hip, a comfortable partner from past battles. He'd left his guns back at the inn. Bullets wouldn't bother Fenrir. The surest way to destroy him would be to take his head. Even an ancient god might have trouble regenerating a head. Getting close enough to use his sword would be the problem.

And how do you feel about that possibility? He's your father, even if he never filled the role. Declan didn't know. He had an uncomfortable feeling, though, that if presented with the opportunity to lop off Fenrir's head, he might just have a deadly attack of conscience. Deadly because he had no doubt Fenrir wouldn't let a little thing like misplaced emotion stand in the way of eliminating an enemy.

"I have something that'll get rid of your snit with me, Ganymede. How about a compliment? Your plan worked. I, um, entertained Declan like you said, and his pain went away." Daria had evidently decided not to tell Ganymede she'd let the "good times roll" long after Declan's pain had disappeared.

Last night Declan had been okay with letting her think she was just a sexy painkiller, but tonight the whole thing bothered him. Was he feeling guilty? The thought chilled him. Too many emotions could get a vampire killed, slow him down at a crucial moment. "My pain was gone before you even walked into the room." Jeez, did he have a death wish?

Uh-oh. She was going all slitty-eyed on him again. "Then why did you let me do what I did?"

Declan grinned at her. "Are you crazy? I don't know any man, dead or undead, who would've told you to stop."

Ganymede looked extra sneaky tonight. "The thing you gotta remember is that it might not be so easy next time. As Fenrir's power grows, his compulsions will probably be harder to override." He sounded defensive.

Warning flags popped up all over the place. "What aren't you telling us?" The universe might end in a few days, but Declan was sure Ganymede and Sparkle would be plotting to mess up their lives to the very end.

"Look, let's get a few things straight. I can't just make Fenrir's compulsions go away. They're too strong. So the best I can do is sort of . . . manipulate them." Ganymede stared straight ahead.

Declan could almost hear the lie machine cranking out another one in Ganymede's head. "Define manipulate."

"I sort of restructure the compulsion so that as soon as it hits, instead of causing you blinding pain and a need to run to Fenrir, you get this uncontrollable desire to have sex with Daria." He said the last words in a rush.

Well, crap. "Was that what was going on last night?" God, he hoped not. Surprisingly, he wanted the need he'd felt to have been all his own idea.

"Nah. *I* took away your pain last night. Once the pain was gone, you were able to fight the compulsion on your own. By the time Daria came in, you were just a little groggy."

"And why was he groggy?" Daria sounded strangely calm.

"You know, you guys don't have to dissect everything. Why not just accept the great sex and forget about it?"

Declan looked at Daria. She returned his stare. Nope, neither of them felt particularly forgetful.

Daria's sigh said she wouldn't try to kill Ganymede, because the sex *had* been great, but she did want to know everything that had been done to them. "Harpies are curious, Ganymede. It's a weakness."

"Okay, okay. Sparkle might've given me the idea. She knew I could replace one compulsion with another, so Sparkle being Sparkle, she mentioned that a sexual compulsion would make her happy. And if I could leave you a little loopy, bloodsucker, it would make her even happier. I'm all about keeping Sparkle happy." Left unsaid was that he'd been doing a crappy job lately.

Declan couldn't fault him. Knowing what Sparkle could do to a man's body, he thought keeping her happy was smart. "I don't have to point out what will happen if the compulsion hits at the wrong time."

Ganymede had nothing to say to that.

Daria had lots to say. "Oh no. What if you pounce on

me right in the middle of dinner? What will the guests say if you chase me around the dining room, throw me onto the table, and then make wild love to me somewhere between the roast beef and mashed potatoes? You know, that has a certain kinky appeal." Her eyes gleamed with laughter.

Declan grunted. Easy for her to joke about it. She wouldn't be the one playing sex-crazed vampire. Whatever response he might've made died as they reached the church. He stood staring at the crumbling building.

"Call him, bloodsucker." Ganymede's voice was terse, all business now.

A quick glance around showed Daria was gone. She'd be taking off her clothes behind a tree somewhere. He'd do his best to make sure she didn't get involved in what was about to happen.

"Fenrir. I'm here." Declan put out psychic feelers, reaching for his father.

He found the werewolf in a rush of power that shoved him back a few feet. Fenrir was coming.

The werewolf materialized with what sounded like a clap of thunder. Declan recognized it as the release of immense energy. Fenrir was now the size of a full-grown Clydesdale. Cripes, he could pull the Budweiser beer wagon all by himself.

Declan stilled as he thought he heard a startled curse coming from the woods. It sounded male. But when he didn't hear anything else, he dismissed it from his mind. If it was one of the inn's guests, he or she was about to get a hell of a show.

"You can't have Declan, dog breath." Ganymede wasn't intimidated.

Fenrir's massive jaw dropped open in a wolfish grin. "Perhaps you would care to place a wager, obese cat."

Obese cat? Declan did a few mental eye rolls. Great. Two beings with enough power between them to take out New Jersey and all they could do was call each other names. Not very creative ones either. Time for him to step in.

"Why do you need me?" He pushed his coat aside so his hand could rest on the hilt of his sword.

"No questions. All that matters is your presence here."

"You'll tell me because you like to brag. What good is it being the big kahuna if no one appreciates your greatness?" Declan hoped he was reading his father right.

Fenrir's laughter was a low rumble that shook the ground. "You understand me well, my son."

"Give me a break, bloodsucker. We don't need to know why he wants you. All we have to do is put his sorry butt into orbit." Ganymede might sound dismissive, but Declan didn't miss the tensing of his muscles or the way his tail whipped back and forth.

Fenrir acted as though Ganymede hadn't spoken. "I hope you weren't thinking I felt a sudden fatherly impulse."

Actually he hadn't. Or at least the rational part of his brain hadn't. But the other part, the section of his mind in charge of all those emotions he claimed he no longer harbored, had held a pathetic hope that maybe, just maybe . . . Declan shook off that particular stupidity.

"So why?" Out of the corner of his eye, Declan could see Ganymede starting his signature rear-end wiggle, a signal that he was ready to rumble.

Fenrir's glowing wolf eyes looked a little too eager. "I need to complete the number three."

"I hate when scumbags go all mysterious on me." Ganymede's words came out in a low hiss. "Get to the point."

The werewolf snarled at Ganymede. "You would do

well to run from here. You don't have the power to bend me to your will."

Ganymede glanced at Declan. "Why's he talking like a bad actor on late-night TV?"

Declan tightened his grip on his sword. "Explain the number three."

The werewolf began to pace, impatience in every stride. "Three is a powerful number. I need the magic it brings. I have strength without it, but on the day of Ragnarok I'll use the mystical potency of three to bring Loki victory."

"What do I have to do with three?" Declan thought he got it, but he wanted a little extra time to call his power to him. So he let Fenrir rattle on.

"Loki had three children by the giantess Angrboda. I am the eldest. You are of the third generation. The only one. You are needed to complete the second three."

Declan was pretty ticked. So all he meant to his father was a number. "And what will I be doing during your great battle, sitting on the sidelines wearing a number three on my chest and cheering the maniacs on?"

Fenrir stopped his pacing to stare at Declan. "You'll be dead."

Okay, that did it. Sure, he liked to travel as much as the next guy, but he wouldn't be going on this trip even if Fenrir let him use his frequent flyer miles. "Wow, a vampire sacrifice. Do I get the altar and all the great rituals? You really know how to touch a son's heart."

"You *will* come to me."

Fenrir's low rumbling growl raised goose bumps along Declan's arms.

"Has hell frozen over yet?" The old fart had really pissed him off now. "I don't think so, Pop. When I check out it'll be on my own terms. And your little battle doesn't even tempt me." Along with his fury came enough hurt to make Declan even angrier. He'd never expected love from his father, but he sure hadn't expected Fenrir to want him dead.

He sensed the moment when Fenrir launched another one of his powerful compulsions. Bracing himself, he waited for the explosion of pain in his head. It didn't come.

"The compulsion?" Ganymede didn't miss much.

"Yeah."

"How're you feeling?"

"Like I need to find Daria right now." Declan clenched his fists against the desire to forget about Fenrir in favor of having crazy sex in the bushes with his favorite harpy.

"Stay with me, kid." Ganymede actually glowed as he prepared to blast Fenrir.

Kid? No one called a nine-hundred-year-old vampire kid. How old *was* Ganymede? He watched the cat, ready to launch his attack at the same time. Mental images of a naked and welcoming Daria weren't helping his concentration. Declan fought to clear away all inner distractions, naked or otherwise.

Fenrir must have realized they intended to attack, because he hurled a wave of power at them that flung Declan back into the forest. He whacked his head against a tree trunk and slid to a sitting position. "Ow!"

Rubbing the back of his head, Declan rose and returned to where Ganymede was still hunkered down in the same spot. He looked untouched.

"Why didn't you—"

"Impenetrable shields. You'll have them too in another thousand years." Ganymede nodded toward the church. "We attack now while the harpy's distracting him."

"Harpy?" Declan's attention snapped to where Fenrir

was leaping high into the air trying to snag a furious Daria out of the air. She was a little too fast for him.

Fear wrapped icy fingers around Declan's throat. Not for himself, but for Daria. He hadn't felt this particular emotion for centuries. He'd carefully nurtured the attitude that it was all about looking out for number one, or number three if Fenrir was to be believed.

Giving up on the high jumps, the werewolf threw power blast after power blast at her.

Agilely dodging the blasts, she beat her wings madly as she waved her arms at Ganymede and Declan. "Hey, guys, now would be a good time to do something."

Declan glanced down at Ganymede. The cat nodded. Together they launched a wave of energy that would have reduced most things to a dust cloud. But when the air cleared, Fenrir was still standing. The only positive was he didn't look quite so confident.

Daria kept the werewolf off balance by hefting huge chunks of stone from the crumbling church and dropping them onto Fenrir's shield. They didn't penetrate, but they had to be rattling him.

Declan felt a ridiculous pride in her strength. After all, what should it matter to him if she could bench-press a thousand pounds?

Once again Declan gathered his power and this time flung it outward in a blazing ball of destructive energy. It exploded against Fenrir's shield, and Declan had the satisfaction of seeing ripples appear in it.

Ganymede was working a different angle. Suddenly the earth beneath Fenrir began to crumble away, leaving a hole that grew ever larger. Never taking his eyes off the werewolf, Ganymede explained. "He didn't shield the ground beneath him. Not smart. He can do it now, but it'll stretch his power a little thin."

Just when Declan thought they might have a chance at Fenrir, he was hit by a force that felt like someone had taken a baseball bat to his whole body. Ganymede took the same hit, but it bounced off his damn shield.

Declan barely had time to recover before what looked like an arrow whizzed by him. Only his preternatural speed kept him from going to that big blood bank in the sky.

"What the . . ." Those last two attacks hadn't come from Fenrir. Declan glanced around. They'd come from opposite sides of the forest.

"Time to get our butts outta here. The wolf has help." Ganymede faded into the woods.

"Daria, get out of there." Declan only waited long enough to make sure she'd obeyed his shout before following Ganymede.

Once hidden by the forest, Declan moved swiftly toward the spot where he'd seen her enter the tree line. He couldn't picture her running naked back to the inn, so she'd be trying to dress. Fenrir was still bound to the church area, but his two friends weren't. Even now they could be stalking her.

When was the last time he'd felt this kind of urgency? He couldn't remember. Reaching out with senses tuned to the smallest of sounds, he listened. There. Heavy breathing, the sound of a heart pounding. Slowing down, he moved silently until he was close enough to see.

Daria had pulled on her jeans and shoes. She wasn't bothering with her bra. He watched as she shoved it into her pocket. Then she yanked the T-shirt over her head. Once she was done, he stepped up behind her, wrapped his arms around her, and whispered in her ear.

"Don't say anything. It's me."

Too late. She was already past the point where she

could stop her motion as she slammed her elbow into the gut of the man behind her.

Daria winced. "*Me* should've said his name instead of creeping and grabbing." She kept her voice to a whisper as she turned to face him.

He grimaced. "My mistake. I didn't want my voice to give away our position. If we get separated the next time we do this, drop your shields and I'll talk mentally."

The *next* time? He was kidding, right? She was so not ready to do battle with a homicidal werewolf again. "How many are there? I saw the arrow almost get you." She didn't think she'd share her feelings about that.

"Two as far as—"

A terrified screech interrupted him. She met his startled gaze.

He cursed. "Just before all hell broke loose I thought I heard someone in the woods. It could've been the two working with Fenrir, but I don't think so." Even as he spoke he was moving toward the scream.

"It could be a trap." She didn't really believe that. The scream had sounded very human and very scared.

Declan didn't answer as he moved with the silence and speed she'd expect from an ancient vampire. She, on the other hand, moved with the silence of a stampeding water buffalo. Damn. She should've stayed in harpy form. In the air she was a formidable force.

He held up his hand and she stopped. She remembered to lower her mental shields.

"*I see one person. Human. Looks like that Walt guy, the one you said you took care of. I don't sense any danger near him.*" Declan paused to listen. "*Nope. I hear a few sounds, but they're moving away from us. He's lying on his stomach with his hands over his head. Looks like whatever he was try-*"

ing to debunk got a little too real. Guess we need to take him back to the inn." Declan sounded regretful.

Daria nodded. Amazing. A vampire and a harpy agreeing to help a human when there wasn't anything in it for them. There must be some deadly kindness germ at the Woo Woo Inn, and they'd both caught it.

"I'll go see what his problem is. You stay hidden just in case there's something wrong and I need you to bail me out." Declan didn't wait for her agreement.

She smiled. He was learning. He hadn't made the mistake of telling her to stay here where she'd be safe. Smart man.

Declan reached Walt, crouched down, and tapped the man on the shoulder. "Do you need help?"

Walt came up swinging. Declan leaped away from the panicked human.

Finally Walt's frenzy burned itself out and he stood panting. "There was a snake, a freaking snake as big around as a barrel and at least fifty feet long. It had glittery black eyes, and when it opened its mouth I saw fangs that must've been six inches long. It stared at me with creepy hooded eyes as it slithered past. I would've been dead meat if it wasn't looking for someone else." He glanced around frantically.

Since nothing had attacked Declan, Daria edged from behind her tree and joined them. "Hi, Walt."

The debunker's eyes grew wide. "It was hunting for you guys. That's the only thing that makes sense. You were trying to take down that werewolf or whatever it was, and the snake was helping the wolf. They must've come from the same corner of hell, because what're the chances two things that big would be hanging in a forest in New Jersey?" He pressed his palms to the sides of his head. "God, is this all real or am I having a psychotic meltdown?"

Daria sighed. "Why did you follow us tonight? I thought we got things straightened out."

"You told me not to take any more pictures, so I didn't. But that doesn't mean I don't want to know what's going on." A little of his courage was coming back.

She glanced at Declan, who'd wandered over to a break in the trees where everything was flattened. It looked like something enormous had passed by.

"Let's get back to the inn, Walt." Daria figured Declan would have to wipe the guy's memory clean this time.

Declan joined her. "I'd take us back the quick way, but I expended most of my energy on Fenrir. If it's any comfort, I think the immediate danger is over. I'd guess the snake has returned to human form. Something that size would have trouble forcing its way through the trees. It'll regroup and try to get us next time out."

"Next time out?" Of course there'd have to be a next time. They hadn't solved anything tonight. Did harpies throw up? She was thinking that might be a yes.

"Return to human form?" Walt's voice shook.

"The snake's a shifter. The flattened trees and brush back there ended a few hundred feet in. That's where it must've changed." Declan turned to Walt. "Hate to do this, buddy, but I'll have to take all those great memories of tonight away from you."

"It was *you*." Walt looked outraged. "You were the one who took away my memory of what happened with the harpies and the werewolves."

"No. Not Declan, someone else." Daria didn't see any reason not to tell Walt. He wouldn't remember for very long. "Declan isn't the only one who can wipe memories."

"Wait. Wait. Don't do it yet." Walt looked longingly in the direction of the inn. "You don't have to make me forget. I mean, who'd believe me anyway? Besides, I can help you."

"How?" Daria glanced behind her. With the full moon, the woods didn't look as sinister as usual. But the big bads were still out there. And they were scary enough to make even a harpy nervous.

Declan started walking, and Walt tagged along, babbling as he went. "You want to kill that werewolf thing. What'd you call it? Fenrir. Anyway, I'm an expert researcher. Debunking is my business, so I have lots of contacts and research skills. I have sources you'd never imagine. If there's a way to destroy the monster, I'll find it."

"Why should I trust you?" Declan seemed to be considering the idea.

"What do you have to lose? I don't have any pictures, any proof of what I know, so I can't expose anyone. And from what I saw of the battle, you don't have a clue how to waste this Fenrir."

When they reached the inn, Declan stopped at the bottom of the steps. "I'll give you three nights." A smile tugged at his lips as he glanced at Daria. "Hey, three's my number, what can I say?"

Walt nodded before taking the porch steps in one leap and yanking open the door. Daria watched until he'd slammed the door shut.

"Can you trust him?"

He shrugged. "He's right. What do I have to lose? I'm betting he's too scared to cross me right now. And once he leaves the inn, no one will believe his story. If there's even a tiny chance he might come up with a way to defeat Fenrir, I'm giving it to him."

She turned her head to study Declan. He sounded matter-of-fact and way too casual. Anyone who only checked out his gorgeous face and body would miss the real Declan Mackenzie, the vampire whose nine hundred years of life lived in his eyes. The moon cast his face in light and shadow. But even though she couldn't read his expression in the darkness, she was willing to make a stab at what he was feeling.

"It must've hurt to know how Fenrir felt about you."

"Yeah."

She hadn't expected that admission. Good for him. "We can't make people love us any more than we can choose our parents. And sometimes the ones who love us the most come to us in unexpected ways." A prophecy? Who knew. This was all too deep for her right now.

He chose not to comment on her insight.

She didn't say anything else until they'd entered the inn. "What's with the snake? And who checked into the fight on Fenrir's side?" Once again she saw that arrow whiz past Declan's head. And with the memory came a return of the rage she'd felt. It was an attack on someone she cared about, and the caring part scared her witless.

They stopped at the registration desk. No one was there, a silent condemnation of Daria's managerial skills. "I need to get to work." She didn't look at Declan as she shuffled some papers around. "So, how's your compulsion? I assume Fenrir took a shot at one."

"Yeah." He frowned. "For a while there all I wanted to do was find you so we could roll around in the underbrush."

"And?"

"It went away. I guess Fenrir couldn't control it once the battle began."

"Oh."

"The compulsion went away. That doesn't mean I still don't want to roll around somewhere with you."

"Oh?"

"Believe it."

She was smiling as she watched him walk away.

CHAPTER THIRTEEN

Memo: to all harpies
Subject: downsizing
Costs of operation have risen dramatically. The price of
torture implements alone has quadrupled in the last
century. And we won't even talk about how much brim-
stone costs. Regretfully, we've decided to downsize. We
would suggest that laid-off harpies find employment as
really ugly fairies. Those harpies who remain must
shoulder the extra load. Your weekly quotas are now
four victims rather than the previous two. Your glorious
CEO will receive a bonus for thinking of this wonderful
cost-cutting plan.

Remember, we want you to think of Tartarus as your
home. (Unless profit margins drop. Then all bets are off.)

HADES THE LOYAL

Daria needed advice. Her brain cells were rioting in the
street. She wouldn't get anything coherent from them.
This was a job for *The Advice Book*. Everyone else at the
Woo Woo Inn would be working an agenda. The book
was neutral. Talking to a book was weird, but she was desperate. Head bent, she was deciding how to word her
question as she entered the library.

"Shut up, you yellow-paged loudmouth, or I'll break
your spine." The snarled threat sounded serious.

Daria recognized that snarl. She looked up. Eris had
The Advice Book clutched in her hands.

Muffled shouts came from the closed book. "Bad things happen to people who steal books. Help!"

A feeling of inevitability settled over Daria. "Let me guess. You plan to take the book back to Tartarus so you can pass the test."

Eris bared her teeth. She looked beautiful doing it.

"What's it to you, swan butt? Hades's memo said he's downsizing. This book can replace his demon advisers, and it'll work for free. Hades will love it."

"Swan butt?"

Eris attempted a sneer but her lips would only form a sweet smile. "You have a white girlie ass. There's not even one hair growing on it. What's a butt without hair?" Obviously smooth butt cheeks were major DNA flaws.

"It takes a white girlie ass to know one. Have you looked in a mirror since your Sparkle makeover?" Daria winced. Her maturity level regressed to about ten years old when she was around Eris.

Eris chose not to comment on that. "Move outta my way, daughter of Apollo's bitch. The book's mine."

Daria thought it would be fun to punch Eris, but she didn't want the book to get torn in the scuffle. Words would work. "Hades doesn't respect a coward. How much courage does it take to snatch a book that can't fight back? Let me think. Oh, none."

The book interjected a thought. "I won't give advice to Hades, but I will give some to you, potty-mouthed thief. You will not achieve your dream. Na, na, na, na."

Eris's beautiful cheeks flushed. She raised the book over her head. "Let me pass or I'll trash your precious book. See if it can still give sucky advice when it's in three pieces."

"Put the book down, Eris." The voice of reason spoke from the doorway.

Daria turned. Kal stood there, feet spread and gimlet

stare firmly in place. She sucked in her breath. He wasn't wearing his harpy face. And from her changing perspective of their world, she was able to admit he looked damn good.

Eris stared at him. "What is it with both of you? Harpy faces not good enough for you? Real harpies wouldn't let the outside world corrupt them." She zeroed in on Daria. "I'll get you right after I get Sparkle—"

She was in the middle of her rant when he moved. Eris stared blankly at her empty hands.

Kal put the book gently back on the desk. "I wouldn't try snatching it again. I'm going to tell Ganymede . . ." He smiled. "No, I'm going to tell *Sparkle* what you tried to do. She likes taking things away. Make her mad again and you might end up as the wingless wonder of the harpy world."

Eris paled. With one last vicious stare for both of them, she left the room.

Kal looked at his sister, daring her to say something.

"Thanks for helping."

He nodded, then followed Eris out of the room.

Sighing, Daria opened the book. "Are you okay?"

"Did she bend my pages? Is my cover torn? Do I still look pretty?"

Good grief, Sparkle in book form. "You're fine."

"Thank you for helping me. I knew a book reviewer once. And when she had PMS, she got vicious just like that." The book seemed to gather itself. "Now, you came here to ask me a question?"

She nodded and then realized the book couldn't see her. "What should I do?" About everything. About Declan, about the test, about *life*.

"The universe gives us what we expect from it. Expect the best and it's yours." The book paused to ponder.

"What is the best for you? You already know, and so does the universe."

"Uh, thanks." She closed the book. "Well, that was suitably cryptic." Now she just had to make sure the universe survived to give her what she deserved.

With all the secrets of life revealed, she headed back to the registration desk.

Sparkle was waiting for her. She clapped her hands, but her enthusiasm didn't reach her eyes. "Tonight is all new and shiny. Enjoy. And even though everything looks bleak and slightly sucky, a great orgasm with a gorgeous vampire will cheer you right up. Do you think Fenrir will give the compulsion another shot?" Sparkle sounded hopeful as she sat on the registration desk, legs crossed, swinging one foot back and forth.

"I don't know. It didn't work last night. Besides, Ganymede's compulsion doesn't include pain. Without the pain, Declan can concentrate on resisting it." Did she want him to resist?

A great big neon *no.* Okay, all emotion and no brain involved in this one. She wanted him: mind, body . . . heart? Not ready to go there yet.

Putting aside conjecture about Declan's power to resist, Daria stared at her to-do list for the night. The problem was her priorities were all screwed up. Managing the Woo Woo Inn and passing her harpy test—which should be *numero uno* on her list—had fallen behind her current favorites: making love with Declan and saving the universe.

Sparkle looked puzzled. "Why would he want to resist it?"

"Oh, maybe because he's a guy who likes to make his own decisions, or because he's into one-night stands, not multiple love sessions with the same woman." Fine, so that last one might not be true. He'd admitted he wanted

her again. There. She'd found a kernel of joy in an otherwise depressing cornfield.

"Hmm." Sparkle was making heavy-thinking sounds.
Not good.

"Forget about that stupid list and whatever else you're
worrying about. We have important stuff to do."

"Um, more important than saving the universe from a
megalomaniac werewolf and a giant snake? We're talking
an end-of-life-as-we-know-it scenario here." Just in case
the universe *didn't* end on the summer solstice, though,
Daria had given Walt the names of Declan's children to
research. She hadn't gotten too far on her own.

"Hello? We are *not* on the same page, sister. Wake up
and smell the possibilities for tonight, because that's all
that matters right now. I've lived thousands of years, and
I've seen civilization hanging by a thread lots of times.
But people kept on having sex, and civilization kept on
kicking butt. So let's plan for a night of erotic fun after
you get done with all the bad stuff."

"And this wouldn't have anything to do with your winning the bet?"

Sparkle widened her eyes in a credible imitation of
shock and hurt. "This is all about you. I mean, what if
you only have a few more days to exist? Doesn't it make
sense to spend those days with a hot vampire? I know I'll
be spending my final days surrounded by the things I
love—my shoes, my nail colors, and my sex toys."

"Not Mede?"

"He's taken himself out of my personal toy box." But
for all her flip retort, real pain showed in Sparkle's eyes.

Sparkle had one thing right. If Fenrir was still in business
by the summer solstice, Daria wanted to be close to those
she loved: Mom, Kal, and . . . Okay, she'd thought about

adding Declan to her list. He wasn't a positive yet, but she'd definitely like to have him nearby if the end came.

"I bet you haven't eaten anything tonight. Breakfast is over and Katie's already left. Let's go into the kitchen so you can at least get some coffee and cereal to keep your energy high." Sparkle's sly smile hinted that Daria would need it for her night of sexual excess.

Rather than wasting her time arguing with Sparkle, Daria followed the empress of erotic energy to the kitchen.

Where she stopped in the doorway to stare.

Ganymede was on the counter curled up in the middle of a giant salad bowl filled with . . . jellybeans?

Sparkle sighed. "That's not smart, Mede. Any of the guests could walk in. They'd probably complain to Katie. Paying customers tend to go all health conscious about cats in their food. And, well, you know Katie gets homicidal when you camp out in her bowls."

"Hi." Daria gave Ganymede a finger wave. "Uh, maybe it's just me, but it almost looks like you're sleeping in a bowl of jellybeans." And this was Declan's partner? The one he was counting on to have his back? Hoo boy.

Ganymede stared at her. His eyes were in cat mode, all mysterious and inscrutable. "Jellybeans are my meditation candy. When I surround my body with their vibrant colors and softly curved surfaces, I'm transported to another plane. Notice I'm not even talking like Ganymede right now. He'd never use wimpy words like *vibrant* and *softly*. Once on this higher plane, I can see the solutions to all life's problems. Uhmmm, uhmmm, uhmmm."

"That's ridiculous." Oops. Daria hadn't meant to insult the lord of loony logic. Fine, so she had.

"Not really. What's ridiculous is when he tries this in human form. Do you have any idea how many jellybeans it takes to fill a bathtub?" Sparkle was busy pouring two cups of coffee. "I love that you can always get a cup of coffee here."

"But *jellybeans?*"

"*Designer* jellybeans. There's a difference." Sparkle brought the coffee to the table along with a box of doughnuts.

Daria concentrated on stirring sugar into her coffee. Sparkle was many things, but stupid wasn't one of them. Daria didn't know how deeply Sparkle's emotions ran for Ganymede, but they'd obviously known each other a long time. Love blinded a person to so many things.

Time for some honest inner dialogue. Am I putting my whole career in jeopardy because I really want to save the universe or because I really want to save Declan Mackenzie? The jury was still out on that one.

Will I be totally bummed if Sparkle wins the bet tonight? Sure, Daria knew that ugly was the harpy rallying cry, but more and more she wanted to look like . . . like Eris. The superbitch had it all. She was gorgeous. Every male at the inn was probably tripping over his tongue. And the cause of Daria's image crisis? Declan Mackenzie.

When will I have the courage to tell Kal I don't want his magical intervention while we're here? Kal. She had to let him know what was happening. Not a chat she was looking forward to, but he deserved her honesty. He'd always been up-front with her.

"Now let's talk about the outfit you have on." Sparkle held her coffee cup to her lips while she stared at Daria from narrowed eyes. "As cute and sexy as those jeans and top are, I seem to remember you wearing the same thing last night. And I won't even comment on those shoes. I'm sure *I* didn't put them in your closet."

"What?" Daria blinked.

"How about that delicious gold dress with the Manolo Blahnik sandals? High heels make a woman's legs sing."

"I can't run in heels that high. And the dress would get ripped to shreds if I had to change suddenly." But that outfit might make Declan into her own personal ball of putty. She knew exactly what shape she'd mold.

The old Daria would have sneered at Sparkle's efforts to make her sexy. The new Daria thought she'd go to her room and change as soon as she finished her coffee and doughnut.

"Holy shit, I've got it." Ganymede leaped from the bowl a second before every jellybean vanished. He looked around. "Doesn't that guy *ever* sleep?"

Sparkle looked ticked. "We're talking important fashion issues here, Mede. Be quiet."

"Sorry, babe, but this is life-and-death stuff." He jumped onto the table. "I've got a plan for getting rid of Fenrir."

Daria didn't know how reliable any plan would be that came from someone who meditated in a bowl of jellybeans.

"Here's the plan. Daria snatches Fenrir and carries him to Tartarus."

Daria waited for elaboration. Silence. "That's *it*? Did I miss the part where an army of kick-ass mercenaries helps Daria take out the big bad?"

"Hey, I'm not into details. I just come up with the winning concepts." Bounding from the table, he padded to the door. "I'll find Declan and fill him in."

Sparkle watched him leave. "Ganymede is such an all-powerful kind of guy, he forgets the rest of us have limitations." She frowned. "Wait. I can stop being his cheerleading squad of one. It's over. I don't have to think he's great anymore."

"Yeah, well—"

Sparkle looked determined to turn in her pom-poms. "Let's have a girl-to-girl chat about men and sex."

"You know, I really have to get some things done. Ganymede hired me to—"

"Keep me amused." Sparkle's laughter brimmed with suppressed excitement. "Ganymede knew I'd get bored if I didn't have a sexual challenge going on, so he chose you to be that challenge. I mean, who else but me could hook a harpy up with a hot and happening vampire who only wants a woman for his personal happy hour? Not that there's anything wrong with that. An hour of sizzling sex could energize even the dreariest person." She cast Daria a pointed stare.

Daria looked for something to break. Sparkle's head was out. Too hard. "What if your victims don't want to hook up with anyone?"

"Never happens." Sparkle had on her business face. "Everyone wants someone, even if they don't know it."

"I didn't." *I do now.*

"*Especially* you." Sparkle looked exasperated. "For a smart woman, you take a long time to get the point. You do *not* want a harpy mate. You *do* want Declan. I've seen the way you look at him."

"I—"

"You do *not* want to be ugly, even if you think that's what you want. You just want to please your mom and fit in with the rest of Harpyville; ergo you have to turn yourself into a disgusting mess."

"How did you know about—"

"I know lots of things, sister. When I accept a challenge, I find out everything about my—"

"Victim?"

Sparkle shrugged. "Whatever."

"And your point to all this is?"

"Forget about your stupid test and give yourself permission to indulge your sensual nature. You have the rest of your existence to be a heartless and hideous predator. Oh, and just for your info, you're not doing too well on the heartless part."

Daria wouldn't give her the satisfaction of agreeing. "How'd you find out about my test?"

Sparkle sighed. "What part of I-find-out-everything wasn't clear?"

Confused, Daria tried to think of a way to refute what Sparkle had said. But you couldn't refute the truth. Her thinking ended when Eris rushed into the kitchen.

"I won't take it anymore. You can't keep me like this, you stupid whore."

Sparkle glanced at Daria. "Does the woman know how to stroke my ego, or what?"

Eris bounced up and down while big fat tears rolled down her face. Of course, she looked adorable. "No one takes me seriously now. I told this jerk that I was hauling his butt to Tartarus for a personal interview with Hades, and he laughed. At me! Then he pinched my ass." She yanked at her hair, but it fell right back into place. "So then I broke his nose." Satisfaction glimmered in her tear-filled eyes.

Sparkle frowned. "Did he mention his lawyer?"

"Change me back to what I was." Eris punctuated her demand with a kick to the table leg.

Sparkled watched coffee slosh out of her cup. "Uh . . . let me think." She grinned. "No."

"Bitch, bitch, bitch, bitch." If harpies could foam at the mouth, Eris would be the soapsuds queen.

"Thank you, thank you, thank you, thank you." Sparkle beamed. "So few people recognize my true nature."

Practically vibrating with frustrated rage, Eris turned her fury on Daria. "And don't think just because I look like this I'll let you carry off the biggest prize, cow."

"Cow?" Daria raised one brow.

Eris was on a roll. "Your mother might be one of the three most powerful harpies, but she's nothing but a cheap slut for spreading her legs for Apollo. You and your twin will never be accepted no matter how hard you try because of who spawned you."

Daria shook her head. "See, now you made me mad." She punched Eris in the stomach.

The other harpy sat down hard, clutching her stomach as she gasped for air.

"I wanted to break your nose or loosen a few teeth, but you would've liked the way it messed up your face. So I had to go for the next best thing. This way you have to listen to me talk while you make all those wheezing noises."

Sparkle clapped her hands. "This is so cool. I haven't had this much fun since I hooked up two demon sisters with the same troll. They fought like cats over that guy. Never understood why. Trolls have zero sensuality."

Eris's face was bright red as she tried to suck in some air.

Daria bent over so she was almost nose-to-nose with the other haspy. "I don't care who you carry off. Just. Stay. Out. Of. My. Way."

Eris scooted away from Daria and then scrambled to her feet. She dove for the door, where she paused, evidently reclaiming her courage now that she was close to escape. "You'll both be sorry. I'll fly away from this place with an entity so powerful, Hades won't even notice what you drag in, Daria."

"More powerful than Declan and the werelion? Hey, you impressed me like crazy with those two." Daria knew she shouldn't be goading Eris. The harpy was a vicious enemy. But Eris was so much fun to goad, and Daria needed some fun in her life.

Eris shifted her anger to Sparkle. "And you'd better write a will leaving all your shitty shoes to that stupid cat, because I'm asking Mom to take care of you. There won't be enough of you left to fill a dustpan once she sees what you did to me." Her eyes had a feverish gleam.

"Bring her on, sister." Sparkle glanced at her watch. She didn't look freaked out at the thought of Aello descending on the Woo Woo Inn. "As entertaining as this conversation is, I'm late for my sensitivity session." She grabbed Daria's hand. "Come with me. I'm not done talking to you." Her gaze flicked over Eris, and then returned. "You're invited too. It's been a long time since I met anyone who needed my session more. Probably Vlad the Impaler was a little lower on the sensitivity scale, but not by much."

Sparkle swept past Eris, dragging Daria along with her. They left Eris growling and snarling behind them.

"I don't know how powerful you are, Sparkle, but just a friendly warning. Aello is as mean as they come, and she'll be ready to tear this place apart when she gets a look at her daughter. She isn't someone you want to face alone."

Sparkle guided her toward the library. "Alone? Why would I do that? Mede will be with me." She blinked. "Oops. I forgot." She got that sad look again.

Ganymede would have to spend maxi-minutes in his empty jellybean bowl to come up with a solution to the trouble that followed a visit from Aello. Only Mom and Ocypete were her equals in power.

Relieved, Daria saw Declan and Ganymede standing by the registration desk. She let Sparkle pull her over to them.

Declan watched Daria approach and then glanced away. He knew his eyes had that hungry-wolf look. Not a good thing. Before meeting Daria, he'd had a handle on who he was—a cold, passionless bastard who only came alive when something or someone engaged his senses. It wasn't a great way to live, but he got a certain comfort from the centuries-long sameness of it all. But now she'd kick-started his emotions in a big way. His passion was alive and laying waste to his self-image.

"Yo, babe, talk some sense into the bloodsucker here. He's not buying into my plan." Ganymede curled his body around Sparkle's legs.

"Don't *ever* call me babe again. You don't have the right anymore." Sparkle's emotions were bubbling dangerously close to the surface.

"Leave Sparkle and Daria out of this, cat. You know, I've heard a bunch of stuff about your supposed power. The word is that not many entities can stand up to you. So where was that power back at the church? From your rep, I expected a little more flash-and-boom. All you did was crouch inside your safety bubble and kick up a little dirt around the werewolf. And now you're passing the job to someone who's a lot less powerful than you." Fear fueled Declan's anger.

"A *lot* less powerful? I have my moments." Daria looked semi-insulted.

Ganymede's tail whipped back and forth. "I already told you I'm not allowed to kill Fenrir. The Big Boss is *the man*, and when I hit his radar because I was breaking too many of his stupid rules, he clipped my wings."

Daria winced.

"That means the best I can do is slow the wolf down. Sorry."

Wow, Declan was impressed. He wondered if anyone

else had ever heard Ganymede apologize. So no help from Ganymede. He forced himself to meet Daria's gaze. "There's no way I'll let you try to carry Fenrir off." A second after he said it, he knew he'd made a mistake.

"*Let* me?" Daria's anger skewered him. "Last time I looked, I had this thing called free will. That means I can do whatever I want."

He stomped on his temper long enough to try a little logic. "You felt Fenrir's power. Do you really think you can just swoop down and carry him off?"

A smile tugged at her lips. "No. But telling a harpy she can't do something is a guarantee she'll want to do that exact thing. It's part of our genetic makeup."

"I hate to say you're wrong, Mede, because I know how upset you get when someone tells you that, but you're wrong. No way can Daria handle Fenrir." Sparkle's smile said, "You're wrong, wrong, wrong, and I *love* saying it."

Ganymede hissed.

"I can if I get some help. In harpy form, I've got the strength to pick him up and carry him away." Daria glanced at Declan.

Sparkle sighed. "It'll take more than just strength. Unless he's unconscious, he'll hit you with so much power, you'll be nothing more than feathers floating in the breeze."

She'd need help. Declan fought past an unfamiliar protective instinct to string a few thoughts together. "Here's what we need: more nonhumans to fight Fenrir and his cronies, along with a way to disable him so Daria can take him to Tartarus. Hades is powerful enough to hold Fenrir forever."

"This will mean chipped nails, won't it?" Sparkle didn't look like she was sure saving the universe was worth nail damage.

"Hey, greatness requires sacrifice. I read that some-where." Ganymede glanced toward the parlor. "I think all the weirdos who belong to your sensitivity group are waiting for you. While you're talking, I'll contact a few people to help us." He padded away.

Sparkle motioned them toward the library, and Daria followed her. Declan followed Daria. He could lie to him-self and say he only wanted to talk about their plan, but he was way beyond self-deceit. His senses clamored for her scent, her taste, her touch.

He found a place for both of them to sit in a darkened corner while Sparkle began to speak.

"Let's pick up from where we left off last time." Sparkle struck a dramatic pose in front of the fireplace, the shim-mer of her short black dress a stark contrast to the flames. "To make it in today's civilized society, we have to be sen-sitive to the feelings of others." She motioned to one of the werelions. "How do you handle it when someone takes your parking spot at the mall?"

The werelion frowned. "I drag the jerk out of his car and eat him."

There was a small gasp from the few humans in the room. Most of the nonhumans nodded their heads in agreement.

The werelion looked uncertain as his wife jabbed him with her elbow. "I guess that wouldn't be too sensitive, huh?"

Sparkle shook her head. "The correct way to handle the situation would be to patiently explain to the other driver that you saw the parking spot first. He'll respond as a sensitive person should by moving his car."

"What if he doesn't?" The werelion was determined to cover all his bases.

"*Then* you eat him."

One of the werewolves waved his hand in the air. "Talking about eating, has anyone seen any little, helpless animals running around in the woods?"

Harvey the werechicken winced.

Sparkle looked a little ticked. "You just ate. How about showing a little sensitivity for Katie. She can't hang around all night cooking for you."

Suitably chastened, the werewolf subsided.

Declan had heard enough. He leaned close to Daria and whispered, "We can come up with another idea to stop Fenrir." He knew she didn't want to listen to what he was saying, but it needed saying anyway. "I don't want you hurt."

Something seemed to soften in her eyes, but it could've just been a trick of the dim lighting. "If your dad gets his way, we'll all do a lot of hurting. This is the only idea we have, so until someone suggests a better one, I say go for it."

He controlled his frustration. "If you belonged to the Mackenzie council, I'd know how to handle this. I'd . . ." He raked his fingers through his hair. "Okay, so I'd let a member of the council do it. But you're different, you're . . ." Words failed him, as they seemed to do more and more when she was around.

She smoothed her fingers over his arm. "I understand. If everything were reversed, I'd be arguing every step of the way."

"You're confusing my life, lady." Declan knew his smile said this was a good thing.

"Your *boring* life. Harpies are action addicts. We live for excitement. Whether this works or not, let's enjoy the ride, Mackenzie."

She squeezed his hand and he wrapped his fingers

around hers. "If Fenrir gives you a hard time, he'll find out a pissed-off Mackenzie isn't someone to mess with."

Vampires weren't good at conversations loaded with emotional undertones. They were solitary creatures who usually talked to their meals as little as possible. So now that he really wanted to steer the conversation toward light and cheerful, Declan found that all he knew was dark and deadly. Luckily, Daria was better than he was at small talk.

"Where do you live?" She kept her gaze fixed on their clasped hands.

"Florida. I like the warm weather and the great beaches. Nothing like a moonlit swim. A lot different from life in the Highlands. How about you?"

She shrugged. "I've done most of my training in Montana. It has lots of wide-open spaces where no one notices me practicing picking up cows. I almost feel like Montana is where I belong, but my real harpy home is on a small Greek island."

He couldn't help it, he laughed. "You practice by picking up cows?"

The corners of her mouth turned up. "Doesn't everyone practice? What about you? Didn't you practice pouncing on people?"

Declan tried to look offended. "The Mackenzies never pounce. We work our sensual magic on women, and when the moment comes to feed, we make sure it's an erotic masterpiece." He frowned. "Of course, then we have to erase their memories, but I've always hoped that on some level the women remembered."

Daria wasn't smiling anymore. "And I guess you've had a blast over the centuries working all that 'sensual magic.' How about men? Don't you ever feed from them?"

"Not often. The centuries have pretty much deadened my emotions." *Until you.* "So the only thing that makes life worth the effort is my senses. Sexual pleasure allows me to use them all." He touched the tip of his finger to her lips, letting the soft warmth of them seep through his fingertips and along his nerve endings.

"Oh." Daria sounded like she didn't know whether to be outraged at his story or aroused by the possibilities.

Satisfied, he sat back. There was jealousy in that one word. He was glad. Should he be ashamed of his emotion? He smiled. Not when it felt so good.

"I'll forgive you for ignoring my awesome sensitivity session if you tell me you were whispering about sex." Sparkle spoke right next to his ear.

Startled, Declan turned to where Sparkle crouched beside him. "We were making plans to attack Fenrir."

"Of course. I could tell by your expressions that you were deep into a conversation that was totally *not* sexual." Sparkle shifted her attention to Daria. "You know, this plan to snatch Fenrir is the best thing that could happen to you. If you pull it off, your test score will be off the charts."

"Test score?" What the hell was she talking about?

Daria shot Sparkle an angry glare. "What Sparkle is trying to hint about in her own subtle way is that I came to the Woo Woo Inn to snatch someone as part of my harpy test."

"Test?" Why hadn't she said something sooner?

She stared at him.

"Okay, I get it. You really were thinking about flying off with me."

Daria jerked her hand from his. "Yes."

"And Eris is here for the same thing? This *test*?" Why was he so mad? He'd suspected from the beginning she was here to snatch someone. Harpies didn't show up at places like the Woo Woo Inn just for a little R & R.

"Right. Now I need to get some air." Without giving him a chance to object, she walked away.

"Hmm. Did I say the wrong thing?" Sparkle's expression said it had been exactly the right thing.

"As a matchmaker, you stink." He started to follow Daria.

Sparkle put her hand on his arm. "She would've told you eventually. I just got full disclosure out of the way so you guys could get on with the sex. You live life while you have it, Declan."

He stared at her and then nodded. She dropped her hand. Declan watched her walk away.

"Take me for a run, please, please, please?" Trouble stopped beside Declan and leaned against his leg. "That werebunny watches me all the time. Then when I go outside, he chases me."

Declan glanced around in time to see Mel sneaking from the room. He frowned. Yes, the way the wererabbit left definitely qualified as sneaking. What was he doing here in Sparkle's sensitivity group? He didn't strike Declan as someone who gave a damn about other people's feelings.

Mel was heading for the porch as Declan looked for the three werewolves. They were slowly making their way from the room. He smiled at Trouble. "Let's take care of your werebunny for the night."

He stopped the men before they got to the door. "Hey, guys, I know you're looking for some good hunting."

All three pairs of eyes brightened. "We need something we can sink our teeth into." The tallest one grinned at his own joke.

Declan nodded toward the door. "Did you see the guy with the blue shirt and khaki pants?"

All three heads nodded.

"He's a wererabbit. Not your usual nervous bunny, but a fluffy-tailed fighting machine. He'll give you a good workout if you hurry. I bet he'll change as soon as he gets past the tree line."

"Wererabbit?" The three glanced at each other, and then they were gone.

Declan smiled as he looked down at Trouble. "Go ahead and take your run. I don't think the werebunny will be paying much attention to you tonight."

Trouble sat beside him smiling a doggy grin while his tail thumped a tattoo on the floor. "You helped me. Someday I'll help you."

"You're a cosmic troublemaker, kid, and I bet if you ever decide to stand up to Mel, you'll find you have all the power you need to take him out. Just something to think about."

Trouble nodded, but he looked doubtful.

Declan forgot about Trouble as he headed for the porch and Daria. He found her staring into the darkened woods. "I just sicced the werewolves on your friend Mel."

"It couldn't happen to a nicer guy. I'm almost certain he's my judge." She didn't even glance at him.

"We need to talk."

"I was going to tell you about the test. Eventually." She sounded a little defensive.

He shrugged. "We haven't known each other long enough for me to expect you to tell all your secrets." Sure he did.

"My mother, Celaeno, is one of the big three in the harpy world. As far back as I can remember, the only thing I wanted was to be like Mom. This test is my first step. I have to snatch someone evil and powerful, someone who'll impress Hades." She smiled but didn't meet his gaze. "At first I thought you might be the one."

"And now?"

"Not so much."

"Why not?" When you go fishing, you don't always catch a trophy fish. She might not give him the answer he wanted.

She finally made eye contact. "You're a friend. I don't hunt people I like. That shouldn't make any difference to a harpy, but I guess it does to me."

Not a bad answer, but not quite what he was looking for either. He didn't want her lumping him in with other people. And what was with the words *friend* and *like*? Pretty tame. He'd prefer ones like *lover* and . . . Yeah, he supposed *like* was an okay word for the moment.

"Be honest, Daria. You don't think you can take me. That's the real reason you didn't try."

Her anger flared, and she opened her mouth to blast him. Then she must've seen the laughter in his eyes. She relaxed and smiled. "If I wanted you, vampire, you wouldn't have a chance."

In the silence of the night something tenuous moved between them.

"Hello, Declan, we've been looking for you." A woman's voice shattered the moment.

He turned.

She was beautiful in a way that screamed *nonhuman*. You could add strange to the description. Her long hair was parted in the middle. Half of it was black, the other half white.

Declan shifted his attention to the man standing beside her, tall and slim—there was something scary about him. Declan met the man's gaze. It was his eyes, a weird shiny black that creeped him out. Not a reaction he'd felt often in the last nine hundred years.

Daria tensed beside him. She felt it too. A sense of danger he could almost touch.

Declan smiled, showing lots of fang. "Do I know you?"

The woman returned his smile, and Declan swore the air around them dropped ten degrees. "I'm disappointed, Declan. I hoped you'd recognize the family resemblance."

The man spoke, his voice a sibilant hiss. "This is your aunt Hel, and I'm your uncle Midgard."

CHAPTER FOURTEEN

Daria moved closer to Declan.

Midgard grinned, and the snake lived in his smile. "Please don't run away. We have a lot to talk about."

"Go inside, Daria." Declan never took his gaze from his newfound relatives.

There he went again, telling her what to do. He wanted her to run inside and hide while he faced the two of them by himself. Wait, there were some powerful entities inside the inn. All she had to do was scream at the top of her lungs.

"You're getting ready to scream. I can tell from the look in your eyes." Hel shook her head, and her hair rippled around her shoulders. "All we want to do is talk to Declan. We're reasonable beings."

Declan's laughter was harsh. "You know, I somehow can't work up a lot of reasonableness when it comes to dying. Oh, and there's that little matter of your brother killing two of the Mackenzie council members."

Midgard shrugged. "Your *father* did what he had to. Their deaths were the only things that would draw you back here in time for the summer solstice. Since he didn't have the strength to come to you, he made sure you would come to him."

"A phone call would've done the same thing." Daria's opinion.

"Reception is poor a mile down." Hel taking Daria way too seriously.

Midgard went on as though no one had spoken. "Fenrir has a great deal of pride, so he forbade us to interfere until now." What went unsaid was that Fenrir had called in his brother and sister because time was running short. Midgard seemed relaxed as he sat down on the porch step.

Daria wasn't fooled. A snake might look benign as it lay curled in the grass, but it was always ready to strike. "You can't expect Declan to walk quietly to his death." Midgard could count on *her* not staying quiet if they tried to take him.

Hel seemed surprised as she looked at Declan. "Of course we do. It's a great honor to be the one who insures your grandfather's triumph over the other gods. Besides, you won't die right away. You'll live to see the gathered forces of Loki. Your sacrifice will take place right before the battle."

"Wow, what a relief." Daria hoped they got sarcasm.

"Call me clueless, but I could've sworn you guys were trying to kill Ganymede and me back at the church." Declan didn't seemed moved by thoughts of the honor Fenrir was trying to bestow on him.

Hel sighed. "If I'd wanted to kill you, you'd be dead. We only wanted to distract you from your attack on your father. I would love to get rid of Ganymede, but he has certain skills that make killing him difficult."

Since neither Hel nor Midgard had made any threatening moves, Daria chanced another question. "It seems like a coincidence that Fenrir just *happened* to be bound here in New Jersey and that Declan just *happened* to visit the Woo Woo Inn last year. What were the chances? I mean, this is a long way from the land of the Vikings."

"There are no coincidences."

Midgard paused to let his dramatic statement sink in.

Daria wondered if he was an actor when he wasn't slithering through the woods in giant snake form.

"Loki has the power to view what the gods do even though he's imprisoned in a cave. He saw them bind Fenrir beneath the earth in a place where they thought none would find him, in a place far from his home." Midgard scanned the inn's lawn as if searching for the ice and snow of his homeland. "They didn't know he was able to link with us. We waited centuries for this summer solstice to draw near and our brother to begin gaining power."

Hel picked up the narrative. "I'm the Queen of Death and as such have some ability to manipulate the future. I knew the name of the woman who was destined to marry Thrain Mackenzie. When I found out she was looking for property to buy, I used my power to point her in this direction." She stared up at the inn. "It's worked out well for her. And once the Mackenzie was here, you were within our reach."

Daria frowned. "Seems like a convoluted way to go about things. I think I'd be a little more direct."

"You don't understand, everything has to go according to the prophecy. Oh, if you're thinking of telling the Norse gods about our plans, forget it. The prophecy says they'll turn a deaf ear to all warnings." Midgard looked impatient. "Only two things remain for the prophecy to be fulfilled. Fenrir must escape his binding and Declan must be sacrificed before the battle. You can't stop what will be."

"Wanna bet?" Daria was committed to carnage if they made a move toward Declan.

There were lines of tension around Declan's mouth. "Have you seen the battle?"

Hel looked away. "No. It's hidden from me. That is a

concern." The air seemed to shimmer with power as she returned her gaze to Declan. "Will you go with us to your father?"

Here it comes. Daria knew Declan was about to give them a big fat no. She got ready to become harpy.

"So you can complete the final step in your plan to destroy the universe?" Declan took Daria's arm and backed toward the door. "Count me out."

Hel smiled. "I hate resorting to threats, but if you take another step toward that door I'll bring the place down before you can get inside. Lots of people will die."

Declan didn't have to look at Daria. She dropped the mental shields between them.

"Damn, I left my sword inside."

Daria winced. Instant guilt. He'd come out to the porch because of her.

"I'm going to lead them away from the inn while I instant message Ganymede about what's happening. It'll give him time to try to shield the inn from my loving relatives. I hope he has enough power. While they're concentrating on me, you get the hell out of here. They want me alive, but you're expendable." His expression said her death would bother him. A lot.

And even with doom and destruction barreling down on them, she felt good about that. Daria nodded as she focused on keeping her mind blank. He'd go all alpha if he knew she had no intention of obeying him.

Daria was ready when Declan made his break. He moved with that dizzying speed vampires could produce. Zigzagging across the lawn, he disappeared into the woods.

At the same time, Daria became harpy. Sparkle could kiss another outfit good-bye. She rose into the air and followed him.

Glancing back, she was in time to see Midgard change

into his snake form and slither toward the trees. She hoped no humans were looking out the windows.

"What do you think you're doing?"

Declan's fury rattled around in her head.

"Helping you, partner." Worry poked at her. Midgard moved fast for all his size. And Daria didn't have a clue where Hel was. *"What's your plan?"*

He was silent for a few angry beats. *"Would it do any good to tell you to get your butt back to the inn?"*

"Nope."

"There's an old ruined mansion out here somewhere." Resignation sounded in his voice. *"I'll try to lead Midgard into it. He's too big to move fast once I have him inside."*

"Have you let Ganymede know what's happening?"

"Yeah. He's setting up some kind of protection for the inn."

"What should I do?"

"Watch for Hel."

Daria saw the old mansion looming dark among the trees and swooped down.

For just a moment she thought about what she was doing. She was shucking the commitment of a lifetime in favor of trying to keep a vampire safe. It was either love or lunacy. She'd prefer to believe it was lunacy.

She spotted Declan slipping through one of the mansion's broken windows. Midgard took the more direct route through a wall.

Daria was pretty much able to follow the action because the roof had big gaping holes in it. Declan didn't seem to be having any trouble eluding Midgard, but Hel would have to show up eventually, wouldn't she?

"Don't you think we've given Ganymede enough time? Shouldn't we head back now?" Hey, Daria was all in favor of tactical retreats. Living to fight another day had real meaning to her.

Without warning, Hel appeared behind Declan. She'd timed her show of support perfectly. Midgard had gotten close enough to demand Declan's complete attention. She had her bow ready, and the arrow pulsed with a red glow. It might not kill Declan, but it'd be a major owie and might allow her to carry him off to the loving arms of Wolf Daddy.

Oh, shit. Daria couldn't alert Declan without making him take his attention from Midgard. With her huge wingspan, she couldn't fit through the hole in the roof, so she resorted to what she'd done when fighting Fenrir. Ripping off a chunk of roofing, she flung it down at Hel.

Daria didn't know who was more surprised when the missile struck, Hel or her. It was a direct hit that knocked Hel down. Yes! The almighty Queen of Death hadn't shielded herself. There was something to be said for low-tech attacks.

Declan glanced behind him and then, before either Hel or Midgard could recover, rose into the air.

"Let's get out of here."

This time she obeyed him. Flapping her wings, she made for the inn. He caught up with her quickly.

"You fly."

"Airport security's a bitch."

She grinned before glancing back. No pursuit yet. Even if Ganymede made the inn into a fortress, outside activities would be dangerous from now on. Cindy and Thrain were about to take a major income hit.

He gave her a thumbs-up, and for a moment something that looked a lot like boyish excitement shone in his eyes. She felt a connection to him that should throw her harpy heart into a panic. It didn't.

Daria searched the area below her. "We're almost at

the inn. I'm landing behind that tree. Give me your shirt. Then we'll go inside."

He followed her down. Even as he hit the ground, he was ripping off his shirt and handing it to her. After changing back to human form, she pulled it over her head and then yanked on the bottom, trying to make it cover more of her.

He took her hand and sprinted toward the porch. "I just sent a mental SOS. Ganymede knows we're coming. He's lowering his shield."

Daria had a quick impression of only a few cars still parked in front of the inn before Declan flung open the door and pulled her into the foyer. Ganymede, Sparkle, and Katie waited. She slammed the door shut behind her.

Ganymede wore a strained expression. "I can only shield the whole building for a little longer. Katie is working on something more permanent."

"Katie?" When Declan thought of a superhero stepping in to save their butts, the cook didn't come to mind.

"You bet. Just call me Broom Woman." Katie held up her weapon of choice.

"It looks funny, sort of glowing and shimmery. Scary." Daria didn't look as if she trusted brooms that glowed and shimmered.

"Tell you the truth, it sort of scares me too." Katie cast a suspicious glance at her faithful kitchen helper. "It wasn't always mine, you know. Belonged to a wizard with more power than I'll ever have. Hate to admit it, but I've been afraid to tap into its full power." She glanced at Ganymede, who was laboring a little as he tried to shield the inn from whatever lurked outside. "Now might be a good time to try. I've called up a protection spell. Let's give it a road test." Without waiting for comments, Katie pulled open the door and slipped outside. She left the door ajar, and Declan could hear her chanting.

Daria looked worried. "Will she be able to do it?"

"Yeah, I think so. That's the good news." Ganymede was crouched on the floor, looking like the weight of the world rested squarely on his cat shoulders. "The bad news is I struck out with the two people I wanted here with us. Holgarth's at some wizard convention in England. They have the damn convention center shielded, so I couldn't get my message through."

Ganymede looked depressed, but not about Holgarth. "I can't stop cursing. It's part of who I am. There're no candy bars, cakes, cookies, or pies left in the inn. I bet Chill started on my ice cream."

Impatient, Declan got him back on track. "What about your other friend?"

"Not a friend. Edge is the cosmic troublemaker in charge of death. He's working down in Texas with some paranormal police force. But he's deep undercover. Blocked all incoming messages." The strain of the shield Ganymede supported was starting to show.

The cat's fur was damp and Declan could see his muscles quivering. Whatever Katie was planning had better kick in soon.

Daria walked over to the window. "No giant snakes or death queens in sight. Is anyone watching out back?"

"Got the werewolves on it. They stayed. A lot of the others didn't." Ganymede looked depressed at the thought of all that lost revenue. "I compelled everyone to get their asses back inside the inn as soon as I got your message. Didn't have time to let them all wander back on their own. The humans didn't have a clue what had happened, and the nonhumans resented the hell out of me for using a compulsion on them." He shrugged.

Declan got the feeling he was more worried about his diminishing supply of ice cream than he was the nonhumans' bruised feelings.

"I explained the situation. Most of them threw their things into their suitcases and burned rubber outta here. The ones who stayed are willing to take their chances."

"Any humans stay?" Declan felt Daria join him.

"That Walt guy. He said he had important research to finish. Don't know why he didn't go home to do it." Ganymede looked at Daria. "He said he's close to solving a problem for you."

Just as Declan got ready to ask about the problem, rumbling roars shook the whole house along with a sharp crack of thunder.

Before anyone could react, Katie pushed the door wide. She looked pale and shaken. "Your new security system is up and running. They want you to call them the Guardians." Exhaustion lined her face. "I'm getting too old for this kind of magic."

Ganymede padded onto the porch and down the steps. The others followed him. Everyone looked up.

"Gargoyles?" Declan let a hiss of amazement escape. Along with the gargoyles crouched on each corner of the inn's roof, there was one protecting the porch. Huge, monstrous, and really scary, they glared down with bulging eyes that glowed yellow.

Katie seemed too weary even for her usual snarky comments. "They'll protect everything as far as the parking area. If I did everything right, nothing, no matter how powerful, can get inside the guarded space." She tottered up the steps. "I need rest." She gathered enough energy to glare at Ganymede. "Stay out of my kitchen." Then she disappeared inside.

They all trailed in behind her. Even though it wasn't

dawn yet, rest sounded tempting to Declan. Looking around, he spotted Daria. She still wore his shirt and nothing else. *Mine.* His body was a possessive bastard.

He curbed his first instinct to go to her. She was talking to her brother, and the conversation didn't look friendly.

Declan knew he needed a plan, but right now his brain was drifting in a confused fog. Hel and Midgard wouldn't give up after one setback. And Fenrir would soon be powerful enough to jog up to the inn's front door. Would the gargoyles be strong enough to protect the inn against an assault from a giant snake, a badass werewolf, and the Queen of Death? He'd bet the Guardians had never seen that kind of action before.

He decided to go to his room and change. It would give him time to think about Daria. *Partner.* That's what she'd called him. In his long life, he'd never had a real partner. Sure, Ganymede said he'd have his back, but Declan didn't fool himself about the cat's motivation. Ganymede made self-serving into an art form.

But he got a different feeling from Daria. Declan thought about that feeling as he climbed the stairs to his room—rolled it over in his mind, and decided it was a great feeling.

He was almost at the top of the stairs when the compulsion hit. All he had time to think was that Hel and Midgard must've run back to Fenrir with news of their failure. Then lust brought him to his knees. Literally. He crawled up the last few steps and lay in the hallway trying to control spasms of raging need. Clenching his teeth, he worked to beat back the compulsion.

Then Daria was beside him, her hands touching him in ways he was sure she meant to be comforting but that had a totally different effect on him. "Stop. Touching. Me." His words were forced out through gritted teeth.

"The compulsion?"

He could only nod.

She didn't waste time on long speeches. "My room is closer." Helping him to his feet, she supported him the short distance to her door. Where her body touched his, a blade of searing desire sliced into him. It was all he could do not to groan. When she pushed the door open, he fell into her room.

Daria crouched beside him. "Do you want me to go away so you can fight this?" She bit her lower lip with even white teeth.

He wanted those teeth nibbling him. "Hell, no."

Her smile ignited a fire in him that threatened to burn through the floor and dump him in the room below.

"Good." She stood, slipped out of his shirt, and turned away from him.

Then she walked. The sway of her round little bottom in all its bare glory would have had the same effect on him even if he *wasn't* under Ganymede's compulsion. Want roared through him and emerged as a strangled cry.

She stopped beside one of the posters on her wall.

It was of him. Naked, sitting on a Ferris wheel. He glanced around. A lot more pictures. All of him. All naked. Damn.

"Sparkle decorated this room. You'll notice the similarity to her room."

What he noticed was her beautiful full breasts with perfect nipples that cried for his mouth.

"Sparkle doesn't have eclectic taste when it comes to artwork. But I have to admit each of the posters in this room is inspiring in its own way." She pointed at the one beside her. "Do you think we can capture the same sense of . . . adventure?"

She was teasing him. Her eyes gleamed with laughter as she slid her tongue over her bottom lip. The soft wet sheen of it would've taken him to the floor if he weren't already there.

It was all too much. His twin hungers flared to life. He felt the slide of his fangs and had just enough rational thought to remind himself to feed only one hunger tonight.

"Come here." It was going to have to be the floor, because he would need lots of roll-around room when all his massed sexual energy reached flash point.

She strolled over to him, the swing of her hips advertising that help was on the way. Standing over him, she pursed her lips in thought. "Hmm. Seems we have a problem. I can't do what I want to do with your pants still on."

He growled. Had to get the damn things off. Mumbling expletives, he dragged the pants off and flung them away from him. He'd already kicked off his shoes.

Then he reached up and pulled her down beside him. Declan smiled at her and hoped he didn't look like the big bad wolf. He shook his head. No wolf thoughts allowed. "I can take you to that place in the poster." He rolled onto his side.

"Really? You can create a fantasy?" She looked interested as she slid her hand over his jaw and traced his lips with the tip of her finger.

He laughed. "No. A few of the Mackenzies can do that kind of stuff with a whole story line attached, but it's not one of my talents. I meant I could recreate the setting, allow you to enjoy the same emotional response you got when you looked at the poster." That had to be a first. He'd never promised emotions to any woman he'd been with.

"Mmm. Sounds exciting." She walked her fingers down his chest and stomach before pausing.

His cock was so hard he wanted to beg her to touch it. But that might not be smart right now. Instead, he propped himself up on his elbow before touching her shoulder. She took the hint and rolled onto her back.

As much as he wanted this to be a long and loving seduction, his body was thrumming with the promise of an explosion of epic proportions. Soon. Unless he wanted to humiliate himself and completely destroy his reputation as the master of sexual pleasure, he'd better move fast.

"I don't want to wait either." She smiled at him.

Daria saw too much, understood him too well for his own comfort. It was getting harder and harder to maintain any kind of distance between them. He'd only wanted her body at first, but now he was opting in for the whole package. He closed his eyes. Had he really thought that?

Laughing, she drew his head down and kissed each of his closed lids. "Stop thinking, vampire. Free your senses. They say danger makes lovemaking more powerful. How about testing that theory now?"

Opening his eyes, he said something totally unplanned, so out of character it clogged his throat. Was he stupid? If this didn't kill the mood, nothing would.

"Would you ever consider pursuing another line of work?"

CHAPTER FIFTEEN

Change her work? Give up being a harpy? Where had that question come from? And why now when she was so hot for him her blood was turning to steam?

No was the first word that popped into her mind, followed closely by *maybe*. Maybe with lots of qualifiers. And every qualifier had his name attached.

She glared at him. Was he really under a compulsion? She doubted it or he wouldn't be able to stop right in the middle to discuss her job. That was fine, though, because she had her own compulsion going on.

"No talk, vampire. Time for action." She poked his broad chest with her finger. "Cook me up a dangerous setting."

Satisfaction gleamed in his eyes for a moment before hunger swept it away. Satisfaction? Why? Because she refused to answer his question about her job? If that's all it took to make him happy, then he should feel totally ecstatic in a few minutes.

She watched as his gaze grew unfocused just as it had back in the woods right before he created his wall of Red Hots.

"Sit up and close your eyes." He leaned down to feather a kiss across her lips.

"Why?" All harpies had suspicious natures. But she did sit up. No eye-closing yet.

"I'm changing our setting a little more than I did in the woods. The shift could make you feel queasy."

He'd said the right words. Heaving all over his sensual moment was so not on her to-do list right now. Shutting her eyes, she waited.

Her eyes popped open as she sensed motion. Daria had seen the poster, so she knew what to expect. Still, the shock left her breathless.

They sat facing each other across an open-sided gondola at the top of a very big Ferris wheel. Reaching out, she gripped the sides of the only barrier between them and a long fall to earth. In her mind, the whole thing was made of cardboard that would collapse like cooked spaghetti if it rained. Fearfully, she looked skyward. She released the breath she'd been holding. The moon and stars were out. Then she looked down. *Ulp.* People on the ground looked like tiny moving dots. Or maybe they were just the spots in front of her eyes that would probably show up right before she passed out.

"You're afraid of heights?" He sounded amused.

"I didn't think so." Good grief, she was a harpy. Flying was second nature to her. "Maybe it's a control issue. I'm not in control of this whole Ferris wheel thing."

"Take a deep breath and think logically. Even if the worst happened and we fell, both of us can fly. We'd never hit the ground."

She followed his advice and drew in a deep gulp of courage. Better still, she took a good look at *him*. He was still naked, his toned body exposed to anything she might want to do to it. And she wanted to do a lot.

"We're stuck up here, huh?" This was good, right? No problems with privacy, and the gentle sway of the gondola could even be construed as a sensual enhancement. "What was Sparkle drinking when she came up with the idea of a poster showing you naked at the top of a Ferris wheel?"

He shrugged. "Who knows? But let's make it work for us." Without warning, he moved across to her side.

She squeaked as the gondola swayed harder. "How can we make love without tipping this blasted thing over?" The breeze played with her hair, blowing some of it across her face.

Declan grinned. "Very carefully."

Pulling her to him, he smoothed some strands from her face. Fascinated, she watched the wind lift his hair, exposing the strong line of his neck. The moon shone behind him, creating a halo affect. But Declan would never be anyone's angel, and that's exactly how she wanted him.

Dipping his head, he took her mouth in a kiss that spoke of dangerous hunger and barely controlled need. His tongue tangled with hers as she wrapped her arms around him. Sliding her hands up and down his smooth back, she deepened the kiss, hoping he could feel the reality of all the things she wanted but couldn't explain. Couldn't explain because they were too new, too frightening.

Declan broke the kiss to nibble a path over her jaw and down the side of her neck. He didn't pause where her pulse beat madly but continued on to her breasts.

Flinging her head back, she stopped thinking and just let her senses take over. The wind touched her face, breasts, and every other exposed inch of skin with cool night fingers. Except for the one nipple that Declan covered with his mouth, teasing the hard nub with quick flicks of his magic tongue. *So sensitive.* A pleasure-pain thing. *Like every thought of being with you and then leaving you.*

Daria chased the thought from her mind with speech. "I want to make you feel good."

Jeez, talk about cheesy lines. You'd think when a person was standing at a major fork in her life's path she'd come up with something a little more poetic, words for the ages.

She placed one finger over his lips when he raised his head to answer. "I want to put my mouth on you." Fine, so she wasn't a poetic harpy. She didn't dress up what she wanted in pretty words.

His eyes flared hot. "Since we're courting danger, I'll sit there." He pointed.

She looked. Gulp.

"Lucky for you, I'm *not* afraid of heights." With one lithe motion he rose, stepped onto the bench where he'd just been sitting, and then sat down on the back with his bare feet firmly planted on the seat. He didn't even reach down to brace himself with his hands.

Brave man. He was sitting on the edge of lots of empty air. One careless moment and it was impact earth. The fact that he could fly didn't lesson the fear factor for Daria. "Um, don't you want to at least hang on to something?"

"I'll hang on to *you.*" Something in his gaze said there were several layers of meaning to his reply.

Holding his gaze, she moved to a kneeling position on the seat. He spread his legs and she edged between them. Then he wrapped his legs around her and buried his fingers in her hair. His safety depended on her strength.

His smile was a smoky fire just before it burst into flame. "You'd always be a man's anchor, harpy lady." There was a hint of yesterday in his husky murmur, of his Highland roots and before that the seas he'd sailed as a Viking.

Her hands shook with her need to touch him. She smoothed her fingers over his muscular thighs before cupping his sacs in each of her palms. They lay warm there as she lowered her head to slide her tongue the length of his shaft.

He shuddered, his pleasure a soft murmur of encouragement. Gaining courage from this proof that she was on the right track, Daria traced a spiral staircase on his cock with her tongue, starting at the base and ending somewhere beyond their self-control.

He got a firmer grip on her hair. "This could come to a head quickly."

She tried not to laugh. Laughter could make him lose his balance. Instead she slid her lips over him, taking him deep into her mouth, enjoying the sensual overload—velvety smooth skin, heat, and the scent of arousal.

Skimming her teeth lightly over his erection and then tightening her lips around him got the desired result.

With a groan of lost control, he released her hair, leaned over until he could grip her bottom, and lifted her onto his lap.

Left straddling his hips, she looked down. "Ohmigod, no!" They teetered on the edge for a second until she froze in place, afraid of doing anything that would send him plunging backward.

"Don't worry, I have great balance. A Viking washed overboard fast if he didn't." His voice was a mixture of laughter and desire.

"What're you doing?" She had a horrible suspicion. Amazingly, her terror was mixed with a rush of anticipation.

He buried his face in the hollow of her neck, and his warm breath triggered a rash of goose bumps. "I think you know."

Then before she could marshal the hundred or so reasons why this was a really bad idea, he cupped her bottom and lifted her onto his cock.

Daria had no way of bracing herself, and she gasped at the shock of his erection stretching and filling her. She was wet and already clenching around the hard length of him when he began to thrust into her.

Once again she froze, not even giving in to the urge for one little wiggle. "I'll do the moving. You work on the balance." She was breathing hard, and her words came out in little gasps. The air was cool, but they were both covered with a sheen of sweat.

"Good luck." His eyes gleamed with the joy of what they were doing.

It was incredible what the promise of a spectacular orgasm would drive an otherwise sane harpy to try. With her common sense shocked into silence, she carefully maneuvered her hips and legs until she was kneeling on the narrow ledge while still straddling him.

"There." Triumphant, she lowered herself onto him slowly this time, allowing herself to wallow in every erotic sensation. That lasted for, oh, about fifteen seconds.

Then everything started to whirl out of control. The heaviness built low in her belly as she raised herself off him and then sank back down. Faster and faster, caution giving way to the frenzy of her rush toward climax. She wasn't aware when he grasped her hips to steady them.

Daria knew she was making little sounds of eagerness, but she couldn't control them. He made no sounds, but his grip on her hips tightened.

The final moments were primitive raw sensation as the rocking of their gondola and her own frantic movements pushed her toward . . . toward . . .

Declan threw back his head and bared his fangs, a testament to all that he was. In some part of her mind she noted that he hadn't tried to bite her.

It was coming, coming, coming—

"Do you trust me, Daria?"

Coming, coming. "Yes."

With that, he fell backward into space just as her orgasm exploded with a spasm that curled her insides into a
knot of such intense pleasure, she swore she saw several
lifetimes pass before her eyes.

Somewhere she was aware of Declan's shout and that
they weren't falling anymore. Her legs were wrapped
around his hips, holding him inside her. He was slowly
drifting above the ground.

Drifting, drifting as the spasms grew less and less.

"Close your eyes, harpy lady."

And she did.

When she opened them, she was lying on her side facing the poster that had started the whole thing. Daria
didn't care what Sparkle said, she was taking that poster
with her when she left the Woo Woo Inn.

If she turned over, she knew he'd be there. She wasn't
sure she was ready for that. Any more than she was ready
to analyze some of the undercurrents running beneath
the surface of their lovemaking.

He touched her shoulder. "You didn't become harpy
when we fell."

"I trusted you to do the flying. The flight attendant
didn't serve my drink on time, though."

His laughter warmed her.

She rolled over and smiled at him. "That was beyond . . ." Sometimes words failed.

His grin was all pleased male. "If it wasn't almost dawn,
I'd be exploring every one of those posters with you."

Dawn. Reality closed in on her. "I didn't hear any
sounds of battle, so I suppose the Guardians did their job."

"For now." The truth of their situation made his eyes
look weary. "I'd better leave messages for the two remaining council members before I go to sleep. They'll want to
be here to help."

This wasn't her idea of post-lovemaking chatter, but Fenrir had to be discussed. "What can he do if we bring in some powerful allies and just wait him out? All we have to do is hold him off until after the summer solstice."

Declan rose and then helped her up. He started pulling on the clothes he still had. "Fenrir is goal-oriented. He'd have no qualms about slaughtering innocents to get his way. He won't be bound to the church much longer. We can't just hole up here if he decides to take his battle public. I don't even want to think what would happen if humans got involved with this."

Okay, so now she was officially depressed. She walked to her closet, aware of his gaze on her behind every step of the way. She smiled. "I can feel your eyes, vampire." His soft laughter was wicked in all the right ways.

"So what do you still have to do tonight?" He didn't ask to stay.

She didn't invite him. "I have some things to talk over with Kal. Then I'll try to contact Mom and Aunt Ocypete. It wouldn't hurt to have another two kick-butt harpies on our team." She was making light of it, but she dreaded facing her mother.

He headed for the door as she finished pulling on fresh clothes. Maybe she'd go barefoot for the rest of the night. All of Sparkle's shoes gave her nosebleeds.

Declan waited at the door for her to join him. When she did, he pulled her into his arms and kissed her. There was a gentleness to his kiss that didn't say *dangerous nighthunter*. Not at this moment at least.

He leaned over to whisper in her ear, "Next time, sweetheart, I want to be on top." Then he left, closing the door softly behind him.

Daria grinned. He was such a guy.

Her grin had faded by the time she reached her brother's

door. This wouldn't be fun. He'd wanted to argue with her right after she'd escaped the clutches of the terrible twosome. She'd postponed the inevitable by chasing after Declan when she sensed he was in trouble. But she owed her brother an explanation.

Daria heard his footsteps approach the other side of the door and arranged her expression to mimic the work-obsessed sister he'd expect to see.

Kal opened his door and glared at her.

She didn't wait for his invite before strolling past him into his room. Taking the offensive usually gave you a leg up on the opposition. "It's time we took stock of where we are, Kal."

When she turned toward him, she got a good look at his face. As always happened when she saw him without his magic, his beauty shocked her. He had an uncompromisingly male face, all the strong lines women loved along with a sensual mouth and those incredible violet eyes. Sheesh, who *really* had violet eyes? Not her. Her eyes were plain old hazel without Kal's magic. The only thing that made them special in any way was a thick fringe of dark lashes.

Kal raked his fingers through his blond hair. "I don't have a clue why we spent months getting ready for this damn test. It's like you set out to purposely dynamite any chances you might have of passing. You won't take a shot at Declan, the candidate with the best chance of putting a big smile on Hades's face. And you're involved in something you've chosen not to share with me."

She winced at the hurt in his voice.

"You don't even look like a harpy anymore." He must've seen the accusing expression on her face, because he grimaced. "Yeah, you're right. I don't look like one either. When did things get so complicated, sis?"

Where to start? Maybe Daria needed to work through her feelings about being a harpy. And she owed it to Kal to do it in front of him. "You know I've always wanted to be like Mom. I've tried. No one practiced harder than I did. No one *believed* more than I did. But these last few days have shown me a side of myself that scares me."

He offered her a tight smile. "Tell me about it."

"Sure, I've been around places where humans hung out, but I never really got to *know* any of them. Since I've been here, I've found I like smiling, I have fun helping people, and—" here came the hard part "—I like looking nice."

"So what does that mean?" His expression gave nothing away.

"Maybe we've never fit in with all the other harpies because we really *don't* belong with them."

The silence went on for way too long.

"Why are you showing your own face, Kal?" Might as well get everything out into the open.

"Sophie, the wereleopard I told you about, is someone I want to spend more time with." Kal looked uncomfortable. "She talks to me, even with that horror of a face I've been wearing." He walked over to the couch and collapsed onto it. "That's not enough, sis. I don't want her to be my friend; I need her to be my lover." He almost seemed to sink into himself. "Is that asking too much? After twenty-eight freaking years, I want a woman who doesn't ask to be paid when she climbs into my bed."

Daria blinked away tears. Why hadn't she ever seen her brother's pain? "Hey, I understand. You're not the only one questioning your life goals." Life goals sounded so sterile, but wasn't that what this was really all about?

"So you like Declan?" He carefully skirted the other "L" word.

She nodded. "You and I are twins, Kal. I'm not surprised we're sharing some of the same feelings."

For the first time since she'd stepped into his room tonight, he smiled at her. "Okay, emotional purging over. You came here for something. Out with it."

Daria joined him on the couch. "I don't want you to use any more of your magic on me while I'm at the Woo Woo Inn."

"And when it's time to go?"

She allowed the question to drift free for a moment before answering, "I don't know, Kal. I really don't know."

"What are you and Declan involved in? I saw you come into the inn with him earlier. You weren't just returning from a quiet walk in the woods." He gave her a sharp look. "Ganymede told everyone a wild story that didn't make much sense. Said he couldn't guarantee our safety, and he thought everyone should leave. Not many details. I'd like to know what we're up against, sis."

"I'm surprised anyone stayed."

He shrugged. "Only a few did. The werewolves are up for anything that promises excitement. Eris stayed. She won't leave if you're still here. Mel didn't leave. Don't know why, unless he's the judge. I hope he isn't, because he sure doesn't like you. Walt, that debunker guy, is still here. Again, I haven't a clue why. Sparkle told all the humans who work at the inn not to come back to work until she called them. The cook said she'd stay. Ganymede was pretty happy about that."

"Won't one of the humans tell the police about what's going on here?" Wouldn't the cops get a surprise if they paid an unexpected visit?

"Ganymede wiped the memories of anyone who left."

She'd run out of questions. Time to tell Kal the truth.

Ten minutes later, her brother sat staring at her blankly.

"No one could make that up." He rubbed his hand across his forehead. "You're not bailing, are you?"

"I can't."

"Because of the vampire."

She smiled. "Yeah, but the fate of the universe had a little to do with it too."

"I get your point." He remained quiet for a few moments, then returned her smile. "Guess you can count me in. You'll need all the help you can get."

Leaning over, she hugged him. Right now she didn't care that harpies didn't do much touching. Kal needed to know how much he meant to her. "Thanks."

"What about Mom? This isn't something we should keep from her."

"When I leave here, I'll contact Mom and Aunt Ocypete."

His smile widened. "Better hope she doesn't come."

She shuddered. "Yeah." Mom would *not* be sympathetic to her daughter's identity crisis. She'd tell Daria to suck it up before she kicked her behind all the way back home.

"Let's get rid of the magic." Kal stared unblinking at her as he chanted the words that would strip Daria of her harpy camouflage.

When he was finished, she got up and rushed to the mirror. The face that stared back at her no longer had black rings around the eyes. Gone were her tattoos and piercings. Without any makeup she looked kind of . . . plain. Talk about a blank slate.

"Great." She headed for the door. "I'll keep you in the loop." Pausing with her hand on the doorknob, she looked back at her brother. "Tell your wereleopard you had an extreme allergic reaction to the sesame seeds on your burger bun. That's why your face looked all swollen and gross."

"Will do."

Smiling, she closed the door. She'd give her brother all the help he needed to hook up with his wereleopard. To hell with harpy tradition. Feeling good about herself, she headed back to her room.

She was almost there when Walt intercepted her.

"Glad I caught you. I wanted to give you these." He waved two sheets of paper at her.

"Come on in." She unlocked her door, and he followed her inside. "What did you find out?"

"First, I think I found one of the Mackenzies you asked about. He goes under the name Grim Kenzie, but I dug deeper and found a trail that led back to a Grim Mackenzie." He handed her one of the papers. "Here's his e-mail addy. Sorry I couldn't get a phone number for you. He lives in Alaska. Some kind of wilderness nut. Hope he's the one you're looking for."

Daria smoothed her fingers over Grim's name with fingers that shook. She'd about given up hope of finding any of Declan's kids. Please let him be the right Grim, and please give her the right words to convince him to contact his father.

"And here's the good stuff." Walt handed her the second sheet of paper. "When the gods first realized Fenrir was going to be a problem, they tried chaining him up. Didn't work. He broke all their chains. Finally they ordered the dwarves to make something Fenrir couldn't break. The little guys made a magic ribbon called Gleipnir. When the gods wrapped that around Fenrir, he was caught. It wouldn't break, and it neutralized his power."

Daria looked down at the paper. "And this is?"

"This is what the ribbon was made of."

"The footsteps of a cat, the roots of a mountain, a woman's beard, the breath of fishes, the sinews of a bear, and a bird's spittle. You think Home Depot will have this stuff?" They were in big trouble.

Walt shrugged. "Look, I just do the research."

He'd done a lot better than she had, and she wanted him to know that. "You're a genius, Walt. Endless appreciation coming your way. I'll understand if you want to leave, though."

"Are you kidding? This is the chance of a lifetime." His expression turned sly. "I'm counting on you to make sure no one wipes my memory clean this time."

"You won't be allowed to take pictures. Will anyone believe you?" Humans either made fun of what they didn't understand or tried to debunk it. Walt would be coming from the other side of the aisle this time around.

"Who knows? But *I'll* know it's true. And that's all that counts." He rose and left her staring after him.

Morning light filtered through her curtains, and she suddenly felt exhausted. Reaction to everything that had happened tonight was setting in. But she still had two things to do.

Turning on her laptop, she sent Grim an e-mail. Her tired brain had trouble forming words that would entice this stranger to find out more about his supposed father. She couldn't come right out and ask him if he was a vampire. If he wasn't, her mail would freak him out. When she finally hit SEND, she prayed he'd pick up the phone and call the inn's number.

Now for Mom. If Daria didn't do it right away, she'd find excuses to put it off. Closing her eyes, she opened the mental link to her mother. *"Mom, I need to talk to you."*

"Did you find someone to snatch?"

"No."

"Are you looking for someone to snatch?"

"No."

"*Are you in trouble?*"

"*Yes.*"

"*I'll be there tonight.*"

"*Bring Aunt Ocypete.*"

Her mother broke the link.

No one could pack so much accusation into so few words as well as Mom did. Daria dragged herself into the shower. She was so tired that even the invisible guy who pressed himself against her back couldn't get a rise out of her. Sparkle would be disappointed. After brushing her teeth, she fell into bed.

And just before she fell asleep, she wondered where the hell she'd find bird spittle.

CHAPTER SIXTEEN

Memo: to all harpies
Subject: training expenses
It has come to our attention that several harpies hired
exotic male dancers and then billed Tartarus for their
fees. Male dancers are never part of our training pro-
gram. Give us a break. Putting money in a dancer's
thong does not qualify as practical training in identifying
the human male. And fondling a dancer's butt cannot
be listed as a hands-on experiment to find the best method
of grasping prey. We were not born yesterday. Punishment for those who choose to ignore this memo will be
one year of watching trolls dance naked. You will go
blind.

Remember, she who tries to fool Hades wakes up dead.

HADES THE SHOCKED

"A woman's beard?" Sparkle stared at the list. As of to-
night she'd been free to fix the nail on her index finger.
She'd taken off the bandage, but her nail was still broken.
"I don't know any women with beards." She frowned.
"How about the beard of a female impersonator? Would
that work? What do you think, Declan?"

"Uh, great." Declan couldn't take his eyes from Daria's
face.

Ganymede snorted. "Good luck." He'd remembered
not to say babe. His copy of the list lay on the parlor
floor. "I guess I'm supposed to find the footsteps of a cat.

How the hell will I do that?" He closed his eyes. "Jeez, there go the cupcakes I was saving. I felt them waving bye-bye."

Declan didn't have to burn many brain cells to figure out that this was Daria's real face.

"If you want the footsteps of a cat, you can mix up some cement—there's a bag in the cellar—and walk through it. When it dries . . . ?" Sparkle shrugged. "Cat footsteps."

Daria's new face was thinner, more delicate than the one Kal's magic had created. Someone who didn't know her might glance at her face and make the mistake of thinking she couldn't defend herself.

Ganymede looked at Sparkle with new respect. "Hey, I like that." He glanced around at everyone gathered in the parlor. "So who'll take something else on the list?"

Her eyes were the biggest change, Declan decided. No more muddy brown. Daria's real eyes were hazel with thick dark lashes.

"I'll take the bird's spittle." Eris's angry scowl was firmly in place and aimed directly at Sparkle. It only made her more beautiful. "I'm a bird in harpy form. I'll just spit in a cup and you'll have your damn bird's spittle."

That brought a collective "Ewww!"

Declan thought Daria's real lips were fuller, sexier. The word *sexy* was a favorite buzzword for his body. It immediately took notice.

"Which one on the list will you take, bloodsucker? You have your choice: the roots of a mountain, the breath of fishes, or the sinews of a bear." Ganymede looked around. "All this thinking is making me hungry. I'll be back." He padded toward the kitchen.

Declan blinked. List? Oh yeah. He dragged his gaze from Daria. "I guess I can take care of the breath of fishes."

Surprised, Daria looked at him. "How? Fish breathe through their gills, underwater. Seems pretty impossible to me."

Everyone in the room agreed.

"There're minnows in the pond out in the woods. I'll catch a few of them in a plastic bag. If I seal the bag off, any breaths they have will be captured in the bag."

Daria didn't seem too sure of that. "Even if it works, it's too dangerous for you to leave the inn."

Declan didn't want to remind her they couldn't stop Fenrir by hiding. So he took another look at the list instead. "We still won't have the roots of a mountain or the sinews of a bear. Any ideas?"

Sparkle spoke up. "Cindy keeps a few teddy bears on hand for any kids that visit. We could cut a piece out of one of them."

Walt looked pained. "But that wouldn't be authentic."

"I bet all of this is just symbolic anyway." Sparkle cast an exasperated glance around the room. "I mean, this stuff doesn't exist." Her expression faded to thoughtful. "Do real birds have spittle? Has anyone ever seen it?"

Ganymede padded back into the room dragging a bag of chips. He dropped the bag next to his list. Ignoring everyone, he tore open the bag with his teeth and chowed down.

"None of this makes a lick of sense." Katie the cook-slash-security-expert sniffed as she brushed a few crumbs from her skirt. "It's a recipe for insanity."

Kal rose from his chair to pace. "What do we do with this stuff once we get it?" He included everyone in his hard stare. "And even if we do the impossible and find someone with enough magical power to create this . . ." He turned to Walt. "What is it?"

"Gleipnir. It's a soft, thin ribbon with enough strength to control even Fenrir."

"Right. So even if we had that, who's going to volunteer to tie this werewolf up?" He scanned their faces.

Most of his audience found something interesting to study on the floor.

Ganymede looked up from his chips. "To heck with this magic stuff. I can come up with a battle plan."

Declan pictured Ganymede as a general. He'd probably stop in the middle of the battle to eat a candy bar. That was too scary for him, so he went back to staring at Daria. She caught him this time.

"What?" She smiled at him.

"Your face."

She reached up to touch it. "Yeah, I have one."

"I like it." He thought over that comment. "Not that I didn't like your last one, but this one is really you, so it's special."

"Thank you, Declan Mackenzie."

Her eyes were warm with an emotion he wasn't sure he wanted to put a name to. *You're a coward, Mackenzie.* He was just getting used to his awakened emotions, and the one he felt when he looked at Daria scared him more than an army of berserkers. He understood how to fight the berserkers. He didn't have a clue what to do with his feelings for her.

"Yo, bloodsucker. Why don't you (chomp) run down to the cellar (chomp) and bring up a sack of cement (chomp)?" Who said you couldn't eat and talk at the same time?

"Why don't you bring it up yourself?" Good, Declan could take his frustration out on Ganymede.

"I'm a cat. No opposable thumbs. Besides, I have to run this meeting. Okay, now the rest of you, someone needs to volunteer for the roots of a mountain."

Declan thought about arguing with Ganymede but decided it wasn't worth the effort. Maybe getting away from Daria for a few minutes would clear his mind. He stood and headed for the back of the inn, where the door to the cellar was.

"Wait for me, wait for me." Trouble galloped up and skidded to a stop on the hardwood floor. "I'll come with you." His tail wagged the whole dog. "It's boring here. Ganymede takes me outside, but I can't go far. I can't chase anything."

Declan grinned. "Tough times, pup." He opened the cellar door and peered down into the darkness. When he threw the light switch, nothing happened. "Looks like someone didn't replace a bulb." He shook his head at Trouble. "You stay up here. I bet there're lots of things down here that could get a dog in hot water with Ganymede."

Trouble's ears and tail drooped. "I'll be good."

Jeez, this was pathetic. Declan felt sorry for the kid. Before the Woo Woo Inn and Daria, he would've shrugged and walked away. "Look, let me go down first and check it out. If it looks safe, you can come down."

Trouble sat down, his mouth hanging open in a happy grin. "I'll wait right here."

Declan was busy thinking about Daria as he walked down the steps. The dark wasn't a problem thanks to his enhanced vision. He reached the bottom and spotted the bag of cement. Too late. The guy wielding it had already started his swing. *Crap.* That was his last thought before impact.

When he regained consciousness, he was being dragged across the backyard to where Midgard in human form waited just outside the Guardians' power range. There'd been a clumsy attempt to tie him up, but only an idiot would think rope could hold a vampire.

He studied the dragger. As the dragee, he figured he was owed some answers. He'd get them fast and then free himself before they reached Midgard.

"This is the advantage of being a shifter. First you knock me out while you're in human form. That's smart because your animal form couldn't hold a cement bag. Then after you shove me out the cellar window you change to animal form to do the dragging. One thing I'd like to know, though, is why you're doing this, Mel?"

Mel didn't look back. "*I'm not going to die for you, vampire. They want you. In exchange I get to walk away from this damn place with some extra cash in my pocket. Easy decision.*"

He had to talk mentally when he was in his animal form. Not as powerful as the troublemakers or Fenrir. Interesting.

"If you were that afraid of dying, why'd you stay in the first place? You could've left with the others. And how'd you know I'd go down to the cellar?" They were getting closer to Midgard. Declan needed to cut things short.

"*I had business here. But that guy waiting for you offered me more money. And I didn't know you'd end up in the cellar. I was hanging near the parlor entrance when Ganymede asked you to get that cement. I'm an opportunist. I saw my chance and got there before you.*" Mel didn't elaborate on the "business" that had brought him to the inn.

Hmm. Maybe Mel really was the judge Daria thought he was. Declan sank some subtle energy probes into the ground. Just enough to slow the wererabbit down a little. If he wasn't so pissed, he'd probably laugh at that fluffy white tail bobbing along in front of him.

"So how'd they get to you?" Declan put down more energy, adding to the drag.

The wererabbit was beginning to pant. *"How the hell does someone get this heavy just drinking blood?"* He yanked Declan a few more steps while Midgard paced impatiently along the gargoyles' boundary. *"They talked inside my head. We made the deal, and now I'm delivering you."*

Don't be too sure of that. Declan prepared to burst free and inflict some payback. He only had to feed about once a week, but he could make an exception for the dumb bunny here. "It didn't occur to you that delivering me meant you'd simply die a few days later? I'm the final piece in the puzzle. After me comes the big battle. Then? No more universe, and no more Mel."

"I don't believe that shit."

Declan tensed to make his escape, but a low rumbling growl put everything on hold. It came from behind him, a warning that someone was seriously ticked. Instinctively, he ducked. Just in time, as Trouble launched himself over Declan and onto Mel with enough force to bring a grunt from the oversized rabbit.

Tethered to Declan by a rope around his shoulders, Mel was getting tangled in his own stupidity as he tried to fight off the angry dog.

Declan freed himself and then took stock of the battle. Wow, Trouble had come of age with a vengeance. He'd latched on to one of Mel's long ears and was shaking it like a favorite chew toy.

Since Trouble seemed to have everything under control, Declan turned to stare at Midgard. His uncle looked disgusted.

Declan grinned. "Next time pick someone smarter."

With a muttered oath, Midgard turned and walked away.

When Declan turned back, Trouble had Mel pinned to the ground. The shifter had returned to human form. "You can let him up now. I'll take him inside."

Trouble seemed reluctant, but he finally released Mel. "I did it, I did it. Did you see me do it?" He bounced around his defeated enemy as Declan hauled Mel to his feet and then shoved him toward the inn. "You didn't call me and then I heard a noise, so I sneaked down to see what was happening. He pushed you out the window and then dragged you away. I knew I had to help you because you helped me. And I did, didn't I? I saved you!"

"You're a hero. Everyone will be proud of you." Declan wondered if he'd ever been that young and enthusiastic. If he had, he didn't remember it. Wait, come to think of it, he'd been feeling pretty enthusiastic around Daria in the last few days.

Declan studied Mel. Then he smiled. "You know, I was wondering why you even bothered to take your animal form for this. You're big enough to just heave me over your shoulder and carry me out to Midgard. But now I understand. I bet I couldn't find one muscle hidden in all that flab. You need to spend serious time in the gym."

He got Mel inside, only pausing long enough to find a throw the were could wrap around himself. Then he marched him to the parlor with Trouble trailing behind talking nonstop about his adventure. Everyone grew still, staring at Declan as he shoved Mel into the middle of the room.

"Our friend here bashed me in the head with a bag of cement and then dragged me outside to trade to Midgard for some cash. It seems my relatives were anxious for my return to their loving arms, so they did a mental search until they found a weak link."

There was a collective gasp. Declan glanced at Daria. He smiled. From the expression on her face, Mel might want to ask for police protection.

Trouble was still bouncing up and down, his tongue flapping in the breeze. "I saved him, I saved him. Me. I jumped on top of the rabbit and bit his ear." The dog looked at Ganymede.

Daria interrupted her death stare aimed at Mel to look at the cat. She didn't know if her message would reach Ganymede, but she threw it out there anyway. *"Please don't crush him. He's just a kid, and he wants your praise."*

Ganymede turned to look at her with those strange cat eyes. *"Message received."* Then he turned to Trouble. "You did good, kid. I'm proud of you. Next time I'm planning to create chaos somewhere, maybe I'll let you tag along."

Trouble's big brown eyes grew wide. "I can go with you?" Then he looked around the room. "I can go with him." Unable to contain his happiness, he raced from the room barking excitedly.

Sparkle frowned. "You will *not* take him anywhere dangerous."

"Yeah, yeah." Ganymede stared at Mel. "What should we do with him? We can't turn him over to the cops. What would we tell them? A wererabbit tried to turn one of the guests over to a giant snake? Wouldn't work." He grew thoughtful. "Maybe we need a more permanent solution."

Mel paled. His gaze skittered around the room until he found Eris. "Do something. You hired me. Get me out of this mess."

Eris tried to brazen it out. "I didn't hire you to do *that*. You got caught working for someone else."

Mel wasn't the judge. Daria sighed her relief. Then she stood and walked over to Eris. "What *did* you hire him to do?"

Mel didn't give Eris a chance to answer. "She wanted me to spy on you and report back to her. If you looked like you might snatch someone, I was supposed to stop you. When I told her how many nonhumans were staying at the inn, she decided to come here too."

"You're a dead bitch walking." Daria didn't know what she would've done if the sound of screeching hadn't interrupted her.

"Out front." Declan still held Mel.

Everyone rushed to the window. The inn had floodlights that turned on automatically once night fell, so everyone had a clear view of what waited outside.

Daria took one glance before looking back at Declan. "Aello." This wouldn't be pretty.

"Mommy's here." Eris had reverted to childlike glee. "You'll all be sorry now." She threw Sparkle a vindictive glare.

Mama harpy was so loud, Fenrir probably heard her out by the church. "Tell those freaking gargoyles to let me in. My baby better be okay."

Ganymede stood on his hind legs to peer out the window. "Now, that's ugly." He glanced at Katie. "Call off the Guardians so she can come in."

Katie pressed her lips together and looked disapproving, but she chanted the words that would allow Aello to pass.

Ganymede stared up at Sparkle. "Pick me up."

Scooping the cat into her arms, Sparkle avoided his gaze.

Daria glanced at Declan. He looked grim. Grimness *should* be the expression of the moment.

Then the door crashed open and Aello made her entrance. Everyone in the room fell away from her except Eris. She ran to her mother.

"Look what Sparkle Stardust *did* to me." Her beautiful blue eyes overflowed with tears.

The sound of breaking glass played a counterpoint to Aello's scream of fury when she got a good look at her daughter.

Aello was tough to look at even when she wasn't mad at something, which wasn't often. Now she was a grotesque monster. Daria looked at her and knew she could never achieve that kind of greatness. And surprisingly, she didn't think she wanted to anymore.

Aello swiveled her head to scowl at everyone in the room. Her face looked as if she'd been in the grave a few days too long and her hair was matted and long. If Daria peered closely enough, she could almost see things moving in that hair. Aello had prettied herself up for this visit.

"Who is Sparkle Stardust?"

"She's right here, death-breath." Ganymede sounded barely interested.

Sparkle didn't look as though she appreciated Ganymede giving away her position.

Aello drew her lips away from brown and rotted teeth. "Return my daughter to her former ugliness."

Sparkle opened her mouth to answer, but Ganymede beat her to it. "Your daughter's an idiot, so I think she'll stay the way she is."

Sparkle threw Daria frantic glances. Daria shrugged. She didn't think there was a power on earth that could make Ganymede close his mouth.

Aello responded to the challenge by becoming harpy. Everyone scrambled away from her, and the room seemed a lot smaller with those huge wings taking up so much space. "You and Sparkle Stardust will be playthings for Hades this night."

Ganymede yawned.

Daria moved close to Declan. He still held on to Mel. "What's Ganymede doing? Doesn't he know how powerful Aello is? He's crazy to make her mad." She was starting to worry about the cat and Sparkle.

"He's protecting his woman." He turned away and she almost didn't catch the rest of what he said. "The way I'd protect you."

Something important had just gone down, but Daria didn't have time to think about it because Aello chose that moment to make her move. She spread her wings before leaping at Sparkle and Ganymede.

She smacked up against an invisible wall. Enraged, she screamed her defiance as she gathered herself for another try. *Splat.* Daria smiled. Well, well. And the winner is . . . the cat.

Ganymede looked bored. "Take your daughter and get out of here, harpy. Oh, and don't think you can sneak around and catch us by surprise. Try touching Sparkle or me again and I'll twist off your head. It might not stop global warming, but it'll make the world a prettier place."

Aello ignored him in favor of turning on her daughter. "Snatch someone *now.* Your beauty is a disgrace to the whole harpy sisterhood, but at least you can bring something back to Hades."

Panicked, Eris scanned the room. "There isn't anyone. I can't—"

Mel chose that moment to jerk free from Declan and make a dash for freedom. A few seconds later, the slamming of the door awoke Eris to a possibility.

"*Him*. I can take *him* back." She raced for the door, her mother close behind her.

As both harpies burst from the inn, everyone ran to the window again.

Mel had almost reached the tree line. He'd already become wererabbit and was covering the ground in giant leaps. Eris took harpy form and flung herself into the air along with Aello. The last anyone saw, Mel was disappearing into the woods and the harpies were circling around trying to locate him.

Everybody went back to his or her seat, and for a few minutes no one said anything. Sparkle put Ganymede carefully on the floor. The cat padded over to his list. It had holes in it from Aello's talons.

"So, bloodsucker, did you get my cement?" Ganymede stared at the chips scattered over the carpet. "And I'm still waiting for someone to volunteer to find the roots of a mountain."

Katie grunted. "If it shuts you up, I'll conjure up a few roots of a mountain. Now I have to get the Guardians up and running again."

Sparkle finally found her voice. She glanced at her broken nail as though noticing it for the first time. "Do you see what happens when women totally ignore their appearance? Who wouldn't be bad-tempered if they had to wake up each morning to see a face desperate for moisturizer and teeth that needed at least a three-month supply of those whitening strips." She shuddered. "Did you see that woman's broken and jagged nails? I'll have nightmares for weeks." But she didn't jump up to fix her own nail.

That bothered Daria. She wondered if Ganymede realized how depressed Sparkle was. Or if he even cared. She had to believe he did.

"Let's get that cement." Declan stood.

Daria jumped at the chance to leave the parlor. Once out of the room, she stopped to glance in a mirror. "I'm wearing one of Sparkle's dresses." The gold one. She'd wanted to look special the first time Declan saw her without Kal's magic. "And my face isn't harpy anymore." She felt sort of strange. "There's nothing of the old me left." The scary part was that she couldn't dredge up any nostalgia for the old Daria.

"You have a great face." He sounded fierce about that.

He made her feel warm and wanted. She wouldn't try to push her feelings away anymore. "Mom might not think so. I didn't want to upset anyone after what just happened, but my mother and aunt will be dropping in tonight. Mom won't be any more understanding than Aello was."

He nodded. "We'll deal."

That's all. He'd made it so simple. For the first time in her life, she felt it was okay to share a burden. She didn't have to be Super Harpy with him.

Daria stayed at the top of the steps and let Declan go down for the cement. Sparkle's gold sandals didn't do cellar steps well. Trouble went with Declan. The dog was probably hoping he'd find another bad guy hiding in the dark.

Declan had started back up the steps with the cement bag slung across his shoulder when they heard Katie.

"Can anyone explain why there are two more of those women waiting outside? Did someone put up a sign promising reduced rates for harpies? Who *are* these people?"

Daria sighed as she walked back to the parlor. "That's my mom and my aunt."

She could see that Katie wanted to say something snarky, but instead she glanced at Ganymede.

"Let them in." Ganymede was already padding toward the kitchen for more chips.

CHAPTER SEVENTEEN

Daria held the door open for her mother. "Hi, Mom." An ordinary greeting to an extraordinary woman. If Celaeno wasn't her mother, she'd terrify Daria. Mom wasn't as ugly as Aello, but she was a lot scarier.

"Get Kal. We'll all go to your room." Mom didn't waste time on pesky greetings. Nothing of the shock she must be feeling at her daughter's appearance showed in her eyes.

Aunt Ocypete pushed through the door. "Hi . . ." She stopped to stare. "What happened to you?" All her horror was wrapped up in those four words.

Daria put off answering her aunt for the moment. "Stay here." She left them standing there while she slipped into the parlor.

The meeting had broken up and everyone was milling around. Daria spotted Kal talking to Sparkle, so she joined them.

Sparkle wore her sensual siren expression. "Mmm. You never told me your brother was so yummy, Daria." She slid her fingers over Kal's arm and looked up at him from under her lashes. "We need to discuss battle tactics, hunky harpy." The moment lacked a certain sizzle, though, because Sparkle's gaze drifted to Ganymede as he returned to the parlor.

If Mom and Aunt Ocypete weren't waiting for them, Daria would have stuck around just to see how Kal extricated himself from Sparkle's sexy tentacles.

"I hate to break up the conversation, but Mom wants

to see us in my room, Kal." Daria didn't miss the flare of curiosity in Sparkle's eyes. Glancing around, Daria noticed that Declan was missing. "Where's Declan?"

"He went to get something for Mede. If Mede would take human form, he could get stuff himself, but he likes people to wait on him." Sparkle made a moue of disappointment at Kal. "Go, and I'll catch you later."

Knowing Sparkle, she literally meant *catch*.

Kal followed Daria out into the hallway to where Mom and their aunt still waited. Mom took one look at Kal and sucked in her breath. "Have both of you gone completely crazy?"

Aunt Ocypete didn't say anything at all. She just put her hand over her mouth and looked at Kal and Daria from wide, shocked eyes.

Daria sighed. This wouldn't be fun. Climbing the stairs, she tried to think of something she could say that would make it better for Mom. Nope, nothing came to mind. It wasn't until she was about to push open her door that she remembered exactly what her room looked like.

"Jeez, sis, do you think you have enough pictures of Declan?" He looked around. "Sparkle?"

"Who else?" Daria had forgotten that her brother had never seen her room.

Mom and Aunt Ocypete seemed a little shell-shocked as they sat on the couch. Kal and she perched on the chairs. Kal threw her a worried glance. Yeah, he knew this would be tough.

Mom folded her hands in her lap as she studied them with narrow-eyed intensity. "Tell me why both of you look like humans."

Kal wore a rebellious expression. "I want to have sex with someone who wants me as much as I want her. The harpies won't have anything to do with me because I'm not authentic enough. Human women run screaming from me." He stared at his hands. Even her big brave brother became a boy again when Mom was around. "I can never be the real deal in our world, so I'm choosing to be accepted in this one. At least while I'm at the Woo Woo Inn." He looked up to meet his mother's gaze. "I met this hot wereleopard while I was here. She left when it got too dangerous. I don't know if I'll ever see her again, but I know I want someone."

Daria noted that Kal wanted to have *sex*. She wanted to make *love*. Did that mean she was further along on the relationship evolutionary path than her brother? Thought-provoking.

Mom didn't say anything, she just turned her attention to Daria. "What about you?

Daria took a deep breath. *Here goes nothing.* She started with Sparkle's stupid bet and ended with how she'd asked Kal not to use his magic on her while she was at the inn. She'd left out the part about the universe ending on the summer solstice. No need to rush the revelations.

When she finished, Mom leaned back against the couch and closed her eyes. "I was afraid this might happen if I turned you loose in the human world. But you had to take the test, so there was no way to avoid it." She opened her eyes. "I want to meet this Declan Mackenzie. And I definitely want to meet Sparkle Stardust." Her smile was a terrible thing to see.

Aunt Ocypete hadn't joined in the conversation. She'd gotten up to look out the window. "I'm not sure if this is a neighborly visit, but there's a big snake, a woman with half white and half black hair, and a bunch of giants coming out of the woods."

"What?" Daria, along with Kal and Celaeno, rushed to the window.

Uh-oh. That's all Daria had time to think before Midgard, Hel, and the giants launched their attack on the inn.

The Woo Woo Inn shook with the sounds of exploding energy bursts and the yells of the giants. The Guardians roared their defiance. The blasts of power lasted for about five minutes before the attackers melted back into the forest.

Aunt Ocypete turned from the window, excitement glittering in her eyes. "Wow, did you see that snake? And those deliciously hideous giants could stand with their feet flat on the ground and stare in this second-floor window. I want the one with the horn growing out of his chin." She looked at Mom. "Have you ever seen a snake like that?"

Mom looked thoughtful as she turned from the window. "That wasn't a snake."

"It wasn't?" Could've fooled Daria.

"That was Midgard the serpent. He has to take snake form when he moves on land, but in the ocean he's a sea serpent. The woman was Hel, and the rest of them were frost giants." She threw Daria a hard stare. "Now would be a good time to tell me why they're here."

"Maybe I should be the one to explain that." Declan stood in the doorway, his expression grim.

Mom studied him for what seemed like hours before nodding.

Declan looked at Daria. "I wanted to make sure you were all right after the attack." He smiled. "The Guardians held them off, and since Fenrir wasn't with them, I'm assuming he's still bound to the church. That's the good part. The bad part is they brought those giants with them. Who the hell were *they*?"

"Frost giants. Primitive beings who're enemies of the

gods." Mom moved over so there'd be room for him on the couch. "Sit down. I'm Celaeno, Daria and Kal's mother. And that's Ocypete, their aunt."

Declan nodded at her aunt and then met Mom's gaze directly. He didn't look scared or nervous. Daria awarded him a bunch of points for that. Not many people kept their cool when they met Mom for the first time.

He sat down next to her mother. "Long story short, my mother was a Mackenzie vampire and my dad is Fenrir. He's bound under a church near here. He's about to bust loose and come looking for me. I'm supposed to be the big sacrifice right before he, Midgard, Hel, Loki, and the ever-popular forces of evil take down the other gods. All this is supposed to happen on the night of the summer solstice. If it goes down as planned, the universe ends. No more me and no more you."

Mom looked stunned, not an expression Daria had seen often on her face. "Not a storyteller, are you?"

"Is that what you wanted?"

She shook her head. "No, I like my information concise and accurate." Her expression relaxed a little.

"Good." He smiled.

Daria's breath caught in her throat. Too bad she didn't have time to study all the nuances of that smile. "We need your help, Mom."

Aunt Ocypete moved away from the window, her expression eager. "You want help taking out the bunch we just saw outside?"

Daria's aunt didn't have a lot to say, but when she was pursuing a victim, she was relentless. Aunt Ocypete never came back empty-handed.

Daria nodded.

Declan stood. "Hate to cut this short, but I have some-

thing to do downstairs. I just came up to check on you."
He smiled at Mom. "I'm sure we'll talk again."

Mom didn't smile back. "I'm sure we will."

They all watched Declan leave the room. Daria wished
she could go with him.

"He's a compelling male by human or vampire standards. I understand why you're drawn to him, Daria." Her
mother's voice softened. "I felt that way about your father
once. Apollo is everything harpy men aren't. It was unfortunate for both of you that I was drawn to males outside the harpy world." She looked at her son. "You look
like him, Kal, and you've suffered for it." Her attention
returned to Daria. "You've spent a lifetime trying to mold
yourself into something you thought I wanted." Moisture
shimmered in eyes Daria thought weren't capable of tears.
"I apologize to both of you."

Tears? From Mom? The concept struck Daria speechless. This was the first time Mom had talked to them
about Apollo.

And then the moment was gone, along with Mom's
tears. "I know you didn't want me to see all this." She ges-
tured at her wayward children and then widened her
sweep to include the room with its Décor by Sparkle. "So
that means you want something badly enough to chance
my visit."

Daria nodded. *Careful.* "Kal and I never talked to you
about our father because we figured the subject was off-
limits."

Mom nodded.

"But now the fate of the universe is up for grabs—"

"Along with Declan's fate." Mom didn't miss much.

"Yeah, that too." Daria felt the heat rising in her face.
"A guy who was doing some research for me came up

with a list of things we could use to make a ribbon strong enough to hold Fenrir." She fidgeted, a nervous holdover from a childhood filled with lots of fidgeting in front of Mom. "We're trying to gather those things. Once we have them, we'll need someone with strong enough magic to change them into this ribbon." She gathered her courage to ask what needed asking.

Mom took away the need. "You want me to ask Apollo to do this for you."

"Yes." No elaboration necessary.

Her mother sighed. "I've never asked Apollo for anything. I've never spoken to him since the night Kal and you were conceived. I suppose the fate of the universe and Declan might be reason enough to do so now."

Daria knew her relief must be a bright golden glow around her.

Kal stepped in. "Would you and Aunt Ocypete consider helping us fight Fenrir?"

Daria's aunt didn't need any thinking time. "I love a fight. And when it's over, I'll have my choice of prizes for Hades. That yummy giant with the horn would be perfect."

His mother smiled. "Definitely. I'll have a lot of stress to work out by that time." She was all business now. "Take me down to meet the others."

As Daria walked into the parlor with her mother and aunt in tow, she watched everyone's reaction. It was always the same.

Her aunt looked more like Aello, your typical gross and disgusting harpy. But Mom was different. Her face was terrifying as opposed to ugly. When you looked into Mom's eyes, you saw your death. Her lips were thin, and when she pressed them together, they promised no pity for any victim she chose.

Mom smiled at everyone in the room. Everyone in the room gulped.

Her mother's smile was her most powerful weapon. All of her teeth were very white and very pointed. She gave everyone a preview of what they'd see when the shark opened its mouth just before ripping them apart.

"Hey, everyone. This is Celaeno, my mom, and Ocypete, my aunt. They're going to help us defeat Fenrir." Daria scanned the room. Where was Declan?

There were the usual welcoming words, but underlying the one-for-all attitude, Daria sensed a lot of omigod feelings among certain members of the audience. Namely Walt and the three young werewolves. The others? Not so much.

Kal didn't stick around. He moved away to join another group.

Ocypete could always spot a weak link, so she hurried over to Walt. Daria didn't have time to rescue him.

Sparkle didn't even try to look casual as she made for Daria and her mother. Uh-oh. Daria hoped Mom understood the importance of troop morale here. It wouldn't do to have fellow fighters trying to kill each other. "Mom, this is Sparkle Stardust. Sparkle, this is my mom."

The queen of sex and sin smiled. "I'd love to help you be the best you can be."

The queen of death and despair *didn't* smile. "I'd love to rip out your throat."

Sparkle didn't miss a beat. "Too bad we all can't get what we want." Her gaze flicked to Ganymede.

Since it didn't look like an extreme makeover for Celaeno was in the offing, she turned her attention to Daria. "See, under all that magic you have a face that could be beautiful with the right makeup."

"My daughter doesn't want to be beautiful."

Speak for yourself, Mom. Daria figured if she'd come this far, she might as well go all the way. She wasn't stupid, though. No way would she admit that in front of Mom. But Mom couldn't say too much if Daria lost the bet again tonight. After all, the terms of a bet had to be honored.

For once, Sparkle showed good sense by not contradicting Daria's mother. "You're probably wondering where Declan is. He should be back any minute. He went to collect his fish. Katie has shut down the Guardians for a few minutes."

Daria didn't even have time to feel horrified before Declan walked into the parlor. Every time she saw him was like seeing him for the first time. He was wearing his sexy leather coat, and as he moved she could see the hilt of his sword. At least he'd taken a weapon with him. His dark hair was windblown, and he held a clear plastic bag filled with water. Two minnows swam around inside the bag.

"You can add breath of fishes to your done list, Ganymede." He spotted Daria, her mother, and Sparkle watching him. From the look on Daria's face, she wasn't thrilled that he'd gone for the fish without her knowing. Well, might as well face her now as later. Handing his fish to Katie, he went to join them.

Daria gave him a narrow-eyed stare. "You went alone." Definitely an accusation.

"Everyone else was busy. I was armed, I was careful, and I came home safely. End of story." Declan was matter-of-fact about it, but her concern made him feel good. He'd gone into danger so many times in his life when no one cared whether he made it out or not. Sometimes *he* didn't even care.

Daria pressed her lips together and said nothing. But her eyes said everything. She was mad because she'd been scared for him.

He didn't get time to enjoy that revelation, because Ganymede leaped onto the fireplace's mantel and spoke.

"We're almost done here. We have everything except the woman's beard." Ganymede glanced at the unopened bag of cement. "You lugged that bag out of the cellar for nothing, bloodsucker. Sparkle got to thinking about how long it would take the cement to harden and came up with another idea. Cindy had some clay. It was with the teddy bears. Sparkle just flattened that clay out and pressed my feet into it. Instant cat footsteps."

"Hey, no problem." Declan felt a need for sarcasm. "I almost got myself kidnapped—which would've led to the end of the universe—for that bag of cement."

Cats were good at blank stares. "We need a lady with a beard so we can get this show on the road. Donate. It's for a good cause."

Celaeno leaned close to Sparkle. "*You* have a hair sticking out of your chin. Someone get me a baggie and tweezers."

Sparkle widened her eyes in horror. "I've *never* had facial hair. A hair wouldn't dare grow on my face. This is just a cheap harpy attempt to blacken my character."

"Get me a mirror too." Daria's mom was smiling. "I don't know what your problem is. A chin hair is a harpy badge of honor."

"Ack!" Sparkle grabbed the mirror Katie put in her hand.

Daria winced. Declan saw why. There was a short hair under Sparkle's chin.

"Omigod! Hand me the freaking tweezers." Sparkle put one hand over her heart. "I think I'm having palpitations."

"Let me do it." Before Sparkle could object, Celaeno took the tweezers from Katie and plucked the hair from Sparkle's chin. Then she dropped the hair into the open baggie Katie held. "I'll keep this."

Sparkle didn't respond. She was staring into the mirror with unblinking intensity.

"Yo, ba . . . uh, a hair here and there shows character." Ganymede meant well, but his compliment was a dart to the heart of the Woo Woo Inn's queen of vanity.

She glared at him. "Say one more thing and I'll use those tweezers in new and creative ways."

Ouch. Every man in the room winced.

Walt dragged over a plastic trash bag. "All the stuff is in here."

Celaeno dropped in the hair and then tied the bag shut. "I'll take this to Apollo and ask him to make your magic ribbon. Let's hope he's not in a bad mood and that he's susceptible to feelings of guilt. Ocypete, you can stay here."

"Be careful." Daria touched her mother's hand. "When will you be back?"

"Summer solstice is only a few nights away. I'll be back before that, with or without the ribbon. I won't let you and Kal go into battle without me."

Declan watched Daria as her mother left. He decided Celaeno couldn't be a monster if she inspired so much love. That opinion came from a guy who had lots of experience being a monster.

Once her mother was gone, Daria wandered toward the stairs. Declan followed her. She waited for him. When he reached her, he put his arms around her. It took him a moment to realize she wasn't looking at him.

He turned to see who'd caught her interest. Sparkle was standing close by, still staring into the mirror.

"Hey, Sparkle." Daria waved at her. "See this?"

Sparkle looked a little disoriented. "What?"

Daria reached up and pulled Declan's head down. Then

she put her mouth over his and laid a kiss on him that almost made his knees buckle. When she finally broke the kiss, she glanced at Sparkle.

"Put it in the record books, Sparkle, because that was a certified lust-filled touch."

CHAPTER EIGHTEEN

The last few nights, Declan's awakening had been a three-step thought process: awareness, Daria, other problems. This night was no different. He'd lain in bed a few minutes anticipating seeing his favorite harpy, talking over the day's plans with her, and touching her. Yeah, so he'd spent the most time on the touching part.

Reluctantly, he went on to his checklist of the good, the bad, and the ugly from last night: Celaeno left last night to ask Apollo for huge favor—check and fingers crossed. Mel and Eris gone—check and thank the gods. Frost giants entered battle on Fenrir's side—check and multiple curses. Daria kissed him and then spent rest of night running errands for Ganymede—check and threaten to strangle cat.

There. Satisfied he'd covered all the important events of last night, he rose and got ready for a new night. Before leaving his room, he strapped on his sword. He didn't bother taking his coat. If his weapon shocked someone, too bad.

Declan was halfway down the stairs when his cell rang. As he continued to the bottom of the steps, he pulled the phone from his jeans pocket and answered. "Yeah?" This wasn't a night for wasted words.

"Valgard."

Relief washed over him. He'd been afraid the council members wouldn't make it in time. "When will you be here?"

The silence dragged on for a little too long. "Uh, we'd really like to be there, Declan. You know how we love a fight." False laughter. "But, um, the British government revoked our passports."

"Why?" Declan hoped pissed-off-vampire was coming across loud and clear.

"Uh . . ." Whispered aside. "Why the bloody hell did they revoke our passports?" A whispered answer Declan couldn't hear. "Er, we were the victims of physical and emotional trauma that made us mentally unstable." Valgard's voice brightened. "We could be a danger to ourselves or others." He seemed pretty happy about that. "But we have every confidence you'll defeat this Fenrir."

Declan did some counting to achieve inner calm. Backward. "What you're saying is Sparkle scared the crap out of you last year, and you're afraid if you show up at the Woo Woo Inn, she might steal your equipment again."

Some blustering went on at the other end of the line.

"But you know something? Sparkle wouldn't be able to do a damn thing this time because you've already lost your balls." He closed his cell phone and shoved it into his pocket.

Well, that was a great start to the night. He felt the slide of his fangs and curled his lip back just to express how much he'd like to rip out a few cowardly throats.

He'd only taken a few steps toward the parlor when he saw Daria sitting at the registration desk. She didn't even pretend not to be watching for him. Her smile kickstarted his whole evening.

When he leaned down to kiss her, he didn't think about possible watchers or if this would compromise his uncommitted loner status. Declan was beyond that.

Her lips were warm and soft, her mouth hot and welcoming, his body hard and determined. Tonight they'd make love. In *his* bed and in *his* room, the one without a Sparkle upgrade. No more forest floors or Ferris wheels.

"Is your mother back?" Declan tried to hold up his half of the conversation while his senses pushed and shoved to get his attention. *Hey, did you get a look at that gold dress? It's the kind of dress that looks good coming off. What about that vanilla scent? Bet it's her shampoo. Go take a sniff. Wonder if she tastes like vanilla too? Go on, you know you want to, just a little bite.* Okay, enough. He slammed the door shut on their chatter.

"No." Her eyes clouded with worry.

A week ago he would've grunted and walked away. He didn't do sympathy. But now he shifted into distract-and-cheer-up mode. "Your mom's a tough lady. She'll be back soon. Looks like everyone's in the parlor. Let's see what's going on."

Ganymede was crouched on the mantel when they walked in. Everyone was scattered around the room.

Sparkle wandered over to them. She still wore a sexy black dress, but she didn't seem to have the, well, sparkle she usually had.

Daria nudged him. "She's wearing the same dress and shoes as yesterday."

"So?"

"Sign of serious depression. I'm worried about her."

Jeez, he was a guy. Nothing in his code of manliness addressed how to figure out women's emotional states by the clothes they wore. It was all a mystery.

Sparkle stopped and smiled. Declan narrowed his eyes. Yeah, it *was* kind of a sad smile.

"Ganymede's getting ready to let us all in on his battle

plan." Sparkle shrugged. "Not that I care. Let Fenrir and Loki trash the universe. It's a crappy world anyway."

Daria looked shocked. "Sometimes. I guess." She glanced at Declan.

He raised one brow.

"I thought since you won the bet last night, you might want to demand I wear makeup." Daria looked hopeful.

Sparkle waved a dismissive hand. "Whatever. If that's what you want, we can do it after Ganymede's speech."

"Mind if I tag along?" He didn't know if makeup was such a good idea. Daria already looked great to him.

For a moment, Sparkle seemed to regain her sense of humor. "Men are so predictable. Let me guess. I'd say from your expression, you think you're a guy who likes the natural look." She cocked her head to study Daria. "She's too pale. Good bone structure, though, but pretty ordinary without color and definition."

He bristled.

"She has potentially gorgeous eyes. I'll make them look bigger, more spectacular. Her lips are full and sensual. She needs a lip shine that'll emphasize their kissability."

Declan thought Daria's lips were already emphatic enough. He didn't want any other men noticing their kissability. Was that being possessive? You bet.

He'd just opened his mouth to express his opinion when a booming voice from outside rattled the windows.

"Fenrir the terrible is here." Sounds of hearty cheering. "Son of Loki the trickster, brother of Hel the queen of death and Midgard the serpent, father of—"

Declan couldn't take any more. Ignoring Daria's attempt to stop him, he flung open the door. "Declan, son of a horse's ass, is here."

Fenrir's forces were spread across the lawn behind the

Guardians' invisible line. And Fenrir himself stood in front. In human form.

The reality of their relationship hit Declan smack in the face. His father looked a lot like him. Only bigger. And meaner. And more arrogant. Some of his own arrogance must've come from Fenrir.

Fenrir ignored the horse's ass comment. "I am no longer amused by your insolence, Declan." He sneered as he scanned the front of the inn. "How can you hide away in this veritable mouse hole? I will not insult my army by ordering them to waste their energy destroying this hovel."

Daria edged up beside Declan. "Translation: his army can't get past the Guardians."

"I came here only to show that I am no longer bound to the church." Fenrir looked as if he was savoring his next words. "And to deliver an ultimatum."

"Love those ultimatums. It's my latent need to have a man tell me what to do." Daria.

"If you do not turn yourself over to me after you rise on the eve of the summer solstice, my minions will destroy the town closest to this place." Fenrir smiled but looked kind of wistful. "I would wish you to be late."

Declan saw in Fenrir's smile the resemblance to Dad's wolf form. It was in the teeth and eyes. "Bet if I stuck a pin in you, all that escaping hot air would heat the whole Jersey shore." Was it smart to make his father crazy angry? No, but it felt so good.

Fenrir threw back his head and roared. The frost giants shouted. Midgard the serpent hissed. And Hel just laughed. Declan decided Hel scared him the most.

Declan didn't even wait for all of them to leave before slamming the door shut. When he and Daria turned, everyone standing behind him hurried back into the parlor.

Ocypete lingered. "My frost giant was out there. Did you see him? So big, so savage, so fine. He's mine. If Celaeno hadn't told me to stay here, I'd go and collect my guy right now."

Trying to imagine that mating gave Daria a pain right in the middle of her left eye. She reached out to clasp Declan's hand. No matter how he denied it, facing his father couldn't be easy.

They entered the parlor just in time to watch Ganymede leap onto the mantel again.

"Yo, we don't have time to waste. We have to get our battle plan moving. Here's what I've worked out. First—"

The strains of "Heartbreak Hotel" sounded in the distance.

"Hell." Ganymede's eyes widened. "The last container of Ben & Jerry's."

Everyone waited expectantly as the music grew louder and louder until it stopped in the parking lot.

Ganymede glared at Katie. "Tune up your broom. Make magic circles until you run outta chalk. But figure out how to keep that . . . darn guy out."

Katie set her lips in a thin line of disapproval. "I'll break open my new box of colored chalk right away."

A few minutes later the ice cream guy joined them. He smiled at everyone and then sat in an empty chair. Daria could've sworn there weren't any empty chairs a minute ago.

"The cat's cursed so many times, all my desserts are gone. You owe me for them." Katie didn't care *who* he was.

He smiled serenely. "They'll be replaced. I really enjoyed your devil's food cake. You're an excellent cook."

Katie harrumphed but looked pleased.

Ganymede was one nervous kitty. But he pulled it together enough to lay down his plan. "Harpies, air attack. Werewolves and Trouble, ground attack."

"Me, me, me? I can help?" The dog didn't seem to notice everyone else's lack of enthusiasm.

"Declan and Sparkle, covert action. Katie, annoying spells. And Walt, official battle historian. I'm the general." Ganymede looked at the ice cream guy. "Yo, Chill, you gonna be around?"

"Oh, I'm always around. Call me an interested observer." He watched the cat from those strange eyes. "Now that you have this plan, how are you going to execute it?"

Ganymede looked uncomfortable and grumpy all at once. "We'll figure it out as we go along." He looked back at his fighting force. "One more thing. Fenrir expects Declan on the twentieth, so we'll attack on the nineteenth. Catch him by surprise and kick his . . . behind."

Sparkle made her way to Daria, pausing to throw Chill a death glare. Ganymede watched her but didn't try to approach.

"Let's take care of your face now." Sparkle didn't look at Ganymede as she led them from the room. "I'll get my makeup kit and meet you—"

"In *my* room." Declan seemed certain of that.

"Look, you guys go on up and I'll be with you in a few minutes." Daria hoped Declan wouldn't ask any questions. He must've read her expression, because he simply nodded.

Once they'd left she walked over to Chill. "Hi, I'm—"

"Daria." He smiled. "You didn't want Declan and Sparkle to see you doing a good deed."

"Uh, yeah. How'd you know?" He had the strangest eyes she'd ever seen. No matter how hard she stared, she couldn't tell what color they were.

He shrugged. "Knowing things is my business."

Daria decided he had a really nice smile and a great voice. He made her feel . . . peaceful. "I get the feeling from Ganymede that you can do just about anything."

He chuckled. "I try."

She took a deep breath. "Well, here it goes. Would you—"

"Free the chimney-sweep spirit?"

Okay, she was officially weirded out.

Chill glanced at the fireplace and there was a popping sound.

"Yahoo! Freefreefreefree . . ." The voice coming from the chimney faded into the distance.

Everyone stopped to listen, and then conversation picked up again.

Daria swallowed hard. "Thank you."

"Now I want you to do something for me."

"Sure."

"Go where your heart leads you."

She nodded even though she didn't believe her heart could lead her away from Hades. But as she climbed the stairs to Declan's room, she decided she *did* believe that Chill knew a lot about hearts.

A half hour later, Daria stared at a new woman in the mirror. When she turned, she saw that woman reflected in the eyes of Declan Mackenzie. His expression said it all.

"Like the change, hot bod?" Sparkle glanced at Declan.

"I love all her faces."

"Good answer, vampire."

And if there was cynicism in Sparkle's voice, Daria understood. If she had Ganymede here right now, he'd be missing a few tufts of hair.

Sparkle smiled, a sincere one this time. No slyness, no sexy siren. "Don't feel bad for me. I've seen the best and the worst of men over thousands of years. I never expect too much." She shrugged. "It's easier that way. And Ganymede did what he had to do to stay a cosmic troublemaker. I understand." Her expression said like hell she understood. "Well, I'll leave you guys to it." She closed the door gently behind her.

The door had barely closed behind Sparkle before Declan pulled Daria into his embrace. "I like the lip shine, but I like the lips under it better."

He lowered his head and traced her lips with the tip of his tongue. *Tease.* She slid her fingers into all that sexy hair and pulled him closer. And when she parted her lips for him, he didn't say no.

It was a long, drugging kiss, and when it ended she whimpered her disappointment. But he brushed kisses across her cheek and then tugged on her earlobe with his teeth before whispering in her ear, "Let's set the mood."

First he lit two candles, one on each of the night tables. Then he turned off the lights. Finally he returned to her. "We can't control what will happen in two nights, but we *can* control tonight. That's good enough for me right now." He slipped her dress off her shoulders and then slid his tongue across the swell of her breasts. "Ever since I saw this gold dress, I imagined taking it off you." Reaching around, he slid the zipper down.

She wiggled with lots of *this* and lots of *that* as the dress slid to the floor. Daria stepped out of it. His expression made her smile. She'd smiled more since she'd met De-clan Mackenzie than she had in her whole life. "It'll seem strange to make love without any Red Hots or Ferris wheels."

He paused in his hungry scan of her body. "Would you like something special?"

"You're special enough for me." She wondered how he'd feel if he knew exactly how special. She was getting a little too intense for her own good. Time to lighten things up. "I thought about maybe making love inside walls of mirrors, but it would look like I was wrestling with myself."

His soft chuckle warmed her. "Right. You can tell your friends your man doesn't have much substance. Around mirrors."

She tugged at his T-shirt. "Time to show some skin, vampire."

While he pulled off the shirt, she worked at the button on his jeans. He didn't do any wiggling as he shucked them, but Daria's heart still did a few extra ka-thumps. Major discovery. "You wore briefs tonight."

He grinned, and she tucked the memory away in her special vault labeled Memories of Declan.

"The joy isn't just in the making love part, it's in the peeling back of the layers until you get to the bare truth." He pressed her against his chest as he reached around her to unhook her bra.

Contact with that hard male chest dragged a gasp from her. It was an assault by all her senses at once. Warmth like swimming in the Mediterranean. Smooth skin with a slight sprinkling of dark hair to make the texture more interesting. A scent of whatever made one man special to one woman, and only that woman. And the taste of . . . She slid her tongue across his shoulder blade. The taste of the man she . . .

Fine, *she* knew she was thinking "loved." All the *gods* knew she was thinking "loved." But that was okay as long as *he* didn't know she was thinking "loved." Because in a few more nights when she flew to Tartarus with her prey, Hades would absorb her back into his harpy family like an evil giant amoeba.

As he stepped away, allowing her bra to drop to the floor, Daria saw a look she'd never seen before on his face. *Wonder.* And all those emotions harpies weren't supposed to have welled up. Who was she to put that look on his face? Over the centuries of his life he'd seen women more beautiful than she was, but just with the expression in his eyes, he made her feel special.

Daria held her eyes wide and refused to blink. No stupid tears were going to run down *her* face. She was tough, she was hard, she was . . . a sticky puddle of melted marshmallow.

Keep your hands busy and don't think. It was the thinking that triggered her emotions. She fumbled with her panties—unsexy gray that complied with the Harpy dress code—and finally managed to skim them over her hips and legs. Sparkle hadn't supplied underwear. She'd have to buy . . . Daria closed her eyes. What was she thinking? When she left the Woo Woo Inn to go back to her harpy life, she wouldn't need sexy underwear.

Her eyes were closed when Declan rid himself of his briefs. When she opened her eyes, it was a done deal. *Rats.*

But Oh. My. God. He was the most beautiful thing that had ever come into her life. And that image would have to last her the rest of her existence. Waterworks alert! This time she *did* have to blink to stave off disaster.

Declan didn't tell her how gorgeous she was, he just stared at her. Sometimes words got in the way. This was one of those times.

Scooping her up, he moved to the bed and laid her on the chenille bedspread. Then he joined her. Resting on his side, he propped himself up on his elbow. "I've touched so many women over the centuries, but I've never really *touched* someone until you, harpy lady." He smoothed his fingers over her shoulder and down her arm.

Goose bumps raced in his wake, trying to keep up with his magic fingers.

"Because when I touch you, I *feel*." He thumped his fist over his heart.

No more explanation needed. Flat on her back, she looked up into his eyes, the brilliant blue eyes he'd said all Mackenzies had. Well, tonight she'd work extra hard to turn them vampire-black with passion. Tonight he'd taste her in the most elemental way a vampire could.

Holding her gaze, he gently pushed her onto her stomach. And then with the lightest of touches he swept his hand from her shoulders over her back and buttocks before skimming his fingers down the backs of her thighs and legs.

She curled her toes. A reflex action. Evidently one of her on buttons was located in her big toe, because as it did its curling thing, she felt the first twinge of heaviness low in her belly.

He moved so silently that only the give in the mattress signaled he'd shifted to a kneeling position between her spread legs. Leaning over, he pushed her hair aside so he could kiss the back of her neck. Then he nibbled his way down her spine before clasping her bottom in his large hands.

She sucked in her breath. "You're the best nibbler I've ever known." Fine, so he was the *only* nibbler she'd ever known. Male harpies didn't spend much time on foreplay.

His soft chuckle promised lots of nibbling to come.

He massaged her cheeks as he used his tongue to swirl a pattern of desire in the little indentation at the base of her spine. The heaviness built and she dug her fingers into the bedspread to keep herself grounded.

How could whatever he was doing to her back make everything in front so sensitive? She rubbed her nipples back and forth against the bumpy chenille, feeling the push and scrape as exclamation points of pleasure-pain. She clenched around the sensation.

"You're warned, vampire, I'm turning over. Staring at the bed isn't doing it for me." She mumbled her notice-of-change-in-position into the bedspread.

Declan laughed and then nipped her toe. "Guess you'll never stay where I put you. But that's what I . . . like about you."

She rolled over and met his gaze. His eyes were black. And when he smiled at her he showed fang. Good.

"Hey, I'm still here." She touched her breasts and then touched between her thighs so he'd know exactly what parts were available. "Just giving you a new perspective, unknown territory to explore, untamed lands to conquer, challenging—"

"Shut. Up." Then he swooped down on her breasts.

I'm still here. Arching her back, she forced away thoughts of how long she'd be able to say that, of how he'd feel when she was gone.

Daria gave herself over to her senses. His mouth on her breast, the moist heat, the scrape if his teeth, the pulling sensation that seemed directly linked to that spot between her thighs. She clenched and unclenched, feeling the yearning for his erection to push into her, spread her wide, fill her. *All the way to her heart.*

The pressure low in her body dragged small whimpers

from her. She thrust her hips toward him in a bit of unspoken communication that went like, "If you don't hurry this along, I'm going to explode into teensy tiny pieces of frustrated harpy. Then see how much fun I'll be."

He ignored her. *Sadist.*

To stave off the inevitable explosion, she touched and kissed any part of his body she could reach. And since he'd abandoned her breasts for other fields of pleasure, she couldn't reach much. So she had to satisfy herself with smoothing her hands over his gleaming shoulders, which quickly changed to digging her nails into his gleaming shoulders as he reached the fields of home.

She spread her legs wider, begging, trying to control the tremors starting to rack her body. And if she grew vocal with some of her begging, so be it.

His fingers trembled as he skimmed her inner thighs. She smiled. Small things could give such pleasure. Now if he'd just hurry, hurry, hurry.

He wasn't in hurry mode tonight. His breath warmed her just before he flicked the most sensually sensitive spot on her entire body with his cruel tongue.

She cried out, a low keening wail of exquisite joy. And by the time he stopped his tongue-teasing long enough to push his finger deep into her, she was panting.

In and out, in and out, his finger mimicked the rhythm of sex. Not enough, not freaking *enough*. She pulled herself up far enough to grasp his damp, tangled hair and yank. "Warning. I will *not* survive one more minute. That's a promise. Then you'll have to explain a dead harpy to Hades." Each word was forced out at the end of a pant.

He grunted. It seemed like Mr. In Control was reverting to primitive. Great with her. She was feeling her inner animal too.

Declan slid his body over hers, his skin hot and slick, his arousal a demanding pressure against her stomach. Then he rose over her and she arched to meet him.

She was so wet, so *ready*, that when he buried himself in her, she wrapped her legs around him and ground her hips against his. When she clenched around his cock, every muscle locked into place, squeezing, squeezing, drawing a moan from him.

Her orgasm pounded, pounded at the door, begging for release, screaming for her to let it go, and go, and go.

He began to move. Driving into her and then withdrawing, leaving only the head of his cock inside her, making her craaaazy. Then he repeated the plunge and withdraw over and over, faster and faster, until she couldn't stand the pressure buildup, until her personal escape valve was ready to explode.

A blur of omigod-I'm-almost-there was quickly blotting out any rational thought. *Hang on one more second.* She had something to say. Important. Really important. She snagged the thought a second before it disappeared from her radar.

She yanked his head down to her neck. "Share with me in every way, Declan Mackenzie. I freely give this." The words had been faint, because it was tough to speak when you couldn't breathe. She hoped he'd heard.

He had. She felt the prick of his fangs just as she flung open the door and let her orgasm race free. But no one had told her she'd be riding it.

It launched skyward, and she tightened her legs, her entire body around it, to keep from falling. It spun and bucked, unbearable pleasure rushing at her in wave after wave. She shrieked her pleasure as it tossed her into the stars. Wind whipped her and sensation beat at her. And then with one final buck, it tossed her off.

She fell, but just as he had once before, Declan fell

with her. Daria knew without question he'd always be there to break her fall. Or maybe she only knew it in this half-world between extreme pleasure and reality. A world that didn't put what-ifs or we-can'ts into the equation.

It was a soft landing. Declan moved off her to once again rest on his side. She lay on the bed still trembling, still trying to catch her breath, still fighting tears. She started to turn her head away so he wouldn't see the glistening in her eyes.

He stopped her. "Don't."

She appreciated that he hadn't peppered her with questions, hadn't demanded answers. He just waited.

One tear escaped. Could she escape too from her personal prison of other people's expectations? No, reality was back in control. Hades wouldn't let her go.

Declan still waited.

"I don't want to leave you." *I love you.* She couldn't quite say those last three words, not when she knew her leaving was inevitable. Saying the words would hurt too much.

Another tear escaped. *Renegades.*

"I know you don't." He smiled as he wiped the tears from her cheek with the pad of his thumb. "I love you, harpy lady, and we'll find a way."

She could only nod, her throat clogged with the repressed emotions of a lifetime. Daria hoped he understood.

He rolled onto his back and stared at the ceiling. The candle flame's light leaped and danced across the hard planes of his face, chasing shadows that mimicked the passing of years, ever changing but still the same. Their lives would be like that, flickering moments in time, casting longer and longer shadows until everything sputtered out. Because eventually all things *did* end, even the lives of immortals.

Without looking, he reached over to clasp her hand. "You forgot to shield your thoughts. I promise you that when we finally sputter out, we'll be sitting side by side on the same mantel. And we'll have a hell of a big puddle of wax to prove we lived long and well." He turned his head to grin. "Believe it."

She squeezed his hand. "I believe."

He exhaled deeply before speaking. "I don't care if Loki's whole army plants itself on the front lawn. Stay with me for the rest of the night."

Daria returned his smile. "Sounds like a plan to me."

Then he blew the candles out.

CHAPTER NINETEEN

Memo: to all harpies
Subject: theft of office supplies
Thieves are welcome in Tartarus. Stealing is a respected profession. But it has come to our attention that office supplies are disappearing at an alarming rate. This will impact our profit margin. Be aware that we have installed mini-demons in every office, and they will be watching. Punishment for stealing from the company will be a hundred years of counting the fleas on Cerberus's furry ass.
Special note: Hades expects whoever stole his blue-and-green gremlin to return it immediately. Reliable hole-punchers are hard to find.
    Remember, he who steals from Hades is dead meat.

HADES THE VIGILANT

Daria's dream was fraying around the edges. As she drifted toward wakefulness, only snatches remained—a dark room, trying to reach for a lamp, unable to move, something watching in the blackness. *Sleep hypnosis.* Her half-awake self recognized what held her in the dream.

As she came fully awake, Daria realized this wasn't sleep hypnosis at all. She still couldn't move. Her heart pounded and her breaths came in panicked gasps as she strained against whatever held her.

"A simple binding spell, harpy woman. It will wear off quickly." Fenrir sounded amused.

If she could have moved, Daria would have jumped a foot off the bed. She couldn't even roll her eyeballs to locate Declan's father. Even as the thought surfaced, he moved into her range of vision and sat down on the edge of the bed. He was a huge man, and the bed sank under his weight, threatening to dump her onto the floor.

Despite pounding heart, panicked breathing, and clammy hands, she tried to take stock. Declan's room. She couldn't see him, but she knew he lay beside her on the bed. Daria sensed it was late afternoon, still light outside, even though she couldn't see past the heavy drapes pulled across the window.

Fenrir stared at her from cold yellow eyes, the eyes of a wolf. He and Declan might look something alike, but she'd never confuse the two.

"It was pitifully easy to fool all of you." He settled in to tell her how. "If you remember, when I wanted to escape your pathetic attempts to destroy me, I simply sank into the ground. It's one of my talents." His expression said he had many, many more.

"Get to the point. What're you going to do to Declan?" She wasn't worried about herself. If Fenrir had meant to kill her, she'd be dead.

"I learn from my mistakes." He frowned. "Of course I never make mistakes, only miscalculations. Anyway, it occurred to me I might circumvent your gargoyles by tunneling underground and coming up beneath this place." Fenrir paused to give himself a virtual pat on his back for outstanding brilliance. "And of course I lied about the summer solstice deadline. I never intended to wait that long."

Ganymede had been outfoxed, or maybe outwolfed.

"I came up in your cellar. That stupid dog was there

looking for evildoers." Fenrir's smile said Trouble had
found a doozy. "He also is bound for the moment."

"What're you going to do with Declan, dirtbag?"

Fenrir rose. "I'll take my son now. Then I'll complete
the ritual that will open a portal to the home of the gods.
Once there, we'll bide our time until the summer solstice." His eyes burned with his fervor. "I'll join with my
father, Hel, and Midgard to ensure that the forces of evil
triumph at Ragnarok."

Yeah, yeah, forces of evil, and on and on and on. The
only good part about Fenrir's long litany of his own genius was she could feel the binding starting to recede. If
he talked for a little longer, she'd be free.

Fenrir must've had the same thought, because he
moved around the bed and out of her range of vision.
Daria felt the mattress shift as he picked up Declan. A
moment later he returned to her side of the bed. He'd
wrapped Declan, still in his vampire sleep, in the com-
forter from the foot of the bed and then slung him over
his shoulder.

"I've spared your life and that of the dog-that-is-no-
dog so you can spread the word of my power. No one can
hope to defeat me, so it would be best if you all cowered
behind your gargoyle protectors until I've gone."

Daria sensed that what Fenrir said and what he meant
were two different things. His true message was in his
gleaming wolf eyes. He *wanted* them to follow and attack
him. Fenrir lusted for blood, anyone's blood. And his
overweening belief in his own power wouldn't allow for
any thought that he might get his ass kicked.

She could move enough now to roll her eyes and grit
her teeth. All her harpy rage—and true harpy rage was a
terrible thing—centered on Fenrir. If he hurt Declan,

he'd better hope the universe ended quickly, because she'd hunt him down and tear him apart. For once she gloried in her harpy nature.

Fenrir left the room, closing the door behind him with a soft click. Daria rolled her eyes so she could see the clock. The next half hour seemed like years. Outside the drapes, she knew the sun would be dipping below the horizon. Declan would wake to find himself a prisoner.

Finally she could move and talk. She rolled off the bed, scrambled to her feet, pulled her clothes on, and raced for the door.

"*I'm coming, Declan.*"

They weren't exactly an army of seasoned warriors creeping silently through the forest. Hannibal coming across the Alps with all his elephants would've made less noise.

Ocypete, Kal, and she hadn't taken to the skies yet, but they were ready. Kal wasn't wearing a shirt so he'd have less to shed.

"Your brother's a fine, fine specimen of a man, gal." Katie the cook nudged Daria. She was cooking up more than magic in her imagination. "Might even give up my broom for him."

"Are you still channeling the wizard's power through your broom, Katie?" Daria hoped so. Katie had lots of skills as a witch, but this operation needed some major mojo to make it work. They not only had to rescue Declan, but she also had to snatch Fenrir.

Katie nodded. "The wizard's kind of power is scary. I'll be glad to get back to doing what I do." She hesitated. "No word from your mom, huh?"

"Not yet. But she said she'd be here, and Mom does

what she says she'll do." Daria knew she sounded pretty fierce about that, but she had to believe Mom was okay.

Daria glanced around. Ocypete was walking with Walt, and the debunker looked a little wild-eyed. Made sense. He might be clutching his pad and pencil, ready to record the historical event, but he had to be worrying about Ocypete making him Hades's newest toy. Daria could've told him not to worry. Her aunt had a frost giant already picked out.

Sparkle was nowhere to be seen. But then she was supposed to be a covert force of one. She'd be sneaking up on Fenrir so she could pass her info back to Ganymede. Which would be tough since she wasn't talking to the cat.

Their general and supreme leader was at the front of his forces, still in cat form. Impressive. Really impressive. An army of mismatched entities led by a cat.

It didn't matter what they looked like, though, because nothing was going to keep her from taking back the man she loved. *The man she loved.* She said it so easily in her mind, but she hadn't said it to the only one that mattered. Daria regretted that.

Suddenly Sparkle slipped from the forest to walk beside her. She'd evidently decided Ganymede wasn't worth abandoning her pride as the queen of sex and sin. She was going into battle wearing black leather—a tight little leather top that showed cleavage, leather pants, and thigh-high leather boots. Whip optional.

"Pass this on to the big freaking cheese up front. Fenrir's men are surrounding the church. He took the old altar from the church, set it up outside, and bound your man to it. Declan is one pissed vampire. Fenrir knows we're coming. Sheesh, could you people be any louder? It looks like Fenrir is waiting for us to get there before he does the ritual you told us about." Then she faded back into the woods.

Relief made Daria weak. Even though Fenrir hadn't said anything about killing Declan now, the possibility still sniped at her from a corner of her brain.

Daria picked up her pace until she was beside Ganymede. "Sparkle wanted me to pass on some info. Fenrir and his men are waiting for us at the church. He's bound Declan to an altar, but hasn't done anything else to him yet."

Ganymede nodded and looked up at her. His eyes were way too sad for a cosmic troublemaker who loved a good—or bad—fight.

"Did she say anything about me?" He looked hopeful.

"Um, no." She probably shouldn't mention Sparkle's big freaking cheese comment.

"I love being a cosmic troublemaker. It's the only thing I know how to do. Choices are hard." Ganymede, always so sure of himself, was having a crisis of confidence.

"Look, I'm kind of an expert on this. I always wanted to be a harpy like my mom. No doubts. Until I met Declan." She shrugged. "Now he's the only thing I want." *And I'll tell him that as soon as I'm within shouting distance.*

"But how did you *know?*"

"I guess you have to ask yourself one question and give yourself an honest answer. Which would be easier to replace in your life, your career or Sparkle?" Daria wouldn't go all emotional on Ganymede and talk about love, because he wasn't that kind of cat. Only he knew what his feelings were for Sparkle.

He nodded. "Yeah. Got it."

Daria had only taken a few steps away from Ganymede

when he stopped. Turning toward his army, he did some silent communicating.

"Harpies, take to the air. Come at them from three directions. I'll work with Katie to bring down any shield Fenrir tries to throw up. Werewolves and Trouble, circle the frost giants. You're not strong enough to beat them, so just do enough to keep them distracted. Sparkle will work on Hel. Next to Fenrir, she has the most power. Once someone frees Declan, he can help with Fenrir. Anyone who has time on his or her hands can try to keep the snake from doing too much damage." He stopped to think. "Walt, stay out of the way and take notes."

Ganymede must be a glass-half-full cat, because Daria noticed he didn't mention Mom. Well, Daria was a realist. She didn't have a chance of controlling Fenrir long enough for a trip to Tartarus without that ribbon. *Please be okay, Mom.*

Confidence. Time to bury the old bones of her childhood insecurities—her doubts that she'd ever be good enough—in a big hole with RIP marking the spot. She *would* rescue Declan, they *would* save the universe, and Mom *would* be okay.

Showtime. She became harpy and then launched herself skyward. Below Daria, her fellow fighters shouted as they closed with Fenrir's minions. Then she forgot everything as she searched for Declan.

There. She almost sobbed with relief as she spotted him. Declan was stretched out on the altar naked, just as he'd slept beside her last night. No ropes or chains in sight. Fenrir must be using his power to hold Declan on the altar. Daria narrowed her eyes to determined slits. She'd just see if she could destroy Fenrir's concentration a little.

She dove, the action around her registering as fragmented images. Trouble and the werewolves trying to evade the lumbering frost giants. Sparkle and Hel bitch-slapping each other. Kal and Ocypete tormenting Midgard in his snake form.

Ganymede and Katie's broom blasting power at Fenrir's shield. He'd evidently created protection for both Declan and himself, because she could see the sparks flying each time a blast hit it.

Daria zoomed around the shield, looking for an opening. Then Declan spotted her. He stopped fighting the binding spell and stared at her.

Love. She saw it in his gaze, felt it in her heart, and recognized she was lost forever. She dropped her mental shield. *"I love you, Declan Mackenzie."* There were lots of other things she needed to say, but that was the most important.

Whatever he might have replied was lost, because suddenly the battle moved into fast forward. The noise level rose a few hundred decibels.

She turned her head to look. *Omigod!* Ocypete had abandoned the battle plan in favor of trying to carry off her fave frost giant. He wasn't cooperating. Daria tried to be heard above the shouting. "Aunt Ocypete, stop! We need you up here."

But Aunt Ocypete wasn't one of the top three harpies for nothing. She was selfish and single-minded, all traits the great ones had. So Aunt Ocypete ignored her niece in favor of wrestling with the frost giant.

What to do? Daria wouldn't abandon Declan to chase down her aunt. But intervention came from an unexpected source.

Sparkle left Hel to Kal for a few minutes as she turned her attention to the frost giants. Her expression froze

Daria. Sparkle had been annoying, spiteful, and sex-obsessed, but rarely scary. She was scary right now.

With eyes glowing an eerie amber, she spoke to the giants. "You are in lust with the harpy, Ocypete. She's the only one you want. Nothing else matters. Go to her now. Leave this place and go somewhere far away where you can be alone with her."

As one, all the Frost Giants stopped fighting and lumbered toward Aunt Ocypete. Daria's aunt looked like she'd won the keys to Hades's liquor cabinet. After ordering all of them to hold hands, she grabbed the last one's hand and rose into the sky, trailing giants like the tail of some monstrous kite.

Daria spared one last glance at Sparkle. *Lots of respect coming your way.* The troublemaker might not be as powerful as Ganymede, but in her area of expertise she was tops.

Okay, one section of Fenrir's fighters out of the mix. Daria turned back to Fenrir. Then everything happened at once.

Ganymede and Katie were still peppering Fenrir's shield with blasts, and he was starting to look a little concerned. He grabbed a knife resting beside the altar and before Daria could even shout, "No!" made a cut across Declan's bare chest. Blood welled from the wound.

Frantic with her need to reach Declan, Daria looked over at Ganymede. Something of her urgency must have reached him, because he closed his eyes and concentrated. His cat body trembled with the effort he was about to make.

She looked back at Fenrir in time to see him dip a small brush into Declan's blood. Then he began to chant as he slowly and carefully painted a "D" on Declan's stomach.

She strained to hear what he was saying.

"With his blood I write my son's name. This is my key. When his name is complete, you will open the gate to Asgard, home to all gods and goddesses, so that I may pass through with all who follow me." A sound rumbled from the sky. It sounded a lot like a giant gate starting to open.

Oh, shit. She cast one more desperate glance at Ganymede. He opened his eyes and released his power in one final blast. At the same moment, Daria began the famous harpy death dive. Not much could stop a harpy diving at the speed of a bullet. A nanosecond before she hit the shield, Ganymede's blast shattered it.

Pulling out of her dive, she used the element of surprise to grab Fenrir's knife and drag it across the palm of her hand. As her blood welled up and dripped off her fingertips, she leaned over Declan.

Before Fenrir could stop her, she used her finger as a pen and her blood as ink—A. R. I. A.

Daria. Triumphant, she heard the gate clang shut. Then she turned in time to see Fenrir take wolf form and leap at her. She barely had a moment to admire his really great dental work and his eardrum-popping roar before the force of his charge knocked her flat. Only her harpy strength allowed her to fend off his first attempt to rip out her throat.

Declan's shout cut through the battle noise, and for a second silence fell. "Not *my* woman, you bastard!"

Then Declan was there, tearing his father off her and rolling across the ground with him. Declan was vampire, using his fangs along with the power he'd inherited from the wolf.

But he wouldn't be able to hold Fenrir for long. Daria

dragged herself to her feet and then launched herself shakily into the air. As she scanned the battlefield for help, she saw something that made her want to cry with relief.

Her mother flew out of the night sky. Celaeno raced for Daria, her mighty wings beating the air, a long pink ribbon floating behind her.

Mom circled above her. "Apollo gave me the ribbon, but he made it pink just to tick me off. Sadistic jerk. That's what I loved about him. Help me. Let's get the big bad wolf wrapped up." As Daria joined her mother in descending on Fenrir, she heard the faint strains of "All Shook Up." She didn't have time to puzzle over why Chill was coming here.

Ganymede watched the harpies trying to wrap the stupid pink ribbon around the werewolf. Ribbon, harpies, and wolf were a tangle of hands, talons, claws, and teeth. So far it was Fenrir one and everyone else zero.

He switched his attention to Sparkle. Even though she wouldn't care what he thought, he'd been proud of her when she'd gotten rid of the frost giants. How many times had he taken her for granted? Too many. And now she was holding her own with Hel. But for how much longer?

Ganymede couldn't help her because he was looking for an opening to blast Fenrir into oblivion—to hell with the Big Boss's rule about not killing anything. And if the Big Boss was listening, he could take all Ganymede's candy bars for the next thousand years. He didn't give a damn anymore. Fine, so he owed someone for that last damn and hell.

He added another damn to his IOU tab as the ice cream truck pulled in behind him. "All Shook Up."

Yeah. Fit his mood. How'd Chill get his truck down that overgrown road anyway? Never mind. He knew. The music ended and a few seconds later his personal pain joined him.

Chill gazed over the scene of the battle, calm as a vanilla-dipped cone. "Looks a little desperate for the forces of good." He glanced down at Ganymede and smiled.

"Counting me as part of the forces of good? Forgetting a few things, aren't you?" Like tens of thousands of years doing evil.

Chill shrugged. "We all make our mistakes. Some just last longer than others."

"So why are you here now?" Ganymede's frustration built as he watched the harpies and Declan fail once again to tie up Fenrir.

Why didn't they just make a loop, drop it over his head, and then run around him like a maypole? At least Midgard was one whipped snake, slithering away with Trouble and the werewolves in hot pursuit.

Ganymede looked back at Chill. "If you're here for more damn candy bars, forget it. It'll be a bitch to collect them, because I've run the hell out of treats." God, that felt good. He was just breaking into a great big cat smile when Hel screeched right behind him.

"Ow!" Ganymede yelped as she hefted him high in the air, her clawed fingers digging deep into his body.

"This is one cat who won't have nine lives. I'm collecting on all of them right now."

Sparkle came out of nowhere. She jerked him from the Queen of Death's hands. "He's mine, bitch. Don't touch him again. Go home and count dead people." She glowed with her anger.

And fear. Ganymede had known Sparkle too long,

had . . . loved her too long, not to recognize when she was scared shitless. For him? Something tore inside him, and he knew what he had to do.

At least Hel seemed to have had enough. The battle was lost. With a last furious glare at Sparkle, she disappeared.

Sparkle set Ganymede down and then raked her fingers through her tangled red hair. Her face was dirty and her nails were broken. Sparkle didn't seem to care.

Ganymede met Chill's serene gaze. "You can take your cosmic troublemaker job and shove it. I stay with Sparkle. There're other jobs. Talk radio always needs someone to stir the pot."

And for only the second time in thousands of years, Sparkle Stardust cried, great gasping sobs that made her makeup run and her cheeks blotchy. Swiping at her face, she smiled at him.

For a moment Ganymede stared at her in stunned amazement. Then he got a little teary-eyed himself. Not crying. The former baddest of the bad didn't cry. "You're one gorgeous woman. Pick me up, babe. After this is over, we'll go somewhere and get to know each other again, spend some quality time together."

Chill coughed. "Looks like you saved yourself again, Ganymede. Sacrificing all for love is a biggie. Maybe we'll give the cosmic troublemaker job another try. Remember, no killing."

Ganymede couldn't believe it, but even in the midst of shocked disbelief he tried to bargain. "Cursing?"

Chill shrugged. "They're your candy bars." He glanced past Ganymede. "Looks like your friends need some help."

Ganymede had forgotten about them. Sparkle lifted

him and buried her face in his fur. Then they both stared at where the harpies, Declan, and Fenrir were still fighting. The werewolf was running out of power blasts and the harpies were running out of energy.

Chill shook his head. "Let's get this over with." There was a blinding light, and when everyone could see again, Fenrir was securely wrapped in the pink ribbon.

Ganymede stared, and then he looked over to where Walt was sitting on the ground with his back against a tree. An exhausted Katie sat beside him, her broom across her knees. Walt was frantically taking notes.

"Make sure you get all this." Too bad Ganymede hadn't allowed the debunker to bring his camera.

Chill laughed. "I love playing the deus ex machina card. It's so contrived, and I usually let people decide their own fates." He shrugged. "But I think we need to move on to more important things this time." He turned toward his truck. "Wait here while I get something."

That gave Ganymede a moment to think. So when Chill came back with two cones, he was ready. "You know, I bet this was all a setup, a way to get me to admit my feelings. Besides scaring the crap outta me. Yeah, now it makes sense."

Sparkle was unwrapping Ganymede's cone for him as Chill smiled and started walking back to his truck.

Ganymede shouted after him. "You tell the Big Boss I'm on to him."

Chill climbed into his truck and started the motor. Then he leaned out his window. "He already knows, Ganymede. He already knows." Then the truck rolled away into the forest and was gone.

"Will they be okay?"

Sparkle's question turned his attention back to Declan and Daria. He was just in time to see Daria launch herself into the air, followed closely by Declan, Kal, and Celaeno. She had a trussed-up Fenrir grasped in her talons.

"Yeah, I think they'll be fine."

CHAPTER TWENTY

Hadn't Daria done this once already? Sweating? Yes. Heart pounding? Check. Breathing hard? Uh-huh. Funny feeling in stomach? Definitely. Panic attack all over again.

Turning over Fenrir to his demon keepers hadn't taken nearly long enough. And she'd tried to draw out pulling on borrowed pants, a top, and shoes. Twenty minutes had seemed more like twenty seconds. Too soon it was time to make her report to the CEO of Tartarus. Gulp. Was it too much to hope he'd be taking a conference call when they reached his office?

Daria knew what to expect when she faced Hades. You didn't *resign* from his company. *Hades* was always the doer. You were terminated or fired. Two words that had the same result. You were dead. Period. But she had to take the chance. A lifetime with Declan was worth the risk.

Speaking of Declan . . . "You should've stayed out of Tartarus." Was Daria afraid for him? A definite yes. "Please don't come into his office with me. He hasn't seen you yet. If he doesn't know you're in Tartarus, you have a chance to escape."

Declan pulled her close. "Let me think. Hmm, abandon you in your hour of need? I don't think so."

"Hardheaded vampire." Her grumpy mumble was a mixture of love and worry.

Mom put her hand on her daughter's shoulder. "If the worst happens—and we'll make sure it doesn't—Kal and I will see that Declan is safe."

Left unsaid was that Hades always got what he wanted. In Tartarus his word was law.

Ready or not, she was about to face Tartarus's CEO armed only with her love for Declan Mackenzie and an army of three.

Hades's demon secretary opened the door to his office and they all trooped in.

His desk was the size of the Woo Woo Inn's parlor. Daria suspected Hades used it as a putting green when no one was watching. It was pretty much empty except for a blotter, a photo of the current winner of the Grim Reaper of the Week award, and an out-box. She'd never seen an in-box. His wall held a certificate naming him executive of the year. Daria knew he kept the same certificate and just changed the date each year. She glanced at the chart listing the murderers he wanted his harpies to snatch that week. They were his favorites. Murders involved lots of hate and lust for revenge.

Hades watched them from across that massive desk. He looked the part of the successful CEO—Armani suit, hair perfectly styled, and brown-colored contacts to hide the demonic glow. He folded his hands on top of his desk and smiled at her, a great smile really.

"Welcome back, Daria. I can't tell you how thrilled I am with your first success. Very impressive, young lady." His gaze swept to Mom. "You've raised a wonderful harpy. Remind me of that when bonus time rolls around."

Hades slid his gaze to Declan and his smile widened. "What? Have you brought me a vampire too?"

"No." It was almost a shout, and Daria forced herself to calm down. "He just helped me to bring Fenrir here."

"*No?*" Hades's smiled slipped. He was thinking about that. But then he smiled again. "I suppose I can wait. Most vampires come to me eventually. So how about we elevate you to a level-five harpy?" His smile turned sly. "Your friend Eris is on level one. Her wererabbit didn't impress."

"No." The one word clogged her throat and made her want to gag on her terror.

Hades definitely stopped smiling this time. "You're very fond of that word, aren't you?"

"I . . ." She coughed and tried again. "I appreciate your kindness—"

"Cut the crap. I'm never kind." Hades symbolically took off his gloves by popping out his contacts and glaring at her with red glowing eyes. "Explain your *no*."

She felt Declan step up beside her. He clasped her hand and squeezed. Courage. With his support, along with Mom's and Kal's, she could do this. "I want to leave the harpies." There, she'd said it. She tensed for the expected explosion.

It didn't come. Instead, Hades stared at her for a long time. "You're the first harpy ever to say those words to me." He snapped his fingers and a laptop popped up in front of him. Hades hit a few keys, then looked up from the screen. "There's nothing in your records to indicate why you'd want to leave us." He cocked an inquiring brow.

Okay, legs about to give out. Would Hades mind if she finished this meeting from the floor? "I don't think I'm cut out for the harpy life. It's just that I like to . . . do *good* things."

Hades frowned, and his hands became clawed.

"I like being *nice* to people."

Fangs slid from beneath his lips.

"I care about people's *feelings*."

Horns popped up from his every-hair-in-place head.

Daria threw her arms wide. "I just *love* people." Not totally accurate, but she didn't have time to make her statement more specific.

Hades winced as if the sound of that word hurt. Then he did some squirming in his seat. "That tail is damn uncomfortable."

No one would ever accuse Hades of not being cool. He didn't rant or rave or invoke hellfire. He just cocked his head as though studying a particularly fascinating butterfly right before pinning it and popping it into his display case. "Of course, I can't let you go. It would set a bad example. Too bad. You could've been one of my best. Since you pleased me with your gift of Fenrir, I'll make your termination painless. A firing is much more painful because it, well, involves fire." His smile would've looked almost fatherly, but the fangs ruined it.

Declan moved in front of her at the same time Mom spoke up.

"This is my daughter, Hades. I've served you faithfully. I'm one of your best. But if you kill my daughter, I'll resign. How will you meet your quotas then? And how will you explain our deaths to the other harpies?" She lowered her voice. "And how will you explain our murders to Apollo? Daria is his daughter."

Hades was upset enough to rake his fingers through his perfect hair. He pulled on one horn. A sure sign of agitation. "I can't lose you. But I can't just let your daughter walk away. What about my reputation?"

Kal spoke for the first time. "I think I have a solution." He looked at Daria, something like sadness filling his eyes, before returning his gaze to Hades. "You appointed me as her judge, but you haven't given me a chance to report."

Daria felt like one of the frost giants had stomped right

in the middle of her chest. Her breath left her in a shocked "Huh?"

Her brother shrugged and smiled at her. "Sorry, sis. I couldn't refuse Hades's order. And I did try to keep you focused on the test."

Yeah, he had. But her mind still couldn't process the truth. *Kal* was her judge. Daria tried to feel betrayed, but it was no use. She loved him too much, and he was right, no one disobeyed Hades. Except her. And-lived-to-tell-about-it might not happen.

She looked away from her brother. He should've told her. *Would that have changed what you did?* Daria sighed. No.

"This whole discussion isn't necessary, because my sister failed the test."

Hades narrowed his eyes on Kal. "Failed? Specifics."

Kal dragged a wrinkled piece of paper from the pocket of his borrowed jeans. "Daria broke every harpy rule. She wore clothes that made her look sexy. She wore makeup that made her beautiful. She performed acts of kindness. I've listed a few examples. She saved a dog and a talking book. And she released two trapped spirits."

Hades seemed overwhelmed by Daria's transgressions. "Didn't you do *anything* bad?" He looked torn. "I'm not sure . . ."

Kal wasn't finished. "And the worst thing?" Pause for big finish. "*She* stole your gremlin."

Hades smiled, a huge pleased grin. "That's my girl. For a few minutes I thought you'd left the dark side completely." He stopped smiling. "Now give my gremlin back."

"She can't. She sold it on eBay." Kal was pushing it.

"Get it back!" When Hades thundered, all of Tartarus shook.

After everyone got off the floor, Declan stepped forward. "I can find it for you, but in exchange, I want Daria's freedom."

"You'd bargain with Hades?"

"Yep."

"I like you. Too bad males can't be harpies." He looked at Daria. "Go. You're obviously not harpy material. Just remember me as Hades the Merciful."

They all beat feet out of Hades's office and didn't stop until they were free of Tartarus. Daria hugged her mom and punched Kal before hugging him too. Declan wrapped his arms around her and pulled her close.

Daria's mother cupped her daughter's face in her hand. "No matter what I am to the rest of the world, remember I'm a mom first. I always wanted what would make you happy." She looked at Declan. "Make sure she stays happy, Declan, because I *am* the certified mother-in-law from hell."

Kal grinned and kissed his twin on the cheek. "Sorry about the judge thing. I'll help search for the gremlin. Any ideas?" He glanced at Declan.

"When Aello showed up at the Woo Woo Inn, I saw something blue and green nesting in her hair." Declan shrugged. "Bet there were lots of things nesting in her hair."

Kal nodded. "We'll give you guys some space now. Send a message when you're all loved out and ready for visitors."

All loved out? Daria didn't think that would happen any time soon. She gazed up at Declan. "Do you have any idea how much I love you?"

"Yeah, a little. But I can tell you exactly how much I love you. If I could fill every second of the nine hundred years I've lived with love, and give it all to you at once, it might come close to what I'm feeling now." Declan lowered his head and took her mouth in a long, drugging kiss. "Ready for the flight home? We need to get started on that loving."

She could only nod.

Declan thought being this happy could spoil a vampire. Sitting on a porch swing with the woman you loved was as good as it got. A plus? It was a spring night at the Woo Woo Inn and still too cool for his bloodsucking competition, the Jersey mosquitoes.

Their wedding was in three days, a small ceremony with just Daria's mom, aunt, Kal, and their friends from the Woo Woo Inn.

Daria was stretched out on the swing with her head on his lap. His lap was pretty excited about that. Funny, but even though she'd stayed relaxed through all the wedding preparations, for some reason she seemed tense tonight.

"Anything bothering you, sweetheart?" He smoothed her hair away from her face. Touching her in any way was a sensual rush.

She smiled up at him. "No. I was just thinking. I still owe you a birthday party. We never decided on your birth date."

He got into the spirit of things. "How about today? Today would've been a good day to be born."

Her eyes were soft with her love for him. That love always amazed him.

"Great. And do I have a present for you!"

"Here?"

She held her wrist up to peer at her watch. "It will be in about two minutes."

Before he had a chance to question her, he heard the sound of a car coming up the drive. He searched the night for a glimpse of it. Daria hadn't said anything about guests arriving tonight.

She sat up beside him and took his hand. Hers was trembling. *What the . . . ?*

The car parked and four people piled out of it. They headed for the inn's porch.

Declan stilled. *Vampires.*

There were two men and two women. The man in front stopped with one foot on the porch step. He looked at Declan out of blue Mackenzie eyes, and a smile spread across his face.

Declan slowly stood. The other three vampires crowded around the first. They were all smiling.

Declan *knew*. He turned dazed eyes toward Daria.

She wrapped her arms around his waist. "Walt did the research and I did the contacting." She was crying.

He looked back at the four vampires. His gaze fixed on the man in front. "*Grim?*" It was a question torn from centuries of hope and despair.

The vampire took that final step onto the porch and embraced him. "Hi, Dad. We're home."

Prologue

Oblivion.

Sudden. Unexpected. One instant alive, and then...
Nothing.

Only the unraveling of time—months, years, centuries.

Awareness.

Sudden. Unexpected. One instant nothing, and then...
Everything.

His essence, his *soul*, had returned, and it sought sensation. No sight, no sound, no *body*. But he knew he wasn't the same.

When the memories came, they battered at him, flashing images of another time. Primitive. *Fun.* The hunt, pounding after his terrified prey. The kill, quick and bloody. The feeding, a gorging frenzy. And afterward the mating, all mindless instinct and primal satisfaction. Savage joy filled him. Anticipation. He'd do all that again.

Then the voice, the one he'd always listened to. *Obeyed.* Warning him that he was rising to a new world. No indiscriminate rending and tearing. Damn. He'd have to control the violence, the urge to destroy. Because he was no longer what he had been. He was human.

What was that? He liked the version of himself he remembered better.

And because he couldn't stop it, he allowed the voice to fill him with everything he'd need to know after he rose. Wave after wave of knowledge left his mind reeling—culture, language, history, and on and on and on.

Finally, the voice explained what he was, *who* he was. And things clicked into place. He remembered. *Everything.* Not just the images he'd seen in his mind, but all that had gone before. And the voice became a name. Fin. His earlier joy took a major hit.

Impatience tugged at him. He was the impulsive one. Something he'd have to temper. But not now. He wanted out. Pushing mental feelers through the tons of earth and rock separating him from the surface, he found the male, no, *man* waiting for him above. And with the man was his new body.

Eager, he shot upward, his essence sliding easily from the earth into the empty body. His new home. He didn't bother thinking about what he looked like. Instead he glanced around, searching for prey, for other predators. A habit from that other time—one he'd never lose.

"Wow, this is so cool. It's exactly 11:11 PM on November 11, 2011. Eleven, eleven, eleven. Just like Fin said it'd be." The man looked up from the lighted face of his watch and leaned toward him out of the darkness. "And you're Ty."

Ty clenched his teeth so he wouldn't snarl. Along with so much other knowledge, Fin had emphasized that eating random strangers wasn't good for the image of the Eleven.

"You'd better be Steve." The guy wasn't a danger to him, so Ty glanced away to scan the area again. It looked like they were in some kind of cave. "Where are we?"

The man slapped the side of his head in a gesture Ty didn't understand. "Sorry. I forgot this is all new to you. Yeah, I'm Steve. I'll be taking you to Fin. And you're inside Newgrange."

Ty could see fine in the darkness, but apparently Steve couldn't. The man pulled a flashlight from his pocket and turned it on. The predator stirred in Ty. Humans didn't have good night vision. Advantage, predator. "Newgrange?"

"Yep. We're not supposed to be here at night, and definitely not without a guide. But Fin took care of it."

Ty tried out a smile on his new face. Fin was good at "taking care" of things. The smile faded when he thought about his new name. Fin had a warped sense of humor.

"And Newgrange is a prehistoric passage tomb in Ireland. One of the oldest surviving structures in the world." Steve raked his fingers through short blond hair. "Let's get outta here. Small enclosed places give me the creeps."

You have no idea. Fin did things like this. He'd given Ty a bunch of information down to the tiniest details, like what a watch and flashlight were, but he'd forgotten to tell Ty where he was.

"How old?" Not that Ty cared. He followed Steve down the narrow passage, trying out a few of the curses Fin had poured into him when he banged his head against a low spot at the end of the tunnel.

"Five thousand years old." Steve waited for him to be impressed.

He wasn't. "Fin wouldn't send you if you weren't one of us. So what soul do you have, Steve?" Did he sound friendly? Fin had said not to scare anyone willing to help them.

Steve shot him a nervous glance, the first hint he'd given that he might be worried about being here alone with Ty. "A horse."

Prey. Ty smiled again.

Steve swallowed hard.

Then Ty forgot about the other man as he stepped out of the tunnel and into the Irish night. Raising his head, he stared up at the few stars visible through the cloud cover.

They were the first stars he'd seen in sixty-five million years.

Eternal Pleasure
Coming this July

MARJORIE M. LIU

THE LAST TWILIGHT

A *Dirk & Steele* Romance

A WOMAN IN JEOPARDY

Doctor Rikki Kinn is one of the world's best virus hunters. It's for that reason she's in the Congo, working for the CDC. But when mercenaries attempt to take her life to prevent her from investigating a new and deadly plague, her boss calls in a favor from an old friend—the only one who can help.

A PRINCE IN EXILE

Against his better judgment, Amiri has been asked to return to his homeland by his colleagues in Dirk & Steele—men who are friends and brothers, who like himself are more than human. He must protect a woman who is the target of murderers, who has unwittingly involved herself in a conflict that threatens not only the lives of millions, but Amiri's own soul...and his heart.

AVAILABLE FEBRUARY 2008!

ISBN 13: 978-0-8439-5767-9

To order a book or to request a catalog call:
1-800-481-9191

This book is also available at your local bookstore, or you can check out our Web site **www.dorchesterpub.com** where you can look up your favorite authors, read excerpts, or glance at our discussion forum to see what people have to say about your favorite books.

Jade Lee

Dragonborn

ONE PROTECTOR

When dragon power flows through your veins, when dragon thoughts burn in your mind, you can accomplish anything. Natiya knows, for she carries one of the last eggs in the land disguised as a jewel in her navel. Day by day the Unhatched grows, and when at last it births they will be joined in a sacred and eternal bond.

ONE SLAYER

When dragon power flows through your veins, when dragon emotions trample your soul, you become a monster. So knows Kiril, for one destroyed his cousin. That is why Kiril vowed to destroy dragonkind—and he has almost succeeded. But there is an obstacle he did not foresee: love.

AVAILABLE MARCH 2008

ISBN 13: 978-0-505-52754-7